G000240863

MAGGIE OF MOSS STREET

Also by Pamela Evans

Lamplight on the Thames
A Barrow in the Broadway

MAGGIE OF MOSS STREET

Pamela Evans

HEADLINE

First published in 1990
by HEADLINE BOOK PUBLISHING PLC

10 9 8 7 6 5 4 3 2 1

British Library Cataloguing in Publication Data

Evans, Pamela
Maggie of Moss Street.
I. Title
823.914 [F]

ISBN 0-7472-0252-4

Typeset in 11/12½ pt Plantin
by Colset Private Limited, Singapore

Printed and bound in Great Britain by
Richard Clay Ltd, Bungay, Suffolk

HEADLINE BOOK PUBLISHING PLC
Headline House
79 Great Titchfield Street
London W1P 7FN

To Barbara Levy,
with gratitude
for her advice and encouragement.

Acknowledgement

I would like to thank Mr Robin Wayne N.D.S.F. for informing me about the flower trade. His courtesy and helpfulness have been limitless. Any inaccuracy in the book does not reflect on his expertise in the field of floristry.

Chapter One

Maggie Brightwell's alarm clock was not a thing of beauty or finesse but of grim efficiency. It had a round face with black numbers, a tarnished chrome rim, three dumpy legs and a bell on the top which clanged into action at ten minutes past seven every weekday morning with all the subtlety of gunfire.

Thursday 29th July 1948 was no exception. Its metallic clatter penetrated to the depths of Maggie's slumber as effectively as toothache. Groaning, she silenced the beast, resisted the urge for another five minutes and swung out of bed.

Yawning heavily she padded to the window, squinting against the early sunlight as she drew back the curtains. Eager to taste the freshness of the morning air, she inhaled deeply at the open window only to be disappointed. Untypically high temperatures had baked the capital recently.

The intense heat had kept Maggie awake until the small hours, and although normally a devotee of the dawn, with its clarity and sense of promise, today she felt unrefreshed and heavy-eyed, her skin clammy against her cotton nightdress which fell loosely over her slender form.

Down in the narrow West London street, the milkman was heading this way on one of the new three-wheeler electric milkfloats with its oddly reassuring clunk, hum and rattle. The heatwave meant that most of the windows in the street were open and the distant chink of crockery indicated an early start in many of the houses and flats. Already factory workers were trickling from their homes, clutching their lunch packed in tins or paper bags.

Still drowsy, but now able to trust herself to flirt a little with the bed without succumbing to its charms completely, she sat on the edge to indulge in her allotted 'surfacing' time which would end promptly at twenty minutes past seven. Falling short of the floor, for at seventeen Maggie was only five foot one, her feet swung loosely. Her lack of height, however, had by no means impaired her general development and her trim figure curved in perfect proportion from the tip of her glossy auburn head to her size three feet.

For all her daintiness Maggie was a very tough young woman. Doll-like in appearance perhaps, her face being heart-shaped with a snub nose, deeply bowed mouth, sapphire eyes and china-smooth skin, but remarkable in her mature attitude to life and the self-possession which conferred an added depth and sparkle to her looks. For Maggie's child-hood had virtually ended at the age of nine, cut short for the eldest Brightwell child by the need to care for the youngest, traumatized by the horrific circumstances of their father's death, their mother's grief, and the blitz raining destruction all around them.

Now shafts of early sunlight lit the shabby overcrowded bedroom which Maggie shared with her mother, thus leaving the only other bedroom for her thirteen-year-old brother, Tom. This room, and indeed the whole of the first floor apartment, illustrated the Brightwells' lifestyle exactly: bright and basic; clean and cheap.

The bed was a double one with an iron bedhead, bolstered pillows and a feather eiderdown in a faded gold material. The bulky mahogany wardrobe stood next to the matching dressing table which was littered with a feminine miscellany; hair grips, brushes and combs, a jar of Ponds vanishing cream, a box of powder, cheap scent bottles and lipstick tubes, and a glossy black jewellery box overflowing with inexpensive bangles and beads. Evidence of Maggie's schooldays was manifest in the two pink nightdress cases she had made in sewing classes, one embroidered "Maggie" the other "Dora', and a sampler on the wall with the words "Home Sweet Home" in cross stitch.

Buoyed up by memories of a visit to the cinema the previous evening with her girlfriend Beryl Bingley from the apartment downstairs, Maggie recaptured the magic of Anna Neagle and Michael Wilding as they had enchanted her through every moment of *Spring in Park Lane*. Such beautiful people, such pretty clothes, she thought wistfully. Then, motivated by her daily aim to have herself dressed and ready for the office, and breakfast prepared by the time Mother returned from work and Tom from his paper round, she yawned and stretched and headed for the bathroom.

Weekday mornings ran to a rigid routine in the Brightwell house-hold. At precisely 5.30 a.m. Dora Brightwell crept softly from the flat and walked to one of the nearby industrial areas where she joined an army of other women to clean factory offices. She returned home just after eight o'clock for breakfast with her offspring before seeing them off to their separate destinations, Maggie to the offices of a financier in Holborn where she worked as a junior clerk, and Tom to school when he wasn't, as now, on holiday. He left for the newsagent's at 6.30 a.m. and returned just before his mother.

This daily regime, which also included an evening cleaning stint for

Maggie's mother, had been the pattern of family life since Dora had been forced into the role of breadwinner when her husband became a fatal statistic of the blitz of 1940.

Over the years, Maggie had striven to ease her mother's burden by helping in the house and caring for Tom. But it wasn't until she had left school three years ago that she had felt able to make a real contribution. It was far more satisfying to her actually to help put food on the family table, but she was not content with the limited amount her current financial status allowed her to do for the family, and intended in time to improve matters.

She whizzed through her toilette and hurried to the kitchen, slipping a pinafore over her navy and white cotton office dress which she wore with white sling-back sandals. Her hair curled naturally to her shoulders and was fastened to the side with a slide. She wore just enough make-up to feel dressed, a mere dusting of powder which would be joined by a touch of lipstick after she'd eaten. Filling the kettle she set it to boil on the gas stove, then sped down the stairs to the front door to get the milk from the step.

Flat 11A was one of four in a block and its front door, which gave direct access to the stairs via a small hallway, was at the side of the building. Opening the door she almost tripped over Nelson, their handsome tortoiseshell tomcat with big yellow eyes and a black patch around one of them. Having long since wooed the family into total subservience, he now rubbed circles around her legs and looked up balefully in feigned deprivation. Upstairs he maintained his calculated pathos by serenading her with pitiful miaowing while she pressed her thumb through the waxed cardboard bottle-top to gain access to the milk.

'It *must* be hot for you to stay out all night, eh, boy?' she muttered, setting down a saucer of milk and fondling his head affectionately. Having had his natural instincts curbed as a kitten, Nelson preferred the considerable comforts on offer at the Brightwells' to any that might be found in the local feline community, and on any but the most clement nights he slept peacefully on one of the Brightwell beds.

By eight o'clock the kettle was singing on the stove, a portion of the bacon ration was frying in the pan with some tomatoes, and toast browning under the grill. It was a modest-sized kitchen with a mottled grey gas stove, a deep square sink with a wooden draining board, a larder and a scrubbed-top table. The family ate their meals there and spent time talking and listening to the wireless which stood on top of a free-standing cupboard with cream- and brown-painted doors.

The BBC news announcer had just mentioned the London Olympic games which were to be opened by the King at Wembley Stadium this afternoon.

3

'That'll be exciting,' said Maggie to Nelson who was now tucking into a dish of pilchards. 'But people'll be fainting like ninepins in this heat, I'll bet.'

'One of these days that cat'll make you faint by answering you back,' said brother Tom, entering the room and going straight to the sink to wash his hands.

'Huh, you're a fine one to talk,' she laughed, turning the bacon with a fork. 'You're always chatting to him.'

'He's a good listener, that's why,' joked Tom, his rare show of humour directly related to the fact that he did not have to go to school today, Maggie guessed.

Watching him lather his hands with carbolic soap, she had to admit, despite all her sisterly affection, that he was not at the most attractive stage of his development. He was painfully thin, and patches of freckles and acne vied for prominence on his pale face. His hair was the same shade as Maggie's but whereas hers was wavy and shining, his was straight and greasy and flopped on to his brow in a fringe above spectacles which were unattractively adorned with a corrective patch over one lens. At an awkward age, his limbs seemed to have outgrown the rest of him. His newish grey flannels were already too short, showing several inches of sock, and his bony arms sprouted from his short shirtsleeves as skinny as whippet's legs.

As he turned to dry his hands, Maggie noticed a nervous flush on his neck and knew that he had been the victim of bullying from the other newspaper boys. Thank goodness he was spared the agony of school until September, she thought. He certainly wouldn't have the heart for breakfast-time bonhomie then.

She felt a surge of protective love for her brother whose strange moods could not be attributed entirely to his adolescence, for Tom had not been as other boys since he was five years old. Unlike his sister, who was a good mixer and anticipated each new day with pleasure, he awoke every morning to misery, for he contemplated contact with his peers with such fear and loathing that he was often physically sick before he went to school.

'Breakfast'll be ready in a few minutes,' she said cheerfully, diplomatically ignoring the evidence of his latest humiliation. If anything upset Tom more than being regarded as a misfit by his contemporaries, it was having his family know about it. 'Will you lay the table, please?'

'All right, sis,' he agreed amicably, glancing briefly at the newspaper before putting it down and going to the cutlery drawer.

Being only human, Maggie was occasionally irritated by her brother's unnaturally withdrawn behaviour which caused her mother and herself such worry. But most of the time she was compassionate towards him for in her heart she knew that mere survival for a boy like Tom, in the cruel exuberance of a boy's world, called for huge reserves of courage. She tried to remain optimistic for a better life for him beyond his school days, but wondered if the tough adult world would be any kinder to someone so lacking in confidence and joviality.

Turning her attention back to the stove, she recalled the days when Tom had been a vociferous five year old, as cheeky as a costermonger. 'A proper little comic,' according to his adoring father. Until one day when Maggie and her mother had been queuing for food, a bomb had hit Granny Brightwell's home while Tom and his father were visiting. By some miracle Tom had been discovered physically unharmed in the ruins, having been buried alive for many hours. The poor child had been found pinned under the debris by his father's corpse, while his dead grandmother lay beside him.

Tom's sense of insecurity had increased when both children had been summarily packed off to Devon, their mother conscience-stricken at not having removed them from danger before. But, influenced by reports of Tom's psychological problems, Dora had had both children returned to London immediately the raids had eased off, and they had taken their chances together for the rest of the war.

For several years the extent of Tom's trauma had been manifest in his nightmares. His cries for help would pierce the small hours as he relived the ordeal in sleep, though remaining strangely silent about it during consciousness. And the extravert child with the infectious chuckle had been replaced by a nervous, sullen little boy, lacking the ability to communicate. He was mocked by his peers and despaired of by his teachers who simply could not reach him. He had managed to master the basic rudiments of the three Rs, but was generally accepted to be the dimmest child in his year.

But Maggie knew that he was neither stupid nor insensitive. When he was relaxed at home he showed a lively intelligent mind. The long lonely hours he spent indoors, while other boys of his age roamed the streets in groups, were filled reading adventure books from the library. He also read the newspaper from cover to cover every day, so was quite familiar with the world around him. And whilst he might seem infuriatingly self-absorbed to the outside world, he was never lacking with a helping hand or a kind word for his mother and sister.

Although Maggie always did what she could to help him, this was no longer the simple matter it had once been when no ruffian dared lay a finger on him in her presence. Now he would not tolerate her protection, preferring to be bullied rather than babied. Although this imbued her with a sense of powerlessness, she admired his spirit.

Her reverie was interrupted by the arrival of her mother. 'Good morning, me darlin's,' said Dora, sailing cheerfully into the kitchen in a crossover apron over a cotton dress, her red hair worn short and close to her head in waves. There was a strong resemblance between mother and daughter though Dora carried a little more weight on her petite frame and had a feathering of fine lines around her blue eyes. But at thirty-eight she was still a very attractive woman with the same colouring and keen smile as Maggie. She brushed her brow with the back of one work-worn hand and flopped on to a chair at the table. 'Phew, it's gonna be a scorcher, I reckon. It was ninety degrees at Kew gardens yesterday, so they say.'

'No wonder I couldn't get to sleep last night,' said Maggie, placing a cup of tea in front of her mother.

'Oooh ta, love,' said Dora, guzzling the tea with all the enthusiasm of one who has just emerged from the Sahara desert. 'I was gaspin' for that.' She eyed her children over the rim of her cup. 'Both all right this morning?' It was more an affectionate habit than a question.

'We're fine, Mum,' they chorused as they did every single day. A tedious ritual, perhaps, but this was the sort of caring stability with which they had been raised and on which Maggie hung her life.

'There's crowds o' people about,' Dora informed them brightly. 'All pourin' on to the buses and trains to Wembley for this afternoon's shindig.'

'How exciting,' said Maggie 'They were saying on the wireless that there'll be thousands of people there.'

'I bet there'll be a crowd outside the Stadium too,' opined Dora. 'Hoping for a glimpse of the royal party when they arrive.' She finished her tea and sighed with pleasure, handing her cup to Maggie for a refill. Although the Brightwells were not ardent followers of athletics, they recognised the importance of the Olympic tradition in promoting international goodwill. And having such a momentous event staged on their own doorstep had, naturally, generated a certain patriotic enthusiasm. 'I wouldn't mind being in the stands at Wembley meself. A function like that is sure to stir the blood. They say it'll be a real spectacle, despite the lack of British resources.'

Maggie nodded in agreement, having inherited her mother's sense of occasion. 'I'd love to be there too,' she said, pouring her mother's tea and passing it to her.

'The first-aid people'll certainly be kept busy though if this heat continues,' said Dora, mopping her brow with her handkerchief. 'One bit of a heatwave and we're all on our knees. We're just not used to it in England.'

'I'd rather be there than stuck in a stuffy old office,' said Maggie wistfully, removing the toast from the grill, 'even if it's a hundred degrees.'

'Oh, well, some of us have to work for a livin',' sighed Dora, taking a packet of cigarettes from her apron pocket and displaying them proudly.

6

'And you can't have everythin'. I've had a good start to the day because I managed to get these from one of the women at work. She knows someone who knows someone, you know . . . black-market prices, but still. Damned shortages! It's about time things started to improve.'

'But they are,' reminded Maggie, referring to yesterday's announcement. 'Footwear and furnishing fabrics are coming off ration in the autumn, and that can't be bad.'

'Yeah, you're right,' agreed Dora, who usually managed to take the irritations of prolonged austerity in her stride. 'One of these fine days we'll be able to burn our ration books.'

Working on the corner of the table, Maggie spread the toast thinly with margarine and piled it on to a plate, then filled three more with streaky bacon, fried tomatoes and scrambled dried eggs before sitting down at the table herself, imbued with a warm family feeling.

Over the years life must have been lonely for Mum, coping with two children alone, Maggie thought. It was no wonder that she sought a little light relief with people of her own generation occasionally. And why shouldn't she go to the pub with Mrs Bingley now and then, or to the cinema, or to the Shepherd's Bush Empire? And although Maggie didn't entirely approve of her mother's fondness for a flutter on the horses, she respected her right to it, since Dora's bets, which were placed surreptitiously with a greengrocer in Ashbrook Green High Street, never exceeded moderation or harmed the family budget. Maggie thought that her mother probably just about broke even. Her winnings, which were reasonable since she was a keen studier of form, were always spent on treats for the family, but she never risked enough to sustain any major losses.

Mother had her critics outside the family circle though. There were those people, usually women sheltering complacently in the protective arms of marriage, who thought she was positively sinful to enjoy such common and masculine leisure pursuits. But they never aired their views twice in Maggie's hearing. Mother might indulge in a little escape from domestic responsibility every so often, but no children could be more blessed with parental love than herself and Tom. Anyway, it was fun to have a mother with such a vital spark about her.

As they cleared their plates, Maggie rose and stacked them on the draining board.

'You sit down and finish yer breakfast, luv,' said Dora, 'or you'll be late for work. I'll do the clearin' up when you've gone.'

'I've plenty of time,' said Maggie, though she did sit down and spread some marmalade on a slice of toast.

'I won't let you be late, don't worry,' said Dora. 'You wanna look after a good job like yours.'

7

'Don't worry, I will,' Maggie assured her, biting into her toast. She knew that her "posh job" meant a lot to her mother. As a girl, domestic service had been the obvious choice of employment for someone of her mother's class and education, and she had worked as a housemaid until she had met and married Maggie's train-driver father. But Dora had been quick to spot the opportunities for women of her daughter's generation, and she ardently encouraged Maggie to make the most of them. 'You don't wanna spend yer life skivvyin' to earn a crust,' she warned her. 'Just because we ain't rich doesn't mean you shouldn't talk proper and have good manners.' Although a pronounced cockney herself, Dora strived to practise what she preached as far as longtime habit allowed. 'You get yourself an office job where you can wear smart clothes and meet a nice class o' person. Then you'll stand a chance of finding a man who can keep you in comfort.'

In the same way as Dora wanted a better life for her daughter, so Maggie wanted to improve her mother's lot. She longed to liberate her from her twice-daily cleaning routine. To this end Maggie applied herself diligently to her job and attended evening classes for shorthand and typing with a view to reaching secretarial status with its improved salary. But although Maggie had avoided disappointing her mother by mentioning it, the girl wasn't at all sure that this sort of occupation would ever confer any personal satisfaction, for she found office routine eminently boring. What the alternative might be she didn't know, only that the idea of clerical work in the long term was a gloomy prospect indeed.

Dora turned her attention to the taciturn Tom. 'And what are you gonna do with yourself all day, son?' she asked.

He shrugged his bony shoulders, his grey-blue eyes surveying his mother guardedly through his owlish spectacles. 'Dunno,' he said at last.

'Yer ought to be out and about in this weather, not mopin' about the house on your own all day in the school holidays!' said Dora briskly. 'Make the most of your freedom, son. You'll be tied to a job soon enough.'

Smarting at her mother's brusqueness which bought a guilty flush to her brother's cheeks, Maggie intervened. 'I expect you'll go out for a bike ride, won't you, Tom?' she suggested brightly, as though he were any other normal boy. 'I know you usually enjoy that.'

Mother didn't mean to hurt Tom, of course. But her anxiety about his well-being seemed occasionally to impair her sensitivity. Tom's only friend was a battered old utility bicycle which he rode to neighbouring high streets such as Shepherd's Bush and Hammersmith where he spent time safely out of range of torment from local boys.

Clearly ashamed of his social failure, Tom threw Maggie a grateful look. 'Yeah, I probably will,' he said, his lips twitching nervously.

Dora and Maggie exchanged glances and this time it was Dora's turn to blush, ashamed of her own impatience. Why couldn't she just hold her tongue? she admonished herself. Obviously, the boy couldn't help the way he was. 'Good idea,' she said sheepishly.

They chatted about more general topics until Maggie rose and said, 'Well, it's time I wasn't here.'

'Are you taking the bus to the station or walking?' asked Tom.

Glancing at the clock on the wall, she said, 'I don't think I'll have time to walk.'

'Mind if I come to the bus stop with you? It'll be somethin' to do,' he asked.

'Course not,' she smiled, recognising his need for a respite from his mother's critical eye.

Outside in the fresh air, Maggie sighed with pleasure. Having recovered from her earlier torpor she now felt charged with energy and purpose. The air smelled sweet and the street was buzzing with activity. White-collar workers now headed for the bus or tube; housewives, equipped with ration books and shopping bags, marched purposefully towards the High Street, eager for a place at the head of some queue. Hopscotch games and skipping were already in progress on the pavement.

Moss Street was made up of local authority terraced houses and flats built in the early 1930s. The flat-fronted, angular dwellings offered standard accommodation and were of red brick with tiny front gardens edged with privet, and small yards at the rear. The tenants mostly comprised factory workers, office staff of the lower echelons, shop assistants, lorry drivers, unemployed people and a sprinkling of spivs. The street led directly into Ashbrook Green High Street which was a busy shopping area offering all the basic essentials. For such items as special occasion clothes or jewellery, the locals went further afield to the West End which was easily accessible by bus or tube.

Turning into the High Street past the shabby florist's on the corner, Maggie and Tom were swept up in the sudden change of pace. People hurried in all directions, queueing for and pouring on to buses, dodging across the road through the delivery vans, buses, bicycles and occasional private car. Shopkeepers were busy preparing to open their doors and serve the jovial queues of women that had already formed outside.

'You mustn't take too much notice of Mum,' Maggie said to Tom as she joined the bus queue. 'She can be tactless at times, but she only wants what's best for you.'

'She wants me to be a *real* boy,' he said, head bowed and hands

9

plunged into his trouser pockets. 'Rough, like the others.'

'You know that isn't true,' defended Maggie. 'She's always discouraged roughness in either of us.'

'In speech and manners, yeah,' he agreed. 'But she still expects me to be a man like me dad. And we all know that I never will be.'

'You *are* only thirteen,' she reminded him. 'And you proved your bravery when you were only five years old. Mum knows what you went through then. But she wants you to be happy now. I only wish you'd done better at your lessons, that would have given you confidence. I know you're not really a dunce.'

'I feel so sick with nerves when I'm at school, that me mind just goes blank.'

Such was the power of blind terror, she thought, but said, 'Well, only another couple of years and you'll be finished there.' But what was to become of him then? she asked herself. Who would want to employ a nervous wreck with an abysmal school record?

A bus snorted to a standstill and Maggie moved with the crowd towards it.'See you tonight, Tom,' she said. 'We'll go for a bike ride, if you like.'

His eyes brightened. 'Yeah, I would,' he said.

'Ta-ta,' she called, clambering on to the platform.

'Ta-ta, sis.'

It was only a few stops to Shepherd's Bush tube station and she was still empathising with Tom as she fought her way on to the train and stood in the airless rush-hour crush. Poor boy. If only she could do more to help.

Only when she ascended from the warm, gaseous breezes of the underground into the bright sunlight at Holborn, did her thoughts turn to herself. And as she strode purposefully towards her office, she realised that her sole ambition for the working day was to reach the end of it. Surely there must be more to earning a livelihood than this!

After Maggie and Tom had left, Dora Brightwell sat thoughtfully over a cup of tea and a cigarette. The continual worry over Tom sapped her energy far more effectively than her work with the mop and bucket. With a boy of thirteen in residence this home should be littered with lads and ringing with the sound of boisterous banter. Women with sons of the same age who complained about the constant stream of youths cluttering up the place didn't know how much she yearned for such a normal, healthy exasperation. If Tom was happy in his isolation, she wouldn't worry so much. But he wasn't, so the anxiety persisted.

Dora accepted the fact that some people actually functioned better whilst under stress; she knew that she was not one of them. Being naturally lighthearted she simply couldn't bear gloom. In fact, her instinct was to distance herself from it altogether.

When her dear husband had been killed, instead of feeling compelled to mourn quietly alone, she had longed to surround herself with people in the cheerful ambience of a crowded pub. And when her son had become more of a problem than a pleasure, she had frequently yearned to drown herself in the escapist warmth of the cinema. Did this make her evil or just weak? she wondered. Was there any redemption in the fact that she had not actually succumbed to these urges at the time, when the children had needed her so much? But latterly, as Tom's difficulties had continued and she had felt the lack of a soul mate, her little diversions had helped to retain her sanity. And, of course, Maggie, who had been endowed with enough guts for the three of them, was a great help. What would they do without her?

Dora cleared the breakfast table and washed the dishes, and was just wondering what shopping she needed when Tom arrived back.

'Do you want me to do any errands, Mum?' he offered dutifully.

Dora shook her head. 'No thanks, son.' She liked to do her own shopping even though her arms were sometimes almost dislodged from their sockets with the weight. In fact, she usually trotted off to the High Street every day even if she only wanted one item, for company was food and drink to Dora. She knew all the shopkeepers well and many of the punters.

Tom sat down at the table and read the paper while Dora made a list. Tripe and onions for dinner, she decided. It wasn't really the weather for it but it was cheap and nourishing so it would have to do. Tripe, onions, carrots, lard, a quarter of tea, a piece of cheese . . .

She rinsed her hands and face at the kitchen sink and combed her hair before the tarnished mirror on the wall. Then she collected the ration books from the kitchen drawer and took her brown leatherette shopping bag from the broom cupboard. 'I'm off to the shops now, Tom. I shan't be long. Ta-ta.'

'Ta-ta, Mum.'

Listening to her receding footsteps on the stairs, Tom wandered into the living room and flopped down on the bulky mustard-coloured sofa, which was part of a shabby three-piece suite. He fidgeted absently with the well-worn embroidered arm covers. A puddle of sunlight fell on to the balding red and brown patterned carpet in the centre of the room, bordered by highly polished, beige linoleum. Also in the room was a dark wooden sideboard and a standard lamp with a bulbus yellow shade, edged with a matching fringe. Above the fireplace was a wooden mantelpiece on which stood a plethora of cheap ornaments; more covered virtually every other available surface.

11

Feeling restless, he got up and went over to the window, looking down into the street where his mother was gossiping to a neighbour at her gate. The two women were engrossed in conversation until suddenly Mother threw back her head and laughed in her unmistakable hearty way. Tom watched, yearning to be part of that sunlit world where people laughed with you, not at you. To be accepted as an equal by his peers was the object of his dreams but had no more likelihood to someone of his meagre confidence than the fantasy of someone else wishing to become a film star.

The diagnoses of various doctors who had been consulted over the years was that his communication problem was a result of a traumatic incident when he was five. But he couldn't see the logic in that since his mind was always far too concerned with the present to dwell on the past. At night he lay in bed imagining how it might feel to be part of the outside world instead of living alone on the periphery. He silently rehearsed dialogues he might have with his contemporaries, but when confronted with the actual reality he simply quaked at the knees and clammed up completely. And then the disappointment at his failure would turn to self-pitying anger and he would abandon all hope and loathe the whole world except Maggie and Mother. And sometimes he even hated Mother, too, for her expectations of him.

Maggie was the only person in the world with whom he felt really at ease. She came to him for advice, as though his opinion might actually be worth something. Then he felt strong and confident, his brain clear and bright.

Although frequently beset by a feeling of resentment towards the world in general for his exclusion from it, he knew in his heart that the answer must lie within himself. If only he could find it . . .

Down in the street Mother had progressed only a little on her journey, and was now chattering to a women in carpet slippers and an apron two houses further on. On the other side of the road a gang of boys of about Tom's age sauntered noisily by, playfully shoving each other, kicking stones and shouting with high spirits. He stepped back quickly with the shame of a voyeur, fearful of being seen, the oddity, the outsider.

His misery and frustration often culminated in violent urges which made him want to kick the walls and break the furniture. Clenching his teeth and fists in a desperate effort at restraint, he held on until the fires inside him finally subsided, leaving him powerless against the tears that fell in humiliating streams. His shame was no less for the fact that he was alone in the apartment. He scurried to the privacy of the bathroom, since that was the only room in the house with a lock. Succumbing to the relief of tears until he felt calmer, he then washed his face, combed his hair and went downstairs to collect his bicycle from the hall.

Passing his mother in the street, he slowed down but didn't look directly at her for fear her shrewd eye might somehow perceive signs of his shameful outburst. 'I'm just off for a ride, Mum, I'll probably see some o' the boys from school,' he said jauntily, thinking it was worth a lie just to see the relief on her face.

'Righto, son,' she smiled. 'Have a good time.'

As he turned the corner, he pedalled faster, fearful of having his fiction turn to reality. The boys from school would just love to catch him with lingering evidence of tears on his face. He cycled out of Ashbrook Green, already longing to return to the safety of home.

Chapter Two

At about the same time as Maggie arrived at the offices of Anderson &
Partners, Financiers of Repute, Established 1880, seventeen-year-old
Chloe Anderson flounced dramatically on to the terrace of her riverside
home at Richmond in Surrey, having just taken a telephone call.

'God,' she said, in the general direction of her mother who was break-
fasting in the sunshine, 'some people have no consideration.' She sank
into a chair at the glass-topped wicker table and rested her chin on her
hands, her dark eyes flashing with rage, her long black hair swinging loose
about her arms. 'No consideration at all!'

Chloe's mother, Lavinia, dabbed her mouth with an embroidered
linen table-napkin and eyed her daughter warily across the table, her
brow furrowed at the storm symptoms. As much as she loved Chloe, the
girl could be very tiresome when her interests were threatened. 'Why,
what's happened, dear?' Lavinia asked, twirling her spectacles around
with well-manicured fingers.

'Fiona Barclay-Dawson phoned, that's what's happened,' Chloe
snapped, pouring coffee from a silver pot.

'Isn't she the girl you're going to Wembley with this afternoon?' asked
Lavinia, her hand trembling slightly as she raised her coffee cup to her
lips for she was actually rather frightened of her daughter in this mood.

Chloe had been a late baby. After fifteen years Lavinia and Rupert
Anderson had regretfully resigned themselves to a childless marriage.
And then, when she had been thirty-six and he thirty-eight, the union had
been blessed with Chloe. Such was their joy, their daughter had become
the centre of their world. They could not find it in their hearts to refuse
her anything.

'*Was* going,' corrected Chloe crossly, helping herself to some of the
bacon ration which was on offer with sausages and tomatoes in a silver
serving dish. 'The stupid girl has just telephoned to say that she can't
make it. She's got flu or something. It's probably just a cold.' She
sighed expressively. 'Honestly, what a feeble reason for cancelling an
arrangement!'

'But if she isn't well, perhaps it's better that she should stay at home?'
suggested Lavinia tentatively.

Her daughter sighed heavily again. 'And where does that leave me?' she demanded, her cheeks angrily suffused. 'It's too late to find anyone else to go with, and I'm damned if I want to go alone.'

Lavinia looked suitably sympathetic, having disagreed as far as she dared. 'I would go with you myself, darling, but I can't bear crowds, as you know. Perhaps Daddy will take the afternoon off to keep you company.' She glanced at her watch. 'It's nine o'clock, he should have reached the office by now. Why not give him a ring?'

Chloe tutted. 'It really is scraping the bottom of the barrel to have to resort to one's parents for company,' she said with cruel thought-lessness. 'But I suppose it will be better than not going to the ceremony at all.'

Lavinia was far too used to Chloe's insensitivity to be unduly hurt by her careless talk. 'Don't let your breakfast get cold, dear,' she warned. 'Food is too precious to waste.'

Absently Chloe chewed her bacon. Lavinia noticed how her pink cotton dressing-gown enhanced her dark colouring. Although striking in appearance with her raven hair, sensuous mouth and exceptional figure, her large features made her attractive rather than pretty. She was tall and slim and had an oval-shaped face with a straight arrogant nose, like her mother's. Her eyes were undoubtedly her best feature, deep brown pools which mirrored her volatile nature.

'Oh, well, Daddy dear,' she said, finishing her breakfast and dabbing her mouth daintily, 'it looks as though I shall have to make do with your company for today.' And she excused herself and went inside to the telephone in the drawing room.

But much to her annoyance her father was not able to accommodate her on this particular occasion. 'But, Daddy, you *must* be able to take the afternoon off,' she insisted. 'It is your business, after all. You can do what you like.'

'If I made a habit of doing just that, the business would soon stop providing you with all your nice things,' he said by way of pacifying her for it wasn't strictly true. A man of his means was pretty well a law unto himself but there wasn't a financier in London who would break an appointment with Bradley Hughes of Hughes Construction, a thriving American company which had recently expanded their operation to the UK. 'I have an important luncheon engagement which I am expecting to last well into the afternoon.'

'Oh, Daddy,' she wailed. 'I've got no one to go to the opening ceremony of the Olympics with.'

'Normally I'd do anything in the world for you, pet, you know that,' he reminded her. 'But today I simply cannot help. Can you not ask one of your other friends to go with you?'

Chloe was one of the privileged few who was not burdened by the need to earn a living so could spend her days as she pleased. Although she had been educated at one of the best independent schools in London, her pleasure-seeking had easily outstripped academic pursuits. Various breeches of discipline and abysmal results in her lower school certificate exams had culminated in the school's refusing to continue with her education beyond sixteen. Chloe had been only too delighted to escape the restrictions of the schoolroom, and since her father was more than happy to cater to all her financial requirements, she was content to be a lady of leisure, particularly as she had friends in a similar position.

'Of course not,' she snapped rudely. 'It's far too short notice.' She paused thoughtfully. 'Is there anyone suitable at your office who could go with me?'

'That's a good idea,' said Rupert, grateful for the suggestion for he dreaded the wrath of his difficult daughter. 'I'll tell George the chauffeur to stay with you for company when he drives you there, instead of calling back for you later.'

But that wasn't quite what Chloe had in mind. It was bad enough having to lower one's social sights to zero by considering the idea of a parental companion. Her father's geriatric chauffeur would be about as much fun as a maths lesson! 'Surely you can do better than that, Daddy,' she objected. 'George is a hundred if he's a day. The excitement will probably kill him off altogether.' She twiddled a strand of hair pensively. 'I was thinking more in terms of a young man. Someone with style.'

Rupert balked at the idea of allowing his cherished daughter to become the subject of office speculation. Resorting to deviousness in the interests of self-preservation, he just said, 'If you don't mind having a stranger go with you, I'm sure I can find a suitable companion. You just leave it to me. I'll send someone along with George when he comes to collect you in the Daimler.'

'You're an angel, Daddy,' she said, a smile now sweetening her tone, 'What would I do without you?'

'You'd manage,' Rupert assured her, beaming at her praise.

The general office at Anderson's caught the full force of the morning sun. By ten o'clock the atmosphere already resembled that of a greenhouse. Breathlessness abounded, perspiration flowed and there was a communual beseeching of the clock to hurry towards five o'clock. Maggie was struggling through a pile of invoice-typing, her fingers slipping on the keys, the paper sticking to her hands, and her clothes clinging moistly to her skin. When she was told by the senior clerk,

Miss Bateman, that she had been summoned to Mr Anderson's office, she welcomed the break from tedium.

But she was not unconcerned by the reason for her summons because all but the very gravest staff matters were dealt with directly by Miss Bateman. So what did the old boy want? Had Miss Bateman reported her for her misdemeanour on the switchboard whilst relieving the telephonist the other day? Or had she perhaps told him of Maggie's late arrival at the office one day last week after an incident with an old lady on the tube? But no, Miss Flora Bateman, known privately by her subordinates as Fussy Flo, a middle-aged spinster with a ramrod back, a flat chest, bunned hair and brogues, might be a stickler for office discipline but she was not without a heart.

He must have got to hear about it somehow though, thought Maggie, entering her employer's office with its leather-topped desk and wall-to-wall carpet. 'I'm Maggie Brightwell,' she informed him since they had not had any previous personal contact. She stood just inside the door and threw him a quick hesitant smile which dimpled her cheeks prettily. 'I understand from Miss Bateman that you wanna see me.' Despite an initial apprehensive tremor, her voice was strong and confident, her chin tilted upwards as she marched briskly towards him, exuding an air of efficiency. Her mother had taught her from an early age the benefit of seeming to be in control of a situation, no matter how petrified you actually were.

Deciding to pre-empt the situation, she said, 'If it's about my bein' late last week, I know it was a full half hour, sir, but there was this elderly lady who came over queer on the tube, you see. She was very shaky, so I went home with her to make sure that she was all right.'

Rupert Anderson found himself imbued with an unaccountable feeling of happiness. It was as though a fresh breeze had suddenly blown through the sweltering office. He was glad to have insisted on dealing with this matter personally, since it was not in the line of business.

'That was very kind of you, my dear.' He leaned back in his chair and fanned his face with a copy of *The Financial Times*. 'But that isn't why I want to see you.'

'Oh!' She nibbled her lip. 'I'm sorry about the giggling fit I had while I was working on the switchboard,' she said, overly informative in her anxiety. 'It must have been nerves or something that set me off like that. It won't happen again, I promise you.'

What a charming young girl she was! Apologetic but not obsequious; self-assured but not offensive.

Rupert's name could not be more appropriate for at fifty-five he was a teddy bear of a man with a square countenance encompassing a broad snub nose, brown button eyes and a wide smile. His general air of kindliness was further enhanced by a shock of bushy white hair. He was a popular employer throughout the firm, though he remained politely distant from the junior staff so as to command respect, something he had learned from his father when taken into the business all those years ago.

'What *am* I on the carpet for then?' asked Maggie impulsively.

Until a few moments ago Rupert had been feeling rather tense about his forthcoming luncheon engagement, and not in the mood for laughter. But now he couldn't help chuckling. 'Why, you are not "on the carpet" as you so amusingly put it, for anything. I simply want to ask a favour of you.'

'Oh! I see.' Maggie stood with her hands neatly clasped in front of her, eying him quizzically across his desk. 'And what might that be?'

'I am looking for someone to accompany my daughter Chloe to the Olympic Ceremony at Wembley Stadium this afternoon,' he explained. 'She has been let down by a friend at the last minute. Since I am informed that you are about the same age as her, I think you would be an ideal companion. Are you happy with the idea?'

Her eyes popped. 'I should say I am!' she enthused 'Who wouldn't be?'

'Good. I have arranged with Miss Bateman for you to go home right away in case you wish to change out of your office clothes. Don't forget to let your mother know of the arrangements since you will be later than usual getting home this evening. My chauffeur will pick you up at your door at about twelve-thirty on his way from here to collect my daughter from our home in Richmond. You can assure your mother that you will be safely delivered back to your home this evening.'

Maggie could hardly believe her luck. Almost a whole day off from the boring work in this steaming office. And for a special outing too. 'Whoopee!' she yelped, overcome by exuberance. She cleared her throat and added more sedately, 'Ta very much, sir.'

'You are very welcome,' he said. 'Just make sure that you have a good time.'

'You bet I will,' she assured him.

He was still smiling as she closed the door behind her. Her enthusiasm had reminded him of the pleasure of giving. Years of indulgence had long since deadened his own daughter's sense of gratitude. Even the war hadn't inflicted too much hardship on her since she had spent most of it in idyllic peace in Kent with her mother at their country house. Local farmers had eased the shortages for them, and even the flying bombs had paid them the courtesy of keeping at a safe distance.

Privilege certainly took the edge off one's appetite for life, he

19

thought. But Chloe could not be blamed for her circumstances any more than he and Lavinia could help doting on her. Chloe demanded of those around her because she knew no other way, the wheels of her comfortable life having always been so efficiently oiled by her parents.

Rupert would sooner use public transport himself to ease the petrol ration so that she could travel in comfort to Wembley, but since this and other sacrifices were not pointed out to Chloe, she could hardly be censured for taking them for granted. Maybe their lavish generosity had been to her detriment. But it was too late now. Neither he nor his dear Lavinia could cope with the tantrums which would certainly ensue from any sudden attempt to impose discipline.

It was no wonder that little Maggie Brightwell's zeal had been such a delight. Rupert was pleased with Flora Bateman's choice of companion for Chloe. He thought that Maggie would be a steadying influence on his daughter, despite the fact she was apparently a month younger.

With domestic matters now safely in hand, Rupert turned his attention to the business of the day. Speaking to his secretary on the internal telephone, he requested the file on Hughes Construction which he needed to study before the meeting if he was to procure a satisfactory result.

Although Maggie felt a little incongruous in the back of the elegant pre-war Daimler as it rolled through the dusty city streets to the select avenues of Richmond-upon-Thames, she was enjoying herself enormously. Fingering the tan leather upholstery she tried to identify the fusty aroma and realised that it was the same scent that she had noticed in Mr Anderson's office: a mixture of lingering cigar smoke and leather. It was the smell of another generation as well as another world.

The car swept into the drive of an imposing white house on a hill overlooking the Thames which gleamed lazily in the sunshine. The grounds of the house seemed like public gardens to Maggie in their magnitude, but she had barely had time to catch her breath at the sight of banks of rhododendrons and roses and the manicured forests of trees and shrubs when a girl in a stylish cream dress appeared, and was ushered into the car beside her.

Maggie smiled warmly at her. 'You must be Chloe,' she said, offering her hand. 'I'm very pleased to meet you.'

Her hand fell limply to her lap at the unveiled hostility of the reply. 'And who the hell are you?' Chloe asked in a cross if cultured tone.

'I'm Maggie Brightwell,' supplied Maggie, with all the cheer she could muster. She wasn't overly concerned about her appearance as a rule, but this well-dressed, elegant creature with long legs and a luminous complexion made her feel about as glamorous as boiled cabbage in her cotton print dress. 'Your father sent me. I work in his office.'

So much for an afternoon out with a young chap who could be relied upon to fawn over her because she was the boss's daughter, thought Chloe furiously. How dare Daddy send such a pretty girl to upstage her? She was obviously some wretched office junior with the social credibility of a tadpole. 'I suppose you've been told to report back to him about my behaviour,' she said.

'Not at all,' Maggie told her, disappointed but not damaged by the other's frostiness. 'He sent me along to keep you company. He seemed to think that you would be glad of it, being that your friend let you down at the last minute.'

Oh, really! Did Daddy have to be quite so undiscriminating when discussing her personal affairs? Now the girl might see her as a social reject and have an edge on the proceedings. For all Chloe's overt arrogance she was not without a more vulnerable side and now felt oddly threatened by Maggie's obvious self-possession. Chloe had a horrible suspicion too that the dratted girl might even feel free to discard her subordinate role just because she was outside the office.

'My friend didn't let me down willingly,' said Chloe, defending herself. 'She's gone down with some sort of summer flu.'

Then she turned away and stared out of the window in silence, leaving Maggie in no doubt as to the pattern she wished to set for the afternoon. Maggie was as sensitive to atmosphere as anyone else, but she had known too much sadness and responsibility in her short life to be intimidated by such bumptiousness.

'Since we are to spend the afternoon together,' she said with an air of resolute cheerfulness, 'might it not be a good idea for us to try to get along? I don't like you any more than you like me, but occasions like this don't come my way very often and I intend to enjoy myself. If you want to sulk, go ahead. You might as well know now, your sour face won't spoil things for me.' And leaving her words to do their work she turned and looked out of the window, from interest rather than pique.

It was amazing what a difference a few miles could make, she thought, absorbing the ambience which might have been that of another planet to Ashbrook Green. Beautiful houses in elegant avenues, quaint cottages with pretty gardens, smart shops with window boxes and colourful awnings, and tantalising glimpses of the Thames were all on view as they wove their way through the charming, upper-class town.

On her side of the car Chloe was fuming at Maggie's rudeness. Had the girl forgotten her position as a mere minion to Chloe's father, and as such very easily replaced? Oh, yes, Daddy was going to hear about this. 'You are not here to enjoy yourself. Merely to keep me company.'

21

Swinging round to face Chloe and noticing the silkiness of her dress and the fine leather of her beige peep-toe sandals, Maggie found it hard to excuse the pouting lips and sullen eyes. 'I *am* only obeying your father's orders,' she said sweetly. 'He told me to be sure to have a good time.'

'Oh!' Chloe was annoyingly deflated. Much to her further annoyance she found herself drawn to this girl who, added to her enviable confidence, also held the attraction of being from another world. Chloe was surprised at her diction which, whilst unmistakably working-class, had none of the roughness to be expected of someone of her station. Curiosity finally prevailed. 'What do you do in my father's office anyway?' she asked.

'I'm a junior clerk,' Maggie explained, 'which roughly translated means office dogsbody. Mostly filing and running errands, a little typing, you know the sort of thing . . .'

Chloe didn't, and thought the whole thing sounded hellish. Seeking to belittle Maggie's occupation and thereby establish her own superiority, she said, 'How frightfully tedious. How can you bear it, day after day?'

'I often wonder that myself,' said Maggie, foiling Chloe with her honesty. 'But anything is bearable if you need the money.' Although aware that some members of the upper classes didn't work, such people were virtually on another planet so far as Maggie was concerned. 'What job do you do?'

'Job!' exclaimed Chloe, as though Maggie was a newcomer to the civilised world. 'I don't need a job. My father supports me.'

'Oh, how very odd,' said Maggie, disconcerting Chloe even more by her refusal to be impressed. 'Whatever do you find to do all day?'

'See friends, go shopping,' she explained, leaning her arm on the open windowsill so that the breeze lifted her hair. 'Tennis and boating in the summer, ski-ing in Switzerland in the winter.'

Maggie thought Chloe had the glamour of a film star. It was a pity she was such a bitch. 'It sounds like fun, but it must get boring after a while,' she suggested. 'I mean, to have no aim in life to create a balance with all that pleasure.'

Oh, really, what did the hoi-polloi know about life? Chloe asked herself. It was all work and wages to them. She emitted a cynical laugh. 'And you, I suppose, have some great aim?'

'Yes, I certainly do,' chirped Maggie.

'Oh, do you, and what might that be?' asked Chloe, her sarcasm moderated by an infuriating interest in this *awful* girl.

'I haven't worked out how yet, but I intend to raise our living standards. For my mother, my brother and myself,' Maggie explained.

Chloe's brows rose scornfully. 'And how can someone like *you* do that?' Why was she bothering to ask? Why did *she*, Chloe Anderson, the daughter of one of the richest families in Richmond, find herself admiring and even envying a common clerk?

'As I said, I don't know yet,' explained Maggie, 'But I'll do it somehow. I don't intend to be a clerk all my life, you know.'

'Perhaps you'll even aspire to the position of secretary one day,' said Chloe sardonically. 'Such an achievement.'

'No, it won't be that,' said Maggie, ignoring the other's sniping in a sudden moment of clarity. 'But I'll succeed in my intention, just you wait and see.'

Loath as Chloe was to admit it, she believed her. And with this came the realisation of why she envied Maggie: it was for her remarkable self-possession which conferred a kind of magnetism. It was an established fact that power went hand in hand with privilege, yet Chloe knew that, somehow, Maggie Brightwell held every ace in the pack.

The discussion ended as they arrived at the Stadium and made their way through the crowds to their seats. Inside the arena the sun blazed down on an atmosphere of eager expectation as the masses waited for the arrival of the royal party. The stands pulsated with the patriotic fervour of many nations, and a communal roar went up when the King, smartly accoutred in naval uniform, went on to the track to shake hands with members of the Olympic Committee.

Maggie's throat ached. 'Hooray!' she cheered, nudging Chloe excitedly. 'Hooray!'

'There's no need to make quite such a noise,' reproached Chloe sulkily.

But Maggie was undeterred and roared even louder as fifty-eight teams of athletes, comprised of six thousand competitors from all over the world, marched into the stadium in a spectacular procession. It was a colourful parade with the British team sporting black berets for men and white for women, and the huge American contingent replacing the long-established straw boaters with soft hats. The spectators were even-handed in their applause and maintained the volume until the teams were all placed in mass formation on the Wembley turf. It was an impressive sight!

Following the King's short speech, the trumpeters of the Household Cavalry sounded a fanfare, and the raising of the Olympic Flag in the arena triggered the sensational release of seven thousand pigeons which circled the stadium in a symbolic gesture of peace. A twenty-one-gun salute heralded the arrival of the torch bearer who received the loudest cheers of the afternoon, and caused such excitement that some of the athletes on parade ran to the edge of the trackside to watch him circle the arena. And soon the flame rose poignantly against the singing of the Olympic Hymn.

In drab post-war Britain this occasion was a spectacle of colour and pageantry which stood out like a diamond in a dustbin. Optimism palpably filled the stadium and Maggie was moved to tears by the emotional impact. 'Isn't it lovely?' she said to Chloe, sniffing into her handkerchief. 'Abso-bloomin-lutely lovely.'

'It's all right,' snapped Chloe. 'But I don't think it warrants the fuss you're making.' Increasing evidence of Maggie's capacity for enjoyment was forcing Chloe more firmly into the role of killjoy, almost despite herself. Normally a sociable creature, she was confused by her feelings. Spite had descended on her with the tenacity of glue and she was a prisoner of her own bad temper. Whilst ardently wishing to enter into the spirit of the occasion, pride drove her deeper into the doldrums. 'It *is* only a sporting event, for goodness' sake, and not the end of a war! There's certainly no call for you to make such a fool of yourself.'

Maggie was rapidly losing patience with this malevolent miss. 'It's far more than just a sporting contest, and you know it,' she said, the sun warm on her back. 'What's the matter? Sore because you're not the centre of attraction for once?'

'Don't be ridiculous,' snapped Chloe.

'You are a bad-tempered brat, Chloe Anderson,' Maggie continued, 'and you can tell your father I said so if you like. If I am ever asked to go anywhere with you again, I shall refuse.' She threw the shocked girl an icy look. 'I'm going to the cafeteria now, to get something to drink.'

To Chloe's amazement, she felt compelled to follow.

Rupert Anderson was concluding a long and successful meeting with Bradley Hughes at the Savoy. 'I think that you and I have a great deal to offer each other on a long-term basis,' said Rupert, drawing on a cigar.

'Sure. I think so too,' said Bradley, feeling pleasantly at ease with this gentlemanly guy whom he knew to have an impeccable professional reputation.

'And I am confident that you won't get a better deal for your finance from any other company in London.'

Bradley nodded. He knew perfectly well that he wouldn't since he hadn't approached Anderson's before checking their reputation as the best in their field. Bradley was also aware of the fact that Rupert Anderson had personal influence with certain people in positions of authority concerned with the distribution of local authority building contracts. With private building regulations still lingering after the war, one had to take such things into consideration when finally placing a business deal of this magnitude.

At twenty-seven, Bradley knew his own mind. Although he didn't care to exploit personal relationships for business gain, he saw no reason not to do so with commercial contacts. A businessman had a duty to his company. He had to look to the future. Anderson's fee for providing the Hughes Company with commercial finance would be considerable. Other financial institutions had been eager with their offers. Anderson would expect this, for the Hughes business was a financier's dream.

Already a thriving company in the USA, rich in assets, Hughes Construction was in the market for capital for a new building development comprising a large council estate in outer London, with all attendant schools and amenities. Even though some remuneration would be made on completion of the first stage of the development, there was still a huge financial commitment to be made in terms of labour and materials. And because most of the company's resources were tied up in other projects, working capital was needed. When seeking commercial finance at this level, Bradley was usually able to negotiate a lower interest rate from a finance company than from a bank. And if a good business relationship was to be forged between his own company and Anderson's, it was to be hoped that Rupert Anderson would show his gratitude by making certain recommendations on Hughes's behalf.

A tall, well-built man with blond hair and blue eyes, Bradley was from Philadelphia. Whilst stationed in England during the war, he had become friends with a London builder called Ray Collins. Already in his sixties, Ray had been struggling to keep his building business afloat in wartime by doing essential refurbishment work. After the war, back home in the States, Bradley had received a letter from Ray offering first refusal on his business which he was being forced to sell because of ill health.

The proposition had not been particularly appealing, given the British building restrictions and the shortage of bricks and skilled labour caused by the war. But realising that these were temporary problems, the idea of helping to rebuild a country he had grown to love had appealed to Bradley. He had taken the idea to his father, Will, who headed the Hughes Company. Will's emotional ties with England were strong because he had emigrated from the north of the country with his folks when he was four. He had sanctioned the project and assigned full control to Bradley.

That had been two years ago; a hard two years during which Bradley had accepted any job at all to keep the UK arm of the Hughes Company ticking over. Anything from domestic repair work to demolishing surface air raid shelters. But now, at last, things were moving and he could see the way forward for real construction work.

'If you give us a good deal, we'll have no need to look further afield in the future,' Bradley assured Rupert. 'Back in the States my father has used the same finance company since he started in business many years ago.'

Rupert beamed. The meeting with this charming, quietly spoken American had proved to be a real pleasure. He was, indeed, a gentleman. 'And I very much hope you will do the same.' He stubbed out his cigar. 'I'll have some figures ready for you in a day or two. Maybe we can meet in less formal surroundings to discuss them?' He took out his wallet to settle the bill. 'Perhaps you might like to come to dinner at my home in Richmond, and meet my wife and daughter?'

'I'd like that fine,' drawled Bradley.

A Daimler in Moss Street was almost as much of an event as the Olympic Games being staged at Wembley. Curtains were twitched aside all along the road as watchers saw young Maggie Brightwell being courteously helped out by a uniformed chauffeur.

Dora couldn't get home from work quick enough to hear all about her daughter's outing. 'And what was the boss's daughter like?' she asked, having been given a colourful description of the scene at Wembley. 'Was she nice?'

Maggie frowned. Even the most generous heart could not call Chloe nice. She was spoiled and arrogant and thoughtless. But to her surprise Maggie heard herself saying,' 'She's different to us, of course, because of her background, but I rather liked her actually.' And to her astonishment she realised that she was speaking the truth.

Chloe's mother was drinking a gin and tonic on the terrace while the housekeeper prepared dinner when her daughter arrived home. Lavinia's dark, greying hair was drawn back into a chignon which made her look rather severe since she had the same strong features as her daughter, apart from her rather nondescript brown eyes. She was wearing a good quality but matronly navy blue linen dress which belted around her thickening waist. Having been informed by a telephone call from her husband of his choice of companion for her, Lavinia had expected fireworks on Chloe's return.

Now, in a bid to lessen the impact of the inevitable explosion by being seen to place her allegiance firmly with her daughter, she said, 'It really was too bad of Daddy to pack you off with some junior clerk. Was she frightfully common? Did you have a dreadful time?'

Mother was right. It *was* too bad of Daddy to burden her with such awful company. And she had had a thoroughly miserable afternoon.

26

Maggie Brightwell was far too sure of herself. All that vulgar yelling and cheering, and her outspokenness was tantamount to bad manners . . .

But to her own and her mother's amazement, Chloe said, 'She's different to us, naturally. But I rather liked her. She's good fun. We got along awfully well.' And to her chagrin, she found herself wishing it were true.

Chapter Three

The girls did not meet again until November. This time the weather brought them together.

A dense, persistent fog, the worst for several years, descended on the country towards the end of the month and lingered for over a week in and around the capital. Visibility was reduced to nil in some areas, causing chaos and disruption for commuters, with delays in rail services and road traffic halted altogether in some places.

By mid afternoon on Monday the 29th, on the eighth day of the fog, those staff who had managed to get into the office at Anderson's had already departed. Maggie, diligently finishing some urgent typing, was the last but one to leave. Donning her camel-coloured coat and brown-and-white-striped muffler, she bade the industrious Miss Bateman good afternoon and hurried from the first-floor office. She made her way down the stone stairs to the main doors and collided with Chloe on her way in.

'Hello there,' said Maggie, instinctively jovial. 'What brings you here on such a day?'

'I've come to see my father.'

'You're out o' luck,' Maggie informed her. 'Everyone has gone home except Miss Bateman, and she'll be off in a few minutes. We've all been leaving early since the fog came, to try to get home before dark.' She paused thoughtfully. 'I gather your father wasn't expecting you.'

Chloe nodded. 'That's right,' she said in a doom-laden voice.

Since the other girl was obviously distressed, Maggie said, 'You seem worried. Is there anything I can do to help?'

Chloe shivered and hugged herself. She was pinched with cold but still managed to look stunning in a red coat with a fur-lined hood. 'Quite honestly, I don't know,' she rasped aggressively. 'Dratted fog! I've been wandering about for ages trying to find this place, and I'm frozen.'

'It's so easy to lose your bearings,' sympathised Maggie. 'I did the self-same thing on the way home every day last week.' She was thoughtful for a moment. 'But why venture out in such weather if you don't have to?'

'I didn't think it could *possibly* be so bad again today. It didn't seem to be when I left home this morning. I met a friend in town for lunch,' explained Chloe, near to tears. 'When we came out of the restaurant and I realised how bad it was, I decided to get a lift home with Daddy.' She chewed her lip and studied her kid-gloved hands, 'Now I don't know what I'm going to do.' And to Maggie's astonishment, she burst into tears.

Placing a sympathetic hand on her arm, Maggie said, 'But there's no real problem, surely! The tubes are still running.'

Furious with herself for showing her weakness to the indomitable Maggie, Chloe shrugged off the kindly gesture and hid her face in her lace handkerchief, sobbing, 'Don't you understand, you stupid girl?' She reverted to type through her tears. 'You can't see a yard in front of you out there. I'll never find my way to the station. I'll just have to go up to the office and 'phone my parents. They'll have to send George to collect me.'

'You can't expect anyone to drive through a pea-souper like this to get you, especially as it will be getting dark soon,' said Maggie, incredulous at such a suggestion. 'It's far too dangerous.'

'What do you suggest then?' snapped Chloe. 'That I spend the night here.'

'No, of course not. I think you should find your way home by public transport, like the rest of us, ' said Maggie crossly. 'Dragging people out in this weather because you're too feeble to make an effort just isn't on. If you weren't so rude, I'd suggest that we walked to the station together. But I don't like to be called stupid.'

Chloe hesitated only a moment. 'I'm sorry, Maggie,' she said, blowing her nose, 'I didn't mean it. I was upset.'

'That's no excuse.'

'I won't be rude to you again,' came the rueful promise. 'Please may I come with you?'

'Come on then, let's get going,' urged Maggie, eager to be on her way, 'or we'll never get home.'

'Thanks,' sniffed Chloe gratefully.

Although the fog caused a great deal of inconvenience, it didn't frighten Maggie. In fact, she had rather enjoyed the community spirit it fostered in the office and on the street. It had also shortened the working day. Naturally, she was concerned for the sick and the elderly for whom the weather was so treacherous, but she was surprised that anyone with Chloe's youth and health should find it worrying. Still, it took all sorts, she thought, mindful of her brother.

Outside, the vapour swirled in freezing banks of yellowish-grey, stinging eyes and setting throats smarting. Recognising that she had reached some sort of a turning point in her association with Chloe,

Maggie assumed an authoritative role. 'Grab my arm and keep your hanky over your mouth. We'll soon find the station, don't you worry. Any station will do. We can always change down the line.'

An hour later they were back at the same office building. 'Well, I'll be blowed,' laughed Maggie, who was frozen to the bone but not down-hearted. 'This fog plays havoc with my sense of direction.'

There was a claustrophobic sense of isolation in the atmosphere. Dark office buildings rose threateningly around them; footsteps and voices echoed eerily in the virtually traffic-free streets; icy globules of moisture suffused their skin and clothes. Morbid news items came uninvited into Maggie's mind: a woman had fallen into the Thames and drowned while walking home in the fog along the towpath; a man had died similarly after misjudging his step in the fog on a canalside up North, according to the morning paper. But she dared not let her spirits flag for a minute because Chloe was already bordering on hysteria.

'I'm so cold, Maggie,' she wailed. 'And I can't breathe. Oh dear . . . oh dear . . .'

'It's only because you're panicking,' admonished Maggie firmly. 'Now stop being such a baby and try not to think about how you feel. You're with me, so you'll be all right.'

She patted Chloe's hand comfortingly. It was hard not be irritated by Chloe's helplessness but she did seem to be genuinely frightened and not just seeking attention. A little hardship would soon toughen her up, Maggie thought.

The resonance of approaching footsteps heralded the appearance of a dark figure emerging spookily from the mist. Chloe shrieked and clung ever closer, but Maggie merely saw the bowler-hatted man in the black overcoat as an ally and said cheerfully, 'Can you help us, mister? We're looking for the station.'

'So am I,' he said amicably. 'Shall we join forces? Three heads are better than one, so they say.'

By the time they finally located the station their numbers had swelled to nine, all seeming like old friends as they hurried into its welcoming lights. The camaraderie had given the ordeal a sense of fun and adventure. Even Chloe seemed to be have calmed down. But Maggie, cast in the role of custodian, made a decision as they approached the ticket office. 'You'd better come home with me, Chloe,' she said. 'To save your folks turnin' out to meet you at Richmond. It might be bad there too. You can go home tomorrow when it's light. One of our neighbours has a telephone, so we can call your parents from there and let them know where you are.'

'Thanks, Maggie,' said Chloe, willingly accepting her commanding role in relief at being spared a journey alone in the present conditions.

'But no more weeping and wailing, mind.' Maggie warned her.

'All right,' promised Chloe, far too grateful to want to risk upsetting her again.

'Everything has its bright side,' said Maggie later when they were safely seated on the tube. 'We've managed to get a seat and that's normally unheard of in the rush hour.'

'I rarely use the tube,' admitted Chloe. 'My parents usually arrange for me to travel by car.'

'You certainly chose the wrong day to strike a blow for independence,' laughed Maggie.

'I'll say,' agreed Chloe, though it had been the pursuit of pleasure rather than emancipation that had sent her out, against her mother's wishes, this morning. She was increasingly impressed by Maggie's sangfroid though. 'Doesn't anything get you down?'

'Of course it does, but I'm too proud to show it,' Maggie told her, unaware that she was held in such esteem by the other girl.

Locating Maggie's home proved only marginally less difficult than finding the station had been, and it was after seven o'clock when they finally arrived, cold, hungry and exhausted. The savoury aroma of mutton stew greeted them in an appetising cloud as they ascended the stairs to be warmly welcomed by Dora, who had also been sent home from work early. 'It's an ill wind,' she laughed, illustrating for Chloe the source of Maggie's positive nature.

With introductions and explanations over, Dora said, 'Now take yer things off and warm yerselves by the fire while I nip across the road to phone Chloe's folks.'

When the girls had thawed out, the Brightwells and their guest ate supper on trays by the fire, making short work of lamb stew enriched with onions, carrots, potatoes, lentils and mouth-watering dumplings, followed by plain suet pudding with treacle. Afterwards they chatted until just after ten o'clock when Dora produced a tray of cocoa and digestive biscuits.

In this companionable atmosphere Maggie watched warmth and civility prevail over the cold, arrogant side of Chloe's personality. Tom and Mother took an instant liking to her. Visitors usually sent Tom scurrying to the safety of his bedroom, so it was a real treat to hear him offering Chloe the use of his bed. 'I'll be happy to sleep on the sofa,' he assured her with a shy smile.

The Brightwells might have been lacking in refinement, but they had no shortage of hospitality. Glowing from a bath, and wearing a pair of Maggie's striped winceyette pyjamas, their visitor climbed between clean, sweet-smelling sheets in Tom's tiny bedroom with a profound sense of well-being, despite the arctic temperatures. As her feet touched the comfort of a stone hot-water bottle, she sighed with contentment.

'Are you comfortable?' asked Maggie, appearing in a red woollen dressing gown and sitting herself sociably at the end of the bed.

'Yes, thanks,' said Chloe. 'Your family are super.'

'Yes, aren't they?'

'Will you come to my house sometime soon?' asked Chloe. 'I'd like us to be friends.'

Maggie wasn't at all sure that her employer would approve of having his home put at the disposal of a junior clerk. 'If you invite me, I'll consider it,' she said, making a joke of it.

'I'm sorry I was so hateful last time,' said Chloe, peering at Maggie over the top of the sheet.

Maggie frowned. 'You were a bit grim, I must say. Why was that?'

'I had a fit of the horrors.'

'I'll say you did! If you get too many o' those, you won't see me for dust,' Maggie warned her, guessing that the darker side of Chloe's nature had not disappeared altogether.

'I know.'

When Maggie had gone Chloe lay awake with the light on, staring round the room. At home she had a warm bedroom four times the size of this one. And hers benefited from soft rugs, an even softer bed and pretty pink walls and curtains. Here, in Tom's room the discoloured wallpaper was peeling with the damp, the bed was lumpy and the linoleum felt like frost underfoot. But she was warm inside from the glow of her newfound friendship with Maggie. Quite why it meant so much to her she had no idea. It wasn't as though she lacked a circle of well-bred girlfriends far more suitable than Maggie, and being at the mercy of her plain speaking wasn't the most enviable experience. Yet somehow, being counted as a friend by her felt like an honour.

Maggie climbed into bed careful not to wake her mother who was emitting rhythmic snuffling sounds. Like their guest, Maggie was mulling over their incipient friendship. Such an association was surprising, considering their inauspicious first meeting and disparate backgrounds, yet it felt natural somehow. What had amazed Maggie was Chloe's lack of confidence for all her swank. She was obviously a victim of over-protection.

Well, she'll get no special treatment from me because of her privileged position, she thought. She must have gathered that by now, yet she still wants to be friends.

Maggie doubted if Chloe's folks would be so keen, though. It was one thing using a junior member of staff as a temporary companion to your daughter. Quite another to allow something more permanent to develop between them.

The girls' contrasting attitudes led to a clash at their very next encounter.

'There is a telephone call for you in my office, Miss Brightwell,' announced Miss Bateman two days later, with a look that might easily have sent a marauding army into retreat.

'Oh dear,' said Maggie nervously, fearing some mishap at home for personal calls at the office were strictly forbidden except in cases of dire emergency. 'Is it my mother?'

'No, it is not,' snapped Miss Bateman. 'It is a young lady who refuses to give her name on the grounds that it is a personal call. Please inform her of our rules. And be quick about it.'

Maggie scurried to the phone and recognised Chloe's voice with a mixture of relief and rage.

'You gave me a real fright,' she hissed. 'I'm not allowed personal calls except in an emergency. I thought something was wrong at home.' Glancing through the glass partitioning, she could see Miss Bateman, having diplomatically vacated the office, throwing her an icy look from the general office. 'I can't stay. Miss Bateman is giving me killer looks.'

'Not allowed personal calls!' exclaimed Chloe with an air of haughty disbelief. 'But that's ridiculous. I didn't say who I was because I didn't consider it to be any of that woman's business, but if she is being difficult just let me speak to her. Once she realises who I am . . .'

'No, Chloe,' interjected Maggie hotly. 'I don't want any special privileges just because I happen to know you. It wouldn't be fair to the others.'

'I'll speak to Daddy about it then,' Chloe stated categorically. 'Get him to alter the rules for everybody. No phone calls indeed! I've never heard such nonsense.'

'Don't you dare say a word,' Maggie warned her, burning under the penetrating stare from the other side of the glass. 'And don't ever ring me here again.'

'How can I contact you then?' asked Chloe impatiently. 'Since you're not on the phone at home.'

'You can ring me at a neighbour's,' Maggie said hurriedly, seeking only to terminate this call. 'We'll organise it another time. I have to go now . . .'

'I called to ask if you would like to come to tea on Saturday,' persisted Chloe.

With concentration now at a minimum, since Miss Bateman had

come into the office and was hovering nearby, Maggie said, 'I usually go to the cinema with a friend on a Saturday.'

'Oh.' Chloe's disappointment was obvious. 'Perhaps I could join you?'

Now that *was* awkward because Beryl Bingley wouldn't welcome the company of someone like Chloe, especially in one of her superior moods. But this was no time for explanations. 'No, that wouldn't be a good idea. It will be better for me to come over to you,' she said in a desperate bid to end the conversation.

'Oh, super,' squeaked Chloe. 'The car will come for you about three, is that convenient?'

By this time Maggie would have agreed to walk naked through fire if it meant liberation from Miss Bateman's disquieting stare. 'Fine. I must go. 'Bye.' She replaced the receiver and turned to face the music.

'The company supplies telephones for the purpose of business, not to serve the social lives of junior members of staff,' barked Miss Bateman.

'I'm sorry,' apologised Maggie. 'It won't happen again.' Too true, it won't, she vowed, because Miss Chloe Anderson was going to be educated as to the ways of the 'other half' when Maggie saw her at the weekend.

'I think it's perfectly beastly of Daddy to ban private phone calls,' effused Chloe on Saturday, having been informed by Maggie of the strictures of a working girl's day. 'Why don't you tell him what he can do with his job?'

Maggie laughed loudly. 'Because I'd be no better off elsewhere,' she said. 'All companies have their rules. Anyway, who would pay my mother for my keep while I found another job?'

Chloe was shocked. 'You mean you have to *pay* your mother for your food?'

'Of course,' confirmed Maggie. 'I can hardly expect her to keep me now that I am working. She had to do it for long enough when I was a child.'

'But what about clothes, who pays for those?' asked Chloe.

'I do, of course, who else? Father Christmas?' chirped Maggie.

'But there can't be much left after you've paid your mother,' exclaimed Chloe, having been told the amount of Maggie's weekly wage.

'There isn't, but I manage,' she explained. 'With careful spending and regular saving.'

'You mean you have to wait until you've got enough saved before you buy something?' said Chloe incredulously.

'Of course.' Maggie was thoughtful. 'But don't you have to wait, too, when you've used all your clothing coupons?'

'Well, no, not really,' she explained a little sheepishly. 'There always seems to be plenty. I think Daddy gets extra ones from somewhere.'

They were in her spacious bedroom. Chloe was lying on her stomach on the bed, her chin propped up on her hands. Maggie was sitting in a pink wicker armchair by the window. Outside, darkness had fallen over the town, but the fog had cleared at last and squares of light shone cosily from the widely spaced houses beneath a blue-black, star-studded sky. Amid the lights at the bottom of the hill, a dark area indicated an expanse of unlit river.

The afternoon had been a thoroughly enjoyable experience for Maggie. Having been driven here in style by George, she had been warmly welcomed by Chloe and her parents. They had had tea by a log fire in the drawing room which was comfortably appointed in autumnal colours. There had been muffins and teacakes and sandwiches as thin as pennies, all served by a maid.

Maggie had assumed that Chloe's parents had welcomed her from pure courtesy and good breeding, since she was sure it could not be heartfelt. As Mother had pointed out earlier, 'You don't raise a girl to be a lady, only to have her mix with people like us.'

But the Andersons seemed genuinely pleased to see her and Maggie liked them enormously. Mr Anderson was especially sweet. Each time she glanced in his direction he smiled reassuringly. Chloe was lucky to have such a kind-hearted father. After tea the girls had escaped to Chloe's room to indulge in girl-talk, something for which they seemed to have an unlimited capacity.

'It's all right for some,' Maggie laughed in reply, knowing that there was no shortage of black-market coupons for those who could afford them. 'But I've no complaints about the way things are for me. My mum thinks that the only way to a better life for a woman is to marry it.'

'I think she's right,' said Chloe.

'The only snag is,' joked Maggie, 'well-heeled gents aren't exactly thick on the ground in the circles in which I move.'

'But I'm your friend now,' Chloe reminded her. 'And I can introduce you to plenty.'

'Good grief!' exclaimed Maggie, throwing her a shrewd look. 'I *do* believe you're serious.'

'Of course. Why wouldn't I be?'

'Because when I get married, it certainly won't be for money,' Maggie declared.

'But, as your mother so rightly says, a good marriage is the only way a woman in your circumstances can better herself,' said Chloe.

'One of the ways, I admit,' said Maggie, 'but I won't accept that it is the only way. It all depends on the woman. Personally, I'd rather do it through my own efforts.'

And that was all Maggie was prepared to say on the subject – another way in which the girls differed. For whereas Chloe bared her soul to Maggie without the slightest hesitation, Maggie was more cautious.

'I know who I want to marry,' said Chloe.

'Oh? Already?' said Maggie in surprise.

'Yes,' said Chloe. 'He's a gorgeous American called Bradley Hughes, a business acquaintance of Daddy's. He's terribly good-looking. Tall and blond with the most amazing blue eyes.'

Maggie narrowed her own eyes quizzically because until now there had been no mention even of a boyfriend. 'And is it serious between you?'

'Oh no, not yet,' exclaimed Chloe. 'In fact, I haven't even been out with him yet. He's been to dinner with us a few times, that's all.'

'But you're talking about marriage,' said Maggie incredulously.

'Yes, I know. Because that is what I have in mind for us eventually,' she explained. 'But he's ten years older than me, so he won't rush things. Fortunately I won't have any trouble getting the parents to approve because he's filthy rich and frightfully charming.'

'But surely it's too early to be thinking about marriage if you haven't even been out with the man?'

'Not really. I want him. And I always get what I want in the end.' She paused dreamily. 'He really is the most dishy man you ever saw. I melt just looking at him.' She gave a blissful sigh. 'As his wife, I'll be the envy of all my friends.'

'Is that important to you? To be envied for your man?' asked Maggie.

'I think it would make the man even more attractive, knowing that he was desired by other women,' said Chloe, and sensing Maggie's disapproval added quickly, 'but I'm very attracted to him anyway. I think he's wonderful.'

'What about him? Is he giving you favourable signs?'

'Oh, yes,' chuckled Chloe. 'I'm receiving all the right signals. He's definitely attracted to me.'

'I'm relieved to hear it,' chuckled Maggie.

They talked and giggled until supper which they ate in an elegant, wood-panelled dining room. The meal, whilst well presented, was typical of the austerity of the times: beef soup, followed by corned-beef hash served with fried potatoes and vegetables. After listening to the wireless for a while, Maggie made a move towards leaving, whereupon Mr Anderson insisted on driving her home since George was off duty this evening.

'There is really no need, 'Maggie assured him, anxious not to cause inconvenience. 'I can easily get the train.'

'Your mother would never forgive us if we let you go home alone in the dark.' He turned to his wife. 'Isn't that right, Lavinia?'

'It certainly is,' his wife agreed, 'Now, not another word, Maggie dear. Rupert doesn't mind a bit.'

And so, once again, Maggie found herself luxuriating in the leather-upholstered comfort of the Daimler, but this time in the front seat next to Mr Anderson, at his request. On finding herself the subject of friendly interrogation, Maggie assumed that he had his daughter's social well-being in mind and willingly answered his questions about her own hobbies, her friends and family. When they drew up outside the flat, he asked if she had enjoyed the afternoon.

'Oh yes, I've had a lovely time,' she said politely.

'Good,' he said. 'I hope we'll see a lot more of you. Chloe needs a friend like you, someone who won't let her have all her own way. I noticed this afternoon the way you stood up to her.'

'It isn't in my nature to let anyone walk all over me,' she said, not considering it her place to make a personal comment about a member of her employer's family.

'I'm afraid my wife and I have always given Chloe everything she's ever wanted,' he confessed. 'And, of course, she expects that sort of treatment from everyone.'

'Well, she won't get it from me,' Maggie assured him.

Ever the gentleman, he leapt from the car and came round to open the door for her, his white hair gleaming in the streetlight.

'There was no need for you to do that, Mr Anderson,' she said. 'It's freezing out here.'

'My pleasure.'

'Goodnight – and thank you for a lovely afternoon.'

'Goodnight, my dear.'

Hurrying upstairs to the apartment, she was surprised to find that the mingled scents of tea-time kippers and dampness were objectionable to her. Accustomed to the stuffy odour of home, she barely noticed it as a rule.

That's what an afternoon of gracious living does for you, she thought. It makes you discontented with what you have. Greeted at the top of the stairs by a furry presence, she picked up Nelson and cuddled him, feeling reassured by the familiar practice.

Lavinia Anderson sat at her dressing table, smoothing cold cream over her face and mulling over the events of the day. Having initially been horrified at the idea of her daughter's social descent, she now admitted to having thoroughly enjoyed Maggie's company. The girl was undeniably working-class, of course, but quite well spoken with beautiful manners, considering. In fact, the girl's determination not to be belittled had a certain dignity. And what enviable self-confidence!

Leaning back her head to work on her neck, she sighed wistfully as all the old regrets at having just one child flooded into her mind. Chloe had always been a lonely soul, and surely she and Rupert wouldn't have indulged her quite so lavishly had there been another. Competition within the home would have given her confidence too, because for all Chloe's bluster, she was often lacking in that area.

Little Maggie Brightwell was a natural leader. Lavinia could see why Chloe was drawn to her because she herself was too. She planned to encourage the friendship for she was convinced that Maggie's forthright manner would be a steadying influence on Chloe.

She creamed her hands, unspoiled by domestic chores, and ran a brush through her waved hair before placing a hairnet over it. Studying herself in the mirror she didn't think that she looked much different now to thirty years ago, since she had not looked young even then. She had never been beautiful and was glad that Chloe had been blessed with exceptional eyes, without which she would have had only the average looks of her mother.

Lavinia's father had been the Andersons' family solicitor and friend, and she and Rupert had known each other since they were children. Drawn together by their reserved personalities, their friendship had blossomed into love in their teens and they had been separated only by the Great War which had forced Rupert to leave his father's finance business to don an officer's uniform. They had married during one of his leaves, the first love for them both, and had enjoyed a long and happy marriage with no inclination towards infidelity on either side. Having been friends for so long before they became lovers, their shared a deep understanding and contentment in each other.

When post-natal complications after Chloe's birth had ended hopes of another child, the disappointment had drawn them even closer together. Side by side they had worshipped her, tailoring their existence to her needs, seeing the world through her eyes. Now that she preferred the company of her own generation, Lavinia filled the empty hours with voluntary work. Visiting the sick and elderly helped to fulfil some need in her.

Meeting Maggie today had appealed to Lavinia's underused maternal instincts. The girl was a refreshing change from Chloe's other friends who were all too full of their own importance to inspire her to any sort of affection. And it wasn't as though Maggie's association with Chloe posed the problem it would have had she been a boyfriend. That would have been immediately discouraged, for an eventual good marriage was vital to Chloe's future happiness.

When Rupert arrived back from Ashbrook Green, Lavinia was sitting up in bed reading, a pink crocheted bed jacket covering her shoulders.

'Well, is Maggie delivered safe and sound?' she asked, smiling at him as he removed his coat and hung it in the big oak wardrobe.

'Yes, safe and sound,' he said, yawning.

'I was just thinking what a charming girl she is,' said Lavinia, resting her book on the eiderdown and peering at him over the top of her reading glasses. 'Not really the sort of friend we'd have chosen for Chloe but having met her I approve wholeheartedly. The way she stands up for herself is so good for Chloe. Don't you agree?'

'I do indeed,' he said, undoing his tie and collar studs.

'I'm not sure exactly what it is about her,' Lavinia said, fiddling absently with her leather bookmark, 'but she certainly has something special. I do hope we see more of her, don't you?'

'Yes, I do,' he said, undoing his braces and hanging his trousers up in the wardrobe. 'She'll do Chloe the world of good.'

Rupert watched Maggie and Chloe from the window as they hurried towards the house across the garden, having been for a walk by the river. They were flushed from the sharp February wind and giggling over some girlish joke when they arrived in the drawing room.

'Hello,' greeted Chloe chirpily, her eyes resting gleefully on the sandwiches and cakes which were set out on an occasional table. 'Tea! Ooh, good, we're starving, aren't we Maggie?'

'Yes, we are,' said Maggie exuberantly, her cheeks glowing prettily, her hair ruffled from the wind.

'Help yourself, Maggie dear,' said Lavinia who was in an armchair by the fire drinking her tea. 'But we don't need to tell you that now, do we? You're practically one of the family. Almost a second daughter to us, in fact.' She smiled across at Rupert who was sitting by the window, nibbling a sandwich. 'Isn't that right, darling? Though we'd better not let her mother know or she'll think we're trying to steal her.'

Rupert smiled and nodded at his wife. Dear Lavinia. How happy she was to have another youngster to fuss over now and then. And how hurt she would be to know just how much Maggie had come to mean to him over these last few months. Just having the girl around made him lightheaded with elation, swept along by the sort of febrile energy he hadn't felt for years. He wanted to give her the things her humble circumstances had deprived her of and drown in her enthusiasm for them. He wanted to fill her life with pleasure.

For weeks he had wrestled with his feelings, tried to tell himself that they were nothing more than a kind of paternal affection. As it was for Lavinia, Maggie was to him the other child they had never had. But now, looking at the two girls sitting together on the sofa, he could delude himself no longer. The bittersweet torment he felt for Maggie was quite different to his love for Chloe.

But why had it happened? He was a happily married man. In over thirty years he had never wanted anyone but his wife, and he loved her still. This thing he had for Maggie hadn't changed that. He felt sick with shame. Why, the girl was just a child. He simply must control his feelings for her.

'Your mother doesn't mind your spending time with us, does she?' Lavinia asked Maggie.

'No, of course not! Mum just wants me and Tom to be happy. She's great!'

'That's good,' said Lavinia, beaming.

A strong sense of domestic harmony washed over Rupert. What a lucky man he was to have such a wonderful family. The last thing he wanted was to hurt them.

Chapter Four

'The flower shop delivery van is outside again,' observed Tom Brightwell, looking out of the living-room window one Saturday morning in April 1949.

'Oh dear,' groaned Maggie.

'There's no fool like an old fool,' tutted Dora, shaking her head disapprovingly.

'All right, Mum, don't go on about it,' urged Maggie, instinctively defensive of Rupert Anderson despite all the embarrassment he was causing her.

'Why don't you let me have a word with him?' suggested Dora. 'He might listen to an older woman.'

'No,' said Maggie emphatically. 'I'll sort it out myself somehow.' Over this last few weeks every vase, bowl and bucket in the Brightwell household had overflowed with best quality blooms. Now, Maggie was not prepared to accept one more reminder of Rupert Anderson's interest in her. Hurrying downstairs she opened the front door just as the delivery man raised his hand to the knocker. 'I won't take delivery,' she informed him quickly as he tried to hand her a bouquet of pink roses nestling glamorously in cellophane tied with white satin ribbons. 'Please return them to the sender.'

'That could make things a bit awkward for me, miss,' said the dark-haired young man who had become a familiar face at the Brightwell door. He drew in his breath, and shook his head. 'Having accepted the order on the phone from a florist in another area, I'm committed to get the flowers to you through our inter-florist delivery service. The customer has paid in good faith so he's entitled to his money's worth.'

'I see.' She chewed her lip, her face pale. 'In that case, please could you take the flowers away and give them to your wife with my compliments?'

'I ain't married,' he informed her, his dark eyes gleaming with sudden amusement.

'This isn't funny,' she snapped, giving him an icy glare. 'I don't want these flowers, or any others that you might be asked to deliver to me. Not now, not ever.'

'Don't tell me, luv,' he said breezily, 'tell the sender. I'm just doing me job.'

She smarted guiltily. 'Yes, of course you are, I'm sorry.' She combed her hair from her brow with her fingers. 'Look, you've done your part and delivered them. Now will you please take them away? Perhaps you have a girlfriend who might like them.'

'No, there's no one I'd want to give flowers to,' he told her.

Maggie sighed miserably. What was she to do about Mr Anderson? For the first few months she had thoroughly enjoyed her association with the Anderson family. Her friendship with Chloe had continued to develop, and Mr and Mrs Anderson had opened their hearts to Maggie wholeheartedly, confirming their approval by including her in family outings, and even allotting a bedroom to her for overnight stays at their home. They had introduced her to another world of concerts, ballet, theatre, and meals in the best West End hotels, and she had basked in the warmth of their obvious affection for her.

But gradually she had begun to suspect that Mr Anderson felt rather more for her than was comfortably acceptable. At first she had thought his lingering glances were a figment of her imagination, and the sudden frequent summonses to his office on trivial matters some new management policy towards the staff. Even when he had begun to offer her regular lifts home from work she had told herself he was just being kind because she was a friend of the family. But when the flowers had started to arrive she could fool herself no longer.

When she had confronted him about them, explaining as diplomatically as possible that she was embarrassed by them, he had plunged her even deeper into despair by telling her that she was very special to him and that he enjoyed giving her things. The fact that his advances seemed as much paternal as passionate, in that he had not actually laid a finger on her, only added to her burden because she felt bound to exercise delicacy in her rejection of him.

It was a particularly difficult situation for Maggie, with him being her employer, and one which was exacerbated by her emotional ties with his family. Although he concealed his feelings for her in their presence, she could feel their insidious pressure and had begun to make excuses not to go to the house, arranging to meet Chloe in town or suggesting that she come to the flat instead, dreading that her friend might see through the pretexts and somehow discover their cause. Despite all Maggie's repudiation of his attentions, Rupert continued to pursue her, seeming oblivious of the pain that would be caused to his wife and daughter should they discover the truth. Maggie guessed that he was suffering from some sort of infatuation which had impaired his reason, for she was certain that he was not normally a salacious man. And now another bouquet. Oh dear . . .

'Your mother, then,' she suggested hopefully, returning to the present and the delivery man.

'Mum died years ago,' he said.

'I'm sorry,' she said politely.

He shrugged his broad shoulders. 'So am I, love, but that's the way o' the world, innit? 'ere today, gone tomorrow.' He gave her a thoughtful look. 'Why not take the flowers anyway, however mad you are with the bloke that sent 'em? I took a lot o' trouble making them up, yer know.'

She glanced at the offending bouquet. 'I can see that, they're beautifully done, but I really don't want them.' She paused, looking at him anxiously. 'It's a long story.'

Up shot his thick, black brows. 'Why not come out with me tonight and tell me all about it?' he suggested cheekily.

Frowning she said, 'You've got a nerve.'

'He who dares wins,' he said, grinning, his crooked white teeth flashing against his dark complexion. 'So 'ow about it then?'

And to Maggie's amazement she found herself considering the idea. She was at a loose end after all. Chloe was entertaining her American to dinner *en famille* and Beryl had a date with a soldier. The company of a stranger for a few hours might be just what she needed to take her mind off things. 'All right then,' she said.

'I'll pick you up at seven o'clock,' he said. And while she was still questioning the wisdom of her action, he pushed the bouquet into her arms. 'Shame to waste all my good work. Ta-ta, see yer later.' And he was gone, whistling cheerfully down the path.

Twenty-four-year-old Jack Radford had every reason to be happy for he had had his eye on the little redhead at 11A ever since he had delivered that first bouquet to her. Deliveries were not normally his responsibility and he had been deputising for his younger brother on that first occasion. But since then he had eagerly relieved young Archie of his duties when there was an inter-florist order for Miss Maggie Brightwell. The fact that "Love, Rupert" was out of favour had given Jack just the opportunity he had been waiting for. What sort of a name was Rupert, anyway? He sounded like a real pansy. A good-looking girl like Maggie would want a man with a proper name. Like Jack, for instance.

Maggie soon discovered that her date for the evening was more than just the delivery boy, and was in fact the proprietor of the rundown flower business on the corner of Moss Street and the High Street.

'I took the shop over when I got demobbed after the war,' he explained as they rattled through the London streets in his black pre-war van, with Radford's Flowers written on the side in dusty white and

45

the riverbank smell of moss clinging to the interior. 'Mum and Dad had run a flower business from there for years until they had an intimate meeting with a flying bomb. They rented the shop from a mate of Dad's and we lived in the flat over the top. The premises were left empty after the folks died, so when I came back from the war I asked the landlord if I could take them over to make a living and a home for meself and me brother Archie who was living with an aunt. Seeing that the landlord owed Dad a favour, he agreed to let us have the place at a low rent without me having to buy the lease. A sort of gentlemen's agreement for the sake of old times.'

'I should think there's plenty of scope to build a business like that up,' she remarked, picturing the dilapidated premises. 'Once the country really begins to thrive again.'

'There may well be but I've no plans to build anything up,' he told her emphatically. 'It's just a wage to me. I live from day to day and I ain't planning to age prematurely by expanding.'

Such lack of enterprise seemed, to Maggie, to be incongruous in an entrepreneur. 'But isn't life a little dull without any sort of a challenge?' she asked.

'Earning a daily crust is enough of a challenge for me, love,' he assured her breezily. 'As long as I make enough to live, I'm 'appy.'

Maggie might not agree with his "live for today" philosophy, but she admired his honesty. He really was very likeable, and handsome too in an earthy kind of way, being of average height with a thickset build. He had a snub nose and wide lips beneath deep brown eyes within his square countenance, around which grew a shock of black curly hair. He was smartly, if a little loudly, dressed in a navy blue suit with a heavy stripe, white shirt and bright blue tie.

He took her to a pub near Shepherd's Bush Green which was packed to the doors until it was time for the last house at the Empire, when it emptied considerably. 'I didn't think a show or a film was a good idea for our first date,' he told her frankly as they sat in a cosy corner by the window. 'You can't get to know someone if yer can't talk, can yer? I 'ope you don't mind a pub.'

'Not at all,' she told him.

'Sorry I can't take you further afield. I have to watch me petrol coupons,' he said.

'That's all right.'

'Now then, tell me about this bloke whose flowers yer don't want,' he said over the rim of his beer-glass.

And feeling completely at ease in his company, she unburdened herself.

'It might be a good idea to leave the job,' he advised her.

'Oooh, that's a bit drastic. I'd have to find another one first and that might take quite a while,' she explained. 'I can't afford to have any time off without pay.'

He nodded sympathetically. 'Umm, I can see yer problem. But while yer seein' him every day, things will only get worse.'

'I suppose you're right,' she said gloomily. 'But I'll have to stay there until I've found something else.'

An idea began to form in Jack's mind. Perhaps he and Maggie could help each other.

'How much notice do yer have to give?'

'A week.'

'Why not come and work for me when you've worked your notice? Clerical work mainly, with some shop work and floristry thrown in.'

'Work for you?' she exclaimed, surprised at such an unexpected offer.

'Yeah, what's so strange about that?'

'Nothing. The offer came as a surprise, that's all.'

No more than it had to him, he thought. Still, it would probably be all for the best. After all, he did badly need help in his office. 'I can't pay you a fortune,' he explained, 'but you'd get a fair wage, and you'd save money in fares over the course of a week. And you could pop home for your lunch to cut down your expenses.'

'But I don't know anything about the flower trade,' she confessed.

'Experience is the best teacher, so they say.'

A mental image of the drab, dusty-windowed shop came into her mind. But oddly enough, rather than repel, the idea excited her. She could soon clean the place up, and the idea of working with flowers produced a frisson she had never experienced over work before. 'Do you need to know immediately?' she asked. 'I mean, are there any other candidates for the job?'

'No, only you, so take your time,' he said. 'But the sooner you get away from your present guvnor, the better.'

'I think you're right.' She narrowed her eyes. 'Who does your office work at the moment?'

He drew on a cigarette and grinned. 'I do, after a fashion.'

'Does that mean that you weren't actually looking for someone, that you created the job to help me out of this jam?' she asked.

His gaze moved over the firm curves of her figure etched against a green sweater which she wore with a grey pleated skirt. Her flame-coloured hair cascaded to her shoulders in a shiny cloud, and her blue eyes sparkled with affront at the suggestion of charity. She really was something special. It was no wonder her boss had fallen for her. Since Jack was basically an honest man, he replied, 'Let's just say that you prompted me to do something I should have done long ago. I hate doing the paperwork and I never seem to find the time. We'll be helping each other if you accept.'

She was still uncertain.

'Don't be afraid to say no if you'd rather not,' he assured her amicably. 'It's no skin off my nose. I realise that a girl like you might want something more glamorous.' He leaned towards her across the table. 'But I'll willingly sort that boss of yours out either way. He won't pester you again when I've finished with 'im.'

'No!' she said adamantly. It had taken all her energy to stop Mum from interfering. The situation with Rupert must be dealt with personally for, despite everything, he was a good man and she was sorry for him. 'That is something I must handle myself. But I would very much like to come to work for you.'

Chloe and her parents were entertaining Bradley Hughes to dinner in their home.

Over the meal he glanced across the glittering dining refinements, the silver and crystal, wafer-thin china and starched white linen, to Chloe. She was particularly striking this evening in a flame-coloured taffeta dress which revealed the creamy texture of her shoulders, her long dark hair worn loose and contrasting vividly in the glow of the lit candelabra.

Surely no man could be unaffected by the signals she had been transmitting to him these past few months? Her sultry beauty excited him unbearably. Those frequently pouting lips, the eyes that burned demandingly, made these dinner parties intoxicating affairs for him. As well as her overt sexuality, he admired her elegance and breeding. She was his idea of the perfect English rose. Had she been older, he would have reacted positively to her body language long ago. But as a friend of her parents he felt it right to proceed with caution. She was the apple of their eye and, even though he knew they liked and respected him, he wouldn't want to take advantage of their hospitality.

She smiled across at him. 'Cream,' she said, her voice girlishly seductive.

'Thank you.'

He took the silver jug, his eyes meeting hers, their fingers touching briefly. It wasn't difficult to see why her parents spoiled her. She was having the same effect on him. Her dark voluptuous beauty was like a magnet to him. He wanted to be with her, to make her happy, whatever the cost. He had been coming here for nine months and seeing her with her parents. Now he needed to be with her alone.

Later, when Lavinia and Rupert were out of the room briefly and he and Chloe were alone in the drawing room, he said, 'I was wondering if you might like to go out with me sometime soon? We could go to the theatre perhaps and have a meal somewhere afterwards.'

She hesitated just long enough not to seem too eager. 'Why, that would be lovely, Bradley, thank you.'

He beamed with relief. 'You let me know what you'd like to see and I'll get some tickets.'

'I'll do that,' she said happily.

'But why leave your job, Maggie?' asked Rupert Anderson on Monday morning in his office. Wishing to tell him personally of her resignation, Maggie had bypassed Miss Bateman by insisting that she wished to see him on a matter relating to Chloe whose friendship with her was now common knowledge. 'If it's money you're after, I'll match any offer you've had.'

Maggie guessed that this show of innocence was his way of living with his uncharacteristic behaviour. And whilst pitying him, she knew that kindness was not going to help matters in the long run. 'Of course it isn't money, Mr Anderson,' she said, continuing to use this formal term as she had throughout the whole sorry business. 'I am leaving because you have made it impossible for me to stay. And don't play dumb. You must realise that you have made a nuisance of yourself.'

He flinched and moistened his dry lips with his tongue, his eyes heavy with humiliation. He reminded her of a guilty schoolboy at the mercy of a teacher. 'I am too old for you, is that what you mean?'

'Yes, of course you are too old for me,' she said with unusual severity. 'You don't need me to tell you that! But more importantly, you are a married man and I happen to have a great deal of affection for your wife and daughter.' She stared sadly into his eyes and shook her head. 'Look, I am flattered that you have chosen me to have a crush on. But it's just a fantasy, can't you see that? I am eighteen years old. I like going out to dances and the cinema with people of my own generation. I like noise and fun and late nights. We have a language of our own, just as you have with people of your age. It's only natural.'

'I never meant you any harm,' he said with childish recalcitrance, 'I love you and I have only ever wanted to make you happy.'

'No,' she corrected firmly, 'it is your happiness you have been pursuing, because the only way you can possibly make me happy is by acting your age and behaving like the father of my best friend.' She was sitting facing him across his desk. She was flushed; he was pale, with two spots of colour staining his cheeks. 'What do you think all this would do to your wife if she were to find out?'

Clasping his head in his hands, he said, 'Oh God, Lavinia. I don't want to hurt her.'

'So what do you have in mind then?' rasped Maggie, impatient with his continued refusal to face facts. 'You claim to be in love with me, yet you don't want to hurt your wife. Supposing I had reciprocated, what would you have done then? Would you have been willing to leave your wife for me?'

He lit a cigar with a shaky hand. 'What is the matter with me?' he asked in a cracked voice, evading the question. 'I have never looked at another woman in over thirty years.' He pressed his fingers to his temples and closed his eyes as though in pain. 'I didn't ask for this to happen, Maggie. Help me, please.'

'I can't,' she said, determined to stand her ground. 'This is a dangerous game you're playing, and for all your dramatics, what it boils down to is the fact that you want to have your cake and eat it too. You can't behave as you have and not hurt someone, even if it is only yourself. You're lucky that I'm only leaving my job. A different kind of girl might have been tempted to make real trouble for a man in your position. You could have lost the people you really love – your wife and daughter.'

'Yes, yes, I know that,' he said, but it was clear that the need to satisfy his obsession overruled all other considerations. 'But please don't deny me the pleasure of seeing you every day. I promise I won't bother you if I can only see you.'

'No!' she snapped. 'Because that won't help either of us. I can't trust you to keep your word while you are in this state.'

'How you must despise me,' he said tremulously.

'I will do if you continue to be so pathetic,' she warned him. 'But, no, I don't despise you. I think you are basically a good man who is undergoing some kind of aberration.' She rose to go. 'Now, you must come to your senses. I want you to promise not to try to contact me.'

'All right,' he mumbled reluctantly.

'Good. I'll give my official notice to Miss Bateman right away.'

'Thanks for not making things awkward,' he said, rising to see her to the door.

'That's all right.'

As she made her way back into the general office she felt drained of energy, the harsh manner she had felt compelled to adopt leaving pity in its wake. How could a respected and dignified man like him have undergone such a transformation? Where was his pride? For all his money and position he was as helpless as a baby against his own emotions. Poor man!

As Andersons' week ended on a Thursday so did Maggie's employment with them, and she started at the flower shop on the Friday. Minutes after her arrival, she questioned her wisdom in leaving her secure job so hastily.

The interior of the shop itself was reasonably tidy and well stocked, with fresh flowers adorning the window and lined up in metal buckets on the floor. There were racks of seeds in packets and various display units containing florist's sundries: small wicker cradles and cribs for new baby presentations; china vases and pots in varying shapes.

At the back of the shop was the small office which was barely accessible for the mountains of paper that littered the desktop, the shelves and floor. Loose piles and tied bundles of tea-stained invoices, mud-splattered bills and dust-covered letters, vied for attention from every corner of the room. An exploration of the desk revealed an ancient typewriter and telephone. 'What,' she asked of Jack in shocked despair, 'am I supposed to do first?'

'The obvious, of course,' he said cheerfully, apparently unperturbed by the parlous state of his clerical affairs. 'Put the kettle on for a cuppa tea.'

'Tea?' She was stupefied at such peculiar priorities.

'Tea for me, ta,' he said with a grin. 'You'll probably find some coffee somewhere if yer prefer that. I'll pop down to the workroom and ask me brother to hold the fort in the shop, then we'll sit down with our tea and I'll run through my system with you.' He grinned. 'Not that I have much of a system, as such.'

Maggie simply could not place tea-making before the task in hand. 'But surely I ought to make a start on the work before we have a tea-break?' she suggested.

'Everything is clearer after a cuppa,' he told her.

'Oh, well, you're the boss,' she sighed, going into a tiny kitchen adjacent to the office and dusting a prehistoric kettle before filling it and placing it on the gas ring.

'I'll just go and get Archie,' said Jack. 'I shan't be long.'

On being introduced to Archie, Maggie instantly perceived that he did not share his brother's agreeable nature. In fact, Archie Radford was one of the most objectionable people she had ever met. He was a lanky twenty-year-old with an oily skin, a thin weasel-like face and dark eyes that burned with some inner resentment. He had the same swarthy colouring as Jack, but Archie's lips were thin, his nose long, his hand-shake limp.

But Archie was the least of her concerns as she spooned tea from the packet into a chipped enamel pot. Ah well, perhaps Jack was right and the job would seem clearer after some refreshment.

It didn't. The day went from daunting to downright ridiculous. The premises, comprising shop, office, kitchen, staffroom and toilets on the ground floor, and a cool storage room and workroom in the basement, felt more like the home of an unrehearsed comedy farce than a commercial enterprise. And instead of getting to grips with the paper-work, Maggie found herself conditioning the new stock of fresh flowers from Covent Garden market by crushing the hard stems and cutting the soft stems to allow them to absorb the water before placing them in buckets. She made tea, answered the phone, ran up and down the base-ment steps with messages, and served customers in the shop in the absence of the brothers who were busy in the workroom below.

Even at this early stage she could see that Jack's lack of business acumen did not extend to his skills with flowers and plants. Fascinated, she spared a few moments to watch him as he worked with moss and wire frames to produce tasteful and imaginative wreaths for a funeral order. This was a whole new world to Maggie and she was amazed at the variety of frames available for the floral tributes. There were dogs, bibles, dartboards, teddy bears, harps. Covering the frames with moss, he then wired the stem of each individual flower and fixed it firmly into the moss, edging the arrangement with ferns.

But it was his expertise with wedding displays that took her breath away. Artistically arranged and wired into bouquets were fresh yellow daffodils and pale narcissi; hothouse roses with velvet-textured petals in rich shades of red; pink and white carnations; lilies of the valley; freesia. Posies and sprays, baskets and bunches in myriad hues, combined to form one wave of glorious fragrance.

Taking a break from this feverish activity, he instructed his brother to do the deliveries while he went on foot to a nearby hotel to see the manager about the flowers for a wedding reception the next day.

'Sorry to throw you in at the deep end, Maggie,' he said for she was to be left alone in the shop, 'But I won't be long.'

Staring at him incredulously, she said, 'But supposing I wasn't here? Who would serve the customers then, with both you and Archie out at the same time?'

'Nobody. We'd put the Closed sign up while we were gone,' he informed her airily. 'Orders must come before passing trade because we've committed ourselves to them.'

'And send all your counter trade to the nearest opposition,' she said in astonishment.

'That's right,' he said. 'As long as I make a living, I don't begrudge anyone else doing the same.'

Even Maggie's inexperienced eye could see the obvious drawbacks of such an arrangement. 'It's a peculiar way of running a business, if you ask me,' she remarked.

'But no one is asking you,' he pointed out bluntly but without ran-cour. 'No one dies or is hurt because our shop is closed occasionally during trading hours. All that happens is that we lose a little money and the customer is a little inconvenienced. And where's the harm in that?'

Put like that there was no argument, so she just said, 'Oh, well, you know your own business best. But don't blame me if I lose you customers because I don't know the trade.'

'You'll soon get the hang of it.'

It was the general lack of organisation that was so irritating, for the actual floristry could not be faulted. And yet, as the day wore on, Maggie found that she was enjoying herself enormously, despite the cold moist atmosphere, her aching feet, chafed hands from working with damp material, and the untouched paperwork.

There was joy to be had in working with such emblems of emotion. Nothing carried a caring message quite like flowers, to bride, hospital patient, lover. Even the sadness of last respects was sweetened by their presence. Maggie also enjoyed the personal contact this work gave her with the public. Already she could begin to relate to the business and understand its purpose, whereas at Andersons' she had been a mere cog in an unfathomable machine.

I think you've done me a favour in driving me away, Mr Anderson, she decided.

When the sign on the shop door was finally turned to Closed, wilting unsold blooms were disposed of while those in good condition were put into fresh water and stored overnight in the coolroom. The moss was watered to keep it fresh, the floor of the shop and workroom swept clean of bits of stem, greenery and fallen petals, and the day's takings safely deposited in the nightsafe of the bank. Next Maggie went into the office with a view to making a start on the work in there.

But Jack had other ideas. 'It's time to knock off, luv,' he said, appearing at the office door.

'Yes, I know, but I think I'd better do something here,' she told him. 'Even if I only clear the decks for tomorrow.'

'You've done quite enough for one day,' he stated categorically. 'It's after five-thirty and no time for sensible people to be working.'

'Perhaps if I do just an hour or so now?'

'I admire yer dedication,' he said, peeling off his dark green rayon overall and unrolling his shirtsleeves, 'but absolutely not. Tomorrow is another day. Right now I've a much more interesting suggestion. How about you and me going up West to see a film and 'ave a bite to eat out? Unless, o' course, you already have a date.'

Finally accepting that work was over for the day, she smiled and said, 'I'd like that very much.'

'Seven o'clock suit yer?' he asked.

'Fine.'

'I'll be at your door on the dot.'

They went to see Judy Garland and Fred Astaire in *Easter Parade*, and had supper afterwards at the Brasserie in Lyons Corner House which was pleasantly bustling. The waiters weaved expertly through the check-clothed tables and a convivial buzz of conversation added to the warmth of the atmosphere. They had soup, cheese omelettes, french fries and peas. Jack had a beer, Maggie a shandy. He was a natural wit and entertained her with jokes and impersonations of film stars and radio personalities.

'You are a fool,' she laughed, over coffee. 'Don't you ever take anything seriously?'

'Not if I can avoid it.'

'But surely you have to sometimes?' she said. 'You know, making provision for the future, that sort of thing.'

'While you're thinking of the future, the present is slipping away,' he said, stirring some sugar into his coffee.' Life is too short. I saw enough men die in France to realise that.'

'But the war is over now,' she reminded him. 'Surely we should all be looking forward to the future with optimism.'

'Sure, but that doesn't mean that I have to spend my time thinking about it. Take life as it comes, that's my motto.' He paused thoughtfully. 'But I am prepared to consider the immediate future with regard to your working for me.'

'Oh?'

'I'd like to teach you to drive. It would be useful if you could help out with the deliveries in an emergency,' he said. 'Are you willing?'

'I'll say.'

Jack wasn't the sort of man to stand on ceremony, and when they arrived back at the flat, he invited himself in for cocoa. Tom had gone to bed, but Dora was still up and she and Jack struck an instant rapport. They had a great deal in common since they both followed the horses, enjoyed a game of cards and a visit to the local. It was after two o'clock when the van finally roared noisily away.

'He's seems a really nice bloke,' commented Dora as she and Maggie washed the cocoa cups at the kitchen sink. 'If you play your cards right, you could have a good future with him in the flower trade.'

Maggie agreed wholeheartedly about a future in the flower trade, but she wasn't sure if Jack featured in it permanently. That was something only time would tell.

'So how are things with you and Bradley?' Maggie inquired of Chloe one Wednesday afternoon in May as they sat on the grass near the Serpentine in Hyde Park.

'Fine,' said Chloe, whose relationship with Bradley was progressing very nicely. 'But what of your romance? Do tell.'

The girls saw much less of each other now that they both had steady boyfriends. Their simultaneous embarking upon courtship couldn't have worked out better since it eliminated potential jealousy and hard feelings about the limited time each had to spare for the other. For Maggie it also eased the problem of visits to the Andersons which should help the dust to settle for Rupert, she thought.

Since it was half-day closing on Wednesdays in Ashbrook Green and Maggie had the afternoon off, she had taken to meeting Chloe in town regularly then as they were both keen to stay friends. They usually had a browse round the shops, or a walk in the park, tea somewhere and a chat.

'It's all going rather well, I think,' said Maggie, idly chewing a blade of grass. 'Jack and I get along fine, even though we work and play together.'

'How are the driving lessons?'

'Great fun.'

Now that Maggie had been at Radford's Flowers for over a month, she felt completely at home in the job. Things were more or less under control in the office, but she had discovered a personal preference for floristry and counter work, and welcomed the chance to get into the shop or workroom to learn the basic skills of the job. She was never happier than when up to her elbows in moss and wire, matching shade and shape, creating new ideas for attractive displays, or helping a customer choose the most suitable blooms for their requirements. Last Sunday she had gone with Jack to assist with the floral displays in one of London's exhibition centres ready for the opening of an important exhibition on Monday. It had been a great thrill. Even the eczema on her hands caused by the sap from the daffodil stems had cleared up now that they were no longer so much in season.

But now it was a fine spring day and Chloe was saying, 'You're a bit mean with the personal details. I want to know what he's like.'

'I've already told you,' Maggie reminded her. 'Jack is a nice bloke but too common for your taste, I should think. So don't get any ideas about us making up a foursome with you and Bradley because it would be a certain disaster.'

'Are you in love with him?'

Maggie giggled. She had no more experience of men than Chloe yet she felt so much more mature than her friend with her girlish talk of love. Maggie was a realist. She expected ordinariness from life, not the romantic gift wrapping that the rich could afford and Chloe would automatically receive from her American boyfriend. 'Goodness, it's much too early to say. Anyway, I'm not sure what that much talked about state is supposed to feel like. I quite fancy him and I enjoy his company, but I don't yearn for him or anything, like they do in books. And I don't know him well enough yet to feel I would put his happiness before my own, which is supposed to be the real test of love.'

'It doesn't sound very exciting.'

'It isn't!' said Maggie. 'But I like Jack and he makes me laugh. That's more important than anything else to me.'

The girls didn't pretend that a social disparity did not exist between them. They each had other friends of their own class and didn't make the mistake of trying to make them mix. Other people, they realised, might not wish to transcend the barriers as they had.

'Your turn now,' said Maggie. 'Come on, tell me.'

'He takes me to all the best places,' Chloe said.

'And . . . ?'

'He's a perfect gentleman. Nothing more daring than kissing.'

Maggie grinned at her own thoughts, for the same thing could not be said for Jack with whom she had a wrestling match during each date. Fortunately, she remained intact, but not for lack of trying on his part! 'This Bradley chap sounds almost too good to be true,' she said. 'But how do you actually feel about him now that you are getting to know him better?'

'I think he's wonderful,' said Chloe dreamily. Bradley had oodles of charm and charisma, and was a terrific man to have as a boyfriend. He brought her presents and made her feel like the most important woman alive. She was desperately in love with him and just couldn't wait for things to get really serious between them. As for putting his happiness before her own – well, in all honesty, Chloe couldn't imagine herself doing that for anyone. It was probably a maxim of Maggie's class, she thought, and certainly wouldn't be expected of her. It was for other people to worry about her happiness, not the other way around. 'He's so frightfully handsome, Maggie. I'm mad about him.'

Maggie felt an unexpected shiver of fear for her friend. It all seemed too good to be true. Did happy endings really exist outside of the films, even for people like Chloe? She was thoughtless and inherently selfish, but she could be warm and generous too. And she seemed so naive and vulnerable at times that Maggie worried about her. 'Be careful, Chloe,' she warned. 'Make sure it is him you want and not just his good looks to show off to your friends. That might seem enough now, but I shouldn't think it would last.'

'Of course it isn't just that,' said Chloe, flushing defensively.

Feeling guilty for spoiling her happiness, Maggie put a friendly hand on Chloe's arm. 'Of course it isn't, and I'm very pleased for you.' She scrambled up, brushing her skirt with her hands. 'Come on, let's go and feed the ducks.'

And the two girls walked together in the sunshine towards the lake.

On Whit Monday afternoon Jack's van transported the Brightwell family to Hampstead Heath Fair with Dora in the passenger seat next to Jack, and Maggie and Tom in the back which had been thoroughly scrubbed for the occasion. Jack had suggested making the event into a family outing and Maggie was delighted with his kindness to her nearest and dearest. Not only was he chummy with her mother, but with Tom too, surprisingly, for Maggie had expected Jack's gregarious nature to drive Tom even deeper into himself. But Jack's warmth and lack of pretension drew even the most introverted of people out of their shells.

'Are you coming on the helter skelter, Jack?' asked Tom, as the fair came into view, the striped awnings on the stalls and amusements rising brashly in a riot of colour from this most elegant of suburbs.

'You just try and stop me,' enthused Jack, keen to nurture Tom's confidence. He liked the boy enormously and hated to see his intelligence concealed by a communication problem. 'We'll take the ladies on the Big Dipper, shall we? That'll make 'em squeal.'

'Yeah,' bawled Tom with youthful exuberance. 'And we'll all go on the chairoplanes.'

'Oh, yeah, mustn't miss those,' chuckled Jack.

Every variety of thrill was on offer here. There were coconut shies and carousels; hoop-la stalls and swing boats; a big wheel and bumper cars. There were rides to be had and prizes to be won. Punters strolled past laden with cuddly toys, hideous plaster ornaments and goldfish in bowls. Kiddies squealed with delight on the carousel; grown-ups screamed with fright on the ghost train. Jack won a cuddly rabbit for Maggie on the shooting range and Tom proudly presented his mother with an ashtray he had procured on the roll-a-ball stall.

Maggie thoroughly enjoyed herself taking rides and trying her luck on the stalls. They found a spot on the Heath away from the fair and ate a picnic, and later, as darkness fell and the fairground lights glowed with splendid gaudiness against the darkening sky, they went to a nearby pub and sipped their drinks in the fairy-lit gardens. It had been a perfect day.

But on the way home Maggie was introduced to another, unexpected, side of Jack's nature. Agreeable as he was, he had fixed ideas about certain things and a hot temper, it transpired. The contretemps happened when they passed a fish and chop shop that was open, and decided to take some home for supper.

'You've spent quite enough money on us today,' said Maggie, scrambling from the van and rummaging in her bag for her purse whilst accompanying him into the shop. 'This will be my treat.'

Since he had insisted on paying for everything for the three of them up until now, she considered this to be a perfectly fair suggestion. So she was shocked by his reaction.

'Don't you dare insult me, Maggie Brightwell!' he bellowed, heedless of the heads turning in their direction in the crowded shop. 'I may not be the world's most ambitious businessman, but I'm not so hard up that I can't pay for my girlfriend when I take her out.'

'I'm not suggesting that you are,' she said, scarlet with embarrassment at the entertainment being derived from this drama by the people in the queue. 'But you've been paying for my family as well as me all afternoon. It must have cost you a small fortune.'

'You can't think much of me if you think an afternoon at the fair will bankrupt me,' he barked, his eyes black with anger.

'Shush,' she urged. 'Everyone's looking.'

'Let 'em look,' he roared. 'I'll 'ave you know that I can pay my way.'

Maggie clutched his arm and matched his furious stare with her own soothing one. 'And no one is suggesting otherwise,' she said gently. 'I offered to pay because it would have given me pleasure. You're not the only generous one, you know. But you go ahead if it means that much to you.'

She watched the fury in his eyes flicker and die under her calming influence. 'All right,' he said more amicably. 'But I don't want to hear you talk like that again.'

'Don't worry, you won't,' she assured him.

Realising that the show was over, the punters turned their attention to more pressing matters. 'Gaw blimey, mate,' said one man to the fellow behind the counter, ' 'ow much longer are yer gonna be? 'ave they gone to catch the fish or somethin'?' And a general murmur of agreement went up, the young couple's quarrel forgotten.

By the time they left the shop with their steaming packages, Jack's anger had abated. Maggie forgot all about it as they ate cod and chips, with bread and butter and a pot of tea, in an atmosphere of hilarity at the kitchen table, recalling various amusing moments of the afternoon.

Enjoying a few minutes alone with Jack at the front gate later, Maggie felt utterly content. She enjoyed having a regular boyfriend, they had had a pleasant afternoon out with her folks, and she enjoyed her work. Life was good indeed.

She might have felt less easy in her mind had she known that watching them from his Daimler, parked in the shadows of a nearby side-street, was Rupert Anderson.

Chapter Five

In June 1949 American tennis star Gussie Moran, affectionately known as 'Gorgeous Gussie', caused a sensation among fuddy-duddy members of English society by revealing lace-trimmed panties beneath her white tennis dress on the Wimbledon Courts.

Rupert Anderson, however, was far more concerned about his own outlandish behaviour, and was almost beginning to question his own sanity. After all, what normal person would spend their time in the perverse occupation of mounting a surveillance on a girl who had made an unequivocal rejection of his affections? Who but a man mentally deranged would risk losing the love and respect of family and friends, and an impeccable reputation, by furtively haunting London's back-streets like a common criminal, just for a glimpse which only depressed him further?

More worrying even than his actions was the fact that they were motivated by irrational compulsion rather than actual desire. At his age the last thing he wanted to do was to leave the comfort of his armchair in the evening to take to the streets in pursuit of an impossible dream. Quite apart from the misery of making excuses to Lavinia, there was the actual physical discomfort of sitting for hours in a draughty car just waiting for Maggie to appear. This sort of thing required a young man's constitution. And what was to be achieved by such an aimless activity, anyway? It certainly wouldn't improve his chances with Maggie if she got to know about it.

And supposing she were to suddenly reciprocate? Was he prepared to disappear into exile with her, isolated from everything that he held dear? For that would be the only available option. He would be branded as a dirty old man by family, friends and colleagues whose sympathy and support would naturally go to Lavinia. The very thought of it made him sick with self-loathing.

But this was quickly overridden by powerful thoughts of Maggie which made him sweat and tremble. He was not drawn to her only by sexual desire, he told himself. He wanted to look after her and make her happy. But – and he could deny it no longer – amid all the honourable emotions he constantly paraded before his conscience, he did want to make love to her. The only time in his long years of marriage that he had ever wanted anyone but Lavinia.

His health and work were suffering as a result of his obsession. The frustration and guilt made him irritable, the physical effects of his nocturnal labours exhausted him, and he had lost weight from all the stress. Dear trusting Lavinia's suggestion had been simple. 'I think you should go to the doctor's for a checkup,' she'd advised him recently. 'You're showing all the symptoms of sugar diabetes. But it isn't always too much of a problem these days, as long as it's treated properly.'

Oh, how he would welcome a physical malaise instead of this mental one! And it didn't help to know that the whole thing was merely self-indulgence, requiring only willpower to snap him out of his growing compulsion.

He simply must stop worshipping her from afar and speak to her in person. He would need to catch her when she wasn't with that boyfriend of hers though. Wednesday afternoons she met Chloe in town, he'd heard his daughter say. Perhaps he might leave the office early one of these Wednesdays and meet her on her way home? He trembled with excitement at the thought. Then, when he was calmer, he picked up the internal phone and spoke to his secretary about an office matter, as though that was the only thing on his mind. No one would ever guess at the turmoil going on inside the respectable Mr Anderson.

Maggie was feeling rather pleased with life one Wednesday afternoon in July as she made her way home on the tube after an enjoyable meeting with Chloe. But her optimistic mood had not been derived from the situation in the country as a whole, since the sugar ration had been reduced to eight ounces a week, sweet rationing had been reintroduced at four ounces per head and there was another cut in tobacco supplies. These new austerity measures were a result of Britain's dollar shortage, apparently. The Chancellor of the Exchequer, Sir Stafford Cripps, had disclosed recently that the nation's debt to America and Canada was running at £600 millions a year, one and a half times the total of British gold reserves. Maggie didn't understand the technicalities of it, only the exasperating results. But the people will cope, she thought. We've certainly had enough experience!

And she, personally, had much to be thankful for. She had progressed in all aspects of her work at the shop, and despite Jack's apoplectic reactions to her attempts at the three-point turn, her hopes of soon earning a driving licence were high.

Tom now came into the shop on a Saturday to help with the menial tasks, and Jack had also agreed to employ him in the school holidays with a view to full-time employment when he left school next year.

The only handicap to the harmonious working atmosphere was Archie, a sulky individual who spent his spare time prowling the streets and pubs with a gang of yobs, looking for trouble. He had found a real victim in the vulnerable Tom and continually played on his own seniority. But despite everything, Tom seemed to be improving. He was still of a reserved disposition and almost fainted with fright if he was called upon to serve at the counter, but he was a diligent worker with a surprising aptitude for clerical work.

The sun felt pleasantly warm as Maggie emerged from Shepherd's Bush station, and she decided to take advantage of the fine weather and walk home rather than take the bus. Strolling airily along the busy shopping parade she glanced in the dress-shop windows, calculating how many weeks she would have to save before she could afford something new. Crossing the green she could hear the trees rustling in the breeze despite the noise of the traffic. She proceeded past the Empire and the cinemas, some of which were still bomb-damaged and closed, and deciding to take the backroads route to Ashbrook Green turned into a sidestreet. It was then that the Daimler pulled up beside her.

'Hello there,' she said shakily to Rupert Anderson who was peering at her from the driving seat. 'What brings you to these parts?' As if she didn't know! She had stopped in her tracks with the shock of seeing him and now instinctively moved towards the kerb to let other pedestrians pass.

'I want to talk to you,' he said.

His pallor and bloodshot eyes registered with disturbing clarity. 'I thought you and I had a deal,' she reminded him.

'Just give me a few minutes, Maggie. Please, get in the car,' he implored her.

'Can't you say what you have to here?'

'Please,' he implored her.

He looked old, tired and pathetic, and she was imbued with a mixture of irritation and pity. Although the street was a secondary one, it was a fairly busy thoroughfare and no place for a man in his position to be seen pestering a young girl. She shouldn't care, after all the aggravation he had caused her, but she did. 'OK, but only for a few minutes.'

His expression changed to one of childish delight, weighing her down with unwanted responsibility for his happiness. She felt hopelessly inadequate to deal with the situation. 'So,' she said, inside the car, 'what's all this about?'

He leaned his arm along the back of her seat, making her skin crawl. 'I just wanted to see you, to speak to you. Please don't be cross with me.'

'So it's nothing more than that?' she rasped. 'Well, I'm more than cross – I am absolutely furious.' She met his beseeching gaze, a mixture

61

of frustration and compassion driving her to the brink of tears. 'Please try to pull yourself together, Mr Anderson. You are worth more than this sort of pitiful behaviour. Don't let me lose all respect for you.'

'I love you, Maggie,' he said.

Oh God, she thought, tears burning, what am I to do? Now it was her turn to entreat. 'Please understand, I'm not right for you. Anyway, I have a boyfriend.'

'I know, I've seen you together. He can't offer you what I can,' he said with infantile sulkiness.

The fact that he had been spying on her barely registered against the need to curb his ardour. 'Maybe not, in material terms,' she agreed. 'But I'm not looking for riches in a man. I'm comfortable with him, he's one of my own kind. Ordinary, you know.'

'He's no good for you,' he said, reduced to calumny in his desperation.

'That's for me to discover,' she told him. 'I have to make my own mistakes, as you have undoubtedly made yours during the course of your life.' Her message was implicit. 'Please stop chasing me and go home to your wife before she finds out what you've been up to. She'll be very hurt if that does happen.'

Clutching his head in theatrical remorse, he said, 'Don't remind me. I just don't know what is the matter with me.'

'Second childhood, I should think,' she opined frankly. 'I've heard it's quite common in people of your age.' She winced at her cruel but necessary bluntness. 'You must try to imagine how you would feel if the father of one of Chloe's friends was doing this to her.'

Sucking in his breath, he shook his head as though the analogy pained him, but made no reply.

'I'd like to visit your home again as a family friend,' she said, resisting the urge to comfort him for fear of any misunderstanding, 'but I can only do that when I'm sure that you and I can be friends. So please, please, accept that there can never be anything other than friendship between us.' She reached for the door. 'Goodbye Mr Anderson.'

She scrambled from the car and tore down the street without looking back, tears streaming down her cheeks. Hurting someone you liked was hard. The effect of it lingered well into the evening, something that did not go unnoticed by Jack.

'Do you have a death wish or something?' he roared during her driving lesson as she took a corner too wide, narrowly missing another vehicle.

'Sorry,' she said, and to her dismay began to cry.

'No harm done,' he said, instantly adjusting his mood to her distress. 'But you've done enough driving for one night. Let's go somewhere and talk.'

And so, sitting in the van parked under a lamp post near Maggie's home, she told him about the incident with Rupert. 'I had to hurt him,' she sobbed, 'and it seemed so cruel. He is such a nice man, you see, and he really does think he loves me. I can't seem to make him understand that it can never be like that for me.' She shook her head in despair. 'I just don't know what to do about him. I'm scared his wife and daughter will find out. Chloe is my best friend, I'd hate her to get hurt.'

Jack slipped his arm around her shoulders and drew her closer to him, soothingly. 'I do have one suggestion,' he said.

'I don't want you to go and tell him what an old fool he is, if that's what you are going to suggest,' she said hotly. 'I think he's already painfully aware of that.'

'That wasn't what I had in mind.'

'What then?' she asked, blowing her nose.

'Marry me,' he said, squeezing her tight. 'He couldn't help but get the message then.'

'Oh!' The shock stopped her tears abruptly. 'That's no reason to get married.'

'I couldn't agree more,' he said tenderly.

She felt, rather than saw, his eagerness in the dim light. 'You mean that isn't why you suggested it.'

'It's speeded things up a bit, that's all,' he said. 'I'm not very good at putting these things into words . . .'

'You mean . . .'

'Yeah, Rupert Anderson isn't the only one who's dotty about you,' he said hoarsely. 'You must have guessed.'

'You've made no secret of the fact that you fancied me,' she said. 'But love . . .'

'Just because I come on strong physically doesn't mean that I don't have finer feelings too, yer know,' he explained, a slight breathlessness betraying the emotion he was struggling to conceal. He laughed nervously. 'So what do yer say?'

'I don't know,' she admitted frankly. His proposal had caught her unawares. She had not thought of marriage in terms of the present but as something for the future, whether to Jack or anyone else. And what about love? Did the warmth and affection she felt for him count as that even though he didn't actually set the world ablaze for her? Her down-to-earth nature told her that it probably did.

'I'll never be rich, but I'll do me best to make you 'appy,' he said, in a strange clipped tone, and at her prolonged silence added, 'I'll get down on me knees if you like, out there on the pavement.'

The very idea of Jack humbling himself in such a manner made her laugh. 'No, there's no need to go to such lengths,' she assured him. 'I'd be honoured to marry you.'

And he was unusually restrained as he kissed her in the glow of the street light, as though this new stage of the relationship required additional respect. It was a very tender moment.

Chloe's excitement at being asked to be Maggie's bridesmaid was clouded temporarily by the news that Bradley had to fly to America on family business. His father's longstanding and trusted manager had been found to be furthering his own interests rather than the company's, and the news had so devastated Hughes Senior that Bradley had felt it necessary to leave the UK company in the hands of its British manager while he attended to filial duty.

'I shall miss you terribly,' Chloe said when he called to see her on his way to the airport and found her in the garden. 'How long will you be away?'

'I can't say at this stage. It depends how long it takes to find a suitable replacement for Dad's manager. I'm sorry to desert you, honey, but my folks need me right now. Dad has taken a real knock over this. The guy was like a brother to him, he'd been with the firm for years. Dad wants me to help select a new man, to make sure we don't make another mistake.'

She slipped her arms around him and was instantly aroused since the strong physical chemistry between them was inflamed at the slightest touch. Chloe didn't know how she would survive without seeing Bradley. Curbing her natural impulse to retreat into a fit of the sulks at any reversal, she said in the sexily petulant voice she knew he found attractive, 'You will get back as soon as you can, and phone me lots?'

'Just try and stop me, honey,' he said, trembling at her proximity.

Set against a background of glamorous socialising, the romance in their relationship remained at the same high level as the sexual attraction. Bradley enjoyed courting Chloe. He liked giving her presents and taking her to all the best places. She was fun to be with, sexy and light-hearted. If occasionally he found himself irritated by her need to be the constant centre of attention it was soon overpowered by his desire for her.

They walked hand in hand across the lawns to the trees at the bottom of the garden where they could say a private goodbye shielded from the house. Looking across at the river tinted olive green in the bright July sunshine, Chloe said, 'Will you be back in time for Maggie's wedding? It's still two months away.'

He looked contrite. 'I honestly don't think I will, honey. I'm sorry.'

'Oh, what a shame,' said Chloe with genuine disappointment. 'Maggie means a lot to me. I'd have loved you to be there. You'll like her, I know you will.'

'I guess I'll get to meet her another time.'

64

'You won't get to see me in my bridesmaid's regalia either,' she said. 'And it's the first time I've ever been a bridesmaid.'

'I've seen you in lots of other lovely clothes though,' he said. 'And I can see the photographs. You always look beautiful, whatever you're wearing.'

She smiled up at him. 'Do I? Do I really?'

He grinned down at her playfully. 'You know you do. So stop fishing for compliments.'

Flushing slightly, she giggled. 'Well it's always nice to hear it.'

They were standing under a luxuriant oak tree. Bradley held her close to him and kissed her deeply. 'On the subject of weddings,' he whispered tenderly, 'I know you're still very young, but I wonder if you might consider marrying me? I do love you very much, you know.'

'Oh, Bradley,' she gasped, almost crying with pleasure. 'I adore you, and I'd love to marry you.'

'That's wonderful,' he said, beaming. 'As soon as I get back from the States, I'll speak to your father. Then I'll buy you the finest engagement ring in London.'

'Ooh, I'm so excited,' squeaked Chloe. 'I can't wait to tell Maggie. We'll have a celebration with her and her husband when you get back.'

'Whatever you like, darling,' he said before silencing her with a passionate farewell embrace.

The first time Maggie found herself defining Jack's carefree attitude to life as alarmingly irresponsible was during the run-up to the wedding.

'Who will look after the shop on our wedding day?' she asked. 'Since we'll all be at the wedding?'

'No one. We'll close for the day,' he informed her breezily.

'We can't do that,' she opined hotly. 'It will be bad for business, and we do have a certain duty to our customers.'

'We're running a shop here, not a hospital,' he pointed out with his own peculiar brand of logic. 'Customers will simply go down the road to the opposition.'

'What about orders?'

'We'll make sure they're all ready by the night before and deliver them first thing in the morning. That shouldn't interfere with our day.'

'Shall we have the wedding on a weekday then?' she suggested. 'When the shop isn't so busy.'

'No fear!' stated Jack quite categorically. 'Saturday is the right day for weddings, so that's when we'll have it, providing that suits you.'

'But, Jack, the business must be considered . . .'

'Bugger the business!' he interrupted. 'I only intend to get married once and I want to do it in style, at the weekend, when people are free from work to come and enjoy themselves.'

'People?' she queried.

'Everybody. Relatives, friends, neighbours,' he explained enthusiastically. 'It'll be the biggest knees-up since VE night. Invite anyone you like, Maggie. Don't worry about numbers.'

She chewed her lip, mindful of the fact that the financial responsibility for the wedding reception rested in the bride's camp rather than the groom's. 'I hate to be a wet blanket, Jack,' she said, 'but what about the expense? It's traditional for the bride's parents to pay for the reception, and Mum can't afford a big do. I'll help out, but even so . . .'

'To hell with tradition,' he said cheerfully. 'I wouldn't dream of expecting your mum to pay. That wouldn't be fair, not with her bein' on her own. And I certainly don't expect you to contribute, on what I pay you.' He hugged her, radiating childlike exuberance. 'No, this wedding will be my treat. I am marrying the most beautiful girl in London and I want the world to be there.'

Swimming against this enthusiastic tide of goodwill, her more practical considerations stood no chance of survival. 'All right,' she agreed. 'We'll get married on a Saturday.'

They were married at the end of September on a golden autumn day with hazy sunshine filtering from a misty blue sky. Maggie looked a picture in a full-length white dress with a lace collar and long sleeves, her face framed by a veil falling from a simulated-pearl headdress. Chloe and Beryl, as bridesmaids, were in pink along with two of Jack's little cousins. The small son of a friend of Jack's was a pageboy.

There was an afternoon reception at a local hotel, followed by an evening party with dancing to a band, from which the happy couple departed amid showers of confetti, congratulations and risqué wishes for the night ahead at a hotel near Hyde Park.

'I'll take yer on a proper honeymoon when we can find someone reliable to look after the shop,' Jack assured her as they rolled across London in a taxi. 'But one night in a posh hotel will have to do for now.'

Maggie positively welcomed this sign of temperance from him after weeks of extravagance. 'Don't worry about that,' she assured him. 'You've been generous enough.'

' 'appy?' he asked, cuddling her into the crook of his arm.

'Yes, of course,' she said, smiling into his eager eyes.

'It went off very well, don't you think? Everyone seemed to enjoy themselves.'

'Oh, yes,' she agreed, 'and they'll keep going for ages yet.'

In actual fact, the mood of the wedding reception had seemed to Maggie more like that of a charabanc outing. She had not thought it possible for anyone to have as many friends as her husband, all of whom would have attended the wedding of Count Dracula himself if it involved a party, she suspected. The pound might have been devalued but none of his guests showed the slightest concern for the nation's dire financial state. You couldn't move in the flat above the shop, where the couple were to make their home, for manifestations of their generosity in enough gift-wrapped homeware to supply a market.

Rupert and Lavinia Anderson had been at ceremony and reception, but had left before the party which would have been rather too boisterous for their taste, Maggie guessed. Mercifully, Rupert had conducted himself impeccably as the father of the bridesmaid, with no hint to Maggie of anything untoward ever having passed between them. And when he had offered her his congratulations, she had sensed a tacit valediction. Jack had been right in his prediction, it seemed.

But now, although Maggie was happy at the prospect of a new life, she was also aware of the nagging ache of homesickness. This worried her, for surely it wasn't natural for a woman to be missing her mother and brother on her honeymoon night?

Surprising her with an unexpected show of sensitivity, Jack said, 'You'll be feeling a bit strange, I expect.' He squeezed her hand. 'It's been quite a day.'

'Yes, I do feel a little odd,' she admitted, biting her lip, her free hand clenched in her lap. She was wearing a royal-blue suit with a matching feather hat which covered just the crown of her head.

'It's only natural,' he said kindly. 'Leaving home is a big step for someone still quite young. It's different for me, I've been standin' on me own feet for years. The war toughend me up.' He took both her hands in his. 'But you'll be all right with me. I'll do me best to make yer happy.'

And feeling her tremble with emotion, he hugged her close. He had such a contradictory nature, she thought. Kind and generous to a fault, fiercely passionate and proud, yet easy-going and tender. Most certainly a muddler with an unrealistic view of life, but she trusted him implicitly and didn't doubt his love for her. 'I know you will,' she said, struggling against a lump in her throat.

Later, she lay awake between the crisp hotel sheets long after Jack had gone to sleep. The heavy satin drapes were drawn back a little from the window and the lights from the street shone into the room. It might be only a one-night honeymoon but Jack had certainly done it in style, she thought, looking around the luxurious room. As well as the beautifully upholstered armchairs and stylish writing desk, there was also an en suite bathroom.

She did hope she had made him happy on his wedding night. He was sleeping contentedly enough. The fact that she had found the consummation disappointing was probably natural at this early stage. Perhaps women weren't supposed to enjoy sex in the same way as men, initially. She'd probably learn to like it in time. She felt strangely empty though as she finally fell asleep.

After breakfast the next morning they took a walk in Hyde Park, gloriously autumnal on this bright sunny morning. Coppery gold leaves covered the ground, forming disorderly russet banks in places. The crisp air was peppered with a suggestion of mist as they strolled around the lake, arm in arm, then lingered for a while at Speaker's Corner to enjoy the lively atmosphere of free speech before making their way back to the hotel. A pleasant after-lunch torpor drove them to their room where they made love and slept till tea which they took in one of the sumptuous lounges. Then it was time to return to the less exalted ambience of Ashbrook Green.

Maggie felt no sense of anti-climax. The wedding excitement had been fun, but an ordinary working routine was hardly anathema to her. In fact, her thoughts had already moved ahead before they arrived home. 'Can I come to Covent Garden Market with you one morning soon?' she asked. 'I think it would be good experience for me.'

'Yeah, it would,' he agreed. 'But I leave just after five o'clock and I wouldn't have the heart to drag you out of bed that early.'

'I don't mind.'

'You'll have enough to do for the next few weeks, getting settled into married life,' he said. 'But let me know when you're ready and I'll give you an early call.'

'Great,' she said, filled with optimism for the future. It was going to be such fun being Jack's wife. She couldn't wait to start running her own household, and to learn more about the shop.

But her enthusiasm was dampened the instant they arrived at the flat, which resembled Wembley Stadium after the Cup Final. The Radford apartment, which was old with high ceilings and sash windows, was on two floors and comprised a living room and kitchen on the first floor, and two bedrooms and a bathroom upstairs. The living room was littered with dirty plates, many containing half-eaten sandwiches and cigarette ends, used glasses, cups and saucers and empty cigarette packets. Bread crumbs covered the shabby red carpet, and Archie's clothes were strewn across the bulky brown furniture exactly where they had been discarded.

He himself was lying on the sofa in a blue woollen dressing gown, reading a Sunday newspaper, apparently oblivious to his appalling surroundings. Ignoring him, Maggie followed Jack into the kitchen which almost made her heave. Every single item of crockery and cutlery that the brothers owned must have been put to use. Cups half filled with cold tea;

plates caked with congealed gravy; ashtrays overflowing; beer bottles; broken glass.

Nauseated by the stench of stale beer and cigarette smoke, she opened a window while Jack marched back into the other room to read the riot act to his brother. This apartment had always worn the hectic disorder of bachelorhood, but Maggie had never seen it dirty before. Why hadn't Archie cleared up after the party? Surely he had known they were coming back this evening.

She went back into the living room where Jack was furiously confronting his brother. 'What do you mean by this?' he bellowed, waving a hand around the room.

'I had a few mates in last night after the wedding party. You don't begrudge me that, surely?' said Archie with lazy insolence, making no move to get up, merely looking at his brother over the top of his paper. 'It's my 'ome as well as yours, remember.'

Jack snatched his newspaper and threw it to the floor. 'And I have never said otherwise. I couldn't care less who you have in while I'm not here, as long as you clean up after you. Why, you've not even washed the dinner things from Friday which you promised to do because I didn't have time before the wedding. How dare you insult my wife by letting her come home to a mess like this?' Realising that Maggie had come into the room, he slipped a protective arm around her. 'I'm so sorry, love. I could cheerfully murder the lazy bugger.' He turned back to Archie. 'On your feet, you. And get this place cleaned up.'

Archie moved into a sitting position but still didn't get up. He threw a cold stare in Maggie's direction. 'Let 'er do it. That's why you married her, ain't it?'

Pale with temper, Jack grabbed him by the arms and dragged him to his feet. 'No, it bloody well ain't! Now get on and make this place fit for a lady. It's a fine welcome you've given Maggie.'

'She don't deserve a welcome,' sneered Archie. 'Just because you're letting her make a fool of you, doesn't mean that I have to do the same.'

Jack's arm tightened around Maggie, and feeling him trembling she realised that he was restraining his temper to spare her further embarrassment. 'Take no notice of him,' he urged her, and she could see his humiliation. 'My brother can be very stupid when he wants to be.' She guessed that he was aiming to remove her from the firing line before he really gave vent to his feelings when he said, 'Come on, love, let's get you out of here while Archie and I clear up. I'll take you round to your mother's.'

But Maggie was made of sterner stuff. This had not been an act of laziness on Archie's part but a deliberate attempt to hurt her. She knew that if her marriage was to stand any chance of survival under the strain of sharing a roof with him, which she had agreed to do in the absence of any immediate alternative, she was going to have to establish her position immediately. It was bad enough working with his surliness; she was darned if she'd tolerate it in the place that was to become her home. 'In what way am I supposed to be making a fool of Jack?' she asked, watching Archie become uneasy under her persistent gaze.

'You know very well what I mean,' he declared, his eyes dark with resentment.

'If I knew, I wouldn't be asking.'

'It's obvious. You married him to get yer hands on his business,' he informed her.

The idea was so ludicrous that Maggie laughed. 'If I did, I must want my brains tested,' she told him. 'The way this business is being run, all there'll be in a few years' time is debts!' She turned to Jack, who knew her opinion only too well. 'No disrespect, dear.' She turned back to Archie. 'So you can rest assured that the business is the last thing I'm after.'

Archie didn't seem to have an answer to that. Two spots of colour suffused his pale, greasy face and he mumbled, 'That remains to be seen. But since you've managed to worm your way into our home, you can earn yer keep.'

She put a restraining hand on Jack's arm as he made to intervene physically. 'I'll do my share,' she said, looking directly at Archie. 'I'll keep the place clean and cook meals as well as continue with my job in the shop. I'll see to the laundry and the shopping. But I will not be a skivvy. You will be responsible for washing the dishes after all meals and you will leave nothing around for me to pick up. This is your home, sure, as you pointed out, but it is also mine now and I'll thank you to respect that.' She paused for breath, her mouth twitching with tension. 'You can please yourself whether you abide by my rules, and if you decide you'd rather not, then you can see to your own meals and your own laundry. If I do them for you, in either event, it will be as a favour not a duty.'

Flabbergasted, he snorted 'Humph' and marched to the door.

Her voice was high but firm as she demanded, 'And where do you think you are going?'

'Out!' was his laconic reply.

'Not until you've helped clear up this mess, you're not,' she informed him brightly. 'I'll make a start in the kitchen. You two can get cracking in here.' She marched from the room with all the resolution of a bargain hunter at a sale, leaving the brothers staring after her, Jack with admiration, Archie with a mixture of anger and shock. She turned at the door. 'Let's make it snappy, shall we? I'd like some time to unwind before bed. I have to be up early in the morning as I'm going to Covent Garden with Jack.'

'Tomorrow!' he queried. 'I thought you were going to leave it for a few weeks.'

'So, I've changed my mind,' she said, her outburst releasing the tension and charging her with renewed energy and confidence. 'I'll be coming tomorrow.'

'Right, fair enough.'

Within seconds the flat was a hive of activity. Dishes and pots were scoured until they sparkled, mats were shaken, carpets brushed, floors washed and polished, shelves dusted and clothes put out of sight. Archie had lapsed into an angry silence but he did as he was bid. And to welcome his bride rather belatedly to her new home, Jack lit the fire in the living room. The sour air that had greeted them on their arrival was now replaced by the combined aromas of soap, floor polish and glowing coals.

Later, when Maggie and Jack were alone, Archie having departed to the pub, they drank watery cocoa (the milk ration had been cut again) by the fire.

'You were magnificent, the way you stood up to him like that,' Jack complimented her. 'You should have let me deal with him for behaving so despicably.' He paused thoughtfully before continuing a little defensively, 'He had an unsettled adolescence, losing Mum and Dad like that.'

Maggie understood Jack's need to defend his brother, even though she, personally, found it difficult to excuse such behaviour. 'That's as maybe,' she said, 'but one sign of weakness on my part and he'll make my life hell. I'm not prepared to let that happen.'

'It's time he had a place of his own,' Jack said apologetically, 'but with accommodation being so short in London, I don't like to push it for the moment.'

'I accept that,' she assured him. They had gone into all this before the wedding and she was not about to change her mind about letting Archie stay on, as much as the idea annoyed her. Neither was she going to allow herself to be intimidated by him. 'There's no need for you to feel guilty.'

'If he gives you any trouble while I'm not around,' he said, 'be sure to let me know. I'll soon sort him out.'

'Archie is one problem that I have to handle myself,' she said, eyeing him over the rim of her cup in the firelight glow. 'But don't worry, I'll manage.'

Finishing her cocoa, she rose and threw her husband a wicked grin. Since lovemaking was to be such an important part of marriage, she wanted to learn how to make it good, not simply endure it. 'Now, how about bed as we have to be up early in the morning?'

And Jack didn't need a second bidding.

71

Chapter Six

'Isn't it exciting to be out so early?' Maggie said to her husband just after five o'clock the next morning as they set off for Covent Garden Market.

'You wouldn't think so if you had to do it all the time,' he laughed. 'But, yeah, there is something special about being out and about at this time of day.'

Maggie shivered and hugged herself for there was no heater in the van and the air was damp and cold, with a light mist hinting at sunshine to come. The sleeping streets of Ashbrook Green were dim and silent, the only sign of life coming from the newsagent's shop where the lights burned as the papers were sorted and marked for the morning deliveries.

The contrast as they passed through the West End and approached the market was startling. The narrow streets of the hinterland were crammed with vans, trucks, cars, buyers, barrow boys. Porters, working with handbarrows or just with boxes of flowers and fruit piled on their flat-capped heads, delivered purchased goods to customers' vehicles, while the men known as pitchers unloaded incoming produce to the market.

There was noise and clamour all around them. A sense of communal anticipation permeated everything as palpably as a storm, increasing Maggie's heart-rate and accelerating her movements so that she leapt urgently from the van. Hurrying towards the main theatre of activity with Jack gripping her hand tightly, she noticed, in the early greyness, the lit windows of the pubs already open for business.

And suddenly the very essence of cockney London pulsated around her, thrilling her with its harsh vitality. London's oldest square, with its fine portico walkways and Italian-style piazza designed by Inigo Jones in the seventeenth century, was packed to capacity for a few hours every morning with people of the horticultural trade.

Jostling through the crowds towards the flower market past a plethora of beans and beetroot, parsnips and plums, the air was scented with the sourness of cabbage and the freshness of citrus. Mountains of bright oranges were banked against piles of shiny green apples; melons and pineapples bunched exotically among ripe pears. It seemed hard to believe that the setting for this thriving commercial enterprise had once been a real garden belonging to Westminster Abbey where the first gardeners had come to sell their produce in the early seventeenth century.

In the crowded flower market Jack swaggered among the sellers with aplomb, studying blooms, arguing about prices and ordering from his list. There was a multitude of shades and smells as hothouse blooms and seasonal ones vied for supremacy. Maggie was particularly impressed by the aromatic and dazzling chrysanthemums in bronze, white, yellow and mauve; roses of many colours; carnations, lily of the valley . . .

She soon realised that strong language was as natural as breathing here. 'I should have brought some ear plugs for you,' Jack laughed as he proudly introduced her to all and sundry, the cheery warmth of their welcome illustrative of his popularity here.

Finally, with the business complete, they went to a small cafe in a sidestreet and ate a hearty breakfast of bacon and sausage, and doorsteps of bread and margarine, all washed down with mugs of strong tea. It was not the grandest of places and was crowded with tough-looking men who swore loudly and wiped their plates with their bread. But it was clean, the food was delicious and Maggie was enjoying herself immensely, last night's altercation with Archie almost forgotten.

On the way back to the van a hazy sun was rising and illuminating the dignified contours of the Opera House which seemed to be watching over the loud, littered streets like a genteel maiden aunt.

'Well, did yer enjoy yerself?' asked Jack, as they trundled home with the heady scent of their load filling the van. 'Not too boisterous for yer, I hope?'

'Certainly not,' she assured him. 'I loved every moment. I must come again sometime. Since I'll be staying in the flower trade it's a good idea for me to learn every aspect of the business, don't you think?'

'Sure, as long as you don't start tellin' me how to run things,' he warned her with the frankness she had come to expect of him. 'In the home you reign supreme. I'll abide by your rules and accept your way of doin' things without question. But in the shop we do things my way. Right?'

She gave a mock salute. 'Yes, sir,' she laughed. But for all the levity of their mood she knew that he had taken the opportunity to make a serious point. And that worried her for she hated to see potentially good business wasted as it was at Radford's every day. The flower trade thrived in London and their shop was in a prime position for passing trade. Wedding orders and display work could also be increased substantially with a little effort.

But that wasn't what Jack wanted. So all she could do to avert future financial problems was to try to minimise expenses that the business couldn't afford. But this was not easy because Jack, for all his good humour, was a very determined man when it came to his own affairs, and deaf to any opinion except his own. It didn't seem to have occurred to him, for instance, that the friendly arrangement he had with his landlord, which allowed them to live for such a ridiculously low rent, might not go on forever. One of these days that husband of mine is going to be forced to face up to the realities of life and his financial responsibilities, she thought.

On Monday afternoon Rupert Anderson sat at his desk, staring gloomily into space. His obsession with Maggie had come to a painful ending on Saturday when he had watched her take her marriage vows. A moment of paternal pride in his daughter, who had attended Maggie so beautifully, had unexpectedly forced him to see himself through the eyes of the younger generation. They would think him old, wise and respectable, he realised. Of course Maggie hadn't wanted him as a lover!

As well as the shame and humiliation as he recalled his appalling behaviour, there was also a feeling of relief. It was good to be back in control of his life again. Maggie would always occupy a special corner of his heart but not as a lover. Only Lavinia would ever be that. And because he and his wife had always enjoyed such a close relationship, he knew that he was going to have to tell her about Maggie or have his guilt come between them forever. In telling her he knew he risked losing her for, to his mind, he had been unfaithful as surely as if he had physically committed adultery. This was why he had spent the weekend unsuccessfully trying to pluck up courage to confess.

Now, with a trembling hand, he picked up the telephone and dialled his home number.

'Lavinia darling, are you busy?'

'Not especially, why?'

'I'm taking the rest of the day off and coming home.'

'Are you not feeling well, dear?'

'I'm fine but I need to talk to you. Is Chloe at home?'

'No, she's gone to see a friend.'

'So we'll have the house to ourselves. Good.'

'It all sounds very mysterious.'

'I'll explain when I see you.'

He did not insult Lavinia's intelligence by moderating his feelings for Maggie in the telling. But seeing his wife's pain, he wondered if he should have remained silent altogether.

'I shouldn't have told you,' he said, stung by her pallor, the hurt in her eyes, 'just to ease my own guilty conscience. But I didn't see how we could continue if I wasn't completely honest. We've always been so open with each other I couldn't bear the idea of having betrayed you.'

Lavinia didn't speak for a long time but just sat still, deeply engrossed in thought, her whole being seeming to have crumpled under the blow. At last she said, 'You were right to tell me. I'm devastated, of course, how can it be otherwise? I'm not sure I know how to handle it, any more than you did.'

They were sitting either side of the hearth in the drawing room where a log fire burned low, the light fading in the advancing afternoon. Outside, the embers of a bonfire emitted dying wisps of smoke for their gardener had been burning garden rubbish. Leaden with guilt, Rupert did not feel worthy to comfort his wife but his love for her had never been stronger than at this moment.

'I don't know what to do to ease your pain,' he said. 'Nothing actually happened, of course, but I think it would have if she had wanted it. I can't lie, not to you, dear. All I do know is that it is over. I have only ever really loved you, as Maggie was at pains to point out. I never doubted that, even when all this was going on, but that didn't stop me from feeling as I did about Maggie.' He sighed and clapped his hands to his head. 'Oh God, it has all been like some terrible nightmare. Me of all people, charging all over London like some lovesick schoolboy. Can you imagine it?'

The idea of her dear staid Rupert in the role of Romeo did take a little getting used to, she had to admit. And suddenly this, coupled with the tension, reduced her to semi-hysterical laughter which infected Rupert too. They clung together, laughing and crying, until the hysteria finally abated. 'Thank God it's over,' he said at last.

'Yes,' she agreed, not doubting the finality of his words.

'What about us though, darling? Does this mean it's over for us too?' he asked.

'Do you want it to be?'

'Of course not! That's the last thing . . .' He turned towards her and thought that she had never looked lovelier. Her eyes were warm, her skin smooth, her voice gentle. He wanted to bury himself in her homeliness and be nourished by their mutual devotion as he had for so many years. 'But I can see that you might not wish to continue. You've been hurt . . .'

'If you think I'm going to throw away thirty-odd years of marriage because of one near miss,' she interrupted crisply, 'then you don't know me as well as I think you do,' But although she was making light of what had happened, she had been horribly shaken by it. All these years she had taken him for granted, never once considering the possibility of his finding any other woman attractive. He was only human, after all. It was time she took a good look at herself and their marriage. The world was full of desirable young women, and they might not all be as unresponsive and decent as Maggie.

'I think she has behaved splendidly,' she remarked thoughtfully. 'A different kind of girl might have exploited the situation horribly. You are, after all, a very rich and respected man.'

'Yes,' he agreed, 'Maggie is quite a girl.' And experiencing a frisson with the utterance of her name, he felt a moment of panic. But it was fleeting for he was in control now.

And seeing that sudden light in his eye, Lavinia accepted the fact that Maggie would always be special to him. But the thought held no threat. She knew the danger was over.

Rising, she went over to the window and drew the blinds before going to him and slipping her arms around him. 'Chloe won't be back for ages,' she said with a slow grin.

'Do we *have* to go tomorrow night, Maggie?' asked Jack miserably one Friday evening in late November. 'Quite honestly, the last thing I fancy on a Saturday night, after a busy day in the shop, is an evening out with your stuck-up friend and her boyfriend. He's bound to be as snobbish as her.'

'Chloe is all right when you get to know her,' Maggie defended. 'And as neither of us has even met her fiancé yet, you shouldn't pass judgement on him.'

'Oh, come on, Maggie, make some excuse,' Jack wheedled, slipping his arms around her from behind as she stood at the cooker prodding the potatoes which were going to be served with liver and onions for their evening meal. 'We'll have much more fun at the local. They have good turns on down there on a Saturday night.'

'No,' said Maggie firmly, determined not to succumb to her husband's charm as he nibbled her ear lobe. 'I have promised Chloe that we shall be there and I am not going to let her down. I wouldn't normally agree to a foursome, since you and she don't hit it off, but this particular outing to celebrate her engagement to Bradley means a lot to her. Anyway, it's very good of them to invite us. Remember that he's insisting on its being his treat and Pinks Club in the West End will cost the earth.'

Maggie had only seen Chloe a couple of times in the two months since the wedding. With a home and husband to look after as well as a full-time job, Maggie's spare time was severely limited. But she had made the effort on two occasions because she had no intention of losing touch with her friend, despite Jack's dislike of her. Chloe and he had clashed at their first meeting and subsequently brought out the very worst in each other. Separately, Maggie found them to be pleasant, reasonable people. Together they were impossible.

The sense of inferiority in Jack's nature, which Maggie blamed for his fear of accepting too much business responsibility, was inflamed by Chloe's superior social status, and he made a great performance of trying to belittle her. She, threatened by his aggressiveness towards her, defended herself by attack in much the same way as she had on first meeting Maggie. The result was continuous sniping between them.

The simplest course open to Maggie would be to keep the two apart indefinitely. But since she had been endowed with a great deal of persistence, she felt that they should be exposed to an occasional meeting in the cause of fostering mutual tolerance.

'It's all show,' grumbled Jack. 'He's got more money than sense.'

She swung round and laughed loudly. 'That's rich, coming from you!' she said, wagging her finger at him playfully. 'Why, you're the biggest show-off in London. Our wedding reception was a prime example of that.'

At least he had the decency to look sheepish, Maggie was pleased to note. 'That was different,' he claimed hotly. 'I was marrying the most beautiful girl in London. I had every reason to show off.'

'Flattery will get you nowhere,' she warned him hotly.

'Ooh, Maggie, you're even sexier when you're angry,' he teased, covering her face with kisses, the issue in question losing ground against more pressing concerns.

'Our meal will be ready in a few minutes,' she said meaningfully.

'The food can wait,' he said, easing her towards the door.

'Archie is in the living room,' she reminded him.

'So what? The living room isn't what I have in mind.'

Forcing herself to respond to his mood, she said, 'Only if you promise to be nice to Chloe tomorrow night, and to wear the dinner suit we've hired without making a fuss.'

'Oh, come on, Maggie,' he reproved. 'That's blackmail.'

'So it is,' she grinned, drawing back and attending to things on the stove.

'You're a wicked woman, Maggie Radford,' he rebuked her, laughing, 'but OK, I promise.'

'In that case, I'll turn everything down,' she conceded with a smile. Despite her very best endeavours, Maggie had been unable to find any real fulfilment in the intimate side of her marriage, though she took pains to conceal this from Jack. It was still early days. She was sure things would improve in time.

As they were dining in style Maggie had splashed out on a new dress for the occasion, an emerald-green taffeta evening gown with a boat-shaped neckline and fitted bodice and a skirt which flared below the hips. Her freshly washed hair fell loosely to her shoulders and her flawless skin was embellished with just enough make-up for that 'special' look. Wearing the silver shoes she had bought to wear with her wedding dress, and clutching a small silver evening bag and a gift-wrapped package for the newly engaged couple, she followed Jack through the restaurant at Pinks Club towards the table where their host and hostess were waiting.

Introductions were made and Maggie and Jack took their places at the candlelit table which was adorned with an arrangement of pink and white flowers. An impressive diamond engagement ring was waved under Maggie's nose and duly admired with as much enthusiasm as she could muster, given that she was reeling from the impact of her quite phenomenal physical reaction to Bradley Hughes.

Chloe had not exaggerated in her description of him. He was, indeed, extraordinarily handsome – tall, blond, blue-eyed, lightly tanned. But what was happening to Maggie seemed to be beyond mere physical attraction, though there was indeed a strong erotic draw. This felt like an ethereal force extracting the essence of her from her body and pulling her towards him, seeming almost to transcend reality. It was an exquisite but alarming experience and she knew, instinctively, that he shared it.

'What would you like to drink?' asked Bradley of his guests, his attention lingering on Maggie.

'Just a shandy for me, please,' she said.

'Something a little stronger later, perhaps,' he suggested. 'I've had some champagne put on ice.'

'How lovely,' she said, avoiding his eyes and hearing a girlish ring to her voice. She handed Chloe the package. 'Just a little something from Jack and me, to mark the occasion.'

All credit to Chloe she was graciousness itself in receiving the embroidered linen tablecloth and napkins, though Maggie guessed that the gift was a humble offering to a couple like them. 'Why, thank you both very much indeed,' she said effusively, her eyes sparkling as she smiled into her fiancé's eyes, adding, 'Isn't this linen just beautiful, darling?'

'It sure is,' said Bradley, smiling across the table from Maggie to Jack. 'Many thanks to you both.'

'We'll use it at our very first dinner party,' chirped Chloe excitedly.

Since dinner parties at home were not a feature of the Radfords' less exalted social life, the well-meant comment only served to illustrate the gulf between the two couples, producing a painful silence.

'I'm glad you're pleased,' said Maggie at last.

'Who wouldn't be?' replied Bradley in a well-meant but banal response.

She smiled gratefully at him and for a few agonising moments their eyes met. It did not seem possible to her that their acute empathy was invisible to the others, but around them events seemed to be progressing ordinarily if a little awkwardly, since nobody seemed to know what to say to break the ice.

To Maggie's surprise and pleasure it was Jack who finally eased things on their way. 'Of course, Maggie and I are old hands at the marriage game. If you need any advice . . .'

There was a burst of laughter and Bradley asked, 'How long has it been, exactly?'

'Two months,' said Maggie.

'You sure look good on it, both of you,' observed Bradley, 'I was sorry I missed the wedding.'

'You missed a good do,' remarked Jack.

Drinks were served, food ordered and the strain in the atmosphere greatly lessened. Jack introduced the subject of the recent spate of air crashes around the world which took them through to the first course. And as the wine flowed, so did the conversation.

Pinks Club was one of London's most fashionable nightspots, successfully blending intimacy with luxury. The small tables, set in alcoves, surrounded a circular dance floor where well-dressed couples were dancing to a small band, with a male singer crooning 'Baby, It's Cold Outside'. Soft pink lighting suffused the ambience, adding a final touch of glamour. Chloe, in fine form this evening, led the dancing after the soup course. 'Come on, Bradley,' she said, tuggling provocatively at his arm. 'Let's dance.'

'Sure, honey.' He rose, glancing across at Maggie and Jack. 'Come on, you guys. We are not going to let you sit down all evening, you know.'

Jack was to the waltz what Hitler had been to world peace, but Maggie smiled graciously and said, 'Just wait until later. Then there'll be no stopping us.'

When the others were out of earshot, Jack said, 'I'll have to have a good few more drinks before I get on the floor.'

'I know that,' Maggie assured him absently, her real attention focused on the other couple, sailing gracefully into the dance. 'But you're making a real effort, love, and I appreciate that.'

He grinned, remembering the circumstances under which his promise had been secured. 'Well, a deal is a deal, after all,' he said. 'And I suppose Bradley isn't such a bad sort of a bloke, for an American. Anyone who's prepared to put up with Chloe deserves a medal in my book.'

'Now then, don't spoil it by being horrid about Chloe,' she warned him, still looking towards the dance floor.

'Sorry,' he said, attending to the contents of his wine glass.

Since Bradley had the air of a man who excelled at everything, it was more or less a foregone conclusion that he would be good dancer. And he was. He and Chloe made a handsome couple, Maggie thought. The dark, well-cut lines of formal dress looked good on him, and she was stunning this evening in a red satin off-the-shoulder dress, her hair swept up into a pleat and decorated with a red rose. She looked almost foreign, with her raven hair and dark complexion more noticeable still in contrast to his fairness.

The music was smoochy and the couple danced in close proximity. Maggie watched as Chloe smiled up at Bradley, then snuggled into his shoulder. As they turned so that he was facing the table over her shoulder, his eyes met Maggie's and once again she was drawn under his spell. As the couple moved into a position which brought them both into profile, Chloe looked up at Bradley, said something and giggled. He hesitated for a moment before joining her in the joke and for a spilt second Maggie thought she saw a touch of irritation in his manner, so fleeting it seemed almost subconscious. Just an over-active imagination, she admonished herself.

There was no fish course, since food rationing still persisted, but the main course was delicious, Steak Diane with a variety of vegetables, followed by sherry trifle. After a toast to the newly betrothed, both couples took to the floor, Jack now sufficiently well-oiled to manage something vaguely reminiscent of a quickstep.

Back at the table they were all flushed and breathless but imbued with party spirit. While the waiter served coffee, the band struck up a slow waltz. 'It's time for a change of partners, I think,' suggested Bradley. 'Come on, Maggie. Let's show them how a waltz should be done.'

She looked dubiously from Jack to Chloe, since she doubted if Chloe's refined style of dancing would stand up to the strain of a turn around the floor with Jack. But her husband surprised her with a benign champagne smile and instructions to, 'Go and enjoy yourself, luv. Me and Chloe'll sit this one out. It 'ull give us a chance to get to know each other better. Ain't that right, Chloe?'

And she, pink and pliant with champagne, hiccuped and said, 'You bet.'

Although Maggie was a married woman, she was also an eighteen-year-old girl with very little experience of men. So it wasn't surprising that she was confused and worried by the stab of longing which Bradley aroused in her as they took to the floor. She had never been stirred this way before, not even by Jack. And for someone just two months married, this was a devastating occurrence. Staring over Bradley's shoulder she fixed her glance on Chloe and Jack, who were engrossed in conversation at the table, to arm herself against the power of Bradley's beguiling eyes and generous mouth. For the one prevailing fact in the muddle of her emotions was that the incipient bond between herself and Bradley must not be allowed to develop.

'It all seems to be going off rather well,' she said, looking up at him and feeling slightly calmer with the emphasis resting firmly on propriety. 'Even Jack seems to be enjoying himself, and socialising on such a grand scale isn't really his thing.' Realising that this might sound ungrateful, she added, 'It's very good of you to lay it all on for us. We're really being spoiled.'

'I'm glad to see you enjoying yourselves,' he said, smiling down at her. 'You mean a lot to Chloe, you know. More than any of her other friends, I think.'

'I'm flattered.'

'She talks about you all the time,' he informed her. 'I get the idea that she kinda admires you.'

'Heavens, I can't think why!' exclaimed Maggie. 'She's the one with all the prestige. I'm just an ordinary working girl.'

Ordinary was the last thing Maggie was, Bradley found himself thinking, but said, 'You're very independent, I understand. I think that's what appeals to her.'

She laughed. 'I don't know about that, now that I'm a kept woman.'

'Hardly that,' he pointed out. 'Chloe tells me that you still work full-time in the shop. And that you sometimes leave the house at the crack of dawn to go to market with Jack.'

'Yes, that's right,' she said. 'But I only go to market occasionally.'

'You don't find it too much,' he queried, 'with the home to run as well?'

Detecting implied criticism of Jack, which she was not prepared to tolerate from anyone, she said, 'Good Lord, no.' She would never betray her loyalty to her husband by letting it be known that she spent as much time as she did in the shop for fear that left entirely to her husband's devices, the business would soon cease to exist. 'I work from choice. It's difficult not to be fully involved when you live over the job. But I enjoy it. I'm afraid I'm one of those infuriating people who thrive on work.'

'I know the feeling,' he said lightly. 'I'm a bit that way inclined myself.'

'Chloe and I are very different,' she explained, deliberately keeping her friend in focus to curb her attraction for this man. 'I suppose the odds against us becoming friends were probably quite high. But somehow it seems to work. I have become very fond of her and I would hate to see her hurt.'

His eyes narrowed quizzically. 'That sounds like a warning to me,' he said.

'No, of course not,' she said, knowing that her remark had been a warning to herself more than to him. Bradley had done nothing out of place towards her, but she knew he was as attracted to her as she was to him. It was as though by establishing her loyalty to Chloe she could somehow extinguish this strange chemistry that existed between them. 'Chloe is my best friend. I'm bound to be protective. Her parents have always given her everything she has ever wanted and as a result she can be very demanding. I am about the only person who doesn't let her have her own way. In fact, I am quite hard on her at times. But underneath all that self-interest, Chloe is a very vulnerable girl. She needs a lot of loving, somehow.'

'I guess I know that,' he said.

'Yes. Yes, of course you do. I'm being presumptuous,' she said, flushing slightly. 'I'm sorry.'

'Don't apologise,' he said. 'I guess I'm glad Chloe has someone like you looking out for her.'

She looked up at him, and the instant their eyes met she was certain that he was struggling against the same feelings as herself. The thread of understanding drew tautly between them, drawing them together and creating unbearable tension. Maggie's skin was burning, her legs felt weak. She looked over his shoulder, avoiding his gaze. 'I don't see so much of her now that I'm married,' she said meaningfully.

'I don't suppose you do.'

'Chloe tells me that your wedding is planned for next summer,' she said through dry lips.

'That's right.'

'I hope you'll be as happy as Jack and I.'

'Thank you, Maggie.'

Almost as though there was a tacit agreement between them not to put their mutual attraction into words, they continued the dance in silence. Feeling him tremble against her, she moved back slightly and fixed her gaze over his shoulder. When at last the dance ended, she was both relieved and disappointed.

That night Maggie lay awake long after Jack had fallen into the heavy sleep of the inebriated. She watched the undulating shadows on the ceiling and turned the events of the evening over in her mind until her brain ached with tiredness. She had always lived to a certain set of rules and was not given to fantasising. This business with Bradley Hughes was not her style at all. But it *had* happened. *Something* had happened. Something so powerful it had done more than unsettle her. It had terrified her! And now she felt empty and alone, as though the heart had been ripped from her marriage. Desperately she tried to convince herself that nothing had changed, that Jack was the only man for her. But it simply wasn't true.

Somehow she must put this evening behind her. She must work at her marriage and make it good. Jack was her husband, Chloe her friend. She mustn't let either of them down. She fell asleep desperately clinging to these thoughts.

Bradley was too restless even to go to bed, and sat smoking a cigar in an armchair by the fire in his Hampstead drawing room, a spacious but homely room with well-stocked bookshelves, hand-carved occasional tables, beige leather easy chairs and a red Axminster carpet.

He tried to focus his thoughts on Chloe and their life together. But a redhead with dancing blue eyes obstructed his vision. Maggie Radford was the most fascinating woman he had ever met and he desired her like no other woman before. And to exacerbate the situation, he knew instinctively that she wanted him with equal ardour. He wanted to know all about her, what lay behind her verve and strength, her compelling personality.

What was the matter with him? Since meeting Chloe he had looked at no one else. For months she had mesmerised him with her dark eyes and her gorgeous body. He had been as eager to marry as she. Now he could think of no one but her best friend. So what happened now? Nothing! Maggie was a married woman, for Godsake!

The strength of the rapport he had felt with her rather frightened him, because it seemed beyond his control. If he had been looking for an affair with a married woman, he certainly wouldn't have stayed so close to home.

His thoughts focused, at last, on Chloe. She was a beautiful woman and he was a lucky man. Guilt weighed heavily on him as though he had betrayed her by feeling the way he had this evening. But he hadn't asked for it to happen! He didn't want to feel like this about Maggie.

Until a few hours ago marriage to Chloe had been all he had wanted. It would be like that again. He would love her and make her happy, and put Maggie out of his mind. He glanced at his watch. It was three o'clock. Knowing that Chloe had a telephone by her bed, he dialled her number. 'Hi, darling, it's me.'

'Hi, Brad,' came the sleepy reply.

'Sorry to wake you.'

'You can wake me any time,' she said suggestively. 'But is there something wrong?'

'No nothing, baby. I just called to tell you I love you.'

She sighed. 'I love you too, Brad.'

'I don't think I can wait till next summer to get married,' he drawled in his strong American accent. 'How about bringing it forward?'

Chloe's voice rose excitedly. 'How romantic!' She paused. 'It will take a bit of organising, of course, being such a big wedding. But I'll soon talk Mummy and Daddy round. They can never refuse me anything.'

'That's great.'

'Seeing how happy Maggie and Jack are has made you impatient, has it?'

He winced with guilt. 'Maybe,' he said, forcing a laugh.

'We'll talk about it tomorrow.'

'Sure.'

'Love you, Brad,'

'Love you, too.'

He replaced the receiver and lit another cigar. He felt better for having brought the wedding forward. It would be easier to cast Maggie out of his mind if he was actually married. He must forget this evening and concentrate on his life with Chloe. She was the one to whom he would devote himself.

Chapter Seven

One day in August 1950, Dora Brightwell was put into an awkward position by her much-loved son-in-law's generosity . . .

The friendship between Jack and Dora had blossomed with time and he breezed in and out of her flat as casually as if he were her own son. This particular morning he had taken a break from the shop to bring her a racing tip and have a chat about form. Finding her a little weary with the warm weather, he said. 'It's time you gave up charrin', Ma. You ought to be taking things a bit easier now.'

'For Gawd's sake, Jack,' she objected hotly, 'I'm only forty.'

'I know that,' he said, raising his hands defensively against her fiery response. 'And I'm not talking about yer age, but the stage of your life. It can't have been easy raising the kids on your own, but you've made a good job of it. You shouldn't have to do such rough work now.'

They were sitting at the kitchen table over tea and ginger biscuits. The morning paper, open at the racing page, lay next to an ashtray, an opened packet of cigarettes and a box of matches. Nelson was snoozing on Jack's lap.

'Needs must when the devil drives,' she said, cradling her cup in her hands and peering at him over the top. 'And charring is the only work I know.'

'I tell you what I'll do,' he said thoughtfully, absently fondling Nelson's head, 'I'll pay you what you earn charring and you can be a lady of leisure.' He warmed to the idea excitedly. 'What do you say to that, eh, Ma? No more getting up at the crack of dawn and turning out again at night. You can please yerself how you spend the day. And I'll see to it that you ain't short o' cash.' He beamed triumphantly at her. 'Well, what do you think?'

Dora thought it was the most ridiculous scheme she had ever heard. Firstly, she would go crazy without a purpose to the day. And secondly, her son-in-law's reckless benevolence terrified her, especially with Maggie expecting a baby at the end of the month. The flower shop was a good little business, with 'little' being the operative word. From the way Jack indulged his nearest and dearest you would think he owned Selfridges. He always acted from the very best intentions, but even so . . .

'It's very kind of you to offer, Jack, but . . .'

'Kind be buggered,' he interrupted. 'It's me duty. You're me family now.' He was completely unaware that he had offered her anything but glad tidings. 'I won't hear another word about it. Give in your notice whenever you like. And don't worry about cash, I'll see you're orlright.'

What was there to say against such genuine kindness but 'Thank you'?

But immediately he had gone, Dora went to the telephone, which Jack had insisted on having installed for her in case of emergency, and called Maggie.

'I don't want to give up me job,' Dora told Maggie at lunchtime when she called in in answer to the desperate telephone summons. 'It isn't the charring I'd miss, but the company.' She shook her head worriedly. 'I didn't have the heart to tell him, because he's so kind. I'm no business-woman but even I can see that if he carries on throwing his money about like this, he'll land you both in the cart.'

And Mother didn't know the half of it, Maggie thought. Jack drew money from the business like water from the tap. And usually for the benefit of Maggie and her kin. Presents and treats abounded. West End shows; meals out; gifts for no particular reason. Last month he'd surprised them all with tickets for Frank Sinatra's London debut at the London Palladium and an expensive supper afterwards. Jack was a kindhearted man, but he was also an irresponsible one.

'Don't worry, Mum,' Maggie assured her, 'I'll talk to him about it tonight. And don't leave your job unless you really want to.'

'I don't want to hurt his feelings,' said Dora. 'He's very good to me.'

'He's good to all of us,' sighed Maggie. 'But he doesn't think things through properly. If only he would let me run the business, I'd build it up to such an extent that we could offer you a nice interesting little job within the firm eventually.'

'You can't take the man's job away from him,' exclaimed Dora.

'Not the job, just the responsibility,' she pointed out. 'I'm the one with the business mind, not Jack. And he knows it.'

'You won't have so much time to spare for the shop after the baby is born,' Dora reminded her.

And that was something of great concern to Maggie. For, whether Jack cared to admit it or not, the business had come to rely on her. As well as becoming a proficient florist, producing adventurous and bold new designs, she had also learned how to recognise good stock at the market, and had acquired a confident and courteous manner with the customers. Even the appearance of the shop had improved under her imaginative touch. It still might not be the smartest shop around, because Jack refused to spend any real money on decoration, but a little re-arrangement and some extra cleaning had brightened it up no end.

Since leaving school at Easter, Tom had proved to be a real asset as a full-time assistant especially these last few weeks when a slight rise in Maggie's blood pressure had resulted in the doctor advising her to take a rest in the afternoons until after the birth. In addition to coping with the routine shop tasks like cleaning buckets and flowerpots, sweeping and washing floors and running errands, Tom's clerical ability was improving to the extent that he was even teaching himself to type on the office typewriter in his spare time.

The fact that he could be trusted with much of the routine paper work meant that Maggie could spend more time where she was at her happiest, at the nucleus of the business. Her energy and commitment had resulted in an increase in the turnover. But although Jack complimented her on this, he still refused to accept her views on major policy.

A misguided entrepreneur Jack certainly was, but he was also an uxorious man. Warm-hearted and considerate, he pursued nothing more harmful outside the home than a game of billiards, an occasional pint in male company, and a bet on the horses.

'Yes, I expect I'll be a bit pushed for time at first,' said Maggie in reply. 'But once I get into a routine I should be able to combine motherhood with the shop. Living on the job is going to be a great help.'

'And at least you don't have Archie to look after now,' Dora mentioned.

'No, thank goodness.' Immediately her pregnancy had been confirmed, Jack had scoured London to find his brother a place of his own. 'We'll need his bedroom for the nipper,' he'd confided to Maggie, 'and you'll have enough to do with the baby to look after without having Archie to cater for too.' It had all been done in due consideration to her but the business had paid: key money on a flat in Shepherd's Bush, and a rise in salary for Archie to cover the additional rent. It could never be said that Jack Radford did not look after his family's present needs; it was a pity he did so at the expense of their future security. But Maggie had been very relieved to see Archie go for she had never felt comfortable with him in the home. In addition to his appalling manners there was something threatening about him. Evil intent always seemed to be lurking in those expressive eyes of his. 'I was only saying to Chloe the other day on the phone, how good it is not having him around in the flat.'

'How is she?' asked Dora, for she liked her daughter's friend.

Maggie laughed. 'Full of ante-natal discomfort at the moment! You know Chloe, she isn't over-endowed with patience. Still, at least we are able to comfort each other, even if it is only on the phone.'

'When's she due?' asked Dora.

'About a month after me.' Maggie sighed. 'I really must try to find time to see her. Chatting on the phone isn't quite the same.'

Chloe and Bradley had got married at the beginning of the year and had moved into Bradley's house in Hampstead, with a weekend place in Kent. Although Maggie was still determined not to let her friendship with Chloe lapse, she had accepted the fact that her husband and friend were best kept apart, and meetings with Chloe were usually woman to woman affairs. The fact that she poured all her energy into the business and her marriage left Maggie with little time to dwell on her attraction to Bradley.

And right now she was concerned with the immediate problem caused by her irresponsible husband. As much as she wished to rescue her mother from her twice-daily drudgery, this was not the time since the business simply could not afford passengers at present. With Jack's blessing, Maggie had made small payments to her mother throughout her marriage, and to do more than this right now would seriously overtax their resources. Bankruptcy would assist no one, she reminded herself.

Heaving herself from the chair, she said, 'I must go, Mum. I'll talk to Jack tonight.'

'Do be careful of his feelings, luv,' Dora warned. 'His heart is in the right place, remember.'

'I won't be too hard on him,' Maggie promised, pecking her mother on the cheek and clumping wearily down the stairs. This sort of weather did not suit her advanced stage of pregnancy.

'But surely you must hate the idea of your own mother turning out every morning when the streets aren't even aired?' Jack exclaimed later that evening, having listened to what Maggie had to say.

'Of course I want something better for her, that has been my ambition since I was old enough to consider such things,' she reasoned. 'But we simply can't afford it at the moment. And the way you spend money, we'll not be able to help her when she's old and really does need it, because all we'll have left is debt.'

They were sitting at the table by the window in the small living room, having just finished their evening meal. Maggie had waited until they had eaten, for she knew neither would have an appetite once she had said her piece. It was easy for Mum to tell her to make Jack's feelings a priority because she did not know the extent of his uncontrolled spending. As if his prodigality with respect to those already present was not enough, superfluity directed at those yet to come had poured into the flat since the confirmation of her pregnancy, mostly in the form of unsuitable toys and games. Even a tricycle big enough to accommodate a three year old had found its way into Archie's old room, which they had made into a nursery. It was crazy!

'That doesn't say much for your faith in me,' he said, staring gloomily out of the window.

She reached for his hand, gripping it as though to assist communication. 'Jack, my darling, you are twenty-six years old and about to become a father. You are not a child with endless pocket money. I know that you want the best for me and mine, but too much today means too little tomorrow, and that spoils my pleasure in your generosity. We have a good business, we make enough to live modestly with occasional treats. If we work hard and expand, one day we might be able to afford a different kind of lifestyle. But that time is not now.'

'I don't want a different kind of lifestyle,' he said. 'I just want to make you and your family happy the way we live now.'

'You don't need to spend money to do that,' she informed him. 'Can't you see that?' She paused thoughtfully. 'We already stretched ourselves in taking Tom on but at least he does earn his keep. We cannot afford to pay anyone who will not do that. And that's all there is to it.'

'We'd manage somehow if we paid yer mother,' he said. 'We always do.'

'But the business, as it is at the moment, can only stand so much strain for so long. Mum would be worse off if we couldn't keep up the payments, because she would have given up her job. And, anyway, she would hate to lose her independence,' she pointed out, moving away from the table and easing her considerable weight into one of the shabby leatherette armchairs. She waved towards the room. 'And there are other things to be considered too. This flat, for instance. I know it's convenient for the shop, but I would like our child to grow up in a house with a garden.'

He began to pace the floor with his head down. 'OK, you want a house, we'll get one,' he said, his temper rising. 'We'll get a mortgage.'

'The repayments on a mortgage would be a damned sight more expensive than the rent we pay on this place,' she pointed out. 'We really would have to economise then.'

'If that's what you want, we'll do it,' he said.

She shook her head, her body damp with perspiration from the sticky, airless weather and the effort of this ordeal. 'No. Now isn't the time. We need to expand the business first, build the turnover on this shop and then open another, maybe several eventually. Then we'll be able to service the mortgage repayments on a house quite comfortably. To do it now would mean drastic cuts in our budget which would make you really miserable. All I'm asking of you is that you cut down all this unnecessary spending and concentrate on expanding the business. We have to look to the future, Jack, for the sake of the baby.'

He turned to the open window and looked out, his back to her. 'You

91

know how I feel about that, Maggie. We are about to have a baby, to become a real family. Expansion will drain us of time and energy. It will ruin our family life. I am not prepared to let that happen. I want less business responsibility, not more.'

'I'll take the responsibility,' she urged. It was so infuriating to be forced to waste such a great opportunity. 'I'll run things. And I'll make sure that our private life doesn't suffer.'

'And I'd take orders from you, I suppose?' he snorted, swinging around to face her. 'No fear!'

'It wouldn't be like that,' she assured him. 'You'd still be the boss. I would just be in charge of the expansion plan.'

'Yeah, and I'd have to account to you for every penny,' he snapped. 'Oh no, Maggie. I may not be a high flyer but I still rule the roost in me own shop.' He lit a cigarette and sat down at the table. 'Anyway, you're going to have to spend less time in the shop when the baby comes.'

'I know that,' she agreed, 'but I'd use the time I do have downstairs differently if we were to start building up. I'd get out and about finding new business. I'd give Tom more responsibility in the shop.' She almost added, 'And get Archie to do a fair day's work instead of spending so much time picking on Tom and trying to find ways to fault him,' but she stifled the remark for Jack tended to be defensive of his brother. 'Anyway, even with things as they are at the moment I shall have to spend the best part of the day in the shop because I doubt if you'll want to manage without me.'

'We agreed you'd work part time,' he said.

'Yes, and that still stands, with or without expansion plans.'

Jack inhaled deeply on his cigarette. 'You can forget expansion, Maggie,' he told her firmly. 'I'll watch my spending from now on, but I'll not be pressured into a life of misery. I want to have time to enjoy my wife and baby.'

She could have screamed in frustration. It just didn't make sense to under-use their potential in this way. 'You still would have,' she persisted, 'and it would mean a better life for all of us.'

But she had pushed him too far. 'No,' he yelled, 'and that's final.' He ground the stub of his cigarette into the ash tray. 'I'm going out for a game of billiards.' He paused and eyed her darkly. 'Unless, o' course, you think that's too extravagant.'

'Sarcasm doesn't suit you, Jack,' she told his back as he marched from the room and thundered down the stairs. She heard the front door slam and his footsteps receding towards the billiard hall at the end of the High Street. Then suddenly the sounds happened in reverse and he burst back into the room and was on his haunches at her chair, taking her hands in his. 'I'm sorry, luv, I shouldn't have lost me temper. Sorry to spoil your plans for building the business up, but it just ain't in me to do it. I promise to be more careful with money though.'

She could have wept with disappointment, but she knew she must concede defeat, for the moment anyway. 'All right, Jack,' she said wearily.

'I'll stay home with yer tonight if you'd rather,' he offered amicably. 'With you being quite near yer time.'

'And have you miss your weekly billiard game?' she said. 'Of course not. Be off with you. No more lavish spending, though.'

'I promise,' he said.

And he was as good as his word until the end of the month when Maggie gave birth to a beautiful daughter. And then the staff and patients of the maternity ward of Ashbrook Green Hospital watched in amazement as what seemed like most of Covent Garden flower market appeared at Maggie's bedside, along with a large bottle of Chanel and an expensive doll for the baby.

Oh, well, thought Maggie. I suppose it's forgiveable in the circumstances. And she was far too thrilled with baby Katy to reprimand him.

As Maggie had predicted, living on the job proved to be an absolute godsend over the next few months, for matters requiring her attention downstairs in the shop did not cease to arise just because she was in the throes of motherhood. She became an expert at living a double life and capitalising on every moment. Those idle spells she had hitherto taken for granted were now put to good use. Shop matters were dealt with while the baby slept, nappies boiled while she fed, the stairs scaled in seconds, and Maggie learned to vacuum the carpet with one hand whilst holding the baby with the other. Katy was a very contented child and Maggie adored her, taking pleasure in her daily needs. Both parents monitored her progress with childlike enthusiasm.

She thrived on their attention. But as she grew more active, it became obvious that proper arrangements must be made for her during working hours. For it was no longer safe to leave her upstairs, even for a few minutes, while Maggie attended to business downstairs. Nor did she think it would be conducive to the baby's well-being to bring her into the shop while her parents worked.

After lengthy discussions and much studying of figures, the Radfords decided to employ a nanny from Wednesday to Saturday since Maggie was less essential in the shop at the beginning of the week. This seemed to be the most practical arrangement because Maggie was of far more value to the business than the wage of a nanny.

It was this decision that supplied the fulfilment of an ambition for both Maggie and Jack. For Mrs Dora Brightwell became official nanny to her granddaughter for a wage slightly exceeding her previous one. This way, with her being a productive member of the team, Dora's salvation from the rigours of the mop and bucket was a legitimate business expense.

The decision to employ her proved to be a wise and happy one for them all. Katy thrived in her grandmother's care, and Maggie got to see plenty of them both, since they were just a flight of stairs away. Dora voluntarily extended her duties to include housekeeping. She shopped with Katy in the pram, cleaned the Radfords' apartment, and the 'something-on-toast' they had hitherto grabbed for lunch was replaced by a delicious home-cooked meal enjoyed in a happy family atmosphere by all except Archie, who declined the invitation to join them.

Absorbed in a joyfully hectic daily routine, life felt good for Maggie. Until one day in the spring of 1951 when the rhythm was dramatically upset by a ten-pound note, missing from the petty cash tin, being found in Tom's overall pocket. Conclusive evidence indeed, and Jack was devastated by it.

'I really trusted that boy,' he confided to Maggie bitterly. 'But he'll have to go, your brother or not. I won't have a thief on the premises.'

Maggie, however, believed her brother when he said he hadn't taken it. 'I don't know who put that money in me pocket,' he said, pale with shock, 'but it wasn't me.'

'I know you didn't,' she assured him. 'And I'll prove it, trust me.'

She confronted Archie in the coolroom the next day where he was collecting some stock for an order to be made up in the workroom. 'Why did you set my brother up?' she asked.

Her direct approach seemed to startle him, for he dropped some daffodils on the floor. Quick to recover, however, he picked them up, flung them roughly back into the bucket, and said, 'Whatsamatta? Can't you admit that your brother is a thief?'

'You know as well as I do that he isn't,' she snapped, flushed with temper. 'Because you stole the money and put it in his pocket, to make trouble for him. Though God knows why. He's never done anything to deserve it.'

Now twenty-three, Archie was a strong man with a solid physique. 'Don't talk rubbish,' he said. ' 'e did it. The proof was there, as plain as the nose on yer face.'

With her hands on her hips, she faced him resolutely. 'If you don't own up to what you've done, I shall tell Jack about a certain incident that took place between you and me in the flat when you were living with us.' Her cheeks were burning at the memory. 'An evening when Jack was out playing billiards.' She could hardly bear to recall the ugly scene when she had had to fight off Archie's advances. Fortunately, she had managed to grab the poker and the sight had been sufficient to cool his ardour.

She had kept silent on the matter rather than cause trouble between the brothers, but now that her own brother's job and reputation were at risk, it was a different matter. But she didn't think it would go that far. Archie had too much to lose from a rift with his brother. A good wage; a rent subsidy; job security . . .

Fear flashed momentarily in his eyes and he emitted a cynical laugh. 'If you mean the time when you made a pass at me,' he blustered, 'go ahead and tell 'im. I'm sure 'e'll be very interested.'

'You're right, he will,' she said, calling his bluff. 'I'll do it now, he's upstairs in the shop.' She headed for the door.

'Wait a minute.'

Turning, she winced at the venom in his eyes. 'Well?' she said.

'What makes you think 'e'll believe your story?' he said briskly, but there was uncertainty in his voice now.

'Because he knows I would never lie to him,' she said simply.

Archie's thin lips tensed. 'Your brother was askin' for it,' he rasped. 'Just who does he think he is anyway, lordin' it around the shop like 'e was God's gift to us all? The sooner 'e's out o' the way, the better I'll like it.'

As the full impact of his jealousy registered, Maggie felt an unexpected moment of compassion for him. It was a very insecure man indeed who saw her timid brother as a threat. 'But why do you hate him so?' she asked.

'I just don't want 'im around, spying on me,' he mumbled miserably.

The air in the coolroom was dry and cold to keep the stock fresh. Maggie shivered but her skin burned. All around them on slatted wooden shelves and the green-painted stone floor were buckets of flowers and greenery. Overhead in the ceiling the cooling unit hummed noisily into the electric tension.

'It sounds to me as though you've got a guilty conscience,' she declared.

'Think what yer like.' He wiped his wet hands on his grubby green overall and folded his arms, staring at her.

'You had no need to go to all this trouble to get Tom dismissed, you know, because he never breathes a word about you,' she informed him, 'not about the times when you slope off and leave him to cover for you when Jack and I aren't around.'

' 'ow do you know about that?' he asked, trapping himself.

'I didn't until now,' she said.

'You tricked me.'

'That's right,' she said. 'You can't expect other people to play fair when you fight dirty.'

Archie plucked a red tulip from a nearby bucket and squeezed its delicate petals cruelly in his hand before hurling it to the ground and crushing it beneath the sole of his shoe. 'Oh, well,' he said, throwing her a look of contempt, 'it seems I've no choice but to go and face the music before you make matters even worse for me. Then I'll get off to the Labour Exchange.'

Maggie watched him walk to the door, his footsteps echoing against the old stone walls which were painted a gloomy shade of green. 'Wait a minute, Archie,' she called.

He turned and waited in silence.

'Why not let me tell Jack what happened?' she offered. 'I'll soften the blow by explaining that you felt threatened by Tom. You'll not lose your job, I'll see to that, as long as you promise to leave Tom alone in future.'

Archie's surprise was mingled with doubt. ' 'ow do I know that I can trust you not to mention anythin' else to Jack?'

'You don't,' she said firmly. 'You'll just have to thank your lucky stars that I'm daft enough to give you another chance, and hope that I don't spill too many beans. What other choice do you have?'

'None, I s'pose,' he mumbled. 'But thanks.' And, obviously embarrassed, he hurried away.

Maggie picked up the remains of the crushed tulip and gently placed it in water with the others in a gesture of insane optimism, for it was battered almost beyond recovery. Maybe her action was a product of that same streak of recalcitrant hope in her nature that had led her to assist Archie just now. She really didn't know, for she had acted entirely on impulse. She closed the coolroom door and made her way upstairs to the shop to break the bad news to Jack and the good news to Tom.

Chapter Eight

Chloe sat by the drawing-room window looking out across the immaculate front garden, beyond which lay an exclusive Hampstead avenue with large traditional houses and trees gloriously adorned with autumn colours. Not that the sight of russet leaves and ripe red berries affected her in the least. She was far too preoccupied with thoughts of her disappointing marriage to Bradley. They had seemed like the perfect couple, so what had gone wrong?

Their courtship had been filled with glamour. It had throbbed with excitement and sexual desire. There had been no rivals for his attention then. Now their daughter Daisy, and Bradley's business, seemed to mean more to him than Chloe when surely she should come before everything else? He had become so serious, so boringly home-loving. The party to which they had been invited this evening was a prime example. He had refused to go with her when absolutely everyone in their social circle would be there. His excuse was some stupid business meeting, but sometimes he declined for the simple reason that he did not want to go out partying as often as she did. And he was only thirty-three, for Godsake! At this rate he'd be an old man by the time he was forty.

To add insult to injury, when she had reminded him that she was the sort of woman who needed to socialise most evenings, he had suggested that she attend certain functions without him. 'I don't feel the need for so much gallivanting as you, honey,' he had told her amicably. 'But you go ahead and have fun. You'll be with friends who'll look after you, you don't need me along.'

The fact that she no longer really enjoyed her husband's company and knew that she would have far more fun without him, did not diminish her fury at what she saw as his neglect of his responsibilities. Dammit! As her husband, it was his duty to escort her socially. Her parents had always given her everything she wanted, and so should he.

It was September 1953. Nanny had taken three-year-old Daisy to the park, Bradley was at the office, and the afternoon stretched emptily ahead for Chloe. She toyed with the idea of calling Maggie for a chat, but guessed she would get short shrift for her friend wouldn't have time for anything as frivolous as idle conversation during her sacrosanct business hours. Anyway, Chloe's claims of boredom were anathema to Maggie. She would simply tell her to stop complaining and do something useful with her time.

Chloe watched an unattractive, middle-aged woman walk past the gate in the direction of the Heath leading a fashionably clipped poodle. Even from this distance Chloe was able to discern the woman's serenity. She looked perfectly happy with her lot though how anyone could actually take pleasure in walking with only a smelly, sniffing animal for company was quite beyond Chloe's comprehension. But the woman's capacity to do this highlighted her own feeling of emptiness, her constant yearning for some inner satisfaction which she saw in others and which seemed unrelated to social status or material comfort.

Maggie was a prime example. Why, the poor girl had the most boring and irresponsible husband imaginable; she was forced to slave in that cold dismal flower shop as well as raising a child, and she had a positive rabbit hutch for a home. Yet her ability to enjoy life was a constant source of envy to Chloe. And for all the latter's superior status, she felt the poorer of the two and sensed that their friendship was of more value to her than it was to Maggie who was always too busy to feel lonely.

Flicking idly through the newspaper, Chloe's attention was caught by a wedding photograph of a pretty darkhaired bride and a handsome fair groom. 'John Kennedy Marries Jacqueline Bouvier' the caption read. The couple's happiness seemed to leap from the page, filling Chloe with jealousy. It was hard to believe that it had once been like that for her and Bradley.

Vaguely aware that the man in the picture was some sort of an American politician, her thoughts turned to a recent family trip to Pennsylvania to visit Bradley's parents. She was their only daughter-in-law, Daisy their only grandchild, and as such they had both received a great deal of attention. The memory warmed Chloe. She needed that kind of VIP treatment.

The thought of her daughter, blonde, blue-eyed Daisy, brought a smile to her face. But whilst Chloe loved her, she knew that her patience with children of that age was very limited, unlike Maggie who spent every minute of her spare time engaged in the most mucky and exhausting parental pastimes, like pushing her daughter on the swings in the park and playing ball with her. And if that wasn't punishment enough, the Radfords, complete with Maggie's mother and brother, had taken the child to Hampstead Heath Fair on August Bank Holiday Monday. Maggie had apparently gone on the swingboats and the carousel with Katy, and the whole gang of them had stuffed themselves with toffee apples and candy floss. It all sounded positively revolting.

Maggie was setting a bad example to Katy, in Chloe's opinion. She was going to have a real little ruffian on her hands if she wasn't careful. At least Daisy was being properly raised with a well-trained nanny to care for her, to take her for sedate walks in the park and to see to it that she avoided any rough company and kept herself clean.

Bradley was no help at all with regard to the refinements of Daisy's upbringing. He had actually been amused by a recent tree-climbing episode, instead of reprimanding the child. And he claimed to enjoy accompanying his daughter to the park at a weekend. In fact, he insisted on it, no matter how many times Chloe reminded him that that was what they paid Nanny for.

Last week there had been a shameful incident in the park when Bradley, if you please, had been asked by the park-keeper to alight from the roundabout on which he was actually riding with Daisy, in view of the fact that he was over fourteen years of age. How shameful for a man in her husband's position to disgrace himself like that in public! Chloe had been glad she had not been there to witness the incident though she had certainly made her opinion known on the subject when father and daughter had come, spluttering and giggling, to tell the tale. 'You're a thoroughly bad influence,' she had rebuked him angrily. But he seemed to think the whole thing was some sort of a joke.

Returning to the present, she decided to remind her husband of his marital obligations. Reaching for the telephone, she dialled his London office. 'Hi, darling, it's me,' she said. 'Now, about the party this evening . . . I know you have some silly old business meeting but I'm sure you can change it to another time. The party will be great fun. There will be some show biz people there – that new singer that everyone is talking about, Frankie Farringdon, for instance. He sings with dance bands and there's talk of him making a record.'

There was an uneasy silence down the line. 'That silly old business meeting is actually very important,' Bradley told her wearily. 'I can't put it off. But you go, honey, and have a good time. We'll go out somewhere special together at the weekend.'

'It's your duty to go with me tonight,' she snapped.

'Maybe it is, but you'll just have to let me off this time,' he said more firmly. 'I have to attend to business. I'm real sorry.'

Chloe felt the familiar surge of violent fury which always consumed her at moments of frustration such as this. It started at her toes and hissed through her body like steam in search of escape. 'Damn you!' she rasped. 'Don't I mean more to you than business?'

'Aw, come on, honey,' he said more sharply. 'I do have a living to make.'

'Why can't you do it during the day like everyone else?' she demanded.

'Because the sort of lifestyle we enjoy doesn't come from working nine to five,' he informed her.

'I think it's just an excuse because you don't want to go to the party.'

'Come on, honey, give me a break,' he said, controlling his temper. 'I don't want to go to the party, I admit it. But I am not using the meeting as an excuse. I really do have to see a guy about business.'

'Damn business,' she hissed.

'You can damn it all you like,' he told her, his patience cracking, 'but it won't alter anything. Someone has to put the jam on our bread.'

'I'll go to the party alone, then,' she said threateningly, as though he had not already suggested this.

'Do so with my blessing,' he said with genuine sincerity, his co-operativeness infuriating her even more. 'I don't want you to miss the fun because of me.'

'I will then,' she said, slamming down the receiver violently.

Trembling with rage she could contain herself no longer, and pummelled her head with her fists until she was sore. It was a child's tantrum in a woman's body, for Chloe was quite unable to cope with even the mildest form of adversity. Eventually finding relief in self-indulgent tears, she managed to sob quite dramatically for a while. Then she went upstairs to her wardrobe to choose a gown to wear to the party this evening.

Bradley replaced the receiver after speaking to his wife and sank gloomily back in his chair. He and Chloe seemed to be becoming less compatible with each passing day. They had everything a couple could want: money, position, good health and a beautiful daughter. So why wasn't their marriage working? Once, the mere thought of being with her had been enough to set him tingling with pleasure. Now, he was beginning to dread going home for fear of yet another confirmation of his failure to make her happy.

Lord knew her happiness was his prime concern, but to concede to her every demand only bred further discontent. No sooner had he given in to her on one point than she was sulking about another. What was he to do to save his marriage? She seemed to find fault with everything he did. She resented the attention he was forced to pay to his work, and she even seemed to be jealous of the time he spent with their daughter. Yet when he and Chloe were alone together they no longer seemed to have anything to say.

Although he was loath to admit it, just lately Daisy seemed to be their only mutual interest. And they didn't often agree about her. Chloe was a good mother, but she was not a very loving one. She wanted the best money could buy for her daughter with minimum personal involvement, whereas Bradley resented missing a moment of his daughter's childhood. Doing things for Daisy was not a duty to him but a joy.

He turned his mind to this latest disagreement. Had he been wrong to stand his ground about his business meeting? Was he really at fault because he could only sustain a limited amount of the flamboyant socialising that Chloe enjoyed? Always with the same crowd, mostly old schoolfriends of hers and their partners; endless superficial chatter which they saw as the last word in wit. It wasn't as though he neglected her. They went dining and dancing and to the theatre. He had bought a country house so that she could ride whenever she wished. And he still remembered to give her flowers and presents.

Bradley worked long exhausting hours. The UK arm of his company was growing fast. The livelihoods of many people rested on his shoulders: architects; accountants; clerks; carpenters; plumbers; bricklayers; builder's labourers. If he failed to obtain necessary contracts, the company could not fulfil its obligation to these people. If Hughes UK did not construct to the highest standards, public safety was at risk. And if the company did not prosper, Chloe and Daisy could not have the comfortable lifestyle they were used to. So he made sure that his firm did thrive. And if that meant sometimes talking business until midnight and depriving his wife of his company at some goddam party, then so be it!

After all, Chloe would be the first to complain if she had to cope with an irresponsible jerk like Jack Radford for a husband. Maggie defended him to the hilt, of course, but it was obvious that she did the worrying for two in that marriage. Bradley's mood lightened at the thought of Maggie. Although he never allowed it to develop, he still felt something extra for her, though they had slipped into a sort of brother- sister-in-law role consistent with Maggie's close friendship with Chloe.

He glanced idly through the window into the yard which was crowded with trucks, cement mixers, earth-moving equipment and vans, all bearing the company name. The three-storey office building, which was the company's head office, had been considerably extended since Bradley had taken over the yard but was already beginning to burst at the seams again.

In the fight against postwar austerity in the building trade, Bradley had set up construction units in the provinces, complete with managers to run them. He expected national expansion to escalate even faster during the next few years, especially when the restrictions on private building were lifted. The Conservative Government had attacked the urgent housing problem by reducing controls on local authority building which had resulted in a record number of new homes being completed this year, a good proportion of which were Hughes Homes. It was great to see this island rising again from the ruins of war. But there was still a long way to go.

Speaking to his secretary on the internal telephone, he asked, 'Is everything in order for my dinner engagement this evening?'

'Yes, I have confirmed with Mr Reynolds and booked a table for two at Claridges,' she informed him efficiently.

'Excellent. Thank you.'

'It's my pleasure, Mr Hughes,' she said, for Bradley's own courtesy and consideration was reflected in his staff's attitude towards him.

He replaced the receiver thoughtfully. Mr Reynolds was the vendor of some prime building land in outer London, and this evening Bradley expected to clinch a deal. An important deal for his company and in turn his family. If only Chloe could understand this and stop her constant opposition. He sighed heavily. It was no use blaming her for the way things were between them. It took two people to make or break a marriage . . . Well, he wasn't beaten yet. He would simply have to try harder to make it work.

Maggie loved Sunday and made it into a real family day. It began with tea and biscuits in the marital bed, with Katy padding into their room and snuggling between her parents while they lazily perused the Sunday paper. Mother and Tom came to lunch, to which Archie was invited but never accepted. An afternoon outing was part of the ritual. Sometimes the park; sometimes the zoo or a trip to the Thames to watch the boats. Then back to Dora's for tea which was usually cooked meats with salad, bread and butter, and home-made apple pie.

'The Bigleys have bought a television set,' Dora announced with unveiled envy, one such Sunday tea-time in February 1954.

'Blimey!' exclaimed Jack. 'They're going up in the world. Cyril must be doing plenty of overtime at the factory.'

'A television set isn't so unusual nowadays,' remarked Maggie conversationally, helping herself to more apple pie. 'Lots of people bought sets for the Coronation last year, and it seems to have started a craze.'

'We'll have to get one, eh, Maggie?' said Jack, eying his wife cautiously.

'I'm surprised you haven't bought half a dozen sets already,' she laughed. 'Given that thrift isn't exactly your middle name.'

'What's a tellawishon?' asked Katy, drowning her portion of apple pie in evaporated milk.

'Like the wireless but with pictures,' explained Tom.

'You remember, pet,' Maggie reminded her, 'they have one at Daisy's house in Hampstead. We watched the Queen being crowned on it last year.'

'Oh yeth, I 'member.' Katy cut into her pie with her spoon, frowning thoughtfully. 'When can I play with Daisy again, Mummy? I haven't seen her for a long time.'

'Oh, sometime soon, I expect,' said Maggie with deliberate vagueness. Chloe was not a great welcomer of playmates for Daisy, especially exuberant ones like Katy who harboured such shocking notions as playing in the street and sliding down the banisters. Daisy's exposure to other children was regulated through a nursery group run by two Hampstead ladies of impeccable reputation.

Chloe made it very clear that she preferred to see Maggie unencumbered by offspring – because children dominated things and ruined adult conversation, she said. And since Maggie liked to spend most of her spare time with her daughter, her contact with Chloe was mostly on the telephone.

'I'll tell her about my new scooter when I see her,' cooed Katy happily, her cheeks still glowing from an energetic session in the park. Her tiny fingers were barely able to hold the spoon, for she had inherited the daintiness of her female lineage. She was the image of her mother with a shock of auburn curls and blue eyes dancing in her tiny freckled face. 'A little doll,' people called her, 'with her mother's looks and her father's soft ways.' Indeed, she was already showing signs of Jack's impulsive generosity. Her most cherished toys regularly disappeared into the welcoming arms of the more astute infants in the community.

Now she raised her eyes to her father. 'I think we should get one of those tellawishon things, Daddy.'

'You think that, do you, princess?' he said affectionately.

'I do, Daddy, yeth,' she lisped, with all the solemnity of a bride taking her vows.

'We'll have to see what we can do then, won't we?' laughed Jack. He winked wickedly at his wife. 'But we'll need to speak to Mummy about it first.'

'Go on with you, Jack Radford,' Maggie chuckled. 'When did my opinion ever count for anything once you'd set your mind on buying something?' She paused and sipped her tea. 'Anyway, in this particular instance, I am in favour of the idea because I think we should move with the times.'

Indeed, it was virtually impossible not to be infected with the current mood of optimism which was sweeping through Tory Britain where consumer spending was rising along with employment. After years of drabness, it was exciting to see the bare shabby shops being refurbished and well stocked. Food rationing was expected to be abolished sometime this year too.

'I second that,' said Dora.

'I guessed you would,' laughed Maggie, since it was a foregone conclusion that the installation of a set in the shop-flat would be quickly followed by one at Mother's place, courtesy of Jack.

Maggie's approval produced a burst of febrile enthusiasm for the much vaunted invention. 'They have turns, jugglers and acrobats and that,' said Dora excitedly. 'And guessin' games and kiddies' programmes. It beats me how it works. I mean, fancy bein' able to see people who are miles away. It'll be like havin' the cinema in our own front room.'

The sound of the telephone in the hall gave rise to further discussion.

'I suppose people thought that the telephone was incredible when it was first invented,' said Tom.

'It still makes me jump, even now,' laughed Dora, as she headed for the phone.

The call was for Maggie. It was Chloe just ringing for a chat. She was at a loose end apparently. Bradley had taken Daisy to the park and they weren't back yet. Maggie couldn't understand why she didn't like to go out with them on a Sunday afternoon. It seemed sad that Chloe felt lonely enough to seek conversation at such a family time of the week. She missed many of life's simple pleasures through not opening her heart to them, in Maggie's opinion. When she rejoined the others who were still chattering excitedly about the proposed purchase of the television set, she felt blessed.

That same evening in a small flat in Shepherd's Bush, Archie Radford was trying to convince himself that his failure to sustain a relationship with a woman did not matter to him.

'Bloody women,' he raged, having just waited an hour outside the cinema for a date who hadn't materialised. 'You're better off without 'em, mate. A night out with the lads is much more fun, anyway.'

But at twenty-six, he was finding it increasingly difficult to find companions to go to the pub or the billiard hall with, since those that weren't already married were courting strong. 'Blimmin' fools, the lot o' them,' he muttered to himself, a pastime he indulged in with growing frequency as the amount of time he spent alone escalated. Eligible women were becoming rare. All but the teeny boppers seemed to be attached.

Throwing his coat over the back of a chair, he went to the mirror above the fireplace and studied his reflection in search of a clue to his lack of sex appeal. Admittedly he didn't have Jack's good looks, but surely he wasn't so bad as to be repulsive to the entire female population?

He was tall with a good body. And what did it matter if his skin had never recovered from the ravages of teenage acne? His eyes were clear and could smoulder quite effectively if he put his mind to it. He pursed his lips sensually, simultaneously lowering his eyelids, and was pleased with the sexy effect. His hair was always a problem, being straight, but if he backcombed the front into a quiff and used plenty of grease, it looked quite stylish. His teeth came up white too if he brushed them regularly. He was fastidious about personal cleanliness when he was meeting a girl, and he wore all the latest gear. So what was wrong with him?

It pained him to recall the number of rejections he had had, some on the initial approach, others after just a few dates. It humiliated him even more to admit that he was still a virgin. Oh, he boasted like all the rest of the boys in the pub, but that was just from self-preservation. He'd never live it down if they ever discovered the truth. Most times he could lie to himself quite successfully too, but this evening the truth was miserably persistent. It's unnatural, he told himself. Unnatural!

Moving to the window he looked down into the lit street. It wasn't crowded, for this was a backroad and it was a cold night. But those people who did hurry by were all in groups or couples. Snatches of inaudible conversation and laughter drifted up to him, then ended abruptly with the slam of a front door which felt like a physical blow. Even when surrounded by company, Archie had always felt isolated somehow, but his loneliness had increased since Maggie had appeared on the scene, excluding him from his home and making him feel like an interloper in his own brother's shop. And as for that pansy brother of hers with his stupid nervousness and his blank stare . . .

Well, Maggie could invite him to the flat for Sunday dinner until she was blue in the face, but he would never go. Nor would he go to her mother's place for Sunday tea, or to any other of the boring family occasions to which he was invited. He wasn't that desperate for company. Let 'em feel rejected by him. Let 'em have an inkling of what it felt like.

Leaden with despair, he went to his tiny slit of a kitchen and made some cocoa. 'Bloody woman, letting me down like that,' he said, referring to his date for this evening. Driven by a surge of violent frustration, he threw a cup and saucer into the sink, smashing them into tiny pieces. 'Women,' he muttered bitterly, smashing more crockery in the sink, 'they want murdering, the lot o' them.'

Blinded by narcissism, he couldn't see that it was aggressive self-absorption that was to blame for his downfall rather than any physical defect. For in his desperation for admiration and love, he was a daunting challenge indeed for any woman.

Chapter Nine

'Well, I think we've just about finished, don't you?' said Jack Radford to Maggie on the eve of the Chelsea Flower Show in May 1954, as he cast a final critical eye over the seedsman's stand on which they had been working.

A glorious array of mixed flowers in reds, pinks, blues, whites and yellows spilled from hanging baskets, burst from pots and rose gracefully from earthenware vases, transforming the tradestand into a dazzling kaleidoscope of colour.

'Yes, I don't think we can do any more to improve it,' agreed Maggie, glancing around the damp showground, buzzing with a frenzy of last-minute preparations for the opening tomorrow which would be preceded by the traditional Royal Visit. 'But I do hope the weather cheers up for the visitors.'

During the last three weeks this pleasant but commonplace London park in the south grounds of the Royal Hospital, well-known home of Chelsea Pensioners, with its roomy lawns and weathered trees, had been transformed into a miracle of colour and creativity. Flowers of every shade and variety clasped the ground, climbed walls, sprouted from window boxes and adorned the tradestands and bandstand alike. A marquee had been erected on the tennis courts and the hitherto plain grassland was now resplendent with complete gardens which seemed to have been there forever.

Maggie and Jack had been here for a week, intermittently, working on displays for the numerous stands, and adding their florist's skills to those of the growers to convert various verges and slopes into dazzling ornaments for this highlight of the horticultural year. Now their work was finished and they could slip away, leaving the fruits of their labours to be enjoyed by the many gardening enthusiasts who would walk these paths during the next few days.

Jack looked up at the leaden sky, from which spasmodic rain had dripped for most of the day, and responded to her remark. 'It doesn't look too hopeful. But it'll take more than a drop o' rain to spoil this shindig.' He smiled at her affectionately for they had worked well together on this project 'Come on, luv, let's go home and get changed into some clean dry clothes.'

They trudged back to the van in companionable silence, both dressed in Wellington boots and mud-spattered mackintoshes. It had been a hectic week, with them dividing their time between Chelsea and the shop which had been left in the care of Archie and Tom.

On the way home Jack asked Maggie if there was anything wrong. 'You seem a bit quiet,' he remarked.

'I'm all right,' she lied. She should have told him there and then about the bombshell that had come in this morning's post, but she was cold, wet and tired. She'd been on her feet since seven this morning and it was now seven at night. Anyway, she needed time to think about the situation, because as sure as God made little apples it would be up to her to find a solution.

It was a week later before Jack finally heard the news. On Wednesday June 2nd, the day that eighteen-year-old Lester Piggott thrilled the country by becoming the youngest jockey ever to win the Derby, when he rode the American-bred Never Say Die to victory at Epsom.

Jack and Dora were ecstatic, having backed the horse. Typically, he immediately blew his winnings on presents for the family. When he arrived home from the local a little tiddly that night, Maggie said, 'I hope you've enjoyed your celebrations, because I really do think that the party is over now.' And she handed him the letter which had been addressed to them both.

'Oh my Gawd,' he said, as the contents registered. 'That's torn it.'

'It certainly has,' she agreed, referring to the fact that their landlord, Mr Berry, was about to put the shop and the flat up for sale. 'But you must have expected something like this to happen eventually. It was obvious that he wouldn't let us stay on at such a low rent indefinitely.'

'I thought he would increase the rent,' he said, lighting a cigarette shakily. 'But I didn't except a bleedin' eviction.'

'He *is* offering us first chance to purchase the property,' she pointed out. 'So I suppose he is being fair.'

'Me a property owner, never!' Jack declared. 'I ain't prepared to take on that sort of a burden.'

Maggie was inflamed by anger. 'What suggestions do you have then?' she asked, aggressive with anxiety. 'Bearing in mind that we don't stand to lose just our living, but our home too?'

They were in the living room with the windows open for it was a warm night. The traffic on this road had increased dramatically this last few years, and Maggie could feel the fumes and dust in the back of her throat. What now of her little house away from the main road? She had hoped that the rise in trade, consistent with the increase in affluence generally, might have made that possible quite soon. But even if Jack were to have a more mature attitude towards these things, she doubted if they could afford to take up the option that Mr Berry was offering. The shop might not be the most glamorous establishment in London, but its prime position made it a valuable property for any entrepreneur, now that the country was on the move.

'We'll put up a fight,' he suggested.

'Without ammunition?' she riposted. 'It was a private arrangement. We don't even have a proper rent book.'

'We'll rent another shop with living accommodation,' he said.

'You can't just walk into any shop and rent it like you did with this one,' she reminded him sharply. 'There are things like leases to be considered. And they cost money.'

'I suppose you're right,' he said gloomily.

His feebleness in the face of adversity hit a raw nerve in her. All the financial worry and frustration he had caused her over the years now culminated in a loss of the tolerance she had taken pains to exercise throughout her marriage. Hot, angry tears burned her eyes. She wanted to strike at him for his wastefulness, his lack of foresight. If he had shown just a little more thrift, and had not opposed her suggestions for expansion, they might have been able to make an offer on this place.

'The only option open to us is to find employment, and try to find a home to rent,' she said coldly. 'I expect Mum will put us up temporarily if we haven't found somewhere by the time Mr Berry wants us out of here.' The words were wrung painfully from her as a last resort which she didn't, in her heart, see as a viable proposition. Jack would find it difficult to work for someone else. He was used to fitting business round his personal life, rather than the other way around. An employer would want someone committed to set hours and profit, not a rebel like Jack who swanned off to the races or to visit a friend during the working day if the mood took him. How long would he last in any restricted position?

'I'm blowed if I fancy working for someone else,' he told her. He lapsed into thought for a few moments, then snapped his fingers victoriously. 'I'll tell you what I'll do, luv. I'll make Mr Berry an offer for the place. He's sure to let us have it below the the market price, us being sitting tenants. We'll get a mortgage. If it means an economy drive to meet the repayments, then that's what we'll do.'

A flicker of optimism raised her spirits. The possibility of their getting the sort of mortgage they would need was only faint, but Jack's agreement actually to shoulder the responsibility of one must surely aid their chances.

But not by very much, it seemed, for Mr Berry insisted on the full market price, his only concession being with regard to time. He would hold the property for them for three months before offering it on the open market.

During the next few weeks they approached several mortgage companies, all to no avail. Their net income was simply not sufficient to service a loan of that magnitude.

'I just don't know what we are going to do,' Maggie confided to Chloe one day on the telephone in a rare unguarded moment. 'It's a worry and no mistake.'

'I'm sure something will turn up,' said Chloe, seeing an opportunity to help her friend with minimum effort on her own part. She would put the problem to Bradley this very day. If anyone could help Maggie and Jack, he could, with all his money. 'Try not to worry too much,' she added, and was rewarded with an inner glow at her own benevolence.

In fact, Chloe had been feeling a little more generous towards life generally this last few weeks since she had found a pleasant diversion from her disappointing marriage. And why shouldn't she see another man? Frankie Farringdon was fun. He was exciting. He made her feel good. Bradley hadn't done that for a very long time.

Having listened to what his wife had to say about her friend's problems, Bradley knew that he would have to approach the matter with extreme diplomacy or the Radfords would refuse to accept help, which would mean hardship for Maggie and her daughter. And they were Bradley's only concern in all this. For although he did not dislike Jack Radford, he disapproved of his irresponsible attitude to life which had caused this crisis. Goddammit, the man must have known he couldn't live on cloud nine forever.

It was obvious that any offer of assistance from Bradley would need to be disguised as a business proposition of value to himself as well as them, if it was to stand any chance of acceptance. The easiest option would be for him to buy the premises and let them stay on as tenants. But was it a good idea to allow Jack simply to potter along, under-using the business and depriving his wife and daughter of financial security? He thought not. An incentive was needed to force Jack to face up to his responsibilities.

Bradley had been pleasantly surprised at Chloe's altruism, and even more amazed by her sensitive handling of the subject. It was nice to know that she could care about someone other than herself. 'I could have asked Daddy to help them,' she had explained, 'but that would smack of charity because both my parents are very fond of Maggie. Since you don't know her so well, she's less likely to put up opposition to your suggestions. You know how independent she is; she'd never have let the problem slip to me if she'd thought I might enlist help on her behalf. And that wretched husband of hers will probably have the cheek to reject anything, hinting at charity after living on the back of his land-lord for years and giving Maggie nothing but worry throughout their marriage! How you deal with it is up to you, but please do something. We can't stand by and let Maggie lose everything.'

Little did Chloe realise that he would willingly let Maggie have the money she needed as a gift if that were possible. If anyone deserved to be helped, Maggie did, the way she worked. It would make him feel closer to her somehow. Especially as he planned to use his own personal funds rather than those of his company. But the Radfords would never know that. 'Leave it to me, Chloe,' he had assured her. 'I'll see what can be done.'

Now it was an evening in July and he was in the Radfords' living room, sitting opposite the couple who were observing him curiously.

'What did you want to see us about, exactly?' asked Maggie. 'Chloe wasn't specific on the phone. She just muttered something about you having a business proposition for us.'

'You've come to the wrong place, mate,' said Jack, aggressive with guilt for he was only too well aware that he was to blame for their troubles. 'About the only proposition we can consider is one from the council offer-ing us accommodation.'

'I'm not so sure about that.' said Bradley, opening his briefcase on his lap and purposely adopting a business attitude. 'All I ask, at this stage, is that you hear me out.'

Jack began to bluster ungraciously about not having time to waste on a pointless exercise. Maggie, looking a picture in a simple cotton dress in green floral print, her hair taken back in a pony tail, rested a gentle but restraining hand on his arm. 'Listen to the man, please, Jack,' she said persuasively.

Bradley watched as Jack stopped talking and looked into his wife's face, his whole being seeming to soften. Then he turned to Bradley and the latter perceived a man wracked with guilt for bringing trouble on the woman he obviously adored. To Bradley's surprise he felt a lump gather in his throat.

'Fire away then, mate,' Jack said.

Bradley cleared his throat. 'It's no good pretending that my being here has nothing to do with the fact that Chloe and Maggie are close friends,' he began, voice high with nervous apprehension in his eagerness to per-suade them to accept help. 'Or that Chloe has not told me of your prob-lem. What are friends for, after all, but to rally round . . . ?'

'We won't take charity,' interrupted Jack predictably, but was once more silenced by the composed and beautiful woman beside him, her shrewd blue eyes resting on their guest.

'But having said that,' Bradley continued as though Jack had not spoken, 'the proposal I have for you is a business one of benefit to my company as well as to you.' He paused only for a moment. 'Within my construction business we operate our own finance company through which we arrange loans, primarily for people purchasing our houses, though the service can sometimes be extended beyond that. For this function we receive a commission from the lenders who in turn receive interest on the loans, though the entire transaction, including repayments, would be done through us. I am telling you this to eliminate any idea of charity from your minds.' He looked from one to the other. 'I understand from Chloe that you are looking for a mortgage on these premises.'

'We *were* looking,' corrected Maggie. 'But we've been forced to give up on the idea. We can't meet the payments they were asking.'

'That is where I might be able to help,' said Bradley, his feigned uncertainty belying the hours of thought that had gone into this proposition.

Maggie's eyes brightened, but only momentarily since facts must be faced. 'I think not,' she told him, her tiny hands clasped together on her lap. 'The last few weeks have proved conclusively that we simply do not have the means to repay such a loan.'

'Perhaps not,' said Bradley with all the persistence of a salesman. He had purposely worn a business suit to add credence to the interview. 'But your shop has a great deal of potential, yeah?'

'Oh yes, we have plenty of that,' said Maggie, turning towards her husband as though daring him to disagree 'Isn't that right, Jack?'

'Well I . . .' He was hesitant, vulnerable in the trap of his own making. 'I dunno so much about that.'

'Oh, come on, man,' said Bradley, irritated by this groundless obstruction. 'Main road premises in London – of course there's potential! The standard of living is rising in the country as a whole. People have got jobs to go to and money to spend.' He paused to assemble his thoughts since he had been thorough in his enquiries into the floristry trade. 'Cut flowers and plants are a popular commodity, and the growth of the inter-florist delivery service has been phenomenal since the war. Is that not so?'

Maggie threw her husband a warning look, then turned her attention back to Bradley. 'Yes, you are quite right. There is tremendous scope in the retail flower business. Do please continue.'

Bradley took a sheet of paper from his briefcase and glanced at it, though he knew its contents off by heart. 'I have taken the liberty of working out a scheme that might be just what you need,' he said, peering at them over the top of the paper. 'I can probably get you a one hundred per cent mortgage at a special low-start monthly repayment.'

'Oh!' Maggie was flushed with fresh hope.

'What's the catch?' asked Jack.

'There is none,' said Bradley. 'But obviously there are certain conditions. The low monthly repayments will only be temporary. As you begin to realise the full potential of your business, the instalments will increase. At the end of one year, and I think that is long enough for some improvement to be seen, the situation will be reviewed and the payments adjusted accordingly. This way, you get your loan and my company gets its commission cheque.' He tapped his pen on his chin and added an authoritative edge to his tone for the purposes of credibility, for an offer of this sort was unlikely to occur in the harsh real world of finance: 'But I must warn you that we shall expect a reasonable increase each year until you reach the standard repayment.'

'Why, that sounds like the answer to our prayers,' exclaimed Maggie, filled with energy and hope. 'Oh, Bradley, you don't know what this means to us.'

But Jack was not so sure. In fact, the solution seemed more frightening than the problem itself. Now that property ownership seemed likely to become a reality rather than just an idea, its awesome obligations weighed heavily on him. Maintenance would become his sole responsibility, whereas at present Mr Berry reimbursed him for any painting and decorating. And what about major structural problems like dry rot or woodworm? And supposing he couldn't meet the escalating repayments! And just the thought of trying to raise the shop turnover made him tremble. What made Maggie and Bigshot Hughes so sure it could be increased anyway? His heart hammered erratically, he felt sick and wet patches formed icily beneath his arms. 'Hey, not so fast, Maggie,' he said, offering Bradley a cigarette, which he refused, and lighting one for himself with a quivering hand. 'What makes you so sure that I want to accept this offer?' he asked through dry lips, tilting back his head as he inhaled.

Maggie stared at her husband, the light fading from her eyes. What *was* the matter with the man? Even now, with his back to the wall in the firing line, he didn't welcome the cavalry. 'I don't see that you have any choice,' she said.

'Oh, don't I?' he snapped, hearing but not feeling the words. 'Well, that is where you are wrong. I may not be much when it comes to providing me wife with financial security, but I am still master in me own house.' He seemed to be looking at Bradley across some sort of chasm in which his own voice echoed distantly. Everything was brightly lit suddenly: the new contemporary fitted carpet, the recently acquired red three-piece suite with its sleek modern lines and spindly legs, the walnut television set with its double doors closed over the screen, the fashionable wallpaper that made the rest look dismal because he had only ever got around to doing one wall. It wasn't a palace but it was reasonably comfortable and *he* had provided it through *his* business – with Maggie's help. They would get out of this mess together, he and Maggie, without the intervention of some Yank with more money than sense. 'Unlike you, mate, who are obviously so hen-pecked by that toffee-nosed wife of yours that you have to spend your time poking your nose into our business.'

The ensuing silence rocked the room. Maggie's optimism was drowned by a wave of embarrassment and fury. 'I think you owe Bradley an apology, Jack,' she said at last, her throat constricted with tension.

His mind was a maelstrom of fear and uncertainty. He could feel his dear Maggie being driven away from him by his own failure. The means to win her back seemed beyond his reach. All he felt able to do was to hit out, trapped by his own immature attitude. 'I see,' he rasped. 'So now you're taking someone else's side against your own husband?'

She clutched his arm, shaking her head in despair. 'What do you expect me to do when you are so rude to someone who has our best interests at heart? Whether or not he is here at Chloe's instigation doesn't matter. The important thing is that he has the means to save our home and our livelihood. Please don't throw it all away.'

Her voice and slender body trembled, her face worked against threatening tears. Bradley felt like an intruder in the presence of such raw emotion between the couple, yet barely able to stifle the urge to go to Maggie and comfort her.

'I've had enough o' this, I'm goin' out,' barked Jack, powerless to control his appalling behaviour. He rose and marched to the door.

'Jack!' Maggie was up and running after him. 'Jack!'

But he was already thundering down the stairs. 'Oh dear,' she said, turning back towards Bradley and brushing a weary hand across her brow. 'Whatever must you think of us?' She walked back to her seat on the sofa and sat down, biting her lip. 'I'm so very sorry, after you've taken the trouble to come and see us too.'

'Apologies are unnecessary,' he assured her. 'Jack is sure to be concerned. It is a very worrying time for you both.'

She ached with tension, her throat was sore and dry. 'He didn't mean what he said, you know. I think the idea of owning property scares him.'

'I guess you're right,' said Bradley kindly.

An awkward silence fell between them. 'I'd better go,' he said, stuffing some papers into his briefcase and closing it.

'Must you?' said Maggie impulsively, adding quickly, 'I mean, would you like to stay for a coffee?' Quite what had inspired her to

114

extend the invitation she didn't know. Only that at this moment she didn't want to be alone.

'I'd love some coffee,' he said.

Maggie was surprised at how comfortable she felt with Bradley without the presence of their respective partners. 'I don't suppose you feel inclined to keep your offer open to us after the treatment you have received from Jack,' she said, sipping coffee opposite him. 'But I was wondering if I might prevail on your good nature and ask you to keep it on ice for a few days? To see if I can't talk some sense into him.'

'Sure, you take as much time as you like,' Bradley said. 'It takes more than the tantrums of a desperate man to deter me from a good business deal.'

'Thanks ever so much,' said Maggie, relaxing in the pleasantness of his company. 'Only, I just *know* we can really do things with the shop, if only I could get Jack to agree to my plans.'

Bradley was captivated by her enthusiasm. She was so unrestrained in her feelings, so full of life and interest. And love, he thought, since her affection for her husband was obvious. So different from Chloe who never seemed deeply touched by anything. 'Tell me about these plans of yours,' he urged her.

And as darkness blanketed the warm July night and the street noises drifted through the open windows, she told him all about her hopes and dreams for her little family.

Jack stood at the bar of the Black Bear mulling the situation over. His considerable consumption of best bitter had only depressed him further. He was in a no-win situation. It was a matter of choosing the lesser of two evils. Which would be worse, he asked himself: to work for an employer to whom he would have to account for his every move for a fraction of what he earned from his own business, or to accept the Yank's offer which would bring nothing but misery since the conditions of the loan were beyond his capabilities? Jack, my son, he warned himself gravely, you are in deep trouble!

He ordered a whisky in a bid to deaden the memory of his dreadful behaviour back at the flat. Had he really said those things? Had he really slammed out leaving Maggie to cope alone? As if she didn't have enough on her plate right now! Dear Maggie, she deserved better than him for a husband.

Another couple of drinks had him practically crying into his beer with shame. And now you've made things worse by getting drunk, he admonished himself, not too far gone to be lost to all sense and reason. Well, you can't go home to Maggie in this state, that really *would* upset her. He left the pub and staggered down the street.

Dora was sitting in the armchair drinking cocoa and watching a play on the television set her son-in-law had given her. She was wearing a pink candlewick dressing gown over cotton pyjamas and her hair was secured for the night by a thick-weave pink hairnet which had all the glamour of a pan scourer. Dora was an ardent fan of the television and had managed to fit in her bedtime toilette between programmes. Tom had already retired to bed since he was due to go to market with Archie in the morning, now the custom once or twice a week to give Jack a break.

A knock at the front door interrupted Dora's blissful relaxation. 'Oh no, don't say that's bloomin' Nora Bigley come for a chat,' she muttered. 'I want to see the end of the play.' Tutting, she shuffled to the door in her slippers, mumbling, 'I do hope she ain't gonna stay long.'

'Jack!' she exclaimed in surprise, perceiving his condition at a glance. 'Come on in before you fall down, for Gawd's sake.'

Her celluloid heroes were forgotten as she administered black coffee to her erring son-in-law, listened to his soul baring and gave him advice on request. 'I don't see that you've any choice but to accept Bradley's offer and be bloomin' grateful for it,' she said. 'All this nonsense about not being able to make a go of the business . . . It's a case of having to, mate. And you'll have Maggie beside you, and if she ain't an asset I don't know who is. Pull yourself together, Jack Radford, and face up to your responsibilities.'

He was disappointed in her. He had expected sympathy for Dora was his friend and ally. She placed his bets and said nothing to Maggie. She went with him to the races. She understood his easy-going, impulsive nature – or she had seemed to until now. 'Oh,' he said sheepishly.

'It's no good you lookin' at me like that, son,' she warned. 'You and me are mates and I think the world of you, you know that. But I love me daughter and granddaughter too, and I'll not stand by and see them lose their home if it can be avoided. As soon as you've sobered up, you go home to Maggie and show her what you're really made of. Accept the challenge and do yer best, that's all anyone can ask of yer. Listen to Maggie's ideas. She's got a good business head on her, that girl o' mine.'

'And what if we fail and can't meet the repayments?' he asked.

'Well, then, you lose everything anyway, but at least you'll have tried. Now stop bein' such a pain in the arse and go home to your wife,' she commanded.

When he'd gone she sank sadly into her chair. It upset her dreadfully to see him so miserable. Poor Jack. He was a frightened man for all his chat. A brave man too in other ways, his war record proved that. Dora was no psychologist but she could see that it was not courage he was lacking so much as self-confidence. And that would only come from him facing up to his problem. Oh well, it's something that he and Maggie would have to sort out between them, she thought wearily as she toddled to the kitchen, washed the coffee cups and headed for the bedroom.

Maggie's fury towards Jack had abated by the time she got to bed and lay awake, waiting for him to come home. Naturally she wasn't pleased with him for embarrassing Bradley and humiliating her, but the latter part of the evening had had a soothing effect on her. It had been positively cathartic to have someone respond to her ideas rather than evade them as Jack always did. Bradley encouraged her enthusiasm, even seemed to enjoy it. And the conversation had not been entirely one-sided. He had told her about his folks, and how his father had built his business empire in the States. It had been an enjoyable and interesting few hours.

But now she heard the sound of Jack's key in the door followed by the creak of the stairs, the squeak of the floorboards on the first-floor landing as he crept into the kitchen followed by a scraping sound and a muttered expletive, indicating that he had tripped over a kitchen chair.

'I have no intention of going to sleep until you are in bed,' she called. 'So you'll do yourself no good by creeping about down there like a burglar.'

There was a muffled 'Oh' and a few minutes later he appeared, shoes in hand, hair ruffled, eyes filled with remorse.

'You're a pig,' she stated categorically, as he proceeded with careful movements towards the wardrobe and put his shoes inside. 'An absolute pig.'

'I know,' he said, standing beside the bed eyeing her sheepishly. 'I'm really sorry. You deserve better then me.'

'I suppose you've been to my mother's to sober up?'

He nodded. 'How did you guess?'

'It wasn't difficult since the pair of you are as thick as thieves.'

Jack lay down beside her, fully dressed. His head had cleared but he still felt drowsy.

'I hope you don't intend to lie on top of the covers all night?' she said crisply, her red hair shining in the bedside light against her white cotton nightdress. 'Because your weight is pulling the blankets away from me.'

'I'll move in a minute,' he drawled sleepily.

'Too right you will,' she laughed, giving him a hearty shove so that he landed on the floor with a resounding thump. She snapped off her light and turned on her side with her back to him. 'Goodnight. Sweet dreams.'

Her relationship with Jack had never been romantic. They shared a

117

comfortable kind of affection rather than the intense passion which was so susceptible to the agonies of jealousy. Quarrels were never allowed to linger and were usually resolved in this good-humoured but unceremonious sort of way. Maggie saw no point in continuing this particular one until the morning when she would certainly have something to say to Jack Radford.

But that wasn't necessary, as it happened, because quite soon her penitent husband snuggled up against her back and said, 'How would it be if I saw Bradley tomorrow?'

'To apologise?' she asked.

'Yeah, that, and to get the deal sewn up.'

'Do you mean it?' she asked, turning over and facing him.

'I mean it.'

'Oh, Jack, thank goodness!' she exclaimed, hugging him. 'I know you won't regret it.'

And, strangely enough, he agreed with her. Now that he had actually committed himself, he felt a whole lot better.

There was an air of excited hilarity at breakfast the next morning. Both Maggie and Jack were in high spirits and discussed the new project enthusiastically. Katy, sensing something special in the air, became a little over-excited and somehow managed to empty her cornflakes into her lap during a giggling fit. Maggie laughed instead of reading the riot act, which infected Jack, and the three of them howled like hyenas before order was finally restored. It was a time of great warmth and harmony which Maggie blissfully absorbed.

'Will you call Bradley and ask him to come over?' Jack asked her, 'while I take a look at the stock that the boys have brought back from the market?'

'Certainly,' she agreed happily.

Bradley was delighted to hear that Jack had changed his mind. He was eager to set the wheels in motion for he could not rule out the possibility of the property being sold over their heads, despite Mr Berry's promise. Even the most sincere pledges had been known to crumble under the pressure of a hefty financial inducement, and the potential of such premises would not have gone unnoticed by the sharks who could afford to be generous with their offers. A glance at his diary revealed a hectic schedule with little time for a trip out to Ashbrook Green. But today was Friday and he wanted this thing signed and sealed before the weekend for fear Jack might have second thoughts.

'Would it be possible for you both to come to see me here at my office?' he said to Maggie. 'I can fit you in but doubt if I can find time to get out to see you at home. It won't take long, it's only a matter of filling in a few forms. Or will that be too difficult for you both to be away from the shop?'

'There won't be any need for me to come,' Maggie explained. 'Jack wants the loan to be put in his name only. He doesn't want me to be held responsible if our scheme fails. He's quite adamant about it.'

'Well, I suppose that's fair enough.'

'Will this afternoon be convenient?' she asked. 'Only Jack has to take the van into the garage for a service this morning, so he'll be without transport for a few hours.'

'This afternoon will be fine,' he said. 'It doesn't really matter what time since I'll see him in between other things.' He paused thoughtfully. 'But if he wants to come along this morning by bus or taxi, while the van is being seen to, that will be fine too. Just as long as we get the forms done today, so that we can start the thing rolling. The legal work will take a while, of course, but once Jack has signed, we can have a letter of intent to purchase sent to the vendor to secure the property for you.'

'That's marvellous. I'll make sure that Jack gets there.'

'Great, I'll look forward to it.'

'And, Bradley—'

'Yeah.'

'Thank you so much for your help, I can't tell you how much it means to us,' she said with great sincerity.

'It's my pleasure,' he assured her, hoping his emotion wasn't detectable in his voice. 'I'm a businessman through and through. I never let the chance to make a buck pass me by.'

And as he replaced the receiver he thought, Shame on you, Bradley Hughes. Now which particular charity shall you have the interest on their loan paid to?

As Maggie walked away from the telephone she found herself wondering if her friend's husband was as ruthless a businessman as he would have them believe. He was dedicated to his job, that much was obvious from Chloe. But no man who tolerated her petulance so patiently could be all that lacking in heart. Oh, well, he's saved the day for Jack and me, so he's a gem in my book, she decided, and hurried excitedly downstairs to the shop to tell Jack of the arrangements.

Jack was feeling pleased with himself at around noon that same day. He had been to Paddington to Bradley's office, apologised for his misdemeanours of the previous evening, signed all the relevant papers and been informed that the property would be his within a few weeks. And now that the deed was actually done he felt exhilarated, his fears quietened by the fact that he had done the right thing by Maggie. He could hardly wait to tell her.

The morning had been well spent and he had no qualms about missing the garage appointment. Once his mind had been made up, he'd not been able to wait to sign on the dotted line, not even until this afternoon. And the van could be done any time. Maggie would be too thrilled about the shop to be mad with him, even though she had made the garage appointment specially. She was paranoid about the maintenance of the van, in his opinion, and made a lot of fuss about nothing. Still, he loved her just the same.

Today was certainly a red letter day, he thought as he drove home, and some sort of a celebration was definitely in order. Something for them all to enjoy before their economy drive really got underway. A champagne toast in the shop perhaps, including Dora, Tom and Archie too. Yes, that should mark the occasion nicely. He'd get some lemonade for Katy so that she wouldn't be excluded.

Glancing at his watch he observed that the off-licences would be open now. But it would mean a detour because he doubted if the stores in Ashbrook Green High Street would stock champagne since there was no demand for it in the area. The more select region of Ashbrook Grove, on the other side of the hill, was much more likely to have it.

Proceeding over the hill beyond his own manor, he saw tiny terraced houses yield to spacious detached ones, narrow streets widen into tree-lined avenues. Pulling in at a smart parade of shops, he was told by a male assistant in the wine store that he could meet Jack's requirements.

'Special occasion, is it, sir?' the man asked conversationally, polishing the bottle and wrapping it in tissue paper.

'Very special,' said Jack, flush with his new sense of purpose.

'Nice weather for the tennis,' remarked the man casually, glancing towards the window.

'Too true.'

'What do you think of Little Mo's chances in the women's singles finals tomorrow?' asked the man, handing Jack the champagne and taking his money.

Jack was more *au fait* with the usual chitchat in the shops on the other side of the hill, on topics such as horse racing and soccer, but even *he* had heard of the talented American tennis player, Maureen Connolly, who had captured the hearts of people all over the world, and acquired her nickname from the fact that she was only 5 foot 2 inches tall. 'I'm no expert but it would be quite something if she completed her hat-trick this year, wouldn't it?' he said, for Little Mo had been Wimbledon champion for the two previous years.

'It would, indeed,' said the man, ringing up the sale on a noisy cash register and handing Jack his change. 'Enjoy your celebration, sir.'

'You bet,' said Jack, stuffing his change in his pocket and turning to leave. 'Cheers, mate.'

Outside, sunshine bathed the freshly swept pavements and well-kept shops. Even the bustle seems more refined this side of the hill, he thought, observing cultured accents and smart clothes. Noticing the beautiful houses on either side of the road as the van struggled up the hill, he imagined presenting Maggie with one of those in the future. Who was to say what might happen now that he had taken the plunge into property ownership?

A house of traditional style with leaded light windows, situated just beyond the brow of the hill, was particularly pleasing to his eye. Deciding to pull into the side to take a closer look, he pressed his foot on the brake. There was no reaction. Bloomin' brakes, he cursed, they need persuasion before they'll co-operate these days.

He pressed his foot down to the floor and pumped it quickly as the van gathered speed down the hill, pulling at the handbrake simultaneously. Nothing at all happened! Well, what was the matter with the stupid brakes? They usually responded to that particular treatment. Panic rose in him as the van hurtled onwards. Soaked with sweat he felt it leave his control and veer on to the other side of the road towards an oncoming car.

Oh my Gawd, there are children in that car. I *must* avoid them. I *must*!

With one mighty heave on the steering wheel, he altered the van's course, missing the car by inches. 'Thank Gawd for that,' he gasped, just seconds before the van crashed at high speed into a wall.

Chapter Ten

Maggie was immersed in a wedding order in the workroom, in her element. The joy of the occasion for which she was working was a great incentive to her as she added the finishing touches to the pink and yellow roses and white carnations for the bride's bouquet. Using the same basic arrangement for the bridesmaid's posies, she bound the stems of the flowers together with green stem tape then added a pointed-edge frill made of silver paper.

Standing back from the work-table, she turned her attention to the floral decoration for the bridal table at the wedding reception. Fixing a piece of wire netting into a boat-shaped vase, she then arranged a stunning multicoloured display of summer flowers in it: sweet peas; stocks; delphiniums; asters. Smaller versions of this, for the other tables, were already complete and lined up on the workbench which skirted the wall. Heady with the scent and satisfied with her efforts, she transferred the finished order into the coolroom where it would remain until delivery the next morning.

Glancing at her watch to see that it was time to break for lunch, she took a broom to the rubbish that had gathered around her feet as she worked, for it was all too easy for someone to slip on a piece of greenery.

A sudden thrill tingled through her at the thought of Jack's appointment with Bradley this afternoon. The new project was going to make such a difference to their lives. It would be so good to be building for the future instead of living for today. Jack should be back from the garage at any moment, she thought, knowing that he was planning to have a bite to eat at home before going to Bradley's office in Paddington to sign on the dotted line. Oh, what a turning point this was going to be.

It was at that moment that Tom called her to tell her that there were two policeman waiting to see her upstairs in the shop.

Everyone was very kind. The policeman waited until she was sitting down in the privacy of the flat with her mother beside her before actually delivering the news. Vaguely, she heard her mother tell her ashen-faced brother to go out for some brandy, then take Katy to the park and keep her occupied until things had calmed down a little. Mother was crying, Archie was sobbing. Maggie remained dry-eyed, gulping at the brandy and wanting to be sick as the policeman's words echoed in her mind, over and over again.

'He was killed instantly, love,' he assured her. 'He wouldn't have felt a thing. His brakes failed completely, apparently. He lost control . . . swerved to avoid another car, according to witnesses.'

Although Maggie seemed to turn to stone, she was aware of a driving sense of responsibility. She dare not allow herself to succumb to this over-whelming sense of weakness that had turned her limbs to water. She *must* remain strong for Katy's sake. Somehow she had to heave her useless body from this chair and carry on. Through the fuzziness in her head she could hear the telephone ringing unanswered down in the shop. Some-one must have closed the shop and forgotten to switch the telephone through to the flat, she surmised dimly.

Somehow, she was on her feet and in control. 'You can take the rest of the day off, if you wish, Archie,' she said numbly. 'And I shall say the same thing to Tom when he comes back with Katy. I myself have certain duties to attend to: the formal identification, people to notify and so on, but I shall finish the wedding orders for tomorrow whatever happens, even if I have to stay up all night. It wouldn't be right to ruin a customer's special day because of personal grief. It will be too late for them to make other arrangements for their flowers now.'

'I'll stay and give a hand,' mumbled Archie thickly, his face blotchy and eyes sore. 'I'll be better off working than stayin' at 'ome on me own.'

'In that case, it will be business as normal for the rest of the day then. Can you make a start by going downstairs and re-opening the shop, please?' she asked, already subconsciously slipping into her husband's managerial role. 'I'll be with you as soon as I can. There will be a lot to do without Jack.'

'Yeah, righto.'

'Thanks, Archie.' Although her senses were still too dulled by shock for the full impact of her own sorrow to register, she was not blind to the suffering of Jack's only brother. She went to him, intending to embrace him in a gesture of sympathy. But he pulled away and hurried down-stairs, rejecting any personal contact even at this time of mutual grief.

Alone with her mother, Maggie sank stiffly into a chair, holding the cup of hot sweet tea Dora had made. 'I feel too tight to cry, Mum,' she confessed.

'You're still in shock, love, but tears will come eventually,' Dora assured her.

'How will I manage without him?' Maggie asked, glancing through the window into the street, packed and bustling before the weekend. It was a familiar scene – crowds, queues, street traders, traffic – yet it seemed strangely unreal to Maggie.

'You'll cope,' said Dora, 'You've already begun by re-opening the shop.'

'If I don't keep busy, I think I might go to pieces altogether,' she admitted.

'It's best to keep goin',' said Dora sadly. 'But Jack will be sorely missed and no mistake.'

Reminded of the fact that her mother had also received a deep personal loss, Maggie went to her on the sofa and hugged her. 'You and he were such pals, I know you'll miss him dreadfully, Mum. He'll not be forgotten, we'll make sure of that.'

Dora emitted a shaky, emotional laugh. 'That's one thing Jack could never be – forgotten,' she said, tears streaming down her cheeks. 'He was far too much alive for that. Trust him not to wait around for old age. It's just like that daft bugger to go and kill himself through drivin' around with dodgy brakes.'

'It is indeed,' agreed Maggie, guessing that for some reason the van had never reached the garage that morning. And through her stupefied emotions came a stab of resentment for the needless waste of the life of a good and loving man, through his own sheer carelessness.

Somehow, with the help of relatives and friends and her own inherent instinct for survival, Maggie coped with the practical side of Jack's death whilst also stepping into his shoes in the shop, during those dark days immediately following his death.

Chloe and Bradley showed their true colours as friends, the former unselfishly whisking Katy away from the morbid atmosphere to play with Daisy. Bradley had appeared on the scene immediately after hearing the news, and had put himself and his Rolls-Royce at Maggie's disposal, cancelling all his business appointments for the day. His support at the morgue and the undertaker's had been of more value to her than he could ever know. He had also solved the mystery of Jack's whereabouts that morning.

Even in her dazed condition, she could see the poignant irony in the fact that her dear, impossible husband had precipitated his own death by shedding one responsibility for another.

And so it was that thirty-year-old Jack Radford, loving husband and father, muddler, natural comic, war hero, was laid to rest in Ashbrook Green cemetery just a mile from the shop. Maggie closed for the day, and the manor turned out in force to see him off for he had been a well-known and popular man. Banks of people lined the streets as the funeral cortège moved slowly by, and a respectful silence descended on the high street.

Now Maggie's tears were ready to fall and she felt close to hysteria as the coffin was lowered into the ground. But the other mourners saw only a beautiful woman, pale but composed, her hair drawn back beneath the wide-brimmed dark hat which she wore with a plain black suit.

At last it was over and the final guest had gone, leaving her in the flat with just her mother and brother. Katy had spent the day at Hampstead with the Hugheses and was staying overnight. Chloe hadn't been able to face the funeral, but Bradley had been there.

'I think the best thing you can do, Maggie love,' said Dora, as they continued to put their faith in the restorative powers of tea, 'is to hand this whole place back to Mr Berry right away and come back home to live.'

As much as Maggie loved her mother, she knew that the days when she could reside comfortably beneath the parental roof were over. She had become accustomed to her independence. 'But you don't have room for us,' she said, choosing her words carefully to spare her mother's feelings.

'We'll manage,' said Dora cheerfully. 'We always did before you left home.'

'We didn't have Katy then,' Maggie reminded her.

'We'll find space for a little 'un like her,' persisted Dora.

Typically, Jack had never got around to taking out any life insurance so Maggie now had poverty to face as well as grief, because she would only have a home and an income from the shop until Mr Berry's time-limit ran out. He had been very kind, and had told her not to worry for the moment, but it was obvious that her chances of staying on here had died along with Jack. But still she knew that she must search for an alternative to her mother's offer. Apart from anything else, Mum was entitled to some peace and privacy. 'Can I think about it?' she asked.

'O' course you can, love,' said Dora kindly. 'But I think it's probably gonna be your best bet. Mr Berry will want you out of here as soon as the dust has settled. And you won't be able to afford much of a place out of your widow's pension.'

'Mum's right,' agreed Tom. 'Katy can have my bedroom. I don't mind sleeping on the sofa.'

A lump gathered in Maggie's throat at the generosity of these dear people who were willing to sacrifice their own comfort on her behalf. 'Thanks, Tom,' she gulped, hugging him.

'That's all right, sis,' he said, his neck, ears and face turning scarlet.

Maggie smiled warmly at her brother. These last few years had certainly changed him. Maybe he would never be one of nature's extraverts but he no longer isolated himself from the world. And that was an improvement which must be largely attributed to Jack for taking the trouble to get to know him. At nineteen Tom was tall and slim, his owl-like National Health spectacles replaced by a smart pair of rimless glasses. His ginger hair was worn short and brushed back from his fresh-complexioned face without a parting. He had been granted exemption from two years' National Service because of various minor health defects, but his nervous air was noticeably improved.

'I'll let you know in a few days,' Maggie assured them both. 'When I've had a chance to gather my thoughts. Thanks for offering, anyway.'

That night in bed she succumbed at last to the luxury of tears, weeping copiously and draining away the tension until only aching sadness remained. A sadness she knew she must learn to live with as she faced the future without Jack. She fell into an exhausted sleep, knowing that in the morning she must make decisions and plans.

'The reason I have come to see you is to ask you if the offer of a mortgage that you made to Jack can be transferred to me,' Maggie explained to Bradley, surveying him across his desk in his office the next day. 'I know that single women are not seen as a good risk, since we are not usually thought of as breadwinners, but I would like to be considered.'

'I see,' he said, his brows raised with interest.

'It seems a pity for the plans I had for the shop to die along with Jack, since the ideas were all mine anyway,' she said. 'He would have been the first to admit that. And I'm confident that I could make a success of it.'

Bradley's expression was serious, his calm exterior betraying none of the pleasure generated by this unexpected opportunity to help her. He was going to give her this mortgage gladly, but to ensure that she never suspected the truth he must appear to comply with certain procedures first. He leaned back as though giving the matter due consideration. 'Jack died before his application had been processed,' he explained coolly. 'So your request for a loan will be a new one.'

'Oh, I see,' she said. 'But do I have a chance, do you think? Obviously I'd need the low start repayment.'

He leaned forward on to the desk and rested his chin on his hands. 'It is true that women are not looked on favourably in matters of this sort, but that doesn't mean that they are excluded from applying.' His gave her an encouraging smile. 'Bearing in mind the sort of person you are, and the fact that the shop does have terrific potential, I should think you have a good chance.' He could hardly contain his excitement at this project. 'It is certainly worth a try, anyway.'

'Oh, Bradley, I am so grateful to you,' she said warmly. 'It would be such a help if I didn't have to uproot Katy at this point. It's hard enough for her to have to cope with losing her daddy, without the upheaval of losing her home too. When we do leave the flat I'd like it to be for something better. In the meantime I want to keep things as much like before as possible, for Katy's sake, give her a feeling of security, you know.'

She looked very pale and strained, Bradley thought, yet more beautiful somehow. In contrast to her pallor, her hair seemed even richer, its gold highlights caught by the sun through the window, her eyes bluer against the smudges of shadow beneath them. He detected a new strength in her too as she accepted the challenge of sole parental responsibility.

'You mustn't worry too much about Katy,' he advised her kindly. 'Children are survivors, remember. Don't forget to take care of yourself in your concern for her.'

'Obviously Katy is my prime concern, it's only natural,' she explained, absently combing her fringe with her fingers. 'But, tell me, can I be optimistic about getting a mortgage?'

There wasn't a financial establishment in London which would take a chance on a widow of twenty-three with a four-year-old dependant and no collateral security whatsoever. But he said, 'Reasonably optimistic, yes. The biggest thing in your favour is the fact that the shop is in such a good position.'

'So what happens next?' she asked. 'I'm anxious to get things started in case Mr Berry finds another buyer now that Jack is out of the picture.'

His thoughts exactly. 'I'll put the facts to my loan source right away. Once I have an agreement in principle, I'll talk to your bank about advancing a small deposit to Mr Berry as a sign of your serious intentions. I should be able to get back to you by tomorrow with a decision.'

'Tomorrow!' she exclaimed in surprise. 'How wonderful. I thought these things took ages.'

Damn! He had allowed caution to slip in his eagerness to put her mind at rest. 'Completion won't be for a while, of course,' he explained smoothly, 'but there is no reason for a delay on the actual decision. If it is favourable, I'll get you to sign the relevant forms. I'll call you as soon as I have any news.'

'I'll keep my fingers crossed,' she said with a wry smile.

As she rose to leave he noticed that she had lost weight. The plain black skirt which she wore with a white blouse was very loose around her waist. He found himself wanting to look after her but bit his tongue against any personal comment. He was, after all, the husband of her best friend and he would be wise to remember that. Maintaining a business manner he made a suggestion. 'You might think about changing the name of the shop if this does come to be. You'll need to give the place a whole new image if you're to build it up, and a new name might help.'

'That seems a bit drastic,' she said. 'It was called Radford's even when Jack's parents had it.'

'All the more reason to change it,' he said. 'Let people know that you are a new force in the market place. With all due respect to Jack, he hasn't left you with a great deal of room for sentiment so far as business is concerned.'

She smiled affectionately at the memory of her husband. 'That's a fact.' She pondered for a moment, appreciative of his advice. 'I'll certainly think about it.'

Alone in his office he mentally checked the technical details of the loan. The amount she needed to purchase the premises was to be paid from his personal bank account via his company. The repayment would be made to his company and transferred back into his personal account later, minus the interest which was to be donated to charity. Satisfied with the details, he telephoned his bank to arrange a rather large withdrawal. Then he telephoned Mr Berry.

In August, when the premises became legally hers, Maggie knew she must have a serious talk with Archie who, being lazy, moody and aggressive, was a burden to the business. It was a pity his co-operative mood immediately following Jack's death had been so ephemeral.

As his one-time sister-in-law she felt duty bound to keep him on, but she simply could not afford to carry passengers. She had one year in which to prove herself, and by God she intended to do it! This shop was no longer going to be a downtrodden establishment, limping unprofitably from day to day. Maggie's, as it was now known, was going to be one of the best of its kind in London. Katy had known the misery of losing her father; she was not going to suffer poverty too, not with Maggie in charge.

So, bracing herself one August morning, she left Tom in charge of the shop and invited Archie into the office.

'I have mortgaged myself to the hilt to keep this shop,' she explained, 'and it's time you and I had a straight talk about your contribution to the day to day running of the business.'

He gave a nonchalant shrug, lit a cigarette, sat back in his chair with

129

one foot resting on the knee of the other, and said, 'Fire away.'

'Your brother was a good man and a loving husband, but he was an inefficient businessman and he left me penniless with an overdraft at the bank,' she informed him. 'I have a mammoth task ahead of me to make this place viable, which it never was while Jack was running it. Obviously, with a daughter to support and a large loan to repay, I must make the shop a success.'

He eyed her cynically. 'Is all this leading up to me being given the push?' he asked sulkily. 'If so, get on with it and stop beating about the bush.'

Oh, if only it was that simple! she thought, but said, 'You and I have never hit it off, Archie, but I'm not going to sack you.'

'Humph,' he snorted arrogantly. 'That's very decent of you, I'm sure, considering the fact that the business you are now calling yours has been in my family for years.'

Knowing Archie as she did, such an insinuation was not unexpected. 'Your family never owned anything. They simply rented the premises,' she pointed out firmly. 'All I have inherited from Jack is debts, so you can count yourself lucky that he never made you a partner or you'd be liable for them.'

There wasn't much he could say to that so he remained silent, flushing slightly.

'Anyway,' she continued, 'I am now the owner of the whole shooting match. And you are welcome to stay on but you must realise that things are going to be very different around here from now on.'

'I'll bet they are,' he said rudely.

Maggie took a deep breath and counted to ten, clinging tenaciously to her patience. 'Look, why not try working *with* me, instead of against me?' she suggested, her face flushed with the sheer effort of this interview. 'Can't you see that I *must* make a go of it or I'll lose it? Obviously, with such heavy financial commitments I have to run a tight ship. Jack could breeze along in his own sweet way because he didn't have the same burdens as me. If I do as he did, I'll be out of business in no time.'

Archie stubbed out his cigarette in an ash tray on the desk. 'So what are you actually tryin' to say?' he asked.

'If you are going to stay on you must pull your weight, learn to be pleasant to the customers for one thing,' she warned, 'and no nipping out during the working day and leaving Tom to do your work. I want the shop and the workroom kept spotlessly clean. I want the standard of our displays and service to be second to none. In other words, I want you to start earning your wages. And there will be more work for us all because I can't afford to replace Jack for the moment and I am

130

going to do everything in my power to get more orders. I shall try for more display work, more wedding orders, more passing trade. I want us all to pull together and if you are not prepared to do this, there is no point in your staying.'

'What about the market?' he asked. 'Have I got to go every time?'

'Ah, I was coming to that,' she told him, since he had taken over from Jack on that front, albeit grudgingly. 'Since we need to go to market three or four times a week, I think it is time Tom took a turn. He has been with you often enough to know the ropes. I will also go once a week when I shall pay the suppliers. Katy can stay with her granny the night before since I can't leave her alone in the flat. Eventually, if things go according to plan and I open more shops, I shall employ the services of a professional buyer to go to market for us. But that won't be for some time yet.' She paused, looking at him. 'For the moment you'll have to do the market twice a week at the most. Does that suit you?'

He hesitated only a moment. 'It sounds fair enough.'

'I take it you'll be staying then?'

'I might as well.'

'And you accept my new rules?'

'I s'pose so.'

Maggie shook her head. ' "Suppose so" isn't good enough for me,' she informed him briskly. 'If you're in, I want you in wholeheartedly.'

'OK, OK,' he said. 'I get the message.'

Later that morning, while out in the van with the deliveries, Archie wondered why he had agreed to stay on at the shop for he certainly didn't relish the idea of taking orders from a woman, especially one younger than himself. It wasn't as though there were no other jobs to be had, and it wasn't imperative that he stay in the flower trade. Factories were crying out for people and a job in one of those would provide other interesting possibilities too, for they were positively crawling with crumpet.

He warmed to the idea even more. A change of occupation was just what he needed. He'd get himself suited, then tell that upstart Maggie what she could do with her job. Why, he'd take a look through the paper this very day. Two sections of the newspaper were regularly perused by Archie, the situations vacant and the lonely hearts columns, both of which were a great comfort in that they offered hope for a new life, even though they never actually spurred him into action.

Stopping at the traffic lights, he experienced a powerful frisson as two young women strutted across the road in front of him in stiletto heels and tight skirts, their bosoms filling their blouses impressively.

131

They're probably on their lunch break from one of the factory offices, he thought, gazing at them longingly.

A sudden chorus of hooters caught the girls' attention and, turning to the cause, they erupted into a fit of the giggles before mincing on their way. Realising that the lights had changed to red and he was the centre of all the angry attention, he proceeded onwards, smarting with embarrassment. Girls like that, with their tight clothes and provocative ways, ought to be locked up, he thought angrily. He'd teach them to laugh at him. One of these days he'd get his own back.

Maybe he really would write a letter to one of the lonely hearts advertisements, he thought, the scorn of the gigglers emphasising his own loneliness. It wasn't just sex he wanted, but company, love, someone with whom to share his life. His enthusiasm rose to a crescendo in the same way as it had at the idea of a new job just minutes earlier.

But as the cool breeze of reality blew across his dreams, he knew that he would never write to a lady at a box number, or apply for another job. He simply did not have the nerve.

One Sunday morning in September Maggie received a worrying telephone call from Bradley. 'I'm sorry to disturb you at a weekend,' he said, 'but Chloe was taken into hospital last night and I guessed you would want to know.'

'Hospital,' gasped Maggie in concern. 'I didn't even know that she was ill.'

'She's had a miscarriage actually,' he explained.

'Oh no, poor Chloe!' exclaimed Maggie. 'I didn't even know that she was pregnant.'

Now he sounded surprised. 'Oh, really? I thought Chloe told you everything.'

'Probably thought it was too soon. How far was she?'

'Only a couple of months.'

'That explains it then,' she said. 'But tell me which hospital she's in and I'll go and see her this afternoon.'

'It's real good of you.'

'Nonsense, she's my friend. It's the least I can do.'

Chloe was lying back against the pillows, staring gloomily into space, when the nurse ushered Maggie into her private room.

'Hi,' said Maggie, kissing her cheek and handing her a bunch of early chrysanthemums.

'Thanks,' said Chloe without interest, putting them on the bedside locker. Her eyes were shadowed, her lips almost the colour of her face which was dramatically pale against her dark hair.

The atmosphere between them was strained. Maggie didn't feel welcome. It was difficult to know what to say to someone in these circumstances. 'You've been in the wars then,' she said at last.

'Sort of,' said Chloe, avoiding her eyes.

'I'm really sorry about the baby,' said Maggie, sitting down on a bedside chair. 'But you're still young. I know it's a cliché but there's plenty of time to try again.'

Turning towards Maggie, Chloe said in a cold tone, 'I don't want to try again.'

'And that's perfectly understandable,' said Maggie sympathetically, 'but later, when you're feeling better . . .'

'Don't be so bloody patronising, Maggie!' Chloe interrupted crossly. 'I don't want any more children. Not now! Not ever! I didn't want the one I've just lost. I'm glad about the miscarriage.'

'Oh, I see.' Maggie recognised this mood. Chloe always defended herself by attacking, which meant she was feeling as guilty as hell about something. Maggie studied her hands, unsure how to proceed. 'Nature's intervention is all for the best then.'

'Yes,' snapped Chloe.

'And I suppose Bradley is too relieved that you are all right to be disappointed,' remarked Maggie.

'He didn't even know that I was pregnant until I started to lose it,' she said dully, 'so the idea didn't have time to take root.'

'I see.' But Maggie was curious. Secrecy wasn't in Chloe's nature. She was usually too much in need of reassurance to keep things to herself. Especially something as crucial as pregnancy. 'It isn't like you to keep something like that so close to your chest. I'd have expected you to tell Bradley the minute you were overdue.'

Chloe fell into a thoughtful silence for a few moments. 'It wasn't Bradley's baby,' she said at last, staring guiltily at her hands resting on the sheet.

'Oh, Chloe,' gasped Maggie, unable to hide her shock.

'Go on then,' spat Chloe, close to tears now. 'Let's get the lecture over with. Tell me what a wicked woman I am.'

'It isn't for me to judge you,' said Maggie, struggling against a feeling of instinctive disapproval. 'That is something that is between you and your conscience.'

Fear darkened Chloe's eyes. She was obviously questioning the wisdom of her confession. 'You won't tell Bradley, will you?'

'Of course not.'

'Thanks Maggie.' Chloe's mood softened. She reached for Maggie's hand, a watery smile replacing the incipient tears.

'You've nothing to thank me for,' she said, not wishing to imply approval of her friend's transgression by becoming involved in a conspiracy. 'I'm simply minding my own business.'

The arrival of the nurse with Chloe's medication gave Maggie an excuse to leave. She was eager to be alone with her bitter disappointment in Chloe and the ache in her heart for Bradley.

'Will you come and see me at home?' Chloe asked. 'I'll be leaving here in a few days. I know you're busy with the shop and everything, but I need to talk. Can you come when Bradley is at work?'

Maggie sighed, reluctant to become involved in the problems of someone else's marriage. But you didn't desert your friends when they needed you, however badly they have behaved. 'Of course I'll find the time to come over. Let me know as soon as you get home.'

Chloe didn't want advice so much as Maggie's condoning of her misdemeanours, she discovered a few days later when she visited her friend at Hampstead. Having convinced herself that her affair with Frankie Farringdon was perfectly justified in that Bradley no longer made her happy, Chloe seemed more concerned about the cooling of her lover's ardour in the sobering light of her pregnancy than with the breaking of her marriage vows. Maggie found it quite astounding.

'I presume you are in love with Frankie?' she said.

' "Attracted" is more the word,' said Chloe.

'And you'd sleep with him just because of that?' roared Maggie.

'Frankie is a very exciting man,' said Chloe, as though that explained everything.

'Honestly, Chloe,' Maggie ranted furiously, 'you really are the giddy limit! You have a husband who keeps you in the lap of luxury. Why can't you be content?'

'I don't know, but I can't,' she said. 'It just isn't the same as it used to be between Bradley and me.'

'You must be sleeping together,' Maggie pointed out bluntly, 'or you wouldn't be able to fool him about the baby.'

'Occasionally one has to make the effort,' said Chloe with a sigh. 'But Bradley just doesn't "do" anything for me any more.'

'But what about him?' Maggie fumed in exasperation. 'Do you ever stop to wonder if *he* is happy? Or are you too absorbed in your own feelings to bother about his?'

Maggie knew that she was the only person alive from whom Chloe would take such criticism without flying into a rage. But, strangely enough, she actually seemed to need Maggie's recriminations. Maybe they eased her conscience, she thought.

'Bradley and I tolerate each other for the sake of Daisy,' Chloe informed her. 'That's about all there is to our feelings for each other these days.'

'And does he cheat on you?' asked Maggie.

'Not that I know of,' said Chloe, flicking her hair back from her face. She was wearing calf-length black trews with a white sweater, and sitting with her legs curled under her in an armchair by the fire-place in the drawing room. Maggie, in a pale pink sweater and grey pleated skirt, was sitting opposite with coffee and biscuits set out on a small table beside her. Daisy was out with Nanny and Bradley was at the office. 'And he'd better not either!'

'It would serve you right if he did,' opined Maggie hotly. 'What right do you have to expect loyalty from him after the way you have behaved?'

'Well I . . .' began Chloe, her words dying away at the flimsiness of her own argument.

'You can't play by one set of rules and expect him to abide by another, you know,' Maggie pointed out.

'I might have known you'd disapprove,' snapped Chloe. 'I should have known better than to tell you.'

'Yes, you should. But since you have told me, you might at least have the courtesy to listen to what I have to say,' Maggie rasped. 'Frankly I think you are the most self-centred person I have ever met.'

'Why do you bother with me then?' asked Chloe, suddenly stripped of all aggression.

'Heaven knows,' said Maggie. 'It really is time you started putting something into life instead of take, take, take all the time. I don't know how Bradley puts up with it.'

'Not everyone can be a superwoman like you,' Chloe riposted.

'Superwoman!' exclaimed Maggie in astonishment. 'I don't know what you mean.'

'Oh, come on,' Chloe urged. 'Nothing ever beats you or gets you down, everyone knows that. Even when Jack died, you rose to the occasion magnificently. And now you're running your own business. That comes under the heading of superwoman in my book.'

Shocked into introspection by the remark, Maggie's own life came sharply into focus. She herself saw it as a compromise – which she suspected was true for most other people. 'I don't spend all my time yearning for some sort of Utopia, if that's what you mean. But that doesn't mean that I don't have fears and disappointments like every-one else.'

'Really? Do tell.'

'Jack was probably the most infuriating man alive. He was careless, irresponsible and stubborn. But I knew he would have walked through deserts for Katy and me if we had needed him to. So I worked at making a go of our marriage. When he died, I didn't know how to carry on. But I had to for Katy's sake. Making life good for her makes my life worthwhile.' She paused thoughtfully. 'I suppose what I'm trying to say, Chloe, is that the sooner you stop striving for that personal something extra from life, the happier you'll be. It isn't that "something extra" doesn't exist but that it only comes through effort. Take a fresh look at what you have and give the occasional thought to someone else for a change.'

'As I said before, if I am so selfish why do you bother with me?' asked Chloe.

'I suppose it's because I don't choose my friends for their saintliness but because I like them, however impossible they are,' Maggie said thoughtfully. 'When you allow yourself to look outside yourself, you are a really nice person, but you don't do it often enough.' She glanced at her watch and rose to go. 'I must dash. I've a million things to do.' She paused to conclude, 'I can't tell you how to live your life, but I'm sure you won't solve your problems by going to bed with the first man who asks you. Save your energy for Bradley, and count your blessings.'

At the door, Chloe hugged her. 'Thanks for coming.'

'That's OK, but do try to get yourself sorted out or you'll lose him altogether.'

The next day Harrods delivered a parcel to Maggie containing chocolates for her and a doll for Katy. The card read: 'For being my friend, Chloe.' It was a kind gesture, Maggie thought, but one that spoke volumes about the depth of Chloe's insecurity. Lavinia and Rupert Anderson had a lot to answer for in spoiling their daughter as they had.

As Maggie's life as single parent and sole proprietor of Maggie's Flowers got underway, she gave a great deal of thought to the question of priorities. Obviously, Katy was her first concern but the success of the business was imperative if she was to provide her child with security. So a balance had to be found to provide each with the necessary attention. Until Katy started school, in a year's time, the weekday arrangements remained as before, except that Maggie was forced to add Tuesday to her working week. Sundays and Mondays were sacrosanct, though Maggie often turned her mind to paperwork in the evening after Katy had gone to bed.

Having organised her routine, she discussed her business plans with Bradley, who had become a valued mentor since getting her the mortgage. 'I have to make the business grow, and that means finding more customers,' she told him. 'As well as building up local trade, I want to spread my wings beyond Ashbrook Green for display work. Being in the metropolis means that we are near to the big exhibition centres, hotels and concert halls, all of whom use substantial floral displays. There is no law that says the big West End florists have to have it all.'

'Isn't that side of the business very competitive?'

'Yes, but so is anything worth its salt,' she said spiritedly. 'And that isn't going to stop me from entering into the market place.'

It was October 1954 and she was in Bradley's office sitting opposite him, looking every inch the businesswoman in a navy blue jersey suit, crisp white blouse and navy court shoes.

'You'll need to advertise,' he suggested.

'I was just coming to that,' she said, her face animated. 'I realise that I must speculate to accumulate, but I don't want to spend too much money on promotion just yet.' She paused and sipped her coffee. 'So, just to test the market locally, I have had some handbills printed announcing our services. They will be delivered to all the houses in the area. To back them up I plan to run a regular advertisement in the local paper. As for display work, I intend to make personal visits to hotel managers about their foyer displays and table arrangements. What do you think?'

Bradley's generosity in making all this possible for Maggie by financing the business had bestowed on him an unexpected bonus, in that she had begun to look on him as an unofficial business adviser. To his joy she consulted him regularly, though strictly on the understanding that he did not pull any strings for her with his numerous business contacts. 'Sink or swim, I want to do it myself,' she'd told him. But, for all that, she seemed to find their discussions helpful. And since it gave him access to her charming company, she could use him as a sounding board whenever she wished. To his shame he found himself falling in love with her, a bitter-sweet experience for he knew that if she were to detect so much as a hint of it, these precious meetings would be terminated by her loyalty to Chloe.

But having accepted the circumstances, he immersed himself in his role, careful not to destroy her fighting spirit while pointing out the harsh realities of commerce, as he felt duty bound to do.

'I agree about the local advertising,' he said, 'but I think you'll be moving too fast if you approach the classy hotels at this stage. They'll be wary of using someone so small. Test the water with some of the pubs and small restaurants. And don't be disappointed if you wear out a lot of shoe leather before you get a flicker of interest. Most of them will be satisfied with the florist they are already using. It's a matter of breaking in.'

Maggie sighed. 'I suppose you're right.'

But he could sense her impatience. 'You'll get there, Maggie. If I was a betting man, I'd put my shirt on it. One of these days you'll do the flowers for the Promenade Concerts at the Albert Hall.'

137

'Then I really *would* think I'd made it,' she laughed.

'But I wouldn't be much of a friend if I didn't warn you of the hazards of business.'

'I know that, Bradley,' she said warmly, 'and I really do appreciate it.'

He would never know just how much these meetings had begun to mean to her. His faith in her had done wonders for her self-confidence. The task she had committed herself to was a daunting one indeed, and one which gave her many sleepless nights. But Bradley swept away her doubts with his frank advice and assumption that she would eventually succeed. He really was a lovely man.

'I'm happy to be of help,' he said. 'Never doubt that you will make it. Just keep your head and hang on to your sense of humour. You'll need that more than anything.'

How right he was! Local trade benefited from the advertising, but after weeks of aching feet and a sorely diminished ego it seemed that her floristry services were not required by any of the larger London establishments who were, apparently, 'Very well suited, thank you'.

'I'll not give up,' she told Bradley.

'Too darned right, you won't,' he agreed.

But even Maggie's indomitable spirit began to flag slightly against the seemingly impenetrable barrier of opposition to her and her plan for expansion. Shop trade was good and steady, but it was simply not enough.

One morning in early November she drove to Bradley's office to tell him of her decision.

'I know you'll think I'm crazy,' she said, 'but I'm going to move upmarket in my search for new business. I've aimed low and it hasn't worked, so now I'm going to aim high. I *must* get that one order that will put my business into another league.'

Bradley observed her with a mixture of concern and admiration. 'And do you have any particular bigshot in mind?'

'Yes. I'm going to try to get in at the Mallory Hotel. They have recently changed management so this will be a good time to approach them.'

His brows rose for this was a high-class Mayfair establishment. 'It won't be easy,' he warned.

'Nothing worthwhile ever is,' she said determinedly.

'It might be difficult to get in to see the manager.'

'Yes, I know.' Her eyes gleamed wickedly at him. 'And I'm fed up with being fobbed off by secretaries. So if they won't let me in to see him, I shall get him to come and see me.'

And leaving him mulling over that cryptic remark, she left.

138

A week later, smartly dressed in a black tailored suit with a nipped-in waist, and a white blouse with a frilly bib, Maggie dined alone at the Mallory Hotel. The light from the crystal chandeliers subtly lit the pale lemon table linen, the glow from the yellow candles flickering over the table arrangements of chrysanthemums. Fine paintings adorned the walls and heavy gold drapes were drawn across the windows.

Finishing her dessert, Maggie ordered coffee. Nervousness had prevented her from enjoying the meal which was a pity since it had cost the earth. But her conscience was eased by the fact that, in this particular instance, such extravagance was a necessary business expense.

'Is everything to your satisfaction, madam?' asked the waiter as he served her with coffee.

'Excellent, thank you,' she said, noticing his curiosity, for a woman dining alone here was a rare thing.

'Are you staying long?' he asked conversationally.

'Just one night,' she told him.

Upstairs in her room, she went straight to the telephone. 'This is Mrs Radford in room 106,' she informed room service. 'I'd like to see Mr Cooper the manager, please.'

The female voice sounded surprised. 'I'm not sure if he is available at present,' she said. 'Can someone else help you?'

'No, only Mr Cooper will do,' she said, having taken the trouble to find out the manager's name.

'Perhaps you could give me an idea of the problem,' the telephonist suggested politely.

'I am only prepared to discuss the matter with Mr Cooper,' Maggie said, the firmness in her voice belying the fact that her knees were trembling.

'I'll see what I can do then, madam.'

'Thank you.'

Her hand was shaking as she replaced the receiver. What on earth had possessed her to embark on such a crazy scheme? Desperation, she reminded herself. So stop panicking and get on with it.

Mr Cooper looked concerned when he tapped on her door a few minutes later. 'I understand you wish to see me,' he said, his grey eyes resting on her anxiously as she ushered him inside.

'Yes, do sit down.'

He was a thin, immaculate man of about forty-five with brown hair and a neat moustache. He declined her invitation to sit down. 'If you could just tell me what the problem is?' He stood by the polished writing desk, eyeing her warily. 'We like all our guests to be completely comfortable here at the Mallory.'

139

Realising that he wasn't sure whether she was about to seduce him or complain about the service, she handed him her business card.

He read it and eyed her shrewdly. 'I'm sorry, but I don't see sales people without an appointment.'

'I tried to get an appointment but couldn't get past your secretary,' she explained.

'That's because we are quite satisfied with our regular florist.'

'How do you know that I can't do better?' she asked. 'Change can be a good thing. I understand this hotel has recently had a change of management.'

'You are very persistent,' he said.

'Only because I am confident in what I have to offer.'

'I really don't think . . .'

'Just let me show you an example of what I can do,' she said. 'Surely you wouldn't refuse one of your guests a few minutes of your time?'

'Well . . .' He studied his fingernails.

This whole plan had been based on the premise that no hotel manager would want to upset a guest, even one who had tricked him. And if she could just get him to pay attention to her sample . . .

When he looked up, he was grinning. 'And I suppose you just happen to have an example with you?'

'Naturally,' she said jubilantly.

He studied the arrangement in silence for a few moments. 'Well, it's different,' he said at last, 'it's brighter and bolder than the usual run.'

'It's attractive though, isn't it?' she said, casting her eye over the stunning, multi-coloured arrangement of chrysanthemums, carnations and roses, fixed firmly into a small vase. 'Using as many colours as possible instead of just a few of the same family creates a gloriously rich effect that goes with everything.'

'Yes, I can see that.' He studied the flowers again from various angles. 'I must say I like it.' He stroked his chin thoughtfully. 'As I said, I am satisfied with our regular florist and I'm not going to dispense with their services. But I am not obliged to use only one firm. So I am willing to give you a chance. We have a ladies' luncheon booked for next month in our gold suite. Perhaps you might like to quote me for the flowers for that? If we are suited by your work then I may be able to offer you more from time to time.'

'Thank you,' beamed Maggie.

'And Mrs Radford—' he said, turning at the door.

'Yes.'

'—if you are ever looking for a job as a sales representative,' he laughed, 'I'd be happy to recommend you.'

140

'You'd better go home to bed, Tom,' said Maggie a few weeks later as her brother crawled miserably around the shop with a bad attack of flu. 'You're certainly not fit for work.'

'But we're so busy, with the Mallory order and all the ordinary work,' he croaked painfully.

'Don't you worry about that,' she assured him. 'We'll manage. You just get yourself tucked up in bed with a hot-water bottle.'

'Well . . . if you're sure?'

'I'm sure.'

'Thanks, sis.'

But as soon as he was out of sight her face creased into a frown. Fate was certainly in a testing mood. On the eve of delivery of her most important order yet, it had not only sent an unprecedented rush of midweek business, but also robbed her of a valuable pair of hands. She was up against fierce competition at the Mallory Hotel and the job called for total professionalism. Mr Cooper had to be more than pleased with her work if she was to receive further orders. He must be *delighted* with her efforts in his gold room. And all by ten thirty tomorrow morning!

First of all she must persuade Archie to do some overtime this evening, then she would ask Mum to have Katy for the night so that she herself could work for as long as was necessary. The Mallory order was going to be ready if she had to stay up all night to finish it.

It was, in fact, three a.m. when she wired the final bloom into place, swept the debris from the workroom floor and staggered upstairs to bed. Carried along by nervous energy, she was at the hotel bright and early the next morning to set up her displays. Having been given carte-blanche as regards design, and considerable leeway as to expense, Maggie had been able to mix hot-house blooms with seasonal ones to provide variety. She had concentrated on what was becoming her forte, the bold use of colour, to transform this conventional functions room into a hall of splendour.

Brightly coloured chrysanthemums, roses and carnations had been arranged in vases, bowls and baskets of varying shape and size. They banked the platform, bedecked the window sills and added the finishing touch to the tables. Just inside the door Maggie had excelled herself in a glorious multi-coloured display in a Gainsborough basket.

'Splendid!' said the delighted Mr Cooper. 'A really first-class job.'

The success of the assignment proved to be a watershed in more ways than one. Not only did Maggie receive further orders from Mr Cooper but she also received a telephone call from a certain upper-crust lady who had been a guest at the luncheon. She had been impressed with Maggie's adventurous use of colour and wished to discuss the flowers for her daughter's wedding.

Things really began to move after that as news of Maggie's unusual designs spread among London's elite. The floral arrangements for society weddings and other high-class functions all began to come her way, but she never underestimated the importance of the day to day shop trade. She increased the frequency of her local advertisements and discussed with Bradley other ideas to draw attention to her services.

'The shop needs a complete refurbishment if we are to get noticed,' she told him. 'We are situated on a busy main road into central London. If the shop was more noticeable, it would bring in business from passing motorists.'

'You could be right,' he agreed.

'But it's the expense,' Maggie confessed, frowning. 'Things are going well, but I daren't overspend at this stage.'

'No, but you must keep abreast of the competition. A smart shop would be an advertisement in itself.'

'Umm, but I don't have the capital,' she pointed out.

'Why not have the amount you need added to your mortgage?'

'Could that be arranged?'

'Sure it could.'

And so it was that in the autumn of 1955 Maggie and Bradley stood outside a completely modernised Maggie's which now brightened up its corner site. White, gilt-edged paintwork surrounded a contemporary glass shopfront on which her trademark, a yellow chrysanthemum, was superimposed. The name of the shop was printed in gold above the shop window along with the telephone number. Flowering window boxes adorned the windowsills above a white and gold awning flapping gently in the autumn breeze. Outside the premises stood a gleaming white van signwritten in gold and also displaying the yellow chrysanthemum.

'It looks terrific,' said Bradley, 'I'm very impressed.'

'Let's hope it proves to be a wise investment,' she said, surveying the finished effect. 'As well as a rather lavish High Street decoration.'

'Don't worry, it will,' he reassured her, watching her affectionately as she gazed at the transformation. He had called in especially to see the facelift, and Maggie had been working in the workroom when he'd arrived. She was wearing denim jeans with a blue and white checked shirt which made her look even younger than her age. It was over a year since Jack's death and she had lost that bleak look of early grief. She looked healthy now, there was colour in her cheeks, flesh on her bones. She had come a long way in fourteen months, both as a single mother and a businesswoman. 'You take my word for it.'

She grinned up at him, screwing her eyes against the sun and brushing her hair from her face in that absent way of hers. 'I believe you,' she said. 'Though why you have such faith in me is a mystery.'

If only you knew, Maggie my love, he thought, but said, 'Put it down to my business intuition.'

A nearby newspaper hoarding carried the headline 'James Dean Dies In Car Smash' as they went into the shop together.

Chapter Eleven

'I'd rather not hear about your extramarital affairs if you don't mind,' said Maggie sternly one evening in January 1956, when Chloe dropped in unexpectedly and launched into an account of her continuing affair with Frankie Farringdon.

'One affair,' corrected Chloe indignantly. 'Anyone would think I'd had dozens of men, to hear you talk.'

'I mean affairs as in general extramarital happenings,' said Maggie, 'but I still don't want to be told about them.' She set a tray of coffee and biscuits down on a table between them. Whilst she was always pleased to see friends, Chloe's illicit love life came a poor second in comparison to the mountain of paperwork she had to catch up on. 'If you must indulge in that sort of thing, that's your business, but don't expect me to applaud you for it.'

'As if I would,' said Chloe haughtily. 'But if one can't talk to one's best friend about these things, who can one turn to?'

Maybe Maggie should have been glad that Chloe's marriage was failing, since she herself was well on the way to being in love with Bradley. But the fact that she cared for him only served to make her even more furious with Chloe for betraying him without, apparently, the slightest compunction. 'You don't turn to anyone,' she advised her firmly. 'Adultery is something for your own conscience and the least you can do is not involve other people.' She poured some coffee and handed a cup to Chloe. 'But since you do seem to want my advice, I'll just say this. Surely the most honourable thing for you to do is to ask Bradley for a divorce and settle down with Frankie? It isn't fair to deceive your husband the way you do.'

'Frankie isn't interested in long-term commitment,' Chloe said wryly. 'He's a free spirit. Probably because he's an artist. You know how they are.'

Maggie didn't know but doubted if people of that ilk were all as single-minded as Chloe's lover appeared to be. Free spirit indeed! 'So what do you plan to do? You can't go on like this forever.'

'I don't know, but certainly nothing hasty as far as Bradley is concerned,' said Chloe, nibbling a biscuit. 'I'm not sure I'd want to settle down with Frankie on a permanent basis, anyway.'

It was only the fact that Katy was sleeping in the next room that prevented Maggie from losing her temper completely. 'What is it you want from a man, Chloe?' she asked in a controlled voice.

Her friend shrugged. 'I don't know, but certainly something more than I have with Bradley.'

Trembling with rage, Maggie snapped, 'He's useful as a meal ticket and a status symbol though, isn't he? And worth hanging on to for those reasons alone. But you'll lose him one day if you carry on like this.'

But Chloe didn't agree. 'Bradley thinks far too much of Daisy ever to break up our family,' she stated confidently.

'And what about Daisy in all this? Surely it must affect her, if only indirectly?'

'It doesn't affect either her or Bradley in the least,' Chloe explained. 'I do everything that is expected of me as a mother, given that I have an excellent nanny. And Bradley and I have been going our separate ways for years. As you know, I spend a lot of my time at our country place in Kent now, so both he and Katy are used to my not being around all the time. When I am in London and I go out to see Frankie, neither of them misses me.'

'Does Bradley have someone else?' asked Maggie, dreading the answer.

'Business is his only love, as far as I know,' she replied. 'And he seems to worship that.'

Was it any wonder, considering the sort of treatment he got from his wife? Maggie thought, but said, 'Let's change the subject, shall we?' She sipped her coffee as she searched for a less emotive subject. 'I must say I find it hard to imagine you leading the rustic life down in Kent. You've always seemed such a townie.'

'Umm I am really. But I seem to have rediscovered my love of riding. I used to do a lot as a child but lost interest for years. Now I'm finding it great fun again.' She nibbled a biscuit thoughtfully. 'Actually, Maggie, I was wondering if you might do me a small favour?'

'If I can – of course.'

'I want to go to Sussex soon for a weekend with Frankie. He's doing a gig there and wants me to go with him,' she explained, eyeing Maggie warily.

'So what's the problem?' asked Maggie. 'It obviously isn't a moral dilemma.'

'Well . . . I was wondering if you'd mind my telling Bradley that I'm going with you,' explained Chloe. 'I can't pretend that I'm going to Kent because he and Daisy sometimes go down at a weekend.'

'Yes, I do mind very much,' she snapped. 'Don't you dare use me as an alibi!'

'Whyever not?' asked Chloe. 'You won't have to do anything except back me up if Bradley mentions it during one of your business meetings.'

'No! I won't be a party to your sordid little scheme,' she protested hotly.

'Oh, Maggie, go on, please.'

'No!'

'Well,' said Chloe huffily, 'a fine friend you turned out to be.'

Maggie sighed impatiently. She had had a busy day and there was still work to do. This added drain on her emotional resources was almost more than she could bear. 'Look, Chloe, as your friend I will try to help you in any way that I can about other things, you know that,' she said, 'but I will not help you to deceive your husband.' Anyone else might have queried the fervour of Maggie's objections but Chloe was far too self-absorbed to suspect that her friend might have a passion of her own. 'You can't have your cake and eat it forever. One day your playing around will end in tears. And don't come crying at my door expecting sympathy when that happens, because you'll only have yourself to blame.'

Chloe lapsed into a thoughtful silence for a few moments. 'Has Bradley been pumping you about me?' she asked.

'Oddly enough,' Maggie said, driven to sarcasm by Chloe's conceit, 'you are rarely mentioned. The purpose of our meetings is to discuss my business and that is what we do.'

The putdown was lost on Chloe. 'Just as long as he's not checking up on me,' she said, finishing her coffee and rising. 'Well, if you are not prepared to help me out over Sussex, I'll have to try one of my more broad-minded friends.'

'Yes, you will, won't you?' Maggie told her, standing her ground.

'Did you enjoy yourself in Sussex?' Bradley inquired of Maggie a few weeks later at the conclusion of their business discussion.

'Sussex?' She stared at him in bewilderment, having forgotten the conversation with Chloe.

'Sure, Sussex. Chloe seemed to have a good time,' he explained. 'Personally, I prefer London at this time of the year. The coast can be a bit too bleak in winter for me.'

Why, the wicked bitch! Maggie fumed. How dare Chloe abuse their friendship in this way? She struggled to collect herself as his blue eyes met hers quizzically. Why Chloe felt the need to cheat on such a man was quite beyond her understanding. Concern for his feelings rather than loyalty to Chloe led her to say, 'Oh, Sussex, of course. Yes, it was good fun.'

'I'm glad. I expect a breath of sea air did you good,' said Bradley, observing her shrewdly. And Maggie had a horrible suspicion that he hadn't believed her.

Alone with his thoughts after Maggie had left, Bradley admonished himself for having inadvertently put her into an awkward position. The poor girl had obviously been no nearer to Sussex recently than he had. He should have guessed that Chloe's sudden urge for sea air would not have been inspired by the idea of a girls' weekend. But he was far more worried about having caused Maggie embarrassment than he was about his wife's infidelity, since he had learned to accept that.

Sometimes he thought he should divorce her, since their only bond seemed to be a legal one. Daisy was the reason he never did more than think about it. In addition to the inevitable upheaval for the child, there was the fear that the custody might go to Chloe even though she was the guilty party, for courts were often biased towards the mother in these cases, he had heard. He dared not take the chance.

A split between him and Chloe could also result in his losing contact with Maggie who might feel obliged by friendship to take Chloe's side and feel too embarrassed to see him at all. Her lies just now had indicated the direction of her allegiance. Fortunately for Bradley, after the initial shock and pain of learning of her unfaithfulness to him, Chloe's indiscretions left him emotionally untouched which was why he didn't force matters to a head by confronting her with them. All things considered, he felt that the situation was best left as it was. For the moment.

'You've gone too far this time,' raged Maggie on the telephone to Chloe later that day. 'You're damned lucky I didn't tell Bradley the truth.'

'You didn't though, did you?' ventured Chloe anxiously.

'The only reason I didn't,' rasped Maggie, 'was to spare his feelings, not to protect you.'

'I'm sorry, Maggie,' said Chloe, sounding suitably contrite, 'but I'm trying to sort my life out. I needed time with Frankie and I couldn't trust anyone but you to back up my story.'

'You couldn't find anyone else to agree to do it, I'll bet,' said Maggie. 'I told you I didn't want to and I meant it. You should have respected that.'

'Oh, Maggie, don't be sore. A few white lies never hurt anyone.'

'They hurt me,' Maggie informed her furiously. 'You do anything like that ever again, and our friendship is over.'

'Such a fuss,' Chloe tutted.

'I mean it.'

'I won't do it again.'
'You'd better not.'

Maggie's turnover grew steadily throughout 1956. The shop's new look drew more passing trade, the local advertising boosted orders, and personal recommendations continued to come in from London's bon ton. 'Flowers from Maggie's' as it said on her stationery, now regularly embellished such glittering occasions as society weddings, charity luncheons and showbusiness dinners.

But, inevitably, as trade increased so did the workload. As well as employing more part-time staff on a rota basis, she found another pair of hands in her mother after Katy started school. Dora happily divided her time between the shop and Maggie's domestic affairs, which were her domain since Maggie's time was more productively employed in business matters. But even with this boost to the workforce they were no longer able to meet deadlines comfortably.

And so it was that in October 1956 an exuberant eighteen-year-old brunette called Sally Jackson joined the staff as a full-time general assistant. She had been in the flower trade since leaving school, and was a skilled florist. She was also a cockney extravert who would turn her hand to anything at all except the office work. 'Just lookin' at that gives me an 'eadache,' she'd say. As well as working with the flowers, she would willingly clean the floor, serve customers, make tea and run errands.

In addition to her industriousness she was a natural entertainer. Customers and staff alike were amused by her tales of teenage life, for she was very much a child of the times, crazy about clothes and rock and roll music. The shop and workroom echoed to the sound of her crooning in the manner of her idol, Elvis Presley.

As appealing as she was, Tom was somewhat daunted by her as she enthusiastically set about the task of bringing him up to date.

' 'ow old are yer, Tom?' she asked one day quite early in their acquaintance when they had finished work and were getting ready to go home, her saucy brown eyes studying him with unnerving candour.

'Twenty-one,' he informed her warily, his mouth becoming noticeably dry at her proximity.

'Gawd, is that all? You look about forty,' Sally said frankly, without meaning to cause offence. 'It's because you're so old fashioned.'

'Oh dear,' said Tom nervously. 'Am I really?'

'I'll say yer are, mate.' She peered into his face even more thoroughly. 'Yer not a bad-looking bloke reelly. Not in the same league as Elvis, o' course, but who is, in real life?'

'He's an American singer, isn't he?' ventured Tom tentatively, for he had never followed youthful trends or pop culture.

149

'Yeah,' she said dreamily, drawing in her breath and dropping her lids ecstatically, 'Elvis the Pelvis they call 'im. Ooh, just the thought of 'im turns me to jelly.'

'Why do they call him that?' asked Tom, both fearful and fascinated by her.

'Cos he moves his pelvis a lot, o' course,' she explained. 'Wiggles 'is 'ips an' that. Gawd, Tom, 'ave yer bin on another planet or somethin'? Everyone knows about Elvis. Everyone of our generation anyway.'

'Do they?' he asked, pale with worry.

'O' course they do, 'e's all the rage.' She returned to her earlier theme. 'I can see I'm gonna 'ave to do somethin' about you. Yer didn't ought to walk about dressed like that, not a fella of your age.'

Smarting from her alarming frankness, Tom said, 'What's wrong with the way I dress?'

She laughed, her round face dimpling prettily. She was rather ordinary in appearance with tiny features arranged neatly in a small countenance and framed by dark brown hair permed into the latest short curly style. Her real attraction came from her warmth and vitality.

Standing back, she ran a scathing glance over him. 'Nothing is wrong with it if yer wanna look like someone's grandad. I mean, just look at those terrible baggy trousers.' She paused and extended her appraisal to his hair. 'And what about yer barnet? It's *reely* square.' She reached up and tousled his front locks. 'You need to fluff it up at the front and grow some sideburns.'

'Oh dear,' said Tom, shrinking from such flamboyance, 'I don't think that sort of style would suit me at all.'

Before he could say another word, she had whipped a comb from her handbag and was rearranging his hair. 'There yer go, mate,' she chirped in delight. 'That's much better.' She chewed her gum meditatively and brought colour to his face by adding, 'In fact, yer look quite fanciable.' She worked her gum thoughtfully. 'I wouldn't be ashamed to be seen out with yer now.' She paused before clarifying her position. 'Well, not so long as yer got yer gear sorted out too. Cos I wouldn't be seen dead with anyone wearing such stupid trousers.' And leaving him weak from the onslaught, she removed her green overall, slipped into her coat and left the shop, swinging her hips and singing a chorus of 'Rock Around the Clock'.

'Honestly, that wretched girl needs locking up,' he was frequently heard to complain to his mother and sister over the next few weeks. 'It's like having a blimmin' juke box in the place, only worse because she talks as well as sings – if you can call her tuneless racket singing, that is. And she'll break her ankles one of these days, clumping around in those stiletto heels all day. Anyone would think she was at a dancehall instead of a place of work. She spends her dinner hour practising her jiving steps in the staff room, if you've ever heard anything so stupid. She's a blimmin' menace altogether.'

'She's like a tonic about the place,' said Maggie.

'I like her too,' agreed Dora. 'She has me in fits with all her stories of what she gets up to at the Palais.'

'It's all right for you two,' tutted Tom. 'She isn't trying to convert you.'

'Oh, I don't know so much about that,' laughed Dora. 'She's educated me in all the latest songs. And I love watching her dance. She taught me a few steps the other day. You're not "with it" Tom, that's your trouble.'

'Oh no,' he groaned. 'She's got you at it too! The dratted girl.'

But both his mother and sister chuckled between themselves as changes began to be made. Maybe Tom would never match up to Sally's beloved Elvis, but a fluffy front quiff appeared in his hair, his trousers didn't flap quite so conspicuously and he invested in a pair of slip-on shoes. And he was sometimes heard whistling popular tunes around the shop, would you believe?

Archie was humming a tune to himself one evening in January 1957 as he got ready to go out on a date. He could still hardly believe how dramatically his life had changed since Christmas Eve when he had met a girl called Sheila at a dance. He had been alone at the time, in search of female company, and much to his amazement and joy the busty blonde in the slinky black dress had agreed to dance with him. She had been on her own too and they had struck up an instant rapport. She'd recently broken off her engagement, apparently, so was miracuously unattached.

They had been going out regularly ever since, and he felt like a new man. His manhood had finally been established quite early in the relationship, and his cold, lonely existence had changed to one of warmth and fulfilment. He wanted to tell the world how happy he was.

But he had not yet told anyone of his romance. He didn't want to face the ribbing from his mates, or the chummy interrogation from his colleagues at the shop until he was absolutely certain of Sheila because that would make him too vulnerable. Her eagerness certainly indicated that she reciprocated his feelings and she had claimed to love him on several occasions, but he would wait until he had a definite commitment from her before announcing his good fortune to the world.

He finished polishing his shoes, and taking a photograph from his wallet, studied it with pride. It was a picture of Sheila and himself at a New Year's dinner-dance at a London nightclub, taken by the club photographer. What a wonderful night that had been! He pressed the picture to his lips, then put it carefully back into his wallet for safe keeping. It was his most treasured possession.

His head was spinning with excitement as he approached the cinema and saw Sheila waiting outside, the silver glow of the neon lights shining on her blonde hair. He thought she looked beautiful in a red belted coat trimmed with a black fur collar, her hair arranged into the new continental style, the overall effect enhanced by a pair of black patent stiletto-heeled shoes. As he got close to her, her perfume made him heady with desire and he couldn't wait to get settled in the back row.

But there was an unusual coolness about her this evening. She slapped his straying hand and turned away from his kisses, saying she wanted to watch the film. Refusing to allow a germ of unease to develop into fullblown panic, he contented himself with draping an arm around her shoulders, telling himself that it was just her way of sharpening his appetite.

Self delusion became impossible, however, as he walked her home through the frosty streets, because her manner was clearly offhand. And when she insisted on passing their usual "goodnight" venue, some shadowy, bush-covered wasteground, and marched purposefully towards her front gate, he asked, 'What's the matter? Have I done something to upset you?'

She shifted uneasily from one foot to another and he could see in the glow from the streetlight that she was avoiding his eyes. She chewed her lip. 'No, it's nothing you've done.'

Dread weighed heavily on him. 'What then?'

Her house was in a terraced row with privet hedges bordering the small front gardens. A dusting of frost coated everything and the air was clear and raw. She opened her front gate and established herself firmly on the other side of it. 'Look, Arch, it's been great fun goin' out with you,' she said, 'you're a really nice bloke.'

The emphasis on the past tense registered with painful sharpness. Despite the freezing weather he felt a nervous sweat suffuse his skin. 'But why talk as though we won't be going out again?' he said. 'There'll be lots more good times for us.'

In his anxiety he reached over the gate and grabbed her arms, almost without realising it.

Wincing, she said, 'Let go! You're hurting me.'

'Sorry,' he said, releasing her. 'I don't know my own strength.'

Normally when they reached her gate, she invited him in for a cup of something and he, fearing fatherly scrutiny, always declined. Now, with this terrible sense of valediction in the air, he would gladly suffer parental torture if it brought her back to him. 'Aren't you going to ask me in then?'

She hugged herself against the cold and pulled nervously at the fingers of her black woollen gloves. 'I don't think there's any point, not now.' She looked up at him, twisting her mouth wryly. 'Oh dear, I feel awful telling yer. I should 'ave said somethin' before we went to the pictures to save yer spending more money on me.' She shifted awkwardly. 'I couldn't bring meself to tell yer.'

'Tell me what?' he asked frantically, emitting clouds of steam as he spoke.

'I've patched things up with me fiancé,' she said sheepishly. 'So, o' course, I won't be able to see yer again.'

He couldn't have felt worse if a bus had hit him. He was winded and numb, yet bruised to the very core of his existence. She had made his life worthwhile. He couldn't let her go! 'You mean the wedding is on again?' he gasped through dry lips.

'Yeah, that's right,' she said, and the happiness in her tone was like a physical blow to him. 'My bloke came round to my house last night and we made it up. I was gonna phone you at work to let yer know, but thought I'd better tell yer to yer face. I'm sorry it's taken me all night to do it.'

'But it's been so good between us, Sheila,' he said in a stricken voice. 'You said you loved me and I believed you.'

'Well, people say all sorts of things in moments of passion, don't they? I expect you've told lots o' girls the same thing without really meaning it,' she said in a matter of fact tone. 'But I do like yer a lot, Arch, honest, and I'll always be grateful to yer for cheerin' me up when I was down.'

'You used me,' he accused, hardly able to bear the pain.

'No more than you used me,' she challenged. 'We used each other, like people do.'

'I thought we had something special goin' for us,' he persisted desperately.

'We did, in a way,' she conceded. 'We cheered each other up while we were both feelin' low. We had a good time. But it's over now.'

He grabbed the lapels of her coat and drew her to him so that she was forced against the wooden gate. 'I was just a stopgap till your precious boyfriend came back!'

'It wasn't like that,' she snapped, irritated now by his unwanted persistence. 'You asked me out and I was free to accept. Now I ain't. That's all there is to it. So please let go of my coat.'

'I love you, Sheila,' he blurted out desperately, 'you've changed my life. I can't go back to how it was before. I just can't . . .'

'Let go of me, please,' she begged, close to tears.

The front door opened and a man was silhouetted in the doorway. 'What's going on out there?' he boomed.

Archie released her abruptly, glad that he was hidden from view by Sheila and a bushy privet hedge.

'It's all right, Dad, I'll be in in a minute,' she called.

'Make sure you are. It's too cold to be 'angin' about in the street,' he said, before disappearing into the house.

Sheila followed him inside, the slam of the front door echoing with agonising finality in Archie's ears. Traumatised, he didn't move but watched a light come on in an upstairs window, indicating that she had gone to her room. He waited until it was extinguished, then began to walk back to his lonely flat, oblivious of the frost gnawing at his face and ears, unaware of anything except his own despair.

Unable to accept the fact that his one and only love affair was over, he managed to convince himself that Sheila had been forced into her decision, against her will, by her dominating boyfriend. 'Well, he won't get away with it,' he muttered as he turned the key in his door, 'because I ain't gonna let her go.' And as he went into his dismal apartment, with its lingering smell of the pie and mash he'd had for tea, he began to plan his next move.

Maggie was taking extra care as she drove home in her Morris Minor from Richmond, because of the coating of frost that had descended while she had been visiting the Andersons'.

Having a child to care for meant that social evenings were something of a rarity for Maggie. But Lavinia and Rupert had been very kind to her since Jack's death, keeping in regular contact and taking Katy on outings, and she had feared she might offend them by continually being unable to accept their invitations to dinner. 'It'll do you good to get out for a couple of hours for something that has nothing to do with business,' Dora had said. 'Don't you worry about young Katy, she's as happy as a lark with her gran.'

And how right Mother was. Customary as it was for mothers to disapprove of indulgent grannies, Maggie turned a blind eye to this in her own mother, convinced that both Katy and Dora found something in each other that they had lost in Jack.

Now Maggie was reflecting on how enjoyable the evening had been. Fortunately, there was no lingering evidence of Rupert's earlier misdemeanours, and she had found the couple's company pleasantly stimulating. Conversation over dinner had covered a wide range of topics and had included the recent appointment of Harold Macmillan, who had succeeded Sir Anthony Eden as Prime Minister, the latter having resigned for health reasons. Many people had expected Sir Anthony's deputy, Rab Butler, to be appointed. 'They reckon the party ranks would have split if Butler had got the job,' explained Rupert. 'He lost popularity over his weak support for the Suez operations.'

Maggie wasn't a particularly political being, but she took enough of an interest in the world around her to be able to make an intelligent contribution to the discussion. 'I read somewhere that Macmillan rejected a call from the opposition for a general election,' she said.

'Umm,' agreed Rupert. 'Repairs to Anglo-American relations after Suez must be his first job.'

Fragments of the conversations were lingering in her mind as she drove slowly around Shepherd's Bush Green, braking carefully at sudden traffic congestion. Crowds of people were pouring from the cinemas, thronging the pavements along the sidestreets, queuing for buses and jostling towards the station.

Noticing that they all seemed to be either in groups or couples, she felt a stab of loneliness. It didn't matter how much she loved and was loved by Katy and Mother and Tom, or how busy and fulfilling her life was, she was still, at the end of the day, alone with no special someone with whom to share her life.

Had she not been so absorbed in her own thoughts, she might have been surprised to notice Archie and a girl among the crowd of pedestrians taking advantage of the traffic congestion and dashing across the road in front of her.

Quite how it happened Tom was never sure. But somehow, on the evening of 6th February 1957, he found himself accompanying a jubilant Sally Jackson to London's Dominion Theatre to watch the first London concert by America's Bill Haley and the Comets, who had arrived at Southampton on the *Queen Elizabeth* earlier that week to a hero's welcome.

'Don't be such a square, Tom,' she had wheedled when her girlfriend had fallen ill and left her with a spare ticket. 'Please come with me. Yer'll love it when yer get there, honest yer will.'

'But it isn't my sort of thing at all,' he had protested in alarm. Conceding to pressure on the baggy trousers issue was one thing; a rock and roll concert was quite another.

'O' course it's your sort of thing,' she had stated categorically. 'Yer young, ain't yer?'

'No!' he'd insisted. 'I won't go with you.'

But even his most ardent resolve was no match for her bewitching smile and persuasive eyes with dark lashes which fluttered irresistibly whenever she had a mind. And, even though he was barely able to admit it to himself, he was flattered by her invitation. For he was not in Sally's league, with her modern ways and her bright looks and her hordes of friends who thought nothing of telephoning her at work and pouring into the shop to wait for her of an evening.

He could not know, of course, that Sally had decided what she really wanted from life the moment she had clapped eyes on Tom, and was determined to make her wish into reality. Maybe she did have an odd way of going about it, but it didn't do to let a fella know your feelings too soon. Especially a shy one like Tom.

And so it was that he sat beside her now in a youthful audience of three thousand, as in a mood of frenzied excitement they gave the performers an ecstatic reception. Almost as one, the crowd clapped, sang and tapped their feet in time to the beat. They roared and wept, cheered and shrieked, as their heroes gave exuberant renditions of 'Rip it Up', and 'Don't Knock the Rock'.

Initially, Tom's reserved nature deterred him from overtly entering into the spirit of the thing along with Sally, who appeared to have lost all control and was stamping and squealing for joy while he sat stiffly next to her, his ears burning with embarrassment. But gradually his toes began to tap almost of their own volition and somehow he was on his feet with Sally, clapping to the beat. He watched in a kind of bemused delight as the chubby-faced Bill Haley gave the fans an additional treat by playing his guitar from a sitting position, while his saxophonist knelt and the bass player rode astride his instrument. By the final stages of the show Tom had lost all his inhibitions and even joined with the rest in singing aloud to 'See You Later Alligator'.

In the closing moments of the show Sally's exuberance reached a peak and she flung her arms around him. 'Oh, isn't it great?' she said emotionally. And kissed him full on the lips. And Tom was too caught up in the magic of the atmosphere to be embarrassed, and kissed her back. He had never been so happy!

Moving with the crowds towards the exit they held hands, enthusiastically discussing the show. As they walked to the station in the crisp night air, Sally linked her arm through his. 'I told you you'd enjoy it,' she said, squeezing his arm affectionately.

'All right, clever clogs,' he teased.

'Did yer really, though?' she asked. 'You weren't just pretending?'

It had been the most wonderful evening of his life, and he wasn't just thinking about the concert. 'I certainly wasn't.'

'You're really beginning to dig the scene, ain't yer?' she giggled.

And quite frankly, if 'digging the scene' meant being with her, he'd even stoop to the depths of Teddy Boy clothes if it would please her. 'If we are going to go out together again,' he said hopefully, 'I suppose you'll insist on me getting some drainpipe trousers?'

'No need to go to those lengths,' she said. 'Just as long as yer don't wear ones that are too square.'

Engrossed in each other, they stopped and kissed, unaware of the freezing weather or passers-by. The procedure was repeated several more times on the way to Sally's home as they both joyfully experimented with the change in their relationship. Bill Haley, I've a lot to thank you for, thought Tom happily.

A few streets away from Sally's house Archie was furtively waiting for Sheila to come home. Since that terrible night a week ago, he had spent a lot of time in the shadows near her house, trying to catch her alone. But she was always with her fiancé. Tonight, however, he was optimistic because he knew that Wednesday was the night she saw her girlfriends. He was expecting her at any moment. Positioned away from the light on the corner of her street he couldn't miss her.

His heart leapt at the unmistakable click of her high heels and the sight of her blonde hair gleaming against her red coat as she passed under a lamppost. 'Sheila,' he said, standing in her path.

Gasping with fright, she said, '*Archie*, it's you! What the 'ell are you trying to do? Give me an 'eart attack or somethin'. You gave me the fright of me life, creeping up on me like that.'

'Sorry,' he said, trembling with all the old excitement at her proximity. 'I just wanted to talk to you.'

'Oh, yeah? What about?' she asked, eyeing him suspiciously and chewing on gum.

'About us, of course,' he said, intoxicated by the familiarity of her cheap scent.

'Us?' she said quizzically.

'Yeah, you and me.'

'There ain't no you and me, Archie,' she reminded him, 'I told you that last week.'

'I know what yer said, but I know yer only said it because yer boyfriend made yer,' he informed her. 'I know he's bullying yer into stayin' with 'im.'

'Have you gone barmy?' she asked cruelly. 'What do yer think he does? Keeps me in chains or somethin'? You've been seein' too many films.'

'Are yer trying to tell me that yer staying with him of yer own free will?' he asked miserably.

'O' course I am,' she told him cheerfully. 'I ain't daft enough to let any bloke make me do anythin' I don't want to.'

Her words penetrated the protective fiction he had woven for himself. 'I don't believe you,' he said, clutching at the remnants of his fantasy. 'I know you love me.'

'Grow up, Archie,' she said harshly. 'If I loved you, I wouldn't be engaged to someone else, would I? I ain't that stupid.'

'It's me you love, not him,' he persisted, stripped of all pride by sheer desperation.

'I do *not* love you,' she said, angry now at his insistence. 'Can't you get that into your thick head?'

The brief period of sweetness and light he had enjoyed with her made the return to the darkness all the more unbearable. He just couldn't bear to be alone again, with nothing to look forward to. Sheila *couldn't* leave him, he wouldn't let her.

But she was already walking away, her heels resounding in the empty street. He tore after her and, clamping a hand over her mouth, dragged her out of the light into an infill building site where a terrace of four houses was in mid-construction. 'Please don't say those terrible things to me,' he begged, dropping his hand from her mouth but holding her tightly against him, tears streaming down his face. 'I can't live without you, Sheila, don't you understand that? You made my life worthwhile.'

Fear had destroyed her bravado, reducing her to tears. 'I'm sorry, Arch,' she sobbed. 'I didn't mean to hurt yer, honest. There are plenty of other girls. Yer'll soon find someone else.'

And that euphemistically couched but piercing rejection finally hit home, driving Archie beyond the limit of his control. Events seemed to move outside his consciousness after that. He watched them as though from a great distance. He saw himself violently gripping her upper arms and shaking her. He heard the thud of his fist on her face and chest. 'You used me, used me,' he growled, from the back of his throat. 'And I loved you.'

'Archie, please, please,' she wept, struggling to free herself.

'Oh, go to your precious boyfriend,' he said, suddenly thrusting her from him. 'Go to him and get out of my life.'

She staggered from the force of his action but, regaining her balance, she made a stand against him, braver now that she was free. 'You ain't heard the last of this, Archie Radford,' she spat breathlessly.

'Just go, will yer?' he mumbled.

'I'm goin', don't worry,' she said. 'I don't wanna stay around a maniac like you. But my boyfriend will hear about this, and he'll be after you.'

'Oh, get out of my sight,' he said, shoving her dismissively.

As she came back at him with a punch, he grabbed her with one arm and lashed out at her with the other, striking several blows before casting her from him with such force she tottered and fell to the ground, her head crunching against a pile of broken bricks.

'That'll teach yer,' he said, 'I 'ope yer bruises ain't little ones.'

158

He waited for some insulting retort, but it didn't come. In the light from the half moon he could see that she was lying on her back among the builder's rubble but couldn't tell if her eyes were open. 'Get up, yer daft cow,' he said uneasily, 'yer'll get cold down there. Don't lie there sulking.'

She groaned, but didn't answer.

Sick with alarm, he fell to his knees beside her. 'Come on now, get up. I'm sorry I got rough with yer. I was upset, but I won't do it again. I don't wanna hurt yer. Come on now, don't play about.'

She made another groaning sound, but didn't move.

'Come on, I'll help yer up.' Trying to lift her, he saw that her eyes were closed. Oh my Gawd, she's unconscious! he thought. He heard footsteps approaching. Panic consumed him. He ran across the site and down the road, sobbing and nauseous, a cold sweat soaking his clothes, his crepe-soled shoes noiseless against the paving stones.

The rock and roll music was lingering in Tom's mind as he walked home from Sally's house, still glowing from her kisses. How good life suddenly was, and how long the night seemed until he would see her again. Him and Sally. Well, well, who would have guessed that two such opposites would fall in love?

His interest was aroused by a sudden movement in the deserted street ahead of him. The figure of a man appeared and ran down the road as though all hell was after him. But there was no one else around. Instinctively suspicious, Tom hurried after him. But the man had too much of a headstart and disappeared from view.

Breathlessly reaching the building site, and realising that it was from here that the fugitive had come, Tom was puzzled. For if the fellow had been stealing bricks or builder's equipment, he wouldn't have been able to move at such a speed. But why the hurry if he wasn't being chased?

The site was eerie in the moonlight and dominated by the dark shape of the half-built terrace, the ghostly curve of the cement mixer just visible in the shadows. The chap was probably late home and taking a short cut, Tom thought, relieved to have found a plausible explanation. He walked on, but halted at some barely audible sound. All was silent. He moved on. But there it was again. It sounded like someone moaning. Someone was hurt around here somewhere. Oh Gawd!

Tingling with fear he picked his way across the site towards the cry, stumbling on uneven ground and rubble. 'Oh my God!' he gasped, discovering the cause of the sound. 'Oh, you poor thing, let me help you.'

Trembling violently, he knelt down beside Sheila, muttering words of comfort. Gathering his jumbled thoughts and remembering that it wasn't wise to move an injured person, he didn't try to lift her, deciding that his most sensible course of action was to go and get help.

He was about to depart for the nearest telephone to call an ambulance when the scene was suddenly flooded with light from the beam of a torch. Horrified, Tom watched as the injured girl gave a final groan and jerked into stillness. The light blinded him as it was shone into his face. 'Well, what's been going on here then? Been having a lovers' tiff, have we?'

And even then, as Tom urged the policeman to get an ambulance, he didn't realise just how incriminating for him the circumstances looked.

'My brother did not kill Sheila Dawson,' Maggie stated categorically to Royston Slade, the lawyer she had hired on Tom's behalf. 'You do believe that, don't you?'

'Yes I believe that, Mrs Radford,' said the lawyer, a thin harrassed-looking man in his thirties, with warm brown eyes and floppy hair which constantly fell across them. 'But we must face facts. The case against him is strong, found as he was with the girl at the point of death.'

'But his girlfriend, Sally, is willing to testify to being with him all evening,' Maggie reminded him.

'Yes, but technically Tom would still have had time to do the deed,' he said, frowning. 'And that is the line the prosecution will take.' It was two weeks since Sheila's death, and after a great deal of police interrogation Tom had been charged with her murder and was now on remand pending trial. 'And there are no witnesses to substantiate Tom's story about this other man he saw running from the scene. The victim's fiancé has a watertight alibi.' He gave Maggie a reassuring smile. 'But try not to worry too much. The trial won't be for a while yet, we've plenty of time to prepare the best possible defence.' He noticed her pallor, the tiredness around her eyes and the tension gripping her whole body. 'Is it possible for you to get away somewhere for a while? You look just about all in.'

'No, I have a business to run,' she said sharply. 'I wouldn't go away at a time like this anyway.'

'Why not? You won't help your brother by making yourself ill, you know,' he pointed out. 'And there is no chance of the police changing their minds and giving him bail because of the violence of the crime. The victim had been badly knocked about before hitting her head on the brick that killed her.'

Maggie stared at him incredulously. He spoke as though Tom's being found guilty was a fait accompli. Perhaps he had doubts about his client's innocence after all. Wasn't it supposed to be a fact that anyone was capable of murder, given the right provocation?

160

But Tom hadn't killed Sheila Dawson. Maggie couldn't be more sure of that if she had been there in person. He had told her he hadn't and she believed him. It was frightening to realise that the rest of the world, except the few who were close to him, probably didn't.

'Tom didn't do it,' she reminded the lawyer.

'I know,' he assured her.

'If only we could find someone else who saw the man running away.'

'Yes, that would change everything,' he said thoughtfully.

Tom lay on his bunk with his face turned to the wall. He was finding it hard to breathe and a cold sweat soaked the rough material of his prison clothes as he fought against claustrophobia. He knew that if he looked at the locked cell door panic would overcome him completely. He must stay calm, let the symptoms come and think of other things. Daytime in prison was bad, but being locked up at night was the most terrifying experience he had ever had. Enclosed places had always made him feel ill.

The sound of his cell-mate snoring on the lower bunk filled the tiny room as powerfully as the smell of the slop bucket. He forced back the bile as it rose in his throat, knowing that the man below wouldn't take kindly to being woken by the sound of vomiting. The gravity of his predicament flooded into Tom's mind, making his stomach churn. If they could arrest him wrongfully, they could convict him just as easily. Tears burned his eyes. He swallowed hard to dispel them as though the sleeping man might somehow hear him crying. One sign of weakness and the other inmates would make his life even more of a misery.

Thoughts of Maggie and his mother made him want to weep with homesickness. Thoughts of Sally warmed him inside. A few weeks, was that all it was since that wonderful evening they had spent together that had ended in tragedy? He reached for her letter under the blanket and put it to his lips for comfort. Right now he would give anything in the world just to hear her trilling out one of her adored pop songs. In her letter she said she would come and visit him soon. She loved him, she said, and knew he was innocent. Oh God, get me out of here . . .

From the way the conversation ended so abruptly when Dora entered the butcher's shop, it was obvious they had been talking about the murder.

'Don't stop on my account,' she snapped, her cheeks flaming. 'Since it's my son who's copping it, you might at least give me the chance to defend him.'

There was an awkward silence. 'We weren't talking about Tom,

Dora luv,' lied the butcher who didn't want trouble in his shop. 'Were we, ladies?'

'O' course we weren't,' mumbled one of the women.

'Don't lie to her,' said another woman aggressively. 'We were talking about that son o' yours. What do you expect, after what he's done? He wants hangin', he does. None of us is safe in the streets with the likes of 'im about. He was always peculiar, even as a boy.'

An uncomfortable silence filled the shop. 'Take no notice of her, luv,' mumbled someone at last, and the other women gathered around Dora sympathetically for she was a popular member of the community.

Refusing to be patronised, she pulled away and confronted the accusing woman who was stuffing a wrapped package of meat into her shopping bag. 'My Tom didn't do it,' she stated loudly and categorically.

'Why has he been arrested then?' the woman asked. 'The police know what they're doing.'

The pain and tension Dora had suffered these past few weeks now culminated in a furious rage. 'He didn't do it!' she shouted to the gathering in general, angry tears threatening.

'O' course he didn't, luv,' said one woman, without much conviction.

'And if he did,' said another, 'there ain't no call to blame Dora. She's not done anythin'.'

'A man is innocent until proved guilty in this country, you know,' Dora reminded them before marching furiously from the shop.

Walking back to Maggie's with tears streaming down her cheeks, she admonished herself severely. Now then Dora, getting hysterical in public isn't going to help Tom. You must pull yourself together. Oh God, please end this nightmare. Please help us get my boy out of prison.

Chapter Twelve

'Do you think it would be a good idea for my mother and Katy to go away for a while, to give them a break from the gossip?' Maggie asked of Bradley one day in March during one of their business meetings. 'The whole wretched business is getting Mum into a terrible state. She came back from shopping in tears the other day after a quarrel with some women in the butcher's. People seem to have already got poor Tom tried and convicted, and Katy has been having a bad time at school too. You know how cruel kids can be. I have always taught her not to run away from trouble, but she's so young to have to cope with something like this – all the more upsetting because she so adores her uncle Tom.'

'I think it's an excellent idea.' Bradley observed Maggie with concern. She was drawn and grey with worry. The flesh seemed to have fallen away from her bones. 'And I think you should go with them. You've been living on your nerves since Tom's arrest.'

She sighed wearily. 'I can't leave the shop.'

'Surely Archie and Sally can cope for a couple of weeks?' he remarked. 'You have reliable staff to back them up.'

Maggie shook her head. 'I'd feel as though I was deserting Tom somehow, if I took a holiday.'

'That's nonsense. He'd be the first to say you should go. You'll need all your strength for the trial.'

Her pallor deepened at the thought of the ordeal ahead. 'You don't think they'll . . . I mean, they do sometimes . . .'

Seeing the fear in her eyes, Bradley went to her and rested a sympathetic hand on her shoulder. 'No, Maggie, Tom will not be hanged,' he assured her firmly. 'The death penalty is only given in this country in very extreme cases these days, like the murder of a policeman, or murder with intent to rob.'

'Thank God.' She reached up and took his hand in a gesture so natural it was almost unconscious. During the last traumatic weeks Bradley had become a family friend to the Brightwells, and Maggie had grown to feel very close to him. His strength had given her the stamina she needed to provide the support her mother required. 'If only we could find someone to back up Tom's story about the running man, it might not even come to trial.'

Frowning, he released her hand and turned her face towards his, stifling the urge to take her in his arms and soothe her worries away. 'Maggie, you must stop tormenting yourself like this. There is nothing you, personally, can do to prove Tom's innocence. You must leave it to the lawyers.'

Sighing, she leaned on the desk and propped her chin on her hands. 'You're right, I know, but it's so hard.'

'Yes, of course it is,' he said gently. 'That's why I think you should go away for a while. A change of scene might help you to get the case off your mind. I know how worrying it is for you, but you mustn't let your own life end because Tom is in prison.'

'No, I won't let you talk me into it,' she said firmly, 'but I shall organise a holiday for Mum and Katy. I have an aunt who lives by the sea near Brighton. I'll arrange for them to go there. Even if Mum isn't keen on the idea, she'll agree because it will be good for Katy. It won't be very warm by the sea this early in the year, but the change will do them both good. And the gossip is bound to die down sooner or later.'

Back in his seat, Bradley had a sudden idea. 'They can use our country place in Kent,' he suggested. 'It's empty at the moment. Chloe is far too busy shopping for her trip to the States with Daisy next week to want to go to the country.' He paused thoughtfully. 'But it might be a little too isolated for a townie like your mother.'

Maggie considered the offer for a few moments, the colour of her eyes heightened by her blue jersey dress. 'I think they'd probably be more at ease in Brighton, but thanks for offering.'

'That's OK.'

Forcing her mind away from her own problems, she said, 'I expect you wish you were going with Chloe and Daisy to visit your parents, don't you?'

'I guess so,' he said. 'It's always good to see my folks. But I can't get away just now. And I have to go on a business trip to Spain in a few weeks' time anyway.'

'You'll miss them, won't you?'

'I'll miss Daisy,' he said. 'Frankie Farringdon will be the one to miss Chloe.'

There was an awkward silence. This was the first time Bradley had made any reference to the failure of his marriage. 'Oh dear,' she said in embarrassment, 'I didn't realise you knew about that.'

'Oh yes, I've known for quite some time.'

'And you've never said anything to her.'

'I guess it suited me not to.'

'It seems such a tragedy,' Maggie said. 'You two had everything going for you.'

'And it all came to nothing.'

In that moment Maggie knew that Bradley needed her as much as she needed him. She wanted to love him and make up for all the pain Chloe's deceit had caused him. But she curbed the impulse. He was, after all, still married to her best friend. 'I'm so sorry,' she said.

'There's no need to be.' He lit a cigar, surprised at himself for mentioning the parlous state of his marriage. But Maggie's recent problems had brought them closer together. He could feel a change in their relationship hovering beneath the surface. He wanted to stand openly by her side through her current troubles. He wanted to share his life with her, and it was becoming increasingly difficult to keep these feelings to himself. But what about her? Was it fair to ask her to get involved with the husband of her best friend? 'Are you sure you won't change your mind and go to Brighton with your mother? It would be the best thing for you.'

'No, I'll stay at home.'

After speaking to her mother on the telephone from Brighton one evening two weeks later, Maggie cleared the dining table and settled down to do some paperwork. It was good to hear that Katy was enjoying herself, and that Mum was a little calmer. She was glad that they wanted to stay on for a while by the sea.

The silence in the flat was oppressive. Concentration eluded her. She stared around the room, recently refurbished with green carpet and a cheerful cretonne-covered suite. The thought of Tom facing another night in prison gave her the usual stab of sadness.

Aware of another dull ache of misery, she tried to work out why Bradley hadn't called since his wife and daughter had left for the States a week ago. Since Tom's arrest he had been in daily contact with her. It was odd that it should stop so suddenly.

Perhaps his trip to Spain had been brought forward, she thought. Or maybe he was sick with only a housekeeper to look after him. The latter thought sent her scurrying to the telephone.

'Hello, Bradley,' she said. 'Are you all right?'

'Maggie, hi. Yeah, sure I'm all right. Why shouldn't I be?' He sounded strangely distant.

'I haven't heard from you,' she said.

'I've been busy.'

'Oh!' She reeled from the rejection. 'I see. I thought you might be at a loose end with Chloe and Daisy away.'

'Not really.'

'I see. Well, as long as you're all right.' Tears stung her eyes but she gave a forced laugh. 'I'll get back to my paperwork then. Goodnight.'

Abandoning the paperwork, she sank tearfully into an armchair, wondering how she could be feeling so wretched because another woman's husband had been offhand with her on the telephone. After all, her being in love with Bradley was nothing new, and she could usually cope with it. She hadn't felt so bad as this before. It was almost as though they had had a lovers' quarrel. Yet they had never even kissed. Deep in thought she sat there for a long time.

The sound of the doorbell startled her back to reality. Hurrying downstairs, she opened the door to Bradley. 'Can I come in?' he said urgently. 'I have to talk to you.'

'Of course.'

Upstairs in her living room he looked gravely into her eyes. 'I'm sorry I haven't been in touch,' he said.

'Don't apologise,' she said sharply. 'You don't owe me anything.'

'Oh, Maggie,' he gasped, 'I haven't called because I've been trying to work out what to do. You must have guessed that I'm in love with you?'

'Well, I . . . Oh, Bradley.' She sank into his arms.

'I knew I couldn't keep it from you much longer if I kept seeing you,' he explained, stroking her hair, 'but I've missed you so much this week. That's why I was so hateful on the phone. I wasn't sure if you'd want to get involved with a married man.'

'We were both involved from that very first meeting,' she said. 'It had to come to the surface sometime.'

'I guess you're right.'

'But what are we going to do?' she asked a while later as they sat on the sofa together.

'Get married, of course,' he said. 'As soon as Chloe gets back from America, I'll talk to her about a divorce.'

Maggie tensed at this note of painful reality. 'Oh God, Bradley! It's one thing being in love and quite another breaking up someone's marriage.'

'My marriage has been over for years. You know that.'

She got up and paced the room. 'Yes, but it still isn't going to be easy.'

'You and I need time together,' he said.

'Yes.'

'I have to go to Spain on business in a few days' time. Why not come with me?'

She stared at him in astonishment. 'You can't be serious!'

'Sure I'm serious, why not?' he asked. 'It would be the perfect opportunity, while Katy is away.'

166

'But I can't just go swanning off,' she said. 'I didn't feel justified in going to Brighton with my mother and daughter, let alone to Spain with my friend's husband.'

He rose and went to her, taking her gently by the arms and searching her face. 'Do you want to go with me?' he asked.

Maggie didn't just *want* to go with him, she *needed* to. They needed time together, to establish their feelings; to talk; to plan; to love without the intrusions of everyday life and all its complications. 'Yes, I do. Very much.'

'And why do you feel you mustn't?' he asked, his eyes seeming to penetrate her very soul.

'For lots of reasons,' she said.

'Mostly connected with your family,' he surmised. 'OK, so Tom is having a hard time right now. But that doesn't mean that you shouldn't continue with your own life. So you have a business to run. Let it do without you for a while. So you have a daughter and a worried mother. They're both enjoying a holiday by the sea. God dammit, Maggie, you spend your life worrying about your family. You work hard in your business so that they can have a good life. What about you? Don't you have a right to do something you want to occasionally?'

'It's hard to walk away from responsibility,' she told him.

'And you wouldn't be,' he sensibly pointed out. 'You'd merely be taking a short break from it.'

He made it all seem so feasible, but she still had doubts. 'It seems so deceitful somehow, going away together while Chloe is in America.'

'Chloe has been deceiving me for years,' he reminded her.

'But even so . . .'

'If she was around now, I'd tell her. Immediately she gets back, I shall bring the whole thing out into the open.' He looked searchingly at Maggie. 'Would it make you any happier if I telephoned her now and told her?'

'No. There's no point in upsetting her holiday.'

'We must have some time together, Maggie,' he said. 'To sort this thing out.'

'When are you leaving?'

'Three days' time.'

She grinned. 'Well, I suppose I shall just have to brave my mother's disapproval then, won't I? I'll phone her to tell her that I am going away.'

And for the first time in ages, there was a gleam in her eye.

'I can't believe we're really here,' said Maggie a few days later as she and Bradley sipped wine on the terrace of the villa overlooking the Mediterranean Sea which was aflame in the evening sun. 'Perhaps I'm dreaming.'

He leaned across and made her squeal by pinching her arm. 'There! Does that convince you that you are awake and on the Costa Brava, the Wild Coast of Spain?'

She laughed, rubbing her arm. So early in the year the sun was not so intense as it would be later and felt pleasantly warm on her face and limbs, exposed to the elements by a pair of white shorts and suntop. 'Yes, I guess you've convinced me.'

The white-rendered villa nestled in seclusion at the bottom of a pine-fringed cliff beside pale, silky sands. It was situated a few miles from one of the region's oldest resorts, Tossa De Mar, which dated back to Roman times. The property was spacious and comfortable with cool tiled floors, and scatter rugs and softly upholstered cane furniture in pastel shades. The bedrooms had en suite facilities and the kitchen was a tribute to contemporary design and gadgetry. The property belonged to Bradley's company, its prime purpose being to accommodate staff when the firm proceeded with its proposed development programme in the area.

This was Maggie's first trip abroad. Fortunately the passport she had acquired for a trip to Paris with Jack, which had been aborted by his death, was still valid or she might not have been here today.

'And no regrets for having defied convention by coming away with a married man?' he said, moving to the seat next to hers and slipping an affectionate arm around her shoulders.

'There would be something wrong with me if I wasn't happy to be here with you,' she said, shivering pleasurably as his hand caressed her neck. 'I've even managed to calm down a little over Tom. But I do feel terribly guilty about Chloe. She is my best friend, after all.'

'But you know how things are between us,' he said, sipping his wine.

'Yes, but the fact that Chloe cheats on you doesn't give us licence to do the same.'

He turned her face to his. 'This isn't some casual affair, Maggie,' he declared. 'I love you and I want to marry you. I didn't ask you to come here just to take you to bed. I want us to be together away from family pressures.'

'I know. But I hate the idea of being a homewrecker.'

His arm tightened around her. 'Do you honestly think that Chloe and I would have stayed together for much longer if this hadn't happened between you and me?'

'No, I suppose not,' she agreed. 'Ironically, I have been warning her for years that she would lose you one day because of her playing around. I didn't expect to be so personally involved.'

'You are merely the catalyst to force Chloe and myself to face up to the truth,' he said reassuringly.

'Poor Daisy,' said Maggie, looking out across the bay. In the distance a few people dotted the sands, but it was too early in the year for the sun-starved British tourists who were beginning to come in droves every summer to this sunshine paradise with their suntan oil and transistor radios. 'What about her in all this?' As she spoke she recalled the many other times she had uttered these very same words to Chloe, and this produced sudden perspicacity. In her heart she had known for a long time that Chloe's marriage could not last.

Bradley's face darkened at the mention of his beloved daughter. 'It is because of Daisy I have let things drift on this long,' he explained. 'But it can't have been much fun for her living with parents who don't get along. I've always been afraid Chloe might be given custody and would somehow make it difficult for me to see Daisy. Now, I'm willing to fight. But I doubt if it will come to that. I'm hoping to work out an arrangement with Chloe with Daisy's best interests at heart. Chloe is selfish but she isn't wicked. And she does love Daisy, especially now that she's over the baby and toddler stage. Divorce is never pleasant for the children involved, but neither is the atmosphere of an unhappy marriage.'

Maggie sighed, hating to be happy at the expense of another. 'In a perfect world, all marriages would last forever.'

'Umm,' he agreed, thoughtfully looking out to sea. 'But this isn't a perfect world. Anyway, what about Katy? How will she take to the idea of having a stepfather?'

She tensed at the thought of the potential problems which threatened her future happiness with Bradley. Being with him had made her realise just how lonely she had been within herself when she was married to Jack. With Bradley she felt complete and really alive.

Since pessimism wasn't in her nature, she said, 'As long as I make sure she doesn't feel excluded, I should think she'll be fine. She's a very balanced child.' She paused and chewed her lip pensively. 'She loved her father, of course, but she was very young when he died. I've no real worries in that direction.' She gave a wry grin. 'I'll probably have more trouble with Mother. She and Jack were such pals. I can't see her accepting a new son-in-law easily, so you may as well be warned.'

'But it's nearly three years since Jack died,' he pointed out. 'And you are still a young woman. Surely she must have realised that you wouldn't stay single forever?'

She recalled her mother's disapproval on being told that her widowed daughter was going away with a married man, and a Yank too. 'Business trip, my foot,' she'd admonished hotly. 'Once you get out there in the sunshine together, Gawd knows what'll happen. You ought to have more respect for your reputation, my girl! There's enough gossip around, without you adding to it.'

'I expect she does realise that, but I've probably soured her against our relationship initially by coming with you on this trip,' she explained. 'She really was quite shocked. But she's a good sort, she'll soon get used to the idea.' She sighed wistfully. 'In the meantime, my future with you seems faraway, beyond an emotional minefield. I wish it didn't affect so many other people.'

'Now we are back to that perfect world again,' he said.

Lifting her face to the sun she felt its warmth easing the tension that had racked her for weeks. 'Being here with you is close to perfection. It's been such a worrying time at home and I feel more relaxed than I have in ages,' she said, taking his hand. 'Don't let's spoil it with practicalities for the moment. The time to face up to our responsibilities will come soon enough.'

'I'll drink to that,' he said, refilling their glasses.

The next day he drove her to the site of the proposed holiday complex in a car they had hired for the duration of their stay. The site was on the outskirts of a quaint Spanish town whose artistic contours had already yielded to the hand of developers as a holiday resort. Juxtaposed with the ancient stone houses, small colourful shops and narrow winding streets that curved through the centre of the town to the shoreline, were square hotels and apartment blocks, their angular, unimaginative lines incongruous against the charm of the traditional architecture. Uglier and more threatening still was the mesh of scaffolding encompassing the constructions still in progress which flanked the natural curve of the shore.

'Some of the new buildings are so ugly,' remarked Maggie as they drove along the town's perimeter. 'They look like glorified concrete blocks.'

'They serve a useful purpose,' opined Bradley. 'They give holidaymakers from all over Europe a place in the sun for a couple of weeks a year at a reasonable price. And they bring money into the country.'

'Are you planning on building something similar?' she asked.

'No. Our plans are for semi-detached and detached villas,' he explained. 'With gardens and swimming pools.'

'For the better-off holidaymaker?'

'Our properties will be for sale, not for rent,' he informed her. 'There is beginning to be a demand for holiday homes here which I think will increase dramatically in the next few years.'

They arrived at the site, an area of wiry grassland fringed with sandy pine forest. Distantly the town was a splash of colour amid the rugged tree-clad cliffs shimmering in a blue haze and interspersed with dusty yellow patches. The only sound in this idyllic haven was the roar of the sea and the whisper of the breeze through the pines.

170

'So what do you think?' asked Bradley as they surveyed the region.

'It's a beautiful spot,' said Maggie. 'All the better for being outside the town.'

He nodded, looking towards the built-up area. 'That will hardly be recognisable in a few years if development continues at such a rate.'

'Yes,' agreed Maggie sadly.

Arm in arm they strolled around the area in companionable silence. 'It certainly is an interesting project,' Bradley said at last.

'Being purely selfish,' she said, 'will I lose you to Spain for the duration of the construction?'

'Not on your life,' he assured her. 'I'll be sending a manager over to run the job.'

'Will he bring a team of builders with him from England?' she asked.

'Some, but we'll use local labour too.'

They stayed a while longer, then made their way into the town where Bradley had an appointment with the vendor of the land. While he attended to his business, Maggie absorbed the town's atmosphere, observing the poverty existing side by side with unabashed affluence. Bright-eyed, ragged children played in the smelly backstreets while the cash registers of the bars and cafes rang to the businessmen's pesetas as they anticipated a prosperous tourist season ahead.

The market square was alive with colour and commerce. There was something here to satisfy every need and tempt every taste. Fresh-caught fish; flowers and fruit; leatherwork and lace; brightly coloured clothes and souvenirs. The air was filled with the mingled scents of wine and coffee, fish and fresh-baked bread. Tourists were few at this time of the year, and the streets overflowed with the indigenous population, socialising and trading in the sunshine, the foreign sounds filling the scene with mystery and magic for Maggie.

Having no command of Spanish, she used sign language to purchase a hideous yellow tie with a central iridescent pattern for Bradley from a street seller of impecunious appearance. And using her phrase book she was thrilled to obtain a delicious cold chocolate drink from a cafe where she sat at a table in the sunshine.

Bradley was diplomatic about the dazzling tie which she gave to him back at the villa. 'I'll treasure it always,' he said, kissing her.

'But you won't actually wear it, I hope?'

He grinned wickedly at her, his fair hair gleaming in the sun. 'We Americans are not so quiet in our dress as you English,' he laughed, knotting the gaudy garment around his neck and letting it dangle incongruously against his bare chest, for he was wearing only shorts.

Maggie laughed until her sides ached but he insisted on keeping it on. And, somehow, in this sunny carefree land, it didn't seem to matter. 'It has a terrible beauty about it somehow,' she said, as the tie flapped ludicrously. 'I bought it because I felt so sorry for the man who was selling them.'

'You're a real softie, but he wouldn't want your pity,' Bradley informed her. 'The Spanish are a very proud race.'

'They certainly have a lot to be proud of in their country,' Maggie remarked. 'It's beautiful.'

Lunch of paella and fresh bread, salad and wine, was provided for them by a local woman whose services Bradley had procured before their arrival, and eaten on the terrace in a mood of affectionate hilarity. In keeping with local tradition they took a siesta in the afternoon before swimming in the warm Mediterranean waters beyond the villa gardens. Although their mood was one of intimacy, their embraces had not gone beyond the preliminary stages and they had not yet shared a bed. A tacit understanding had sprung up between them that further intimacy would only occur at Maggie's prompting.

They dined out that evening in a restaurant in the town, and later sipped wine together on the moonlit terrace. 'Do you have business to attend to tomorrow?' Maggie asked, a pleasant sleepiness replacing her recent feeling of tense exhaustion.

'No, I shall let the vendor worry about my final decision for a few days,' he explained. 'He is a hard businessman and he is being a little greedy about the price. He needs a few days to cool off, to be a little less sure of me.'

'So you can forget work for a while?'

'I sure can.'

'Perhaps we might do a little sightseeing,' she suggested tentatively. 'As it's my first trip abroad, I am eager to see as much as I can.'

'Sure,' he said. 'Perhaps you'd like to go further afield.'

'I'd love that.'

'Would you like to spend a few days in the capital city?' he asked eagerly. 'Madrid is a fascinating place.'

'That would be wonderful,' she said. 'But isn't it a long way from here?'

'It will be a long drive,' he told her. 'But well worth the effort.'

'Oh, Bradley, I can't wait,' she said excitedly. Caught up in the joy of the moment, the problems of home seemed very far away.

Chapter Thirteen

In America, Chloe was feeling happy too.

'This is the largest municipal park in the whole of the United States, honey,' Lilian Hughes was explaining to her granddaughter as the child stood between her grandparents near the Schuylkill River in Fairmount Park, Philadelphia.

'Can we go on a row-boat please, Grandpa?' asked Daisy, treating him to one of her most winning smiles.

Over the child's head, Will Hughes sought the approval of his wife, Lilian, an attractive woman in her late fifties who was casually dressed in blue jeans and a white sweater. The fact that Lilian did not project the traditional grandmotherly image, her hair being tinted blonde and her face benefiting from the sort of grooming that only the rich can afford, did not mean that she was not a soft touch so far as her granddaughter was concerned.

Lilian nodded approvingly at her husband. 'You haven't taken a vacation from business in honour of our visitors just to stand back and look at things, Will Hughes,' she said in mock reproach. She looked down at Daisy. 'Sure, we'll go out on a boat, honey, but first let's find out if your mom would like to come too.'

'Goodee,' Daisy squealed, bounding across the grass to where Chloe was sitting on a bench in the sunshine.

'I'd sooner just sit here, if you don't mind,' said Chloe, who was in thoughtful mood. 'You three go and have fun.'

'OK, honey,' chorused Lilian and Will.

Turning his attention to Daisy, Will winked and said, 'Your grandma will do the rowing.' He grinned at Lilian. 'Isn't that right, honey?'

'It certainly is not,' she retorted jovially, for this sort of good-humoured banter was natural between them. 'We'll do it between us.'

'I guess I'll just do as I'm told, then,' laughed Will affectionately. 'Like the henpecked husband that I am.'

In reply he received a hearty slap on the back from Lilian. 'If you're henpecked, then I'm America's First Lady,' she laughed.

Basking in the reflected glow of her grandparents' loving association, Daisy was almost beside herself with delight, giggling uncontrollably as she went hand-in-hand with them towards the river.

Watching them go, Chloe thought how much Bradley resembled his father. They both had the same square-shaped jaw, blue eyes and colouring, though Will's hair had turned white. They shared the same purposeful stride too. Compared to Chloe's own parents, Will and Lilian were quite young, both still under sixty. Chloe was fond of them both and felt a stab of pleasure at the sight of the happy trio hurrying across the grass.

This vacation had been Chloe's most enjoyable visit to Philadelphia yet. Hospitality had abounded in the Hughes' splendid home in the high-class neigbourhood of Chestnut Hill. But today Lilian had decided on a programme of sightseeing for her guests, and they had spent the morning exploring America's most historic square. They had been to the impressive Liberty Bell Pavilion and seen the nation's most revered symbol of liberty, and visited Independence Hall where the Declaration of Independence was adopted, and Betsy Ross House where the eponymous lady was credited with making the first US flag.

They had wandered through Penn Square, and visited old Philadelphia with its narrow lanes and beautifully preserved houses and trees. After lunch, in one of the city's many restaurants, they had made their way to this immense epitome of leisure space, over eight thousand landscaped acres catering for every conceivable outdoor recreation.

Now, alone with her thoughts, Chloe reflected on the cathartic effect this holiday was having on her which could only be attributed to the absence of her husband. Relieved of the misery of mutual indifference and pretence, she was full of a sense of tranquillity and well-being. More patient than usual with her daughter's demands, she had reached the point where she was actually enjoying the child's company.

During this stay Chloe had found herself observing her parents-in-law with interest as joy in their relationship exuded from them, filling all around them with a sense of harmony. Daisy obviously felt it too for the little girl had been positively radiant since the moment they arrived. Sadly, Chloe accepted the fact that the magic of Lilian's and Will's combined chemistry was something that she and Bradley would never generate if they stayed together for the rest of their lives.

A chorus of voices calling her name drew her attention to the river where the nautical trio were waving madly at her, Lilian at one end of the rowing boat, Daisy sitting with Will at the other. Like father like grandfather, she thought, sensitive to the fact that Daisy was drawn, from habit, to the male of the couple. 'Hi,' Chloe called, waving her arms enthusiastically, her eyes moistening with a sudden surge of pleasure in Daisy's happiness, a rare occurrence indeed for Chloe.

She's becoming easier now that she's older, thought Chloe, confused by these new and tender emotions. And thank goodness for that! Toddlers are so tiresome.

When the boaters returned, flushed and exuberant, Will and Daisy went to get some ice creams, while Lilian joined Chloe on the bench. It was a fine spring day with pale sunshine bathing the verdant planes, and a light breeze rustling in the trees. After Lilian had chatted for a while about the boat trip, Chloe said impulsively, 'It's been a terrific holiday, Lilian I'll be so sad to leave.'

'Aw, don't even think about leaving yet, honey, we've still a while to go before we have to part with you,' said Lilian. She paused and glanced absently across the lush parkland where walkers explored the hiking trails and cyclists glided by on the paved bikeways. 'Will and I are having a wonderful time. Your visit has done him a whole lotta good.' Her lively blue eyes were thoughtful. 'He doesn't take nearly enough time off from the business, I guess.'

'Doesn't he have a proper holiday then?' asked Chloe.

'Sure, he takes an annual vacation, but that's about all. He's worked so hard all his life, it's time he learned to leave things to his deputies more often,' she explained. 'I'd like to see him taking time out to have fun, do a little fishing, or perhaps play some golf. And it would be good for us to be able to do more things together too.'

'It won't be too long before he retires, I suppose,' remarked Chloe.

'I can't imagine him ever fully retiring,' confessed Lilian. 'And why should he if he wants to stay on? Full retirement doesn't suit everybody. Just so long as he takes more time out for relaxation.' She paused, looking out across the river. 'Still, I mustn't complain. I expect Bradley is just the same. I don't suppose you see nearly enough of him.'

'That's the price the wife of a successful businessman pays,' said Chloe evasively, for how could she tell her husband's mother that the idea of more time with Bradley was abhorrent to her, and the only way their life together was even remotely endurable was because they saw so little of each other.

'Take comfort in the fact that it runs in the family,' said Lilian, patting Chloe's hand companionably, unaware of the effect she was having on her daughter-in-law's conscience.

Daisy and Will were approaching, laden with ice-cream cones for them all. Lilian smiled. 'Will is in his element with young Daisy. It does my heart good to see it.'

'Yes,' nodded Chloe, feeling fraudulent for allowing these dear people to take her to their hearts in the belief that she was the protector of their son's happiness. How shocked Lilian would be to know that Bradley meant little more to Chloe than a stranger in the street.

Allowing herself to face the truth about her feelings for him, whilst

175

encompassed by the sincere affection of his parents, racked her with guilt. Not because she did not love him, for that was beyond her control, but for allowing this appalling situation to continue for so long.

'I wish Daddy was here,' said Daisy, sitting on the bench and licking her ice cream.

'That sure would be good,' agreed Will.

'Wouldn't it too?' agreed Lilian.

'I don't want to go home yet, though,' said Daisy thoughtfully, 'even though I do want to see my daddy, because I'm having such fun here.'

'We'll have to persuade him to take time off to come with you next time,' suggested Lilian.

'Yes, we will, won't we, Mummy?' Daisy threw Chloe a shrewd look. 'Are you having a good time?'

'Yes, I certainly am, darling.' And as Chloe realised just how much she was dreading returning home to Bradley and their pretence of a life together, she decided, at last, that it was time for them to go their separate ways. She would speak to Bradley about a divorce as soon as she got back to England.

The sun was just beginning to rise over Madrid when Maggie and Bradley arrived. They had started out in the late afternoon of the previous day and had made a leisurely drive of it, enjoying the scenery and making several stops before driving through the delicious cool of the night.

Set on a plateau within view of the mountains, the city instantly captivated Maggie. The washed streets were already bustling with the noisy dazzle of the dawn markets and the air was filled with the scent of coffee and burning charcoal. Maggie's first impression was of a glorious mixture of elegance and ugliness, a place of sophistication and squalor where beggars and businessmen spoke the same pure Spanish tongue. There were plazas and parks; splendid hotels and scrubbed taverns; luxury shops and street peddlers. The sounds of traffic, chatter and laughter roared around them.

Bradley had telephoned ahead and booked two rooms for them in an hotel in the centre of Madrid. They booked in, showered, and breakfasted on coffee and rolls on the terrace beneath white-fringed parasols.

Maggie ached with tiredness for although they had taken turns with the driving neither of them had slept. But she was also infected by the vigour of this amazing city which seemed to vibrate from every paving stone and person. 'We need to catch up on some sleep, I know,' she said, spreading apricot preserve on warm crusty bread. 'But I'm far too excited to go to bed right now. I just can't wait to explore. If you'd like to sleep, you go ahead. I'll take a wander around on my own.'

'I think we should stay awake until we drop,' he laughed.

So, hand in hand, they took a tour of the city, observing the fine shops on the Gran Via, and the fascinating little arcades around the Puerta del Sol. They wandered through narrow backstreets where beautiful bare-foot children played while their mothers gossiped at their doors. They drank coffee in the sunshine at the very heart of Madrid, the Plaza Mayor, and ate lunch of seafood, bread and wine in a cool tavern which finally sent them staggering sleepily back to the hotel for a siesta.

That evening, feeling much refreshed, they ambled through the old city, a place of courtyards and old coaching inns, where the elderly snoozed in their chairs on the pavements, young girls paraded up and down, men filled the bars, and children romped in the open until midnight.

It was the small hours when they finally arrived back at the hotel and enjoyed a nightcap on the terrace in the warm air which still pulsated with nightlife around them. The atmosphere between them was more intimate than ever before. They both knew it was time for their relation-ship to progress.

The consummation left them exhausted and complete. Maggie felt renewed and cherished, and so united with Bradley that they might have shared one skin. 'We won't be needing the other room for the rest of our stay,' she laughed gently, as they lay together in the afterglow, listening to the distant sound of music, footsteps and laughter in this vital city that never seemed to tire. Unlike the lovers who fell into a deep sleep.

Maggie's slumber did not remain undisturbed for long, however. Quite soon she began to drift in and out of consciousness, aware of the fact that she did not feel well. At first it was just a headache and queasiness which she ascribed to the unaccustomed oily food. But soon her discomfort became unbearable. Her limbs ached, her neck was stiff, and although she was shivering violently, her skin was on fire. What a time to get 'flu, she cursed, now feeling oppressed by the warm climate which seemed to be choking her.

Despite her efforts not to disturb Bradley, the sounds of her distress in the en suite bathroom brought him scurrying to her assistance. 'You poor darling,' he said, helping her back to bed and producing some pills from his suitcase. 'It's probably a dose of Spanish tummy. A couple of these will soon put you right.'

The pills came back within seconds of her having swallowed them, and she now felt very ill indeed. It was painful to move, yet she couldn't lie still. She wanted to sleep, but her skin felt as though it was brushing against barbed wire, and her throat was now so sore she could barely swallow. Coherent thought was becoming difficult too as she alternated between physical wretchedness and terrifying nightmares. Gradually

177

her surroundings faded. Vaguely, she knew that someone else was in the room. Distantly, she perceived the drone of hushed voices, a mixture of Spanish and English. A doctor was examining her. And then she passed into oblivion, unaware of the drama about to unfold around her.

'Hello, Chloe, how are you?' asked Bradley, a week or so later on the telephone. 'Did you have a good trip back from the States?'

'Quite good, yes,' she said. 'When will you be arriving home?'

'Not for a while yet.'

'Oh, I was expecting you in the next couple of days. And that's a nuisance,' Chloe said impatiently, for she was eager to speak to him about the decision she had made in Philadelphia, 'because I have something important to tell you.'

For the last few days, Bradley had left Maggie's bedside at the hospital only to snatch enough sleep to sustain him and to shower and change his clothes. He had only slipped back to the hotel now because the doctors were with her. She had been admitted to hospital with suspected meningitis, which had now been discounted in favour of a virus which was equally as dangerous. It had been the most terrible time of his life and his nerves were stretched to breaking point. He had telephoned Chloe, out of duty, to warn her of his delayed return, and was in no condition to tolerate one of her petulant moods. 'It will have to wait for a while, I'm afraid,' he said wearily. 'Whatever it is.'

Although his prolonged absence from the marital home was no burden to Chloe, the fact that she was to be kept waiting to discuss with him her plans for divorce infuriated her. 'Oh, will it?' she snapped in her old acid manner. 'Well, I don't think that's good enough. I realise that you're enjoying yourself in the sun out there in Spain, but I need you here. A telephone discussion just won't do, in this particular instance.'

He had not planned to mention the drama of the last few days to Chloe at this stage, but she had pushed him beyond patience. 'Actually, my reason for staying on here is something that you should perhaps know about,' he told her.

'Oh?'

'It's Maggie.'

'Maggie! What's she got to do with it?'

'She's here in Madrid with me, and she's very sick,' he explained gravely. 'The next few hours are critical. The doctors are expecting a crisis. She may not come through it.'

'Oh my God!'

'All we can do is pray.'

There was a silence before Chloe made the inevitable query. 'But how come she's in Spain with you?'

178

'This isn't the time to go into that.'

'Oh, I see.' She sounded puzzled but subdued, the grave circumstances forbidding even her to ask further questions at this time. 'You'll let me know the moment there is any news?'

'Sure. And Chloe?'

'Yes?'

'Her mother isn't expecting her back for another few days, so I haven't told her,' he explained. 'I don't want to worry her unnecessarily. Don't mention it to her, will you? I'll call her myself . . .' He paused, hardly able to utter the words '. . . one way or the other, the minute I know.'

'No, I won't. Just call me when you know anything. And give her my love.'

'Will do.'

Later that day, Maggie's condition worsened. The room resounded to her delirious ramblings while the nurses sponged her with cool flannels. Bradley had been on active service during the war, but he could not remember ever feeling this frightened. Powerless to help, he clasped her damp, burning hand while she stared at him without recognition. All he could do was to remain calm beside her, praying and offering words of comfort he knew she could not hear. And then, suddenly, she slept, breathing evenly and peacefully.

'She be all right now,' said the nurse, in broken English. 'I'll go and get you some tea, Senor.'

The relief was too much for Bradley and his tears flowed uncontrollably. Then he bowed his head in silent thanks. When the nurse came back she advised him to go back to the hotel and sleep. But he just said, 'I want to be here when she wakes up.'

When Maggie awoke, she saw an unfamiliar room with white walls and scrubbed floors. The clinical surroundings were relieved by flowers, which she guessed were from Bradley, arranged in vases around the room. Just before she drifted back to sleep the sweetness of her incipient recovery was enhanced by the sight of him asleep in the chair beside her. Waking for the second time she felt very much stronger, and Bradley too was awake.

'Welcome back,' he said tenderly, taking her limp hand and putting it to his lips.

'It's good to be back,' she said, smiling weakly.

Progress was swift after that and she was released from hospital within a few days, but Bradley insisted on a week of convalescence at the villa. He had telephoned Dora, who was now back from Brighton, and had been warmly assured that Katy would be in capable hands until Maggie's return, whenever that was. Dora's disapproval of Bradley had noticeably lessened in her concern for her daughter.

'No point in rushing back until you are strong enough,' Bradley advised Maggie. 'If you go back to work too early, you'll soon find yourself back in bed.'

And so April 1957 was almost over by the time they sat on the terrace watching the sunset on the eve of their departure. Maggie was still underweight from her illness but attractively tanned from long, lazy days in the sun, her hair bleached to the colour of sand.

'Well,' said Bradley, pouring them both a glass of champagne and smiling at her, 'to us and a long and happy future together.'

'To us,' she said, raising her glass.

Chloe listened in shocked disbelief to what her husband was saying to her in the drawing room of their Hampstead home. It was a weekday morning in early May. Daisy was at school and the housekeeper out shopping.

'You and Maggie,' she exploded at last, 'carrying on behind my back? I can hardly believe it. Well, I've certainly been a naive fool.'

Angry tears burned her eyes. This was the last thing she had expected. Even on learning of Maggie's presence in Spain with Bradley, Chloe had merely assumed she had gone along as a business companion. Maggie and Bradley had been friends for years, she had known and approved of that. If it had been anyone else but Maggie, she might have had doubts. But it had never entered her head because Maggie simply wouldn't *do* a thing like that. But she had, and Chloe was devastated, her eagerness for a new life without Bradley diminished by jealousy and hurt pride.

It made her sick to think of the plans she had made for a civilised parting for herself and Bradley, whereby they could remain friends. Why, she had even intended to give him unlimited access to their daughter. Now, humiliated by his betrayal, and that of someone she had trusted beyond all others, her instinct was to hurt them both, all thoughts of her own freedom and happiness paling into insignificance against the power of this. She did not love Bradley, but he had made a fool of her and for that he must pay.

'We haven't been carrying on behind your back,' he denied. 'Things only came to a head while you were in America.'

'You're not denying that you've slept together?' she rasped, her eyes narrowed spitefully, her fiery emotions darkening her looks against the white linen dress she wore.

'No, I'm not denying that,' he said with determined composure. 'But it only happened recently. We haven't been having the sort of sneaky affair you're implying.'

'You *are* having an affair with her,' Chloe raged. 'And whatever words you use to describe it, that is the fact of the matter. You and my so-called friend have been having a cheap little fling!'

'There is nothing cheap about my relationship with Maggie,' he declared, his blue eyes dark with rage. 'I love her, and I intend to marry her.'

'Over my dead body,' she snarled.' I'll not give you a divorce.'

Bradley gave a cynical laugh. 'I don't think you are in a position to make any objections,' he told her. 'Since you've been committing adultery for years with a certain Frankie Farringdon.'

She was shaken by this. 'I suppose she told you?'

'No, she didn't,' he said. 'Maggie is far more loyal to you than some of your other friends.'

'Be that as it may,' she snorted, 'you've no proof.'

'Maybe not, but I shall get a divorce, one way or another.' He paused thoughtfully and lit a cigar. 'I'd hoped we could come to an amicable arrangement, since we have both known for a long time that our marriage is over. But if it's a battle you want, then a battle you shall have.'

Chloe hated feeling powerless to manipulate him. She was damned if she was going to stand by and let him and Maggie make a fool of her. It was one thing embarking on an independent new life at her own instigation, and quite another being forced into the role of discarded wife, to be scorned and pitied. She simply wasn't going to allow that to happen. She'd make him stay married to her or die in the attempt. How dare he and Maggie find happiness together when it had eluded her for so long?

She paced restlessly to the window and stared across the garden which seemed to mock her in its joyful zest for life. Fresh green leaves burst from every branch and stem: white lilac blossoms gleamed in the sun. Violent frustration welled up inside her and she stifled the urge either to physically assault her husband, or to punch her own head with her fists.

Exercising supreme self-control, she turned to face Bradley who was standing with his back to the hearth, smoking a cigar. He was smartly dressed in a pale grey business suit, his tan deepened by the whiteness of his shirt. He was a handsome man by any standards, but it was a very long time since she had been aroused by his good looks. Only resentment at his unfaithfulness remained, her own transgressions conveniently forgotten. 'I'll fight you every inch of the way,' she informed him coldly.

'But why are you so opposed to the idea of us splitting up?' Bradley implored. 'It isn't as though you are in love with me. And I'll see to it that you don't suffer financially.'

The pain of her injured pride blinded her to the good sense of his words. 'It is your duty to stay with me,' she persisted, 'and I'm not going to let you go.'

He stared at her incredulously. All this from a woman who had treated their wedding vows like disposable hankies! 'And just how do you propose to stop me?'

'I'll find a way.' She looked as stunning and spiteful as an angry cat, her gold hooped earings flashing against her raven hair.

She was quiet and thoughtful for the next few moments before changing her strategy. Fixing her dark eyes on his, she said more softly, 'We could try again, Bradley.'

'It's too late for that.'

Her powerlessness was unbearable to Chloe. She lunged at him with clenched fists. 'You will give her up and stay with me. You will!' she screamed, pummelling his chest.

Bradley grabbed her by the arms and held her at bay. 'Have you no pride?' he asked. 'You are a beautiful and intelligent woman. Don't destroy yourself and all those around you with your selfishness. You don't want me, you haven't for a long time. So let go and give us both a chance of happiness.'

He released her and she stood back, shocked into silence by his frankness. Dragging a handkerchief from her pocket, she dried her crocodile tears. 'No, I'll not make it easy for you,' she said coldly.

'You'll save yourself a lot of anguish if you do,' he said sadly. 'Because I intend to be with Maggie, whatever happens.' He marched across the room, turning at the door. 'I'm really sorry it has ended like this, Chloe. You and I never really made it as a couple, but we might have stood a chance as friends. One of these days you'll find real love and then you'll realise just how much I want my freedom now.' He paused briefly. 'I'm going to the office. I'll arrange to move my things out of here.'

Alone, she sank down into the chair by the window. She had always been able to produce tears easily by casting herself in the role of victim. But she was far too angry now to cry. She hated Bradley for stripping her of any control of the situation. In pre-empting her idea of a divorce, he had made her feel rejected and worthless. But she wasn't beaten yet.

Feeling sick with nerves, Maggie turned her car into Chloe's drive the next day. Whilst understanding that it was unrealistic to expect her friendship with Chloe to continue unchanged, the fact that Chloe did not actually love Bradley inspired her with hope for some sort of continued association. Chloe's attitude on the telephone had given nothing away. 'You and I need to talk,' she had said in an even tone. 'Can you come over as soon as possible? It's more private here than at your place, what with the shop and everything.'

182

Having been shown into the drawing room by Chloe's housekeeper, Mrs Marsh, Maggie was greeted formally by Chloe, their customary peck on the cheek noticeable by its absence. Maggie smarted with compunction, for she was uneasy in her position of 'other woman'. She was invited to sit down, and coffee and biscuits were almost instantly produced by Mrs Marsh.

'These biscuits are rather good,' said Chloe with false nonchalance, offering a plate of brandy snaps to Maggie. 'Do try one.'

Maggie couldn't have swallowed a thing if her life had depended on it. 'Later, perhaps,' she said, taking a sip of coffee to moisten her dry mouth.

The uncomfortable silence rang around them like the echo of a bell. Maggie felt small and unsophisticated against Chloe who had obviously taken pains with her appearance. She was wearing an emerald-green silk dress which emphasised both her superb figure and her striking colouring. Her hair was drawn back into a chignon and her long legs displayed to advantage in green high-heeled shoes.

Having fitted this visit in between a million jobs at the shop, Maggie was casually dressed in jeans and a sweater. In this arrogant mood Chloe reminded her of a cat playing with a mouse.

'Are you quite recovered?' asked Chloe, nibbling a biscuit in the manner of someone who doesn't have a care in the world.

'Yes, I'm feeling much better now, thanks,' she said, as though Chloe was a stranger.

'It must have been dreadful for you, being ill in a foreign country,' said Chloe with unnerving pleasantness.

Deciding that evading the issue would serve no useful purpose, Maggie said, 'I imagine I would have felt just as bad had it happened here, but I was out for the count a lot of the time. Poor Bradley was the one with all the worry.'

Thus exposed the issue stood palpably between them, demanding attention. Chloe sipped her coffee, surveying Maggie with a shrewd eye. Far more upsetting than the thought of losing Bradley was the idea of banishing Maggie from her life. She hated her one-time friend for making it necessary. 'I can't believe that you have done this to me, Maggie. I would have trusted you with my life.'

'Oh, Chloe,' said Maggie emotionally, meeting her friend's accusing stare. 'I'm so sorry. I never intended it to happen.'

'I don't know how you can live with yourself,' said Chloe.

'And I don't know how you can be so morally superior, considering your own track record,' retorted Maggie defensively.

'Now we really are resorting to gutter tactics,' said Chloe. 'Still, I suppose that's natural for someone like you.'

Resisting the urge to slap her, Maggie said, 'You haven't cared about Bradley for years. I doubt if you ever really loved him. Now is the chance for a new life for you both.'

'Don't try excusing what you've done by telling yourself that I don't love Bradley,' Chloe snapped. 'He's my husband and therefore off limits to you, regardless of my feelings for him. You're the one who is usually so good at preaching morals.'

Maggie was full of remorse. 'I can understand you being sore, and I don't feel good about what has happened. But it never would have come about if you and he were happy. A split between you was inevitable, regardless of me.' She wrung her hands anxiously. 'You and I have been friends for a long time, Chloe. I don't want that to end.'

'You're the one who has made us into enemies,' Chloe said coldly, 'and I hate you for it.'

'Do we have to be enemies?' asked Maggie ardently. 'You don't want Bradley any more than he wants you, not really. And he won't stay with you, whether you agree to a divorce or not. So why not accept what has happened with good grace? We could all remain friends.'

'It seems that you don't know me at all,' said Chloe, 'if you think that I'll give up that easily.'

'But what have you to gain by clinging on to something that you don't want?' Maggie implored her. 'You and Bradley are not going to learn to love each other by staying together. If I thought there was a chance of that I'd stand back. But Bradley needs me, Chloe, he really does.'

Chloe poured more coffee from the silver pot, fuming with jealous rage. When she looked up her eyes were blazing. 'Bradley is my husband and the father of my daughter. His place is with us.'

'Ah, yes, Daisy,' said Maggie, wincing with guilt. 'I was wondering when you'd bring her into it. You've always been far too taken up with your lover to bother much about her, so don't use her for your own ends now.' She rose and slung the strap of her bag over her shoulder, meeting Chloe's eyes. 'I am not proud of being in love with a married man but it has happened and I can't undo that. Even if I were to give him up, that would never change. I'm really sorry, Chloe.'

And without waiting for a reply she left the house. Somewhere between Hampstead and Ashbrook Green, she had to pull into the side of the road to try to curb the flow of tears. Oh God, what was she to do?

Chloe was trembling as Maggie's car roared away, the ensuing silence grim with valediction. It had been the most traumatic experience of her life. Although she had shown no sign of it to Maggie, Chloe was consumed with guilt for the misery she felt compelled to inflict on a

184

woman she had loved as a friend for the last nine years. It had been to Maggie she had turned for reassurance and advice all that time. Now all that was over.

But did it have to be? she asked herself. Up until yesterday she had been ready to make a fresh start without Bradley. If she reverted to that plan she and Maggie could remain friends. But pride was all powerful. It nagged horribly inside her, eliminating any sort of reason.

The fact that Bradley and Maggie had betrayed her hurt terribly. What fools they were to imagine they had found real love! Lust was the only truth between man and woman. When that faded they would be left with the same empty shell that was her own life. The thought of the empty years ahead without Maggie produced real heartfelt tears.

'This is an unexpected pleasure,' said Bradley, looking up from his desk that afternoon to find Maggie standing there.

'Your secretary said you were alone,' she explained. 'I persuaded her to let me come straight in. I hope you don't mind.'

He rose instantly and embraced her. 'Of course I don't mind. I'm delighted to see you, surely you know that by now.'

'Yes, I do, of course,' she said, her tone staccato with agitation.

'I'll get you some tea,' he suggested, ushering her into the seat she had occupied so often these last few years.

'Thank you,' she said.

Having asked his secretary for some tea on the internal phone, he said to Maggie: 'What's happened? You're upset.'

'I've been to see Chloe.'

'Oh. I see!' he said, his features tightening.

The tea arrived and Maggie drank hers eagerly for she was parched with stress. She had turned the matter over in her mind until her head ached, but in her heart she knew she did not have a choice. 'I can't go through with it, Bradley,' she said wearily. 'I just don't have the stomach to break up someone else's marriage.'

'But, Maggie,' he said, springing up from his seat and coming to her, his hands resting on her shoulders. 'You mustn't let Chloe get to you like this. You're playing right into her hands.'

She leant against his desk, her head resting on her arms for a few moments in sheer dejection. This trauma so soon after her illness had weakened her almost to the point of collapse. 'I'm sorry, Bradley. My conscience just won't let me,' she said, sitting up.

He went down on his haunches beside her and searched her face. 'Please, Maggie, don't do this,' he begged.

Sighing, she shook her head. 'I've tried to make myself believe that a split in your marriage doesn't matter because you're not happy. I've

185

tried to convince myself that Daisy will not suffer by the break-up. But I can't take the chance.'

'But Maggie . . .'

She raised her hands for him to stop talking. 'I know that you and Chloe have lived separate lives for years, but you do have a family unit of sorts and Daisy lives within that unit, however indifferent you and Chloe are to each other. I can't be responsible for destroying that.'

'But Chloe will keep the house,' he persisted.

'Without you in it,' she said. 'And with Daisy torn between the two of you.'

Beside himself with anguish, Bradley said, 'Maggie, please change your mind.'

'That's not possible, I'm afraid,' she told him miserably. 'It might be different if Chloe wasn't so bitter. But she is sure to be difficult about your seeing Daisy, and that would break your heart as well as your daughter's. If Daisy were to have psychological problems in the future, I would blame myself. I know how devastated my daughter was when she lost her father. No, Bradley, it just isn't on.'

'But Daisy wouldn't be losing me,' he pointed out. 'Quite the contrary, I would try for custody.'

'And then she loses her mother on a full-time basis,' Maggie said. 'Her security would be gone whoever gets custody. She'd be caught in the upheaval of a broken home, no matter how much you try to spare her. I know that this sort of thing does happen, and that separations can be very successful, but I can't have it on my conscience. I think you should stay with it, at least until Daisy is old enough to cope.'

'You're not suggesting that I stay with Chloe,' he said, incredulously.

'Yes, that is exactly what I'm suggesting,' she explained. 'Lead your separate lives, as you have for years, but do it under the same roof, for Daisy's sake.'

'But I don't want to! Please, Maggie . . .'

'You've nothing to lose by staying with Chloe,' she interrupted emotionally. 'Because it's over between us. It has to be. And if you stay with her, at least you'll have the pleasure of watching your daughter grow up in close proximity. One day Daisy will be old enough to understand these things, then you'll be free to do what you like. But not now. Not with me.'

Brittle in his anguish, he blurted out, 'I'm surprised that you haven't put up more of a fight against Chloe. She's won hands down.'

'No, she hasn't, not really,' opined Maggie. 'There can be no winners in a situation like this.' She rose to leave. 'Take care of yourself and of your daughter, as I shall of mine.'

'But when will I see you?' he asked.

'You won't, unless we happen to meet in passing,' she explained. 'And please, please don't contact me.'

'Maggie . . .'

'Don't make this any more difficult for me than it is already,' she implored, her voice shaking. She went to him and kissed him on the lips. 'Goodbye, Bradley, I'll always love you.'

And as he tried to clutch her to him she moved away, unable to speak.

Bradley stood by powerlessly as she walked to the door, small but dignified, her head held high, red hair streaming behind her. She didn't look at him as she turned to close the door, but hurried from the building. Knowing that further persistence would upset her, he moved to the window and watched her walk briskly across the yard to her smart Morris car. Unable to bear the pain of seeing her drive away for the last time, he turned back into the room, heartbroken.

Numbly, Maggie weaved through the London traffic, the May sunshine bathing the dusty streets and glinting on car bonnets and bumpers. Diverting from the main road to a short cut through a prestigious area with tree-lined avenues and grass verges, the scent of lilac blossom wafted powerfully through the window. She knew that she would never be able to smell that particular flower again without wanting to cry.

For the second time that day she pulled into the side of the road to check the copious flow of tears. 'This really isn't good enough, my girl,' she admonished herself determinedly. 'You've a daughter to raise and a business to run. You've a brother who's in trouble and a mother who needs you because of it. So go home and get on with your life, and stop blubbering about something that just isn't possible.'

But it was some time before she was able to compose herself sufficiently to continue her journey.

Situated in the heart of the Kent countryside a few miles from Tunbridge Wells, Bushleigh Lodge, the Hughes country house, was a beautiful old property standing in several acres of grassland, with stables, and gardens surrounding the house. Faced with limestone and cross-timbered beams the house had been completely modernised whilst retaining its original Kentish charm.

Sitting by the window of the oak-beamed sitting room two weeks later, Chloe stared across the verdant landscape, watching the rain and trying to make sense of her life. Now that her anger and jealousy had finally abated she was able to take a more rational view of the situation. And she didn't like what she saw. She had got her way, it was true. The affair between Maggie and Bradley was over and he was staying on in the marital home for Daisy's sake. But after an initial moment of satisfaction at having won the battle, his capitulation gave Chloe no pleasure. Only loneliness in the certain knowledge that she was hated by Bradley and by her closest woman friend.

The rain swept across the gardens and pattered on the windows. Drenched meadows stretched for as far as the eye could see, but the desolate landscape seemed in tune with her mood and cheered her somehow. She was glad she had come to Bushleigh for a few days on her own. The place always acted as a balm to her and she loved it. Finishing her coffee, she went upstairs and put on her jacket, jodhpurs and riding boots. With a brown riding mac over the top, she went across to the stables.

'Going out in this weather, are you, missus?' asked George Brown who had just finished mucking out.

'Yes, I need to get the London fumes out of my system,' she told him as she saddled up her black mare. He and his wife lived locally and looked after the place for them. George came in every day to see to the three horses, exercising them when Chloe was not around. He also took care of the grounds, whilst his wife looked after the house and cooked for the family when they were in residence. 'I'll see you later.'

'Righto, missus.'

The air smelled sweet as Chloe cantered across the wet countryside, the rain stinging her face and seeming to cleanse her and clear her mind. On horseback she was at her best. Chloe accepted the fact that she had no useful skills. She couldn't sew or type, or run a shop like Maggie. But she knew that she was an exceptional horsewoman and this made her feel confident and alive, as though she might have something to offer after all.

Turning her mind to her current dilemma, she remembered her holiday in America and how she had begun to view the prospect of a future without Bradley as an interesting challenge. She had even had some vague notion of opening a riding school here in Kent. So why had she allowed her humiliation to obliterate her plans for independence? She would make an excellent riding teacher. She and Daisy could move to Kent. Daisy could go to school in Tunbridge Wells. There would be no need for the child to be hurt if she and Bradley parted amicably. Perhaps she and Maggie could even be friends again.

The idea gained in credibility by the moment. Her heart raced excitedly and she broke into a gallop. She did not have to have a man in her life. Maggie had managed perfectly well without one for years. And so could she, if necessary. Better to stay single than be with a man she didn't love and who didn't love her. She'd make a completely fresh start. Her affair with Frankie had just about run its course anyway.

Now that she had made the decision she felt reborn. The end of her marriage to Bradley was going to be a new beginning for them all. She would go straight back to London today and tell Bradley and Maggie of her plans. Bradley could start divorce proceedings right away.

'I'm going to set us all free,' she cried jubilantly into the wind, urging the mare on. There was an indescribable intimacy between herself and the horse as they thundered across the rainy meadows. 'I'm free at last.'

At that moment the mare stumbled and rocketed Chloe to the ground with such force that she felt her bones crunch against the earth. The pain was excruciating until she lost consciousness.

'Daisy sends her love,' said Bradley, one day in June when he visited his wife in hospital. 'I'll bring her to see you at the weekend.'

'I'll look forward to that,' said Chloe, smiling weakly for she was still in a great deal of pain.

'And George sends his regards,' he said. 'I don't think he's over the shock yet of finding you unconscious like that.'

'Lucky for me that he did,' she said. 'Who knows how long I might have lain there if he hadn't taken one of the other horses out?'

'How is the pain now?' he asked.

'They are giving me something for it,' she told him.

'Good.'

A silence fell between them. They had run out of conversation years ago.

'The doctor was telling me that you'll be able to get about the house to a certain extent with just the aid of a stick by the time you come home,' said Bradley optimistically. 'So you won't have to be in a wheel-chair all the time.'

'Yippee,' said Chloe sarcastically.

'Medical science is improving all the time. Maybe they'll be able to do something more for you later on,' he suggested.

'My hip is smashed to smithereens, Bradley,' she reminded him. 'About all they can do for me is to ease the pain.'

'Yes, well, we'll all have to try to make life as easy and pleasant for you as we can, won't we?' he said patiently. 'And the doctor said the pain will get less eventually.'

Tears burned her eyes. So much for my plans for a wonderful new independent life, she thought bitterly. Just over a month ago I was all set to run my own riding school. Now I won't even be able to get through the day without help. Suddenly to find yourself dependent on others was a terrifying feeling. She felt so helpless, so very alone. Bradley was being wonderfully supportive but she dreaded the thought of his leaving her to face life alone with her disability in the future. She had to have someone to lean on. That was why she had told the nurse to

189

tell Maggie she wouldn't see her when her friend had telephoned the hospital. As much as she wanted to see her, she dared not put temptation in Bradley's way by letting Maggie back into their lives.

She reached for his hand. 'You won't leave me, will you, Bradley?'

He hesitated only for a moment. She had been in constant agony for over a month, and the doctors had told him that she would be in pain for a long time to come. Her hip was so badly damaged there was nothing they could do. She would not be able to walk properly again because one leg was now considerably shorter than the other. 'No, I won't leave you.'

Outside in the car after leaving the hospital, he picked up his newspaper and re-read the article which had haunted him all day. 'After a three-day trial, the judge sentenced Tom Brightwell to twenty-two years in prison after the jury found him guilty of the murder of Sheila Dawson last February.'

Bradley had suffered vicarious torture these last three days knowing what Maggie would have been going through. More than anything in the world he wanted to be with her, to help her through this terrible ordeal. But he owed it to her not to contact her, for that was what she had wanted.

He sighed as he began the drive home, his promise to Chloe weighing heavily on him. Chloe's fate was one he wouldn't wish on his worst enemy. He saw it as his bounden duty to stand by her.

Chapter Fourteen

'I want to talk to you both about my plans for expansion,' Maggie said to Archie and Sally one day in September 1958, having invited them into her office. 'Because they will mean changes for you both.'

'Changes? Ooh, blimey,' said Sally, who although much matured by her suffering over Tom's ordeal had managed to retain her cheerful manner.

'Opening another shop, are yer?' said Archie.

Nodding, Maggie leaned back in her chair with aplomb, her legs crossed elegantly at the knee. Having just returned from a business meeting with a London hotelier, she was smartly dressed in a sage-green suit which she wore with a cream blouse and matching shoes. Her make-up was modest and her hair worn in a smooth, shoulder-length bob. 'Yes. I've been in business on my own for four years and this shop has done well. Now it is time to expand and also get myself and Katy rehoused. I am going to open another shop and buy a house.'

'Coo,' said Sally.

Archie smoked a cigarette, eying her in quizzical silence.

Maggie had noticed a change in him over this last year or so. He was subdued, preoccupied. Sometimes he almost seemed to be engrossed in a world of his own. She could not bring herself to like the man, but since he was Jack's brother and he did know the flower trade inside out she was prepared to include him in her plans.

'I am offering you the job of manager of this shop, Archie, with accommodation in the flat above,' she said.

A look of surprised pleasure registered in his eyes, but since it was not his policy to seem pleased about anything with regard to his job, he just said, 'Oh, right.'

The offer of promotion she was about to make to Sally was born of affection and respect. Over the past year or so the girl had become almost one of the family. She visited Tom regularly in prison and spent more time at Dora's place than she did at home. Her whole life was planned around Tom's release when she intended to marry him despite opposition from her family, her friends, and even from Tom himself who was worried about her wasting her young years.

191

Turning to Sally, Maggie said, 'I am opening a shop in Ashbrook Grove which I would like you to run for me. There will be accommodation for you in the flat above. I know it has been difficult for you lately living at home, with your parents disapproving of your association with Tom. Perhaps you might consider yourself to be a little young to be in charge of your own shop but I have every confidence in you. You've a good all-round knowledge of the trade and I'll look after the books and take overall responsibility. I shall also employ the services of a professional buyer to go to market for both shops. I am hoping to buy a house just round the corner from there so I'll be on hand whenever you need me. I myself will concentrate on the administration, increasing the flow of business and so on.' She paused and looked from one to the other. 'So, what do you think?'

'Ooh, Maggie,' said Sally, breathless with excitement. 'That's reely t'rrific. I'll work hard and build an 'ome for me and Tom.'

Maggie smiled and turned to Archie. 'Well,' she asked. 'How about you?'

He waited a few moments before uttering a lazy, 'Yeah, you can count me in.'

'Good, I'm glad that's settled,' said Maggie. 'I must say, I'm looking forward to living off the job. It will be nice to have a garden and space for Katy to entertain her friends. I am having the top floor made into a self-contained flat for my mother, and I shall also have my office at home.'

'When is all this due to take place?' asked Archie.

'Within the next few months, I hope,' Maggie informed him.

'I can't wait to tell Tom,' said Sally, who constantly amazed Maggie with her ability to behave as though he was just an ordinary boyfriend she could see every day. 'I'll write to him tonight.'

Seeing further evidence of Sally's faith in an eventual future with Tom illuminated the hopelessness of Maggie's own situation. At twenty-seven years old she felt dead inside. All the job satisfaction in the world could not replace the vitality that been drained from her the day she had said goodbye to Bradley. Not a day passed when she didn't think of him.

He was on her mind later as she drove to Kensington on business. She wondered how things were between him and Chloe now. Perhaps her disablement had brought them closer together. Maggie's only link with the Hugheses was through Chloe's parents whom she still visited occasionally. But they never said very much about their daughter; presumably being tactful because of the rift between the one-time friends. That separation hurt Maggie more than she had expected. For all Chloe's faults, Maggie missed her dreadfully.

Finding herself in a traffic jam, she turned off the main road and proceeded on an alternative route through the backstreets. And suddenly
personal problems were forgotten as she found herself in the eerie aftermath of last night's race riots as workmen struggled to clear the Notting
Hill streets of broken glass and other debris. Petrol bombs and milk
bottles had been thrown at the police, according to the morning news,
when trouble had flared between the white and black communities of the
area. She proceeded cautiously on her way, fearful for her tyres on the
splinters of glass still littering the area.

Surrounded by the after effects of crime, Maggie was reminded of her
brother's close association with the law, and fury welled up inside her at
the terrible injustice he was suffering. How he was able to accept such an
appalling fate so calmly was beyond her. But accept it he had after the
appeal had been unsuccessful, and he now seemed to be concentrating on
making the best of things and aiming for remission which would shorten
his sentence considerably.

Somewhere there was someone who knew that Tom was innocent.
Somewhere a murderer walked the streets a free man. Who was he?
Where was he? These were the questions that haunted her as she left the
stricken area.

Archie finished the fish and chips he had bought for his supper, screwed
the newspaper into a ball and poured himself another cup of tea. Taking
his wallet from the pocket of his jacket draped over the back of the chair,
he removed from it the possession he valued most in the world: the photograph of himself and Sheila taken on that wonderful New Year they had
spent together.

'Well, what do you think o' that, eh, Sheila?' he said, staring at her face
in the photograph. 'High and mighty Maggie is givin' me me own shop to
run.' He put the photograph to his lips, breathing deeply, his eyes filling
with tears. 'I wish you were here to share it with me.' His eyes became
glazed. 'If you hadn't wound me up by goin' back with yer boyfriend, the
accident would never 'ave happened and you'd still be 'ere today.'

He stared deeply into the photograph, smiling as he relived the night it
had been taken. He closed his eyes to make the images sharper. Sheila
would never be dead while he had the photograph to bring her closer to
him.

For the remainder of the year Maggie had little time to ponder on personal problems. Simultaneously with the arrangements for business
expansion and house purchase, she received her most prestigious commission yet: the floral displays for the motor show at Earls Court. A
feather in her cap indeed.

'We'll be doin' the flowers at the Albert Hall for the Proms before long,' laughed Sally, because it was common knowledge that Maggie wanted that prize commission.

'Maybe,' she said lightly.

Just before Christmas Maggie moved into her new house and opened her shop in Ashbrook Green. Situated within easy reach of both shops, her new abode was a large mature house of traditional design with spacious rooms, high ceilings and deep bay windows. Maggie had it converted into two self-contained flats with an office incorporated into hers, and Mother comfortably accommodated upstairs. It was an arrangement of personal and practical benefit, since both she and Mother retained their independence whilst having company on hand if required. And Katy simply adored having her grandmother around. Maggie felt happier with her mother under her roof for she knew Dora had been devastated by Tom's sentence, even if her way of coping was to keep cheerful and carry on as normal.

So as 1958 rolled into 1959 and youngsters twirled their hips to the hoola-hoop craze, housewives clamoured for possession of Formica worktops, and homegrown pop singer Cliff Richard vied for popularity with America's Elvis Presley, three generations of Brightwell women and one elderly cat began life together in their new home.

And when they drank a toast to absent friends around midnight on New Year's Eve, Dora suspected that the tears in her daughter's eyes could not be ascribed solely to the absence of Jack and Tom. Dora had not approved of Maggie's 'carry on' with Bradley, it was true. In Dora's day a woman thought twice about going on a day trip with a man she wasn't married to, let alone to blooming Spain! But she hated to see Maggie unhappy. Oh, yes, the world might see a self-sufficient businesswoman, but a mother's eye was more discerning. Being a widow of long standing herself, Dora knew only too well that there was no substitute for that someone special in your life. The fact that Maggie's someone was married to another would not alter that.

Bradley's New Year toast was a glass of whisky which he drank alone in the sitting room of his Hampstead home in front of the television set. Both his wife and daughter were in bed. Thank goodness for tomorrow when the festivities would finally be over and he could escape to the office, away from his travesty of a marriage!

He and Chloe played their parts well. He was the dutiful husband, she the tragic wife. Chloe was not completely bound to a wheelchair. She could manage to get around the house with the aid of a stick, but the effort required to walk with such an ungainly limp exhausted her and prevented her from venturing much further than the terrace. Bradley did what he could to make her life easier. He pushed her in her chair, took her out in the car and tried to make sure she was not too much alone, employing a resident companion to allow him to attend to his business. But although he did all this with compassion, he could not love her any more than she could love him. So they lived a curious life, together but so far apart.

Now, as the chimes of Big Ben from the television set died away, he glanced around the room, newly decorated and furnished in contemporary style to Chloe's taste. Two plain white walls contrasted dramatically with two boldly patterned blue ones; angular sofas and chairs in royal blue stood on a white carpet. There were glass-topped occasional tables and tall skinny standard lamps. It was very stylish but too cold and clinical for his taste. He preferred the cosy ambience of the drawing room with its large soft chairs and warm red carpet. Still, far be it for him to oppose Chloe's slavish dedication to fashion if it made her happy. She didn't have too much else going for her these days.

He rose and drank a toast to Maggie, silently sending his wishes for all things good for her in the New Year. Guiltily he then made a wish for better things for his wife in 1959 too, and went to bed, relieved to have reached the end of this poignant season for another year.

Damn this time of the year, Chloe fumed as she lay in bed staring at the patterns on the ceiling. Christmas and New Year was for lovers, for people who cared for each other. It had no place in the life of a misfit like her, a married woman with the heart of a single one.

She thought of the New Year parties of the past when she'd danced until three and fallen into bed dizzy with champagne. Now all she had to look forward to was watching Bradley pretend he stayed with her because he wanted to.

Switching on her bedside lamp, she heaved herself up, reaching for a chocolate from the box on the bedside table. This was what she was reduced to, turning to food for comfort. She wondered how Maggie had spent the New Year and felt a stab of pain. 'Happy New Year, Maggie,' she said miserably. 'I've missed you.'

The New Year proved to be very prosperous for Maggie. Her second shop was such a success she had opened another at Hammersmith by the end of 1959. She could now afford to dress well and furnish her home tastefully. She also became one of the first London owners of a Mini.

'It's so close to the ground, it feels like a bloomin' dodgem car,' Dora complained good-humouredly as they ran alongside a double-decker bus during her first ride in it. 'Gawd almighty, we'll be squashed to death in a minute!'

'It only feels like that because you're not used to it,' Maggie laughed. 'I think it's a terrific little car, and here to stay. Trendy, too. They say it's popular with some of the stars.'

As Maggie's Midas touch in business became increasingly apparent, so did her generosity towards her family and staff. The latter were rewarded with regular bonuses. Nowadays, Dora looked after the domestic side of Maggie's household lock, stock and barrel, as well as helping out at either of the shops if necessary. Between Maggie and her mother, Katy never came from school to an empty house.

In return for Dora's valued assistance, Maggie made sure she always had plenty of money in her pocket. The salary paid to her far exceeded the normal rates for similar work, and whilst Maggie would willingly have supported her without Dora making any contribution, this way her mother felt beholden to no one.

Business was good, family relations were excellent. The only lump in the custard was Tom's wrongful imprisonment which enraged Maggie almost to apoplexy every so often and sent her scurrying to the lawyer's office to command him to 'do something'.

It was to this end that one morning in February 1960, she found herself in the reception area of the offices of Slade & Brown. 'I do have an appointment with Mr Royston Slade,' Maggie reminded a young receptionist, having waited almost an hour.

'Yes, I know, and I'm sorry you've been kept waiting, Mrs Radford,' said the girl politely. 'I'm afraid he has been delayed.'

'Can I see the other partner then?' asked Maggie sharply. 'I simply do not have time to sit around here all day.'

'I'm afraid he is fully booked all morning,' apologised the girl, flushing slightly.

'Oh, really,' huffed Maggie, who being scrupulously punctual herself was intolerant of its absence in others. 'How long is it likely to be until Mr Royston Slade decides to put in an appearance?'

The girl bit her lip anxiously. 'I'm not sure,' she said.

'Do you mean to say he hasn't even bothered to call in to let you know?' exploded Maggie.

'Well . . . er . . . no, he hasn't actually.' The girl looked embarrassed and stared at her typewriter as though hoping to draw inspiration from the keys. She raised her eyes to Maggie more boldly. 'I'm sorry, but it really isn't my fault. Perhaps you could come back another time?'

'I could,' snorted Maggie, 'but I'm damned if I will. What are you running here? A punch and judy show or a business. I am a client, you know.'

Perking up considerably, the girl retaliated: 'Mr Slade isn't normally late for his appointments. Something must have happened that is beyond

196

his control.' She studied her painted fingernails. 'Anyway, I'm not personally responsible for his movements. I only work here.'

'Yes, yes, of course you do,' said Maggie, rising to leave. 'But if this is the way Slade and Brown conduct their professional appointments, I think I shall have to find another firm of lawyers to look after my affairs. Kindly tell Mr Slade, when he does pay you the courtesy of gracing the office with his presence, that I shall take my custom elsewhere.'

And she marched from the room, leaving a trail of fire behind her.

'What a way to treat a client,' she fumed to her mother over lunch which they were enjoying together in the dining alcove of Maggie's sunny kitchen overlooking the mature gardens. 'That's no way to do business! No wonder Tom is still in prison while a murderer roams free.'

'Now be fair, Maggie,' admonished Dora whose sense of justice had remained surprisingly unimpaired by the appalling lack of it shown towards her son. 'Mr Slade did everything he could. It isn't his fault the evidence again Tom is so strong. He probably has a very good reason for letting you down this morning.' She helped herself to another portion of stew and dumplings. 'Now eat your lunch before it gets cold.'

Dora's leniency towards Royston Slade for his failure to keep the appointment reminded Maggie of her own solitary position as head of the company. Mother was a gem in the house and an asset in the shop. She was a loving parent and a dear friend. But she was totally lacking as any sort of business adviser because she could never see beyond the human element in anything.

Maggie's own tougher edge didn't mean that she now only saw people as mere cogs in a commercial machine, but assuming sole responsibility for a growing business empire required a firm hand. Bradley would have understood for he also sat in the entrepreneurial hot seat. How she missed his moral support!

'These dumplings are just the thing for this cold weather,' Dora was saying. 'Now eat up, Maggie, and forget all about Mr Slade until after lunch.' After a brief silence she changed the subject. 'Isn't it good news about Princess Margaret's engagement to that Armstrong Jones fella?'

'Yes indeed,' said Maggie.

'He's a photographer, apparently, a nice-looking chap too,' continued Dora chattily. 'I hope she'll be happy. I reckon it broke her heart when they wouldn't let her marry Captain Townsend. Must be rotten to have yer love life interfered with like that. I enjoy a good royal wedding. I hope it'll be on the telly . . .'

Mellowed by good food and the gentle warmth of her mother's company, Maggie decided to forget all about the inconvenience of the morning and look for another suitable firm of solicitors that afternoon.

It was in a more genial mood that she answered the doorbell half an hour later while she and Dora were having coffee.

'Mrs Radford,' said Royston Slade, his warm brown eyes resting on her anxiously.

'Well! You've got a nerve,' she began.

'I really am terribly sorry about this morning,' he said quickly, pushing his untidy hair back from his brow.

'So am I,' she said firmly, but her annoyance was lessened by the fact that he had taken the trouble to pursue her personally rather than just using the telephone. 'Since you're here, you'd better come in.'

They went into Maggie's living room which was comfortably appointed in creams and soft shades of peach with tan-coloured sofas and armchairs. 'The least I can do is explain what happened,' he said.

Maggie waited with interest.

'I was about to leave home for the office, having driven my son to school earlier,' he began, parking his long spindly form in a chair, 'when I got a telephone call from the school informing me that he'd been taken to hospital after taking a tumble in the playground.' He ran a hand over his worried brow. 'As it happened he'd sustained nothing more serious than a sprained ankle, but I didn't realise that at that time. I dropped everything and rushed to the hospital. The casualty department was frantically busy, and in all the confusion I didn't get around to calling the office to explain what had happened until after you'd gone. Er . . .' he gave a wry grin ' . . . not in good humour, I understand.'

Flushing a little, Maggie said, 'Well, perhaps I was a bit hasty. Had I realised the circumstances I'd have been more patient. You know how it is in business? Time is of the essence.'

'Quite so,' agreed Royston, who was expensively but untidily dressed in a grey business suit. His tie was crooked, and his shirt had parted from his trousers in one place at the waist. 'I am a stickler for punctuality as a rule.'

Dora, who had offered him refreshment immediately he came through the door, handed him some coffee which was gratefully received. 'Thank you so much. It's been such a hectic morning, I feel parched,' he said.

He gave the impression of being permanently fraught. Over coffee he explained that he was a widower and his son was twelve rising thirteen. 'I ought to pack him off to boarding school, of course,' he explained, nibbling hungrily on a biscuit, since apparently he had not yet got around to lunch. 'At least then I'd be able to conduct my professional life without the inevitable interruptions of single parenthood. If he was away at school I'd only have the major holidays to contend with.

'I'm soft, I know, but I can't bring myself to send him away. My own abysmal days at boarding school are still too vivid in my mind, that's the

198

trouble. All good character-building stuff, no doubt, but it doesn't suit everyone.'

'Hear, hear,' agreed Dora, to whom the very idea of subjecting a child to the strictures of boarding-school life was criminal.

Royston threw her a grateful smile. 'I daresay there are those who disagree with us.' He sipped his coffee before continuing. 'Having him at day-school does have its problems though.' He paused. 'Still, I enjoy having him around. He'll be off on his own soon enough. He's a good lad.' He produced a photograph of the boy from his pocket and handed it proudly to Dora. 'We have a lady to keep house for us, and she helps me out if Tim is sick or anything, but she doesn't live in. I couldn't bear the idea of another woman living in the house after my wife died.'

'I can understand that,' said Maggie, suddenly liking and trusting him. Previous meetings with him had been strictly formal, and she had never really seen him as a person before. He was terribly nice and had the air of someone who would have sleepless nights if he failed to return library books on time.

'Of course, I don't normally miss appointments because of him,' he explained. 'This morning's fiasco was not the norm, I promise you.'

His frankness led Maggie to mention her own similar circumstances. 'I'm lucky though because I have Mum to help me,' she said, smiling towards Dora. 'I don't know what I'd do without her. Do you not have a relative who could help out?'

Shaking his head, he explained, 'My parents live abroad and my late wife's parents disagree with my not sending him away to school so will not co-operate at all.' He finished his coffee and set the cup down on a polished wood table nearby. 'Still, I didn't come here to talk about my problems, but to apologise and to try to persuade you to give me another chance.'

Maggie tensed as her business with him flooded back into her mind. 'You're forgiven,' she said, 'but I need an appointment as soon as possible.' She paused for a moment. 'Like this afternoon.'

He made a face. 'Oh, dear. This is going to sound really unprofessional, I know, but I have to take this afternoon off to be with Tim, as he's been in the wars. My housekeeper is away for the day or I'd ask her.'

'Where is he now?' asked Maggie, puzzled.

'Waiting for me outside in the car,' explained Royston.

Dora shot to her feet. 'Why, he'll freeze to death out there,' she exclaimed disapprovingly.

'I knew I wouldn't be more than a few minutes,' said Royston defensively. 'He's all right. He's well wrapped up. I wasn't sure if you'd approve of my bringing a child in with me as it's a professional call.'

But Dora was already hurrying up the front path, and appeared a few moments later accompanying a fresh-faced youth with sherry-coloured eyes and a most engaging smile.

'Well, you'd both better take your coats off and make yourself at home,' she said authoritatively. 'There's plenty of stew in the pot. I always make far too much for us.'

'We wouldn't dream of imposing,' said Royston courteously.

'Stew and dumplings, Dad,' said Tim wistfully. 'I'm starving.'

'Well, I . . .'

'No arguments,' said Dora with good-humoured bossiness. 'And when you've finished yer lunch, Mr Slade, you can have a chat with Maggie while Tim comes upstairs with me. That'll save the bother of an office appointment.'

And since it was the perfect solution, she received no opposition.

Unfortunately Royston didn't have much hope to offer to Maggie. 'In the absence of any new evidence there is nothing more we can do for your brother at the moment,' he told her sadly. 'All we can do is to hope he gets full remission which will reduce his sentence by a third.'

'But it's so damned unfair,' she said emotionally. 'When I think that the real murderer is still walking the streets, it makes my blood boil.'

He nodded sympathetically. 'I know, Mrs Radford. But the truth will come out one of these days, I'm sure of it.'

'And in the meantime my brother is wasting his life in prison,' she sighed.

'Bear up, Mrs Radford,' he said gently.

Seeing the warmth in his eyes she realised that he really did care and was not just some unfeeling professional going through the motions. 'I'll try,' she said, and managing a smile, added, 'Do call me Maggie.'

'Certainly, and I'd be much happier if you'd call me Royston.'

When Katy arrived home from school she was greeted by the welcoming scent of Gran's home-made scones. Lovely, she thought, savouring the thought of scones eaten while they were still warm. Mother appeared on the landing. 'Up here, love. We're joining Gran for tea,' she said.

'Goodee,' said Katy, unbuttoning her dark blue gaberdine school raincoat as she hurried upstairs, her cheeks glowing from the cold. She was startled by the sudden appearance of a stranger on his way from the bathroom to the living room. A boy with brown curly hair, smiling eyes and a limp.

'Hello,' he said brightly. 'You must be Katy. There are lots of photographs of you around.'

'Yes, that's right, but who are you?'

'Timothy Slade,' he informed her cheerfully. 'My father is your family lawyer.'

'Oh, I see.' She stared at his foot which was bandaged and clad in a slipper. 'What have you done?'

'Sprained my ankle mucking about in the playground,' he explained, thinking how pretty she was with her auburn hair and sparkling blue eyes.

'Typical of a boy,' said Katy in disdain. 'You always have to be too rough.'

'I expect you're right,' he laughed.

He was rather nice, and good-looking too, she thought. 'Are you staying to tea?'

'Fortunately, yes,' he said exuberantly. 'I can't wait to get at your gran's scones. They look delicious.'

'We'd better get in there then, while there are still some left.' She moved back courteously. 'After you.'

'Ladies first,' he said, ushering her into the room ahead of him.

And well behaved too, for a boy, thought Katy, smiling shyly at him as they joined the others.

That day marked the beginning of a new friendship for both Maggie and her daughter. As Maggie got to know Royston better she found him to be one of the kindest people she had ever met.

Royston slipped into the gap left by Bradley as Maggie's business mentor. And on a personal level they found it useful to pool their resources in their mutual plight as single parents by arranging outings together with the children. They shared many enjoyable family meals, and Dora became a kind of unofficial granny to Tim.

He didn't always wait for his father to visit Maggie before he himself called on Katy, and frequently caught the bus from his home in Hammersmith to Ashbrook Grove. His three-year seniority bestowed on him a certain charisma in Katy's eyes and she thought of him as something between an elder brother and a romantic hero. He was charmed by her high spirits and prettiness, and their circumstances led him to see her as a substitute sister. He was very protective towards her.

Sometimes, if their school holidays differed by a few days, he would meet her from school and they would walk home together for tea. Katy swelled with pride as her credibility with her peers soared, for he was that awesome of creatures, an older boy. It was all very innocent.

Maggie too valued her new friendship. She and Royston discussed romance, neither minding the lack of it between themselves. Whilst Royston had no plans to remarry, he occasionally dipped a tentative toe into less platonic waters than those that flowed between he and Maggie.

But he never seemed to get past the initial stages. There was always some disaster, mainly due to the fact that he tried to be a perfectionist both as a father and a lawyer, leaving little energy for the niceties of courtship. He was prone to such embarrassing mishaps as arriving somewhere with a carelessly unfastened zip or wearing odd shoes, or arriving late and leaving early because of Tim.

Whereas Maggie, as his friend, found these qualities endearing, she could see that they would be extremely irritating to someone seeking a more fulfilling relationship.

'Romance is such a complicated business,' Royston confided to her one day. 'If only it was as easy and enjoyable as our relationship.'

If only life were that simple, Maggie thought, reflecting on the contrariness of nature in this instance. She and Royston had all the ingredients to make a go of it as a couple. They were both single, they liked each other enormously and the children got along well. But fate had not seen fit to bless their relationship with that ineffable magic which would make them anything more than pals. Instead, it had directed her special chemistry towards a man who was not in a position to do anything about it.

Chapter Fifteen

'Katy is trying to pressurise me into letting her go with her friends to a pop concert at the Astoria Finsbury Park. It's at the end of December,' Maggie confided to Royston one day in late November 1963 when they were lunching together at a little place in Ashbrook Grove. 'It's this new group all the kids are raving about, the Worms or Slugs or something.'

'You mean the Beatles,' Royston corrected.

'They're the ones,' she said. 'It's their Christmas show apparently, and it's to be a mixture of concert performance and pantomime.'

'Yes, Tim mentioned it. He intends to go with them, I believe,' said Royston.

Maggie nodded. 'I think Katy has roped him in because she thinks I'll more inclined to let her go if he's there, him being a responsible sixteen year old. She's only thirteen, remember? It seems very young for her to go out in the evening without an adult, don't you think?'

'Normally, yes, but as long as she is taken to the show and collected afterwards, she'll be all right,' he opined. 'And Tim is a sensible lad. He'll see to it that she comes to no harm.'

Reassured by his confidence, she relaxed. 'Yes, I'm sure you're right.' She grinned ruefully. 'How quickly she's growing up. The suggestion that I go with her was greeted with horror.'

'I can imagine,' laughed Royston companionably. 'Parents are not top of the social league at that age. Tim's just the same.'

'I'll be the most popular mum in London this evening though,' smiled Maggie, 'when I tell her that she can go.'

'Why don't we make a joint effort of it?' suggested Royston pleasantly, spooning some sugar into his coffee. 'We could drive them to the show together and have a meal out somewhere until it's time to collect them.'

'Good idea,' she agreed.

Lingering on the subject of their respective offspring for a while longer, he asked, 'Does Katy still want to come into the business with you when she leaves school?'

'She seems to,' said Maggie. 'But I shall make sure she considers all the other options first. How about Tim? Is he still keen on going in for law?'

'Yes, despite all my warnings about the long hard years of study.'

'You're pleased really, though.'

'Oh, yes, I'm proud to have him come into the profession.'

'I'm sure he'll do well. He's a bright lad.' Maggie had become very fond of Tim. As gentle and clever as his father, he was a pleasure to have around.

'I think so too,' said Royston, beaming with paternal pride.

Changing the subject, she asked, 'What do you think about my opening a shop in Knightsbridge next year?'

'The unstoppable Maggie Radford strikes again with shop number six, eh!'

She grinned, for in addition to her other shops there was now a Maggie's in Chiswick and Shepherd's Bush. Now she was ready to move into the heart of central London. 'That's right. I'd value your opinion.'

'Bearing in mind the success you are having with all the other shops,' he said, 'I should think that a Knightsbridge branch would be an excellent idea.'

'They're certainly having their fair share of drama in your homeland,' said Rupert Anderson to his son-in-law a few days later whilst entertaining his daughter's family to dinner at Richmond.

'You mean the murder of Lee Harvey Oswald, the man charged with President Kennedy's assassination?' said Bradley. 'Yeah, that sure was dramatic. The guy just stepped from the crowd and shot him as he was being transferred to the County Gaol. Millions of people watched it on TV.'

'Everyone was talking about it at school,' piped up Daisy, attractively dressed in a pale blue angora dress which matched her eyes. 'I think it's scary.'

'It won't be a happy Christmas for the Kennedys this year,' said Lavinia, immaculate but staid in a maroon jersey dress.

'Can we change the subject, please?' demanded Chloe, looking striking in a scarlet woollen dress, her dark hair drawn back and fastened with a red clip. She had put on a little weight these last few years, but she was still very attractive. 'The whole thing gives me the shivers.'

'Yes, let's talk about something else,' agreed Lavinia, ever in pursuit of a quiet life.

'What do you think about your grand-daughter's latest fad?' asked Chloe, looking from her father to her mother. 'She wants to go to some dreadful pop concert with some friends, would you believe?'

'Ummm, she was saying something about it before dinner,' said Rupert thoughtfully. 'I can't see any real harm in it, as long as she's taken there and brought home by an adult.'

'She's thirteen years old, for God's sake,' Chloe reminded him sharply. She needed her parents' support in this matter because she certainly did not have her husband's. The wretched man still persisted in encouraging their daughter in the most unsuitable activities. Chloe's disability caused her to make an even firmer stand on family issues for fear she might lose control altogether. 'And that is far too young for her to be out at night without her parents.'

'But it isn't as if she'd be roaming the streets or anything,' said Rupert, who found it even harder to refuse his grand-daughter than he had her mother at that age.

Chloe's expression hardened. 'I can see that Bradley and Katy have been working on you to get you on their side,' she snapped, 'leaving me to be the villain of the piece. God knows what rough types will be there. There will probably be all sorts of violence. We don't pay for Daisy's education just to have her mixing with the hoi-polloi.' She looked to her mother for support.

'She does have a point, you know, Bradley,' said Lavinia, whose slavish acquiescence to her daughter by far outweighed her fondness for Daisy. 'Goodness knows what sort of goings on there will be. It will be full of working-class youngsters, and you know how uninhibited they can be.'

Bradley laughed. 'You English and your class system,' he drawled. 'From what I can make out, kids from all walks of life are crazy about the Beatles.'

Throwing her daughter a meaningful look, Chloe said, 'If you've finished your meal, Daisy, you run along to the other room while we discuss the matter.'

The girl slipped from her chair. 'All my friends are being allowed to go,' she said as a parting shot. 'I'll be the only one left out. We're not living in the Dark Ages now, you know.'

As soon as she was out of earshot, Chloe turned on Bradley. 'Of course *you* just want to gain popularity with her,' she hissed. 'And let me be the ogre, yet again.'

In all other areas of the domestic front Bradley conceded to Chloe's wishes because it was simpler that way. They ate food to her taste, and had her style of decor everywhere but the drawing room. But when it came to Daisy, that was a different matter. For he was not prepared to sit back and watch Chloe mould his daughter into a replica of herself. It was all too easy to give in to his wife on every issue now, out of sympathy. But he felt he owed it to his daughter to stand firm where she was concerned.

'That isn't true,' he denied. 'I do not want her to grow up in a sanitised vacuum, that's all. It is good for her to mix with youngsters of

205

all types, not just those selected for her by her privileged circumstances. I honestly cannot see anything wrong in allowing her to do what all the other teenagers are doing.'

'Oh, let her go,' spat Chloe, an angry flush suffusing her cheeks. She was furious with him for goading her into losing her temper in front of her parents. 'And on your head be it if she comes to any harm.'

'She won't,' he stated categorically, 'because I shall deliver her and collect her myself.'

Chloe fell silent for a few moments. 'If you'll excuse me, I'd like to go into the lounge with my coffee,' she said. 'I can't sit at the table for too long, as you know.'

'Here, let me help you,' he said, instantly at her side.

'Thank you, dear,' said Chloe, smiling at him for the benefit of her parents.

Lavinia and Rupert exchanged glances as the couple left the room, a picture of married bliss with Chloe leaning heavily on her husband's arm. But her parents were not taken in that easily. And neither was Daisy, they suspected.

The atmosphere in the cinema was electric. Katy had never experienced anything like this before. Excitement crackled through the auditorium as fiercely as fire throughout the first half of the show, which consisted of relatively unknown groups. And then, to a tumultuous welcome, John, Paul, George and Ringo appeared on stage, smartly dressed in grey Beatles jackets, their group name written on the drums. Girls screamed; some fainted; others tried to climb on the seats or stood in the gangways doing the Twist. Katy wept with joy. Nothing she had seen on television matched this live performance. She felt personally involved with the proceedings, as though the musicians were performing for her alone. Mesmerised by the spectacle, she was unaware of the fact that Daisy Hughes, equally enraptured, was sitting just a few rows away.

Maggie and Royston were back at the cinema half an hour before the show was due to end. Over-cautious maybe, but they were not alone in this. There was already a large gathering outside; many were parents, others were fans hoping for a glimpse of their idols. A party atmosphere rippled through the crowds and British reserve was swept away by mutual interest in the events inside the building. Strangers chatted and couples hugged each other against the cold.

'If the excitement out here is anything to go by, what must it be like inside?' said Royston.

'Perhaps we shouldn't have let them come,' Maggie said anxiously.

'Nonsense! They'll be having a whale of a time.'

It was a clear, bitter night. The neon lights spread a pale glow over the frosty pavements and frozen puddles. Maggie was wearing an emerald green, belted coat and long tan boots. She pulled her collar up over her ears, shivering and stamping her feet.

'We should have stayed in the restaurant a bit longer,' she said, her breath turning to steam in the freezing air. 'We could have had another coffee instead of standing about in the cold.'

'Both of us were too much on edge for that,' he laughed.

'Yes, how fussy we are,' she said, grinning up at him. 'That's what parenthood does for you.'

He bent his head towards her and they laughed together with all the affection of old friends. A breathless hush descended on the crowd as movement by the police towards the doors of the foyer indicated the end of the show.

'Looks like they're coming out now,' said Royston.

And suddenly teenagers poured through the doors in an exuberant chattering stream: dreamy eyed, laughing, tearful. Maggie and Royston kept their eyes on the crowd, fearful they might miss their offspring in the crush.

'There they are,' said Royston, waving his arms madly towards the doors.

Katy and Tim were together among a crowd of their contemporaries who were rapidly dispersing into the custody of waiting parents. Katy was ecstatic. 'Oh, Mum, they were really groovy. Weren't they, Tim?' she said, breathless with admiration.

'It was a great show,' he agreed, a shade less effusively for he was not given to extravagant displays of feeling. 'I think the Beatles will probably be around for a while.'

'Come on, let's go home,' said Royston, putting a friendly arm around Maggie and ushering her out of the crowd. On their way to Royston's car, which was parked in a side street, they could see a heaving mass of people blocking the stage door.

'The group won't be able to get through,' said Katy with concern.

'Don't you believe it,' said Tim.

And as they watched, the solid swarm of people was diffused by the jets of fire hoses aimed on them by the hand of authority.

'Goodness,' said Katy, wide-eyed.

'Wow,' said Tim.

'Come on, troops,' said Royston, gathering his party together to cross the road.

And as Maggie hurried across with his protective hand on her arm, she had no idea that Bradley was just a few yards away, watching her.

* * *

207

Daisy filled the car with excited chatter all the way home. The Beatles were 'fab'; the show had been 'cool'. All that was required of Bradley was an occasional grunt now and then, for which he was truly grateful since he was still preoccupied with the devastating after effects of seeing Maggie again after all this time, and with another man too. Recognising her companion as Tom's lawyer, Bradley noticed that Maggie's association with him had progressed beyond the merely professional.

Why shouldn't she find happiness with someone else? he admonished himself. She was a free agent, after all. Had he really expected a woman with so much to offer to spend her life alone? In actual fact, he had never allowed himself to dwell on the matter because it was far too painful. But now he must try to be happy for her. Oh, but it was hard!

The shock of coming upon her so unexpectedly in the crowd had felt like a hammer blow to his chest. She had looked beautiful. Green was her colour, it contrasted wonderfully with that bright hair of hers.

Normally his daughter's youthful exuberance delighted him. Tonight it filled him with gloom. Daisy was growing up fast. Already she was beginning to have a life of her own. In a few years she would fly the nest altogether, leaving Chloe and him alone. What a ghastly thought! The future stretched miserably ahead for Bradley.

The winter of 1964, whilst not as severe as that of the previous year, seemed equally as cheerless to Maggie. In January she was forced into bed with influenza, but since many of her staff were similarly afflicted she was obliged to leave her sickbed long before she had properly recovered. Still feeling weak and feverish, she drove herself on, personally helping out throughout her network of shops rather than close any. Her burden was increased by Dora's also succumbing to flu which put her out of action for two weeks.

It was towards the end of this gloomy period that Maggie received the sad news, from a tearful Lavinia on the telephone, of Rupert Anderson's death after a short illness. Pneumonia had developed after flu. His heart hadn't been able to take it. Maggie sent flowers, but did not attend the funeral for fear of upsetting Chloe.

February was almost over by the time Maggie felt restored to health. And it was on a rainy day at this time that she travelled to a solicitor's office in Richmond, having had a letter asking her to contact them. They had been rather mysterious on the telephone, wishing to see her personally. Now, the solicitor came straight to the point.

'The late Rupert Anderson has left you a large sum of money,' said the pale, bespectacled man.

Puzzled, she said, 'I think there must be some mistake. I'm not entitled to any of Mr Anderson's money. Surely that should all go to his family?'

'Most of it has,' he explained, pushing his spectacles on to the bridge of his nose. 'This is something that the family knows nothing about. Mr Anderson made a separate arrangement with me about it shortly before his death. The amount is thirty thousand pounds.'

'What!' Maggie clutched her head in horror. 'Oh, my Lord, I can't accept that, it wouldn't be right. Please will you give it to his wife? I can't possibly keep it.'

Shaking his head, he said, 'It is my bounden duty to see that it goes to you. Mr Anderson was an extremely rich man, you know. The amount he wants you to have is a mere pittance compared to the fortune his family has inherited.'

'But I don't need it,' she protested. 'Maybe I'm not in the same league as the Andersons, but I am quite comfortably off.'

The man studied some papers on the desk in front of him for a few moments before picking up an envelope. 'Mr Anderson predicted this reaction from you,' he explained, his brown eyes surveying her impartially. 'And he left this letter for me to give to you personally.' He handed her the envelope. 'I know nothing of the contents, but perhaps it might help.' He rose. 'I'll leave you alone for a few minutes to read it. When I come back, we'll talk about the technical details of transferring the money from my client's fund into your bank account.'

'Thank you,' she said, dazed, and turned her attention to the letter.

Dear Maggie,
Knowing you to be a very independent young woman, I imagine that your reaction to discovering that I have left you some money will be one of horror. But please accept my gift in the spirit in which it is given, with deep affection and respect. I know that you are well off in your own right these days, but I'd like you to have something from me just the same.

I admire your success because it is something you have worked and struggled for, unlike myself who merely inherited a business and a fortune from my parents. I wanted to help you financially after your husband died, when I suspected that you really needed it, but I knew you would never take anything from me while I lived. Money is all I have to offer because my love for you only causes you pain.

Oh, yes, although I stopped bothering you, I did not stop loving you, ever. I am fortunate in that I have a wonderful wife who was a great comfort to me when I told her about my feelings for you many years ago. I love my wife and daughter dearly, and what I feel for you does not lessen that. They are reality, you are the dream. And what would life be without dreams?

209

I can say these things without compunction now because by the time you read this, I will not be able to hurt and embarrass you as I did all those years ago. A lesser woman might have taken advantage of my vulnerability at that time. I acted like a fool. You behaved impeccably and I thank you for it. My family know nothing about this bequest. I thought it would be easier for all of you this way. Please use the money in whichever way makes you happy.

Rupert

Maggie stumbled from the office through a blur of tears, telling the solicitor she would come back later to discuss details. Right now, she needed to be alone with her thoughts. In her haste she left her umbrella in the office, but barely noticed the driving rain beating on her face and soaking her red mackintosh as she walked through the small moist town in her leg-hugging white boots. Although it was still only mid afternoon the lit shops glowed in the crepuscular light. At the top of Richmond Hill she stopped awhile, absently observing the view, her hands plunged deep into her pockets, her wet hair hugging her scalp.

Leaden skies hung blackly over the bare trees on the verdant slopes curving down to the Thames, dark and misty on this dismal day. It was a sad, deserted scene but acutely beautiful with its luxuriant greenery and clear unspoiled contours. It was a landscape she had observed many times before when she had spent time in the area with Chloe. Now, in her highly charged emotional state, its late winter beauty increased her flow of tears. She walked on into Richmond Park, splashing though puddles and squelching in mud.

The fact that Rupert had harboured his feelings for her all these years had been a shock, for his old attraction towards her had been almost forgotten by Maggie. To her it had been one of those youthful traumas that are pushed to the back of the mind. And all these years Lavinia had known and had never given Maggie so much as a sharp word! As a seventeen-year-old girl she had not understood Rupert's lunatic obession with her. Now, as someone with an undying but fruitless love herself, she was imbued with sympathy for him.

Trudging on through the wooded grassland past a herd of deer under some trees, Maggie felt a sudden compulsion to visit Lavinia and confide in her about the events of this morning. Was it not her right to know? She had been a good and loyal wife to Rupert. Surely Maggie's inheritance morally belonged to her? But in her heart Maggie knew that Lavinia would be best left with her memories of Rupert unhampered by a reminder of a contender for his affections.

But what was she to do with the money? Her business was thriving though extra capital was always useful, especially with the opening of the

Knightsbridge shop later in the year. But did she want to use it for business? That was the question in her mind as emotion finally yielded to the enterprising side of her nature. The money had been forced on her and it was her duty to spend it wisely. By the time she got back to the solicitor's office, she was soaked through but she had made her decision.

'Speaking as your unofficial business adviser,' said Royston the next day, having been told of the way in which she planned to use the legacy, 'I feel bound to query the wisdom of your decision to give all the money away.'

'It may not be wise,' she told him, 'but it is what I want to do.'

Royston was a kind and generous man who cared about his friends. And here was one of them blithely intending to give thirty thousand pounds to charity. 'Why not give some to charity, put some into the business, and use the rest to have fun?'

'I don't need the money,' she stated categorically.

'Your business is doing well, I know,' he said, 'but you are expanding fast. And that must surely eat into your capital.'

'If I hadn't been given the money, I'd have managed,' she pointed out.

'Yes, quite so, but since you have been given it, it could be very useful to your business. Expansion doesn't come cheap, remember?'

'I lease all the shops except the first two,' she reminded him.

'Even so, the overheads on the Knightsbridge shop will be your highest yet,' he said, frowning. 'And it will take a while to recoup the setting-up expenses. If you were to put some of your windfall into the business, you could be really sitting pretty.'

'No, Royston, I have made up my mind,' she said resolutely.

'Well, as your friend I'd be failing in my duty if I didn't warn you of the folly of such an action.' His grave expression softened into a grin. 'But I know I don't stand a chance against that determined look in your eye. Go away, woman, and choose your charity before I burst into tears at the thought of all the things you could have done with the money.'

And she left, knowing that she would have his support whichever charity she chose to help.

'I'll come straight to the point,' said Maggie, a week later to a certain Reg Barrett who ran a shelter for the homeless in a derelict house in a rough area of Ashbrook Green. 'I read a piece about your campaign in the local paper and I'd like to know more about your work before I seriously consider making a donation.'

She glanced around his small office on the ground floor of the house with its damp walls, peeling paint and oil heater which battled unsuccessfully against the wet and windy elements of early March.

Reg Barrett, bearded, bespectacled and wearing a duffel coat, looked at her ruefully. 'Basically, the wife and I offer a bed and a meal to twenty-five people per night, and we turn double that number away. It's not much but it's better than nothing, and the place is due for demolition soon. The council only let us have it because it wasn't deemed fit for human habitation.'

'And you are trying to raise the cash to buy another suitable property, I understand?'

He handed her some tea in a chipped enamel mug, his hands encased in grey woollen mittens. 'That's right. A house, a hall, anything with a roof on it. Of course, in an ideal world, we would seek to have something purpose built. Nothing elaborate, just a place where we could cater for basic human needs: warmth, food, beds, showers.' He jerked back to reality. 'That, of course, is just the stuff of dreams.'

There was a tap at the door and an old woman appeared in the doorway, dressed in rags and exuding a foul stench.

'Hello, Vi,' said Reg, apparently unaffected by her miasma which had sent Maggie gasping gratefully into her handkerchief. 'How are you, luv?'

'Not so good, Reg,' said the woman in a bronchial wheeze, giving him a wry grin. 'I don't feel well enough to sleep outside ternight, mate, and yer wife says yer full up.'

Reg sighed. 'That's right. Not a bed to be had, I'm afraid.'

'Me chest is bad, Reg,' she informed him hoarsely. 'It don't 'arf catch me when I breathe.'

'You should see the doctor,' he said, raking his curly brown hair with his fingers.

'I don't want no bleedin' doctor! I just wanna bed for the night. I'm an old woman, I can't take the winters no more.'

He stroked his bushy beard meditatively, his mouth tense. 'Jesus, Vi, I can't make space where there is none.' He sighed and raised his eyes in resignation. 'Come back tonight for a meal and we'll see what we can do.'

Vi cackled happily. 'Ta, Reg, yer a real gent,' she said, and shuffled off leaving evidence of her visit permeating the very walls.

Maggie was greatly disturbed by the plight of the elderly woman. 'She shouldn't be living rough at her age,' she said. 'Has she no family to care for her?'

'Not that I know of,' he said succinctly.

'Surely there would be a place for her in a state home for the elderly?'

'Vi would sooner die,' he said ruefully. 'She's lived on the streets for so long, she doesn't want to conform to the restrictions of a more comfortable existence.'

'It hardly seems possible that this sort of thing still exists in this day and age, in a Welfare State,' exclaimed Maggie, shaking her head worriedly.

'Every society has its misfits,' Reg explained, cradling his mug in his mittened hands. 'These people opt out of the system for various reasons: bankruptcy, broken marriages and so on. Some of the youngsters leave home after a family quarrel then can't find accommodation. Living rough becomes a way of life to them and they can't, or won't, get back into society's mainstream. Many of them take to drink and drugs. Vi's been on the booze for years.' He frowned. 'We do what we can here with our limited resources. It's little enough, but even that will go unless we get a good response to our appeal.'

'Who pays the running costs of the shelter?' she asked.

'We are funded by donations,' he informed her.

'I see, and does that support you and your wife?'

'Good Lord, no,' he declared. 'We both have part-time jobs. The fund isn't such that we can dip into it for our daily bread.'

'Do you live here?'

'No, we've a bedsitter round the corner to give us a break from the place. We have several volunteers working with us on this project and we take it in turns with them to stay here at night so that there is always someone on duty.'

'You certainly have a busy life,' said Maggie. 'You must get very tired.'

'Spare time isn't something we have much of,' he admitted. 'But we choose to do this. I don't get tired so much as despondent.' He finished his tea and rose. 'Let me show you around and you'll see why.'

The tour of inspection revealed a ruin of a property, clean but barely habitable. The four bedrooms upstairs had rudimentary beds crowded into them with stained mattresses and rough blankets; the walls were black with mildew, and water dripped into buckets placed under various holes in the roof. The sanitary facilities consisted of a cracked, stained bath and decrepit toilet.

On the ground floor there was a room vaguely resembling a kitchen with an ancient gas stove, a leaking sink and a wooden table; a canteen furnished with wooden trestle tables; and a shabbily furnished rest room. The whole house had bare floorboards and the smell of disinfectant mingled with the more oppressive odours of dampness, urine and dirty clothes. A few tramps and hollow-eyed youths were sitting in the rest room.

'You stay open during the day then,' observed Maggie. 'You don't restrict your opening hours to the evening and night.'

'We try to man the place during the day,' he explained. 'But it isn't easy because we all do other jobs.'

213

Having made a few enquiries as to Reg's character beforehand, and now having met the man, Maggie was confident about her decision. Back in the office, she wrote out a cheque. 'This should boost your fund,' she said, handing it to him. 'It might even allow you to have something purpose-built. That will be for you to decide.'

'Wow!' he gasped as he read the amount. 'Am I dreaming or are you real?'

'I'm real, all right,' she laughed, glowing with benevolence.

'How can we ever thank you?'

'You have nothing to thank me for,' she said, and left without elucidating.

Walking to her car in the blustery rain, she said, 'I do hope you approve, Rupert.'

In May 1964 Maggie's yellow chrysanthemum trademark appeared on the window of a shop in genteel Knightsbridge.

This was her most ambitious venture yet, for the overheads were enormous, but she expected it to be her most lucrative. The shop was fashioned in the same slick style as the other branches: a modern glassy shopfront with gold lettering, and a smart interior in yellow and white. It was to be managed by a good-looking, well-spoken young couple.

Although Maggie employed the services of a buyer to purchase stock for all branches, she still attended Covent Garden Market occasionally herself for two reasons. Firstly because she didn't want to lose touch with the grass roots of her business. And secondly because she loved the atmosphere of the place. That first visit with Jack had left her enslaved to the chaos, the noise, the whole darned muddle. Soon the market was to move to a more suitable site. Whilst Maggie could see the necessity for this since the congestion in and around the streets between the Strand and Holborn during market hours had long since been a thorn in the side of market traders and the general public alike, she would be sad to see it go for the magic that had grown up over three hundred years would not be transferable, in her opinion.

Katy was already showing a real talent for floristry and was always eager to help during weekends and school holidays. But Maggie was keen to broaden her vision.

'Get some academic qualifications, my girl,' she advised her one Saturday morning just before the opening of the new shop, when Katy was helping her mother with a few last-minute jobs. 'Then see if you still want to come into the business with me. And don't be too anxious to grow up either, that will happen soon enough.' She gave her daughter a sharp look. 'What's happened to your hair, incidentally? You look top heavy with it sticking up like that.'

214

'Mu-um,' admonished Katy, 'it's backcombed. It's all the fashion.'

'It won't do the condition of your hair any good,' Maggie pointed out with the sort of maternal wisdom guaranteed to provoke a scornful reaction.

'Who cares about that as long at it looks good?'

'Good heavens above,' said Maggie, 'you won't be fourteen until August.'

'I am a teenager though,' she chirped. 'And girls of my age don't go about in pigtails any more.'

'I can see that,' laughed Maggie. She didn't disapprove of her daughter's fashion consciousness. The girl could hardly be otherwise in today's youth culture, so different to the austerity of her mother's girlhood. 'Come on, we've just about finished here. Let's go and have some lunch at Harrods.'

'There are some good restaurants in Chelsea, everyone says.'

'Chelsea it is then,' Maggie laughed, willing to indulge her daughter's whim in return for her valuable assistance. Children certainly knew what they wanted these days and were not afraid to speak up. And a voice in the back of her mind said, 'She'd speak up for herself, regardless of the confidence of her generation. She's your daughter isn't she?' As they set off for the trendiest spot in town, Maggie was smiling. Katy was spirited, it was true, but she had her father's kind heart too, and Maggie adored her.

And Katy was thinking, Mum is great, but I wish she had a man in her life. It doesn't seem likely that anything will develop between her and Tim's father, not after all this time. Oh well, that's parents for you. They never seem to know what's good for them. Then her thoughts turned to the more crucial matter of how long it would be before she was allowed to wear eye make-up. All that heavy mascara the older girls wore looked really fab. And hipster jeans, wow!

Chloe and Daisy Hughes were lunching in style that Saturday at one of the capital's most prestigious hotels. Eating out was no longer the easy pleasure it had once been for Chloe now that she had to be chauffeured to the restaurant and helped to her seat like an invalid. She was very conscious of her limp, and only a strong need for some sort of social life persuaded her to appear in public at all. On this particular occasion Bradley had an appointment with his tailor nearby and would be joining them a little later.

'One can always rely on the service here,' remarked Chloe, after a waiter had blended unobtrusively into the background, having expertly served them with the finest Lobster Thermidor. 'And that's so important, don't you think?'

Daisy giggled, 'Oh, Mummy, you are so bourgeois,' she said fondly. 'That sort of thing doesn't interest me a bit. I'd be just as happy eating in a cafe.'

'Really, Daisy,' tutted Chloe, who had recently begun to feel outdated in the company of her exuberant daughter, a devotee of the new teenage pop culture. 'I don't know where you get these ideas from. You go to one of the best schools in London, after all.'

'Don't be such a snob, Mummy,' said Daisy, spiritedly but without malice for she was very fond of her mother.

Choosing to ignore that remark, Chloe steered the conversation to the occupants of the next table, a mother with a daughter about the same age as Daisy. 'Isn't that a lovely dress that girl is wearing?' she whispered, referring to the young woman's rather staid attire.

'It's hideous,' said Daisy cheerfully. 'I wouldn't be seen dead in it.'

'That's a pity,' said Chloe, casting a disapproving eye over her daughter's floral shift which she had insisted on having from Quant's Bazaar in the King's Road, Chelsea. Chloe herself was immaculate in a lime-green dress in the finest sea-island cotton. 'And backcombing your hair on top like that makes you look very common.'

'Better than looking like a frump,' said Daisy, rolling her eyes expressively towards the girl at the next table. 'Like her.'

'That dress she's wearing must have cost the earth,' said Chloe in a low tone. 'You can see the quality from here.'

Daisy gave a nonchalant shrug. Her fair hair was beehived at the top and tied into two girlish bunches at the bottom. 'Who cares about quality?' she asked. 'Grooviness is what matters.'

'I'm not suggesting that you should be unfashionable,' Chloe said.

'You are if you want me to dress like her,' objected Daisy in a whisper.

'You're becoming impossible,' said Chloe, flushing and turning her attention to her food.

Daisy reached across the table and patted her mother's hand companionably. 'Don't be cross, Mummy,' she said. 'I guess things have changed since you were a girl.'

Softened by her daughter's conciliatory gesture, Chloe said wearily, 'Yes, I expect you're right.'

Tucking into her meal, Daisy felt a wave of compassion for her mother who was obviously a very unhappy lady. As soon as she had become of an age to discern such things, Daisy had realised that her parents did not have a good marriage. This saddened her for she loved them both and wanted them to be happy. When they were with Daisy separately they were warm and loving people. Together they became cold and bitter, despite their efforts to conceal it. It was a shame. She looked across at her mother and smiled, before her thoughts drifted on to the more enjoyable matter of her newly acquired Beatles record. She couldn't wait to get home to play it.

Bradley faced his personal assistant, Ted Wright, grimly across the desk. 'I do not want to make a profit out of this particular project,' he said.

'We are running a business here, Bradley,' said Ted, who had been with the Hughes Corporation since it started in the UK and had become a valued friend. 'The company already donates regularly to charity every year, and that is quite enough. We don't need to do more.'

'You mean that we don't need to be seen to do more,' Bradley corrected. Whilst Ted admitted to being a realist, Bradley saw him as a cynic but did not condemn him for it because they made a good team. Ted's practical eye muted Bradley's hypersensitive social conscience which was a target for every needy cause in London.

'That's right,' admitted Ted. 'It's a hard world we live in, mate.'

'Not so hard that we only give to charity to enhance our company image,' declared Bradley, waving a letter from someone requesting an estimate for the construction of a centre for the homeless. 'The guy who wrote this doesn't work for money.'

It was late May 1964 and the two men were in Bradley's office. Although still on the original site of the yard Bradley had taken over in the late 1940s, the Head Office building had been rebuilt and was now a smart modern structure.

'So what?' said Ted, who was ten years Bradley's senior, a sturdily built rough diamond who had been in the construction business all his life and knew it inside out. 'If we were all like him, there would be no money for anyone to donate to charity.'

Bradley swivelled his chair towards the window and glanced at the neat lawns and young trees that fronted the building, smart staff cars replacing the trucks and cement mixers of yesteryear which were now more efficiently housed at a separate depot. 'The site alone must have set these people back, at London prices,' said Bradley, referring to the contents of Reg Barrett's letter. 'I suggest we just charge them for the materials at cost price and labour at the rate we pay the men.'

'And waive our profit altogether?' said Ted who had been made a director of the company some years ago. 'I shouldn't think the board are gonna be too happy about that.'

Bradley studied the letter again. He guessed that Reg Barrett had been deliberately forthcoming with details of his scheme in the hope that sympathy would procure a low price. And why shouldn't he use such tactics? Commerce did not have the monopoly on them. 'We do well enough on other jobs. We can afford to give up our profit on this one.'

Ted grinned and lit a cheroot. He liked this quiet American and admired his dedication to his work. But Bradley was inclined to let his heart rule his head and Ted felt duty bound to put up opposition even if, like now, he gave Bradley his final support. 'No harm in putting it to the board, I suppose,' he said. 'And you'll get my support. The job will go to the lowest tender, of course.'

'We'll have to make sure that our tender qualifies then, won't we?'

'Why does this particular venture mean so much to you?' asked Ted.

'Conscience, I guess,' he said. 'I live in comfort, and I sure wouldn't fancy the idea of sleeping on the street.' Glancing out of the window again he felt a stab of pain at the sudden recollection of that day when Maggie had walked out of his life across the yard. All the concrete and manicured lawns in the world couldn't erase that memory.

Chapter Sixteen

In January 1965 Maggie and her mother found themselves with a crisis on their hands when Tom ended his relationship with Sally.

'He says he doesn't love me any more,' she wept. 'After all these years, how could he do it to me?'

'P'raps it's all for the best,' Dora confided to Maggie later. 'It hasn't been much of a life for her just livin' for Tom's release. At least now she might give herself a chance to meet someone else.'

'Maybe,' said Maggie.

But she didn't. In fact, the girl who had won their hearts with her infectious humour and endless capacity for cheerfulness, changed dramatically, shedding tears continually and losing all interest in life. Her work was done automatically and she spent all her spare time at home in her flat. The suggestion that she might find happiness with someone new only upset her even more. 'I don't want no one else,' she said miserably. 'Tom is my man. He's the only one I want, even if I've gotta wait years for him.'

Maggie and Dora tried everything they could think of to cheer her up: inviting her on outings; offering sympathetic company; Maggie even suggesting that she take a holiday. But the former extravert only withdrew deeper into herself.

'Why don't you have a word with Tom?' Dora suggested to Maggie. 'See if you can find out why he did it. He's always talked to you more than anyone. He can't have jilted Sally for another woman, that's for sure.'

And loath as she was to interfere in such a delicate matter, Sally's continuing decline called for drastic action.

'She's really heartbroken, Tom,' she said to the gaunt face of her brother through a metal grille after the normal greetings had been exchanged. 'Mum and I can't get her to perk up at all.'

'She'll get over it,' he said grimly.

'Maybe, but it's been three months and she's no better.'

'A husband is what she needs, someone who can be with her, love her properly and look after her,' he said, the quiver in his voice betraying the pain he was struggling to conceal.

'You did it for her, didn't you?' she said, searching his face, accustomed now to seeing his cropped hair and rough prison clothes. 'You do still love her.'

'I've no right to tie her to me,' he said, glancing around at the rows of prisoners engaged in hushed conversations through the grille, at the warders watchfully lining the walls. 'She's wasted enough years already, I should have ended it sooner.' He paused for a moment. 'I could barely bring meself to do it. I've lived for her visits. Knowing that she was waiting for me has kept me going. But I had to lie to her and tell her I didn't love her. It was the only fair thing to do.'

Maggie gulped to dispel the lump in her throat. For someone who had been so nervous as a child, Tom had shown immense courage in his ordeal. 'Do you think you are right in ending it?' Maggie asked him, longing to tear down the grille and hug him. 'You've taken away her reason for living as well as your own. She simply does not want anyone else.'

'She will in time.'

'It's been eight years, Tom,' Maggie reminded him. 'I think that proves that she knows her own mind. She's in a bad way. Mum and I are really worried about her. She's like one of the family to us.'

'What is the right thing for me to do, sis?' he asked, his hands clenched tightly in front of him, two scarlet patches on his cheeks standing out against his pale face. 'I've caused her nothing but trouble. She's even fallen out with her family because of me.'

'I don't know what's the right thing, Tom,' Maggie admitted. 'But I do know that you'll cause her more harm than good by refusing to see her.' She shook her head sadly. 'Think about it.'

One evening in the spring, a happier Sally arrived at Maggie's door. 'Tom sends you 'is love,' she trilled. 'I've had a letter from 'im. He wants me to go and see him next visiting day.'

Maggie hugged her, realising that she already thought of her as a sister-in-law. She cursed the grave miscarriage of justice that prevented this from becoming a reality, and inwardly wept for the years of suffering this brave young woman still had to endure.

With Sally back to normal, Maggie was able to turn her attention to an invitation she had received from Reg Barrett and his wife to be the guest of honour at the official opening of the new centre, early in May.

'Guest of honour, eh?' said Dora proudly. 'You are going up in the world. But how come?'

'I suppose it's because I gave them a donation once,' said Maggie airily, as though the sum had been a mere trifle. As far as she was concerned, her offering had been a redistribution of Rupert's money, and she wanted no thanks or glory which was why she had told no one about it except Royston. Out of courtesy to the Barretts she felt duty bound to attend the function though, but only after having obtained their promise not to mention the amount of her donation. 'It's on Saturday week and they are laying on a special lunch at the centre, apparently. You can come with me if you like. I'm invited to take a guest.'

Dora shook her head. 'I've promised to help Sally in the shop for the next two weekends until her Saturday girl comes back from holiday. Why not ask Royston to go with you?'

'Perhaps I'll take Katy,' said Maggie thoughtfully. 'She's old enough to cope with something like that now. And I'll enjoy showing her off.'

'Good idea,' Dora agreed.

The day dawned bright and sunny. Wisely deciding on simple attire, Maggie wore a white shift dress with a green trim, green earrings and shoes, her well-shaped hair curling loosely just below her ears.

Katy, at almost fifteen, was in the uniform of her generation: a skinny-rib jumper and a parentally approved mini skirt. Hardly haute couture, but having managed to prise her daughter out of her hipster jeans, Maggie wasn't complaining.

They arrived in plenty of time for Maggie to have a chat with the Barretts and a tour of the property before the other guests arrived. The shelter was newly built and situated in an area of Ashbrook Green virtually unknown to Maggie, a region near the canal consisting mostly of factories and warehouses. 'We would have had difficulty getting planning permission for a place like this in a residential area,' explained Reg.

Maggie was impressed. It was basic accommodation on two floors, comprising dormitories divided into cubicles for privacy, modern shower and toilet facilities, central heating, a hygienic kitchen, a canteen with laminated tables, and a simply furnished lounge with a television set. 'You've done a really good job,' said Maggie warmly.

'Thanks to the generosity of our benefactors,' he reminded her.

By the time they had finished their tour of inspection, people were beginning to gather in the entrance hall, the walls of which housed various notices about the National Health Service and Social Security. Also on the foyer wall was a small pair of velvet curtains covering a commemorative plaque which Maggie, as the guest of honour, was to unveil.

The hum of congenial chatter lapped pleasantly around Maggie and Katy as the crowd grew and introductions were made. Those present included the mayor and his wife, a sprinkling of officials from the local council, the parish vicar, some business people of the area one assumed had been generous to the cause, and several of the volunteers. It was a gathering of about thirty people.

Reg called for order and opened the proceedings with a brief speech before calling for Maggie to step forward and pull the cord. There was a ripple of applause followed by formal thanks to Maggie from Reg.

It was when she turned to face the company that Maggie found herself staring into the eyes of Bradley Hughes who was on the edge of the crowd with Chloe, in a wheelchair, and Daisy. The shock of seeing him weakened her almost to the point of collapse, but did not diminish the instinctive joy which she saw reflected in his eyes. He smiled and nodded and she reciprocated, dazed. A look of acknowledgement passed between herself and Chloe, but the latter's initial smile soon became an icy stare.

Maggie was far too delighted to see Bradley to wonder why he was here. So violent were the emotions he awakened in her, she feared they would be on show for all to see. It was a relief to note that events around her were progressing ordinarily with no particular emphasis on herself. 'Now perhaps you'd like to come into the lounge for a glass of something before luncheon, ladies and gentlemen,' Reg was saying.

Since this was not a large enough function in which to avoid people, Maggie knew that some sort of a confrontation was inevitable. Already Katy had spotted the Hugheses.

'Mum, isn't that Daisy Hughes over there?' she asked uncertainly. 'It's so long since I last saw her, I can't be sure.'

'Yes, that's her,' said Maggie, being falsely casual. 'And so grown up too.'

'Doesn't she look fab with her hair long and straight like that?' Katy waved madly across the room at Daisy. 'Mind if I go over and talk to her? She's the only person of my age here.'

'You go ahead, love,' agreed Maggie, and watched as Daisy also broke away from her parents. The two girls met in the crowd, drawn together by their youth.

Deciding that this entire function was going to be intolerable if the ice was left unbroken between herself and the Hugheses, Maggie weaved her way purposefully towards them. Waylaid by the Mayor, however, who lengthily extolled the virtues of the centre, she eventually found Bradley alone, Chloe having been drawn into conversation some distance away with the Vicar.

'Hello, Bradley,' Maggie said, pleased to have him to herself but hoping that Chloe wouldn't think her timing was deliberate for she had no wish to exacerbate the situation between them. 'You are the last person I expected to see here.'

'Snap,' he said, smiling warmly.

'I once made a donation to the Barretts' appeal,' she explained. 'What's your connection?'

'We built the place,' he told her.

'Ah, I see.' She could have wept for the joy of being with him. 'You look well.' And indeed he did. But noticing that his fair hair, which was worn fashionably longer than she remembered, was now white at the temples, she realised with a shock that he must be over forty. The contours of his face had deepened with age and lines feathered his eyes and mouth, but he was still a remarkably handsome man.

'So do you.' He moved back and inspected her thoroughly. 'Lovelier than ever. And so smart and fashionable.' Up until then he had been speaking with his mouth. Now his words came from the heart. 'Oh, Maggie, it is so good to see you,' he said, his voice breaking with emotion.

For Maggie it was as though the first rays of spring sunshine were warming her through to the bone. 'And you,' she said shakily. 'And you.'

Chloe was watching them from across the room. Whatever had been between them was obviously still there, despite the years apart, she thought. Her first reaction to seeing Maggie again had been one of sheer pleasure, for she had missed her terribly this last eight years. On the heels of elation came the fear of losing Bradley and finding herself alone. Oh God, how vulnerable she felt in this damned wheelchair which she was forced to use today because of all the standing and ambling about one was expected to endure at a function such as this.

Added to a feeling of dread came envy at the sight of Bradley and Maggie so happy together. They seemed to create their own aura which excluded the rest of the world. Her jealousy was not so much for what they had found in each other as for what she had failed to find for herself. Her loveless existence with Bradley had left her a lonely and embittered woman. All her love was channelled towards her daughter who would soon be independent of her.

But the Vicar, a white-haired man with a rubicund complexion and faded blue eyes, was saying: 'You must be very proud, Mrs Hughes, to have been involved in such a worthy project as this one.'

'My husband is the builder, not me,' said Chloe who had known nothing about this project until the invitation had arrived, and had only accompanied Bradley for the sake of family prestige. 'I cannot claim to have been involved.'

'Behind every successful man there is a woman, so they say,' said the Vicar patronisingly. 'You must take pride in that, my dear.'

'Do they also say that behind every successful woman there is a man?' asked Chloe.

223

The Vicar clearly regretted the remark which had been nothing more then a conversation filler. He guzzled his sherry as though it might provide him with the inspiration he needed to answer her, for he was not at all comfortable with the attitudes of some modern women. 'I'm sure they do,' he said at last.

'I happen to know that our guest of honour here today is a widow,' she said. 'And no one can dispute her success.'

'These old sayings are only words, my dear,' he pointed out, having had time to gather his wits. 'And can apply to either sex.' He glanced around the room seeking escape, for strident women terrified him. 'If you'll excuse me? One must circulate.'

Alone, Chloe tried to fathom out why, when she despised Maggie, she had become hot under the collar on her behalf. Finally deciding that she had been making a stand for womankind generally, rather than Maggie personally, she braced herself to face her one-time friend. It was infuriating to find that she was trembling as she manipulated her chair across the room.

'O levels soon,' said Katy to Daisy.

She made a face. 'Yuk, don't remind me. Isn't it a pain?'

'I'll say. Are you hoping to stay on to do A levels?'

'I'd like to, yes,' confessed Daisy. 'I want to go to university if I can. But we'll just have to wait and see. How about you?'

'I can't wait to leave school,' said Katy. 'I'm planning to leave after O levels. If I can get Mum to agree.'

'What will you do then?'

'I want to go into the business with her.'

'I see.'

'I love your dress,' said Katy, referring to a pink mini dress Daisy was wearing.

'I got it at Birds' Paradise,' said Daisy.

'That's the boutique that used to be a London bus, isn't it?' queried Katy.

'That's right, they have some fabulous gear there.' She lowered her voice confidentially. 'I have to work real hard on Mother before she'll let me have anything from there, though. She prefers me to have boring old high-class clothes.'

'Parents are on a different wavelength, aren't they?' sympathised Katy. 'It was different in their day, so I suppose it isn't their fault.'

They were standing on the edge of the adult gathering, sipping Coca-Cola, completely relaxed in each other's company.

'Do you have a boyfriend?' asked Daisy.

'Not a boyfriend as such, but there is a boy I really fancy,' she admitted. 'He's the son of a friend of my mother's, a lawyer. He's eighteen and really fab.'

'Do you go out with him?'

'No, I think he thinks I'm too young for him at the moment. But we see a lot of each other because our parents are friends.' She pulled a rueful face. 'He's going away to university soon, though.'

They paused briefly before Daisy changed the subject. 'I only just recognised you, we were just kids when we last met.'

'Yes, I had to check with Mum before I could be sure it was you,' admitted Katy. She drew her Coke through her straw thoughtfully. 'What happened between our parents to stop them seeing each other, do you know?'

Daisy shrugged. 'I've no idea. I suppose they drifted apart after Mummy's accident, or had a row or something.' She glanced across the room. 'They seem to be getting along fine now though.' She turned back to Katy, whom she liked enormously. 'I'm really glad you are here today. I thought I was going to be bored stiff among all these oldies.'

'Me too.'

'Let's try to sit together at lunch, shall we?' suggested Daisy.

'Yes, let's,' agreed Katy.

'We can keep in touch independently of our parents now that we are older,' said Daisy.

'Of course we can.'

'Who's your favourite group,' asked Daisy.

'The Beatles.'

'What about the Beach Boys?'

'They're really fab too!'

'Well, Maggie, it's been a long time,' said Chloe, forcing a smile and wishing she felt less emotional for it weakened her position even more. 'How have you been?'

'Oh, surviving, you know,' replied Maggie lightly, though she was unnerved by her confused emotions. Meeting this couple, who both meant so much to her in different ways, had set her nerves on edge.

'Surviving very well, from what I've heard,' remarked Chloe, since it would be noticeably churlish not to comment on Maggie's success. 'I've noticed your Knightsbridge shop. And very smart it is too.'

'Thank you. One has to make a living,' Maggie said casually, though her throat was constricting horribly. 'You're looking terrific.' And she meant it for the well-cut yellow linen dress Chloe was wearing left the world in no doubt that maturity and disability did not alter the fact that she was still a very beautiful woman. She was heavier now, but even so . . . 'Still as fashionable as ever, I see.'

'One has to make an extra effort with a teenage daughter around,' said Chloe with determined levity. 'They can so easily destroy the mature ego if one isn't careful.'

Maggie emitted a dry laugh. 'Don't I know it?' she agreed.

The atmosphere couldn't have been tenser had the years since their dramatic altercation not elapsed. Maggie had often hoped that one day she might be able to renew her friendship with Chloe; now this didn't seem possible.

Feeling the tension crackle around them, Bradley intervened. 'They'll be serving lunch soon, I expect.'

'Yes,' said Maggie, and striving to erase the awkwardness with conversation rather than make a social comment, added, 'It seems a little incongruous though, doesn't it? I mean, all of us who have more than enough of everything, feeding our faces in a centre for those who don't even have a bed of their own for the night.'

'I'm sure the down and outs won't begrudge lunch to the people who made all this possible for them,' snapped Chloe, belligerent in her own personal unhappiness. 'There is no necessity for us to feel that we have to starve or go about in rags just because they do. There is no need for them to live as they do anyway, in this day and age. We are not in the Dark Ages now. People who are too irresponsible to conform to society ought to be damned grateful that people like us do anything for them at all.'

She smarted at her own intolerance. Why am I saying these things when I know nothing about the subject? she asked herself. It isn't as though hitting out at all and sundry eases the pain.

Both Maggie and Bradley listened to her outburst without comment. The knowledge that they both understood her well enough to realise that she didn't really mean what she said made Chloe want to weep for the circumstances that prohibited friendship between the three of them. Oh God, what a mess!

Bradley steered the conversation on to the safer topic of Maggie's business. 'I often see your vans around London,' he said. 'They're very eye catching with the yellow chrysanthemum on the side.'

'Thank you.'

Caught up in the warmth emanating from one to the other, despite the uneasy climate, Chloe's inner turmoil was fanned into rage. If those two were harbouring any ideas about getting back together again, they could forget it. In fact, it might be a very good idea to give them both a strong reminder of the actual state of affairs.

'I've been thinking,' she said to Maggie, excited by a sudden plan, 'we really ought to see something of each other again. That other business was a very long time ago. We are all that much more mature now, and life is too short to let old quarrels linger on.'

226

Although warming to Chloe's suggestion, Maggie was suspicious of her reasons for making it, and even more doubtful about the possibility of renewing a comfortable association between them. 'Maybe one of these days we'll get together,' she said evasively.

But Chloe was desperate to eliminate any chance of a renewal of her husband's affair. 'The sooner the better,' she persisted, glancing across the room to where the girls were chattering happily. 'Why not make a family occasion of it? Bring Katy down to our place in Kent for a long weekend. It's particularly beautiful there in the spring when the orchards are in bloom. If you come next weekend the blossom will still be around.'

Realising just what torture a weekend with Bradley in his marital surroundings would be, Maggie was certain that Chloe's reason for suggesting it had been to make some sort of a point. 'It's very kind of you, but it is difficult for me to get away,' she said.

'Surely you can manage to take a weekend off?' Chloe insisted. She turned to her husband. 'Do persuade her to come, Bradley dear. It will be just like old times.'

Taken aback by the turn of events, he said: 'But if she can't get away . . .'

At that moment fate smiled on Chloe in the form of the arrival of the girls, very chummy and begging to be allowed to sit together at lunch. 'Katy dear,' Chloe said, dispensing with formal greetings in her urgent desire to get her plan underway, 'I'm just trying to persuade your mother to bring you down to Kent next weekend. She's claiming to be too busy. Do try to talk her into it. You'll have such fun.'

Katy threw her mother a pleading look. 'Say we can go, Mum,' she said. 'I'll really love it.'

'Please, Auntie Maggie,' said Daisy, reverting to the title she had used when they had all been such friends. 'I'd be so thrilled if Katy could come.'

Maggie knew that she was trapped. Without disappointing the children and arousing their suspicions there was no way out, since she could not claim to be busy every weekend. She met the challenge in Chloe's eyes. 'It seems I am outnumbered. So thank you very much, we'd love to come,' she said, just as Reg Barrett began to usher them into the new canteen for lunch.

Chapter Seventeen

Despite Maggie's grave apprehensions about the visit, her spirits rose involuntarily the following Friday afternoon as the grime of the city yielded to the sweet country air and the ubiquitous blossom fields, pink for apple, white for pear and cherry. The lightly scented breeze blowing through the car window reminded Maggie of a fruit-picking holiday she had once had in Kent with her mother and Tom. Oh, such carefree times of farmhouse suppers and long days in the fields, when physical exhaustion had been the only problem.

Who could have guessed then the traumas ahead? she thought as Tom's plight came to mind, bringing its usual mixture of sorrow and anger. Her own difficulties paled into insignificance against this. Contending with offensive remarks from a few malicious neighbours, and boycotts to her shops from a few bigots who would sooner die than give their business to the sister of a 'murderer', were nothing compared to his suffering. The weekend ahead may well be a tense, painful time but at least she was free to live her life, however emotionally chaotic it might be. Tom wasn't.

Following Chloe's directions, Maggie weaved her beloved new white Mini through a rustic landscape dotted with red-brick conical oast-houses and villages with gabled houses and timbered cottages. The towers and spires of ancient churches were occasionally etched against the sky.

When their tyres eventually crunched on to the drive of Bushleigh Lodge, past gardens which were a mass of spring flowers and leafy shrubs, Katy exclaimed, 'Wow! What a fabulous place.'

'It certainly is,' agreed Maggie, perceiving a certain welcoming charm about the house which she had never felt when visiting the Hughes' stylish London home. Being roomy rather than huge, and pretty rather than smart, there was a cosiness about it somehow.

Their hosts had obviously been looking out for them and appeared even before the car doors were opened, all casually dressed in jeans and shirts, Bradley pushing Chloe in her chair. The two girls immediately broke into youthful chatter and went off together.

'It's a lovely place you have here,' said Maggie.

'Thank you. We like it,' said Chloe, smiling. 'And we are both terribly thrilled that you decided to share it with us for a few days, aren't we, darling?' She cocked her head towards Bradley who nodded, looking bemused. 'Leave all your stuff in the car. Bradley will bring it in for you.'

The emphasis on the connubial 'we' was acutely noticeable and obviously intended to set the tone for the weekend. Maggie groaned inwardly and applied herself to studying her surroundings to distract herself. The house had been beautifully restored, using a great deal of wood panelling and oak beams. Soft upholstery in warm colours adorned the sitting room, antique furniture filled the dining room, and the stone-floored kitchen was fitted out country style. Various other rooms were situated on the ground floor: a study, a television room, and Chloe's bedroom because the stairs were difficult for her. The whole house was ramped for her wheelchair.

The girls appeared and Daisy showed the visitors to their rooms on the first floor. Maggie found hers to be a charming haven in pink with en suite bathroom. Standing by the window, she looked out across a scene of ineffable beauty. Meadowland spread as far as the eye could see, frequently splashed with the pale shades of blossom and tinged with the blue mist of late afternoon. Its unspoiled loveliness inspired her to cast the problems of the past from her mind and concentrate on making the weekend a success.

Downstairs she found Chloe alone in the sitting room, seated on the sofa. Bradley was seeing to the luggage and the girls were out in the paddock, she explained.

'You're not tied to your chair all the time, then?' she remarked conversationally.

'Oh, no, I can heave myself around to a certain extent,' Chloe explained. She had, in fact, spent time wondering which would be the most effective way to greet Maggie. Initially to display her reliance on Bradley by limping outside on his arm, or make a more dramatic impact by being in her chair? Finally, she had decided that it didn't really matter since she had the whole weekend in which to emphasise the way in which her injury made her dependent on her husband. 'But it is too painful and exhausting to do it for very long.'

'It must be awful for you,' sympathised Maggie.

'Yes, it does get a bit much at times,' Chloe said truthfully, but also using the opportunity to make a point. 'Bradley is very supportive. I don't know what I'd do without him.'

'I can imagine,' said Maggie.

An awkward silence was broken by the arrival of Mrs Brown with some tea which she placed on a small table near Maggie.

'I thought you might like something after your journey,' said Chloe who was a natural hostess under any circumstances, 'and it is a little early for something stronger.'

Taking the opportunity for a few private words while they were alone, Maggie said, 'It is good to see you again, Chloe.'

Taken unawares by a flood of affection for her, Chloe replied impulsively. 'Yes, it is,' she said, gulping on a lump in her throat. 'We used to have such fun. All that soul-baring and giggling . . .'

Maggie smiled.' Oh, what it is to be young! That sort of thing is for our daughters now. They seem very friendly.' She leaned over and poured them both some tea. 'We must keep old differences out of sight this weekend, for their sakes.'

Chloe's eyes widened for she had almost forgotten Maggie's candour. 'As I said last week, all that nonsense is long forgotten as far as Bradley and I are concerned.'

Although smarting at the trivialisation of her affair with him, Maggie didn't blame Chloe for making it. It was only natural that she should feel insecure. She had obviously felt threatened by the unexpected meeting at the centre and this weekend was intended to warn Maggie off. Well, she thought, her marriage is safe from me, no matter how much I still love Bradley. Whatever the truth of the situation between Chloe and Bradley, they did have a family life. Maggie was glad she had not destroyed that. 'I'm happy things worked out for you and Bradley,' she said.

'Things do have a habit of sorting themselves out,' said Chloe meaningfully.

Determined that the past should now be put safely behind them, Maggie changed the subject. 'How many horses do you have?' she asked, glancing through the window at the stables which were situated to the side of the house beyond a yard area. A man was leading around, observed closely by the girls.

'Just two,' said Chloe. 'There's no point in having more now that I can't ride.'

Having been told George's function, Maggie said conversationally, 'It must be fun to ride a horse.'

'Why not have a go while you're here?' suggested Chloe impulsively.

'I wouldn't have a clue where to start,' laughed Maggie.

'That doesn't matter,' said Chloe, enthusiastic despite herself. 'I'll tell you what do do.' At Maggie's querying glance, she added: 'We have a ramp out to the paddock. I really *would* go mad if I couldn't get out to see the horses now and then. I could supervise from my chair, with Daisy leading you on a halter rope.'

'Hey, steady on,' laughed Maggie, relaxing with the improvement in the atmosphere, 'I only said it might be fun to ride. I wouldn't have the nerve to get on a horse, let alone ride one. We didn't all have parents with country houses when we were children, you know.'

'I'll teach you how,' urged Chloe, her face suddenly animated.

Maggie had never seen her so alive, and was filled with compassion. It must be so hard for her not to be able to ride. 'Well, I'm not sure . . .'

'Do say yes,' Chloe urged. 'You'll love it, I promise you. There's no other feeling in the world quite like being on horseback.'

'Oh, all right then,' agreed Maggie doubtfully.

'Tomorrow afternoon,' Chloe said. 'And I shall keep you to it.'

The evening passed pleasantly enough. After a meal of fresh salmon followed by steak and salad then crème caramel, cooked and served by Mrs Brown, the girls went to play records in Daisy's bedroom, while the adults lingered over coffee. 'Do you divide your time between here and Hampstead?' asked Maggie conversationally.

Bradley shook his head. 'I don't come down as often as Chloe,' he said.

Maggie looked puzzled.

'I come with my companion, Joan,' Chloe explained. 'We employ her. I need someone while Bradley is at work. She often drives me here during the week and we stay a few days.'

'Daisy likes to spend her school holidays here, I expect,' said Maggie.

'Not so much as she used to,' confessed Chloe wryly. 'She doesn't like to miss anything that's going on with her friends in town. You know how teenagers are.'

'Don't I just!'

Much to Maggie's surprise, she was really beginning to enjoy herself and ascribed it to the relaxing surroundings and the wine they had drunk with dinner. The evening was concluded with a refreshing stroll in the garden, with Maggie pushing Chloe in her chair, the nocturnal dew clearing her head wonderfully.

While she was getting ready for bed, Katy tapped on her door and appeared, flushed and smiling in blue cotton pyjamas. 'I'm having a fab time, Mum,' she said, perching on the end of the bed and hugging her knees.

'Good. I'm glad you're enjoying yourself, love.' Brushing her hair in the dressing-table mirror, and seeing her daughter's reflection behind her, Maggie observed the signs of incipient beauty. Katy's auburn hair glistened in the light and her figure had begun to curve. She was similar to Maggie in colouring and features, but already taller and more willowy.

'I like Daisy a lot,' chirped Katy. 'We get on really well, yet we're not a bit alike. She goes to a posh school and I don't. She wants to go to university and I don't. Yet I feel I can tell her anything at all. And we laugh at all the same things. Isn't that strange?'

History was repeating itself, Maggie thought. Two girls, with different personalities and from different backgrounds, drawn together by an unaccountable force. For although the class difference was not so great between these girls as it had been between their mothers, it still existed to a certain degree.

It was true that Maggie was a rich woman in her own right, and Katy had never known the sort of poverty her mother had grown up with. Katy had her own room in a comfortable home, nice clothes, a good allowance. She would be encouraged to take further education, not forced out to work at fourteen as Maggie had been. She was informed and socially aware. She had received a state education from her mother's choice, not necessity. She could meet Daisy Hughes on equal financial terms.

But Katy was still the daughter of a nouveau-riche woman of trade, whereas Daisy had the polish of generations of breeding. And despite Maggie's success, she still lived close to her roots, something she attributed to her down-to-earth mother who still preferred cod and chips to caviare, and an evening out at the pub or bingo hall when Maggie could afford to take her to dinner at the Ritz.

Maggie did not see class disparity as any problem for the girls though. How much easier it would have been to resolve had that been the cause of the trouble between their mothers.

'Daisy's mother and I used to be like that when we were girls,' said Maggie impulsively.

'What happened, Mum?' asked Katy. 'Why did we stop seeing Daisy and her parents?'

For an instant Maggie was tempted to tell her the truth, for it would have been a relief to unburden herself. But fearing embarrassing Katy in the light of her tender years and new friendship with Daisy, she just said, 'Oh, we had some silly argument.' She put her hairbrush down on the dressing table and removed her gown to reveal a plain white satin nightdress.

'It's all right between you now though, isn't it?' said Katy, surveying her mother as she got into bed. 'Only I want to stay friends with Daisy, but I wouldn't want to make things awkward for you.'

Quick to clarify the situation, Maggie said, 'You mustn't let my relations with Daisy's parents affect your friendship with her. You are growing up now. You choose your own friends, regardless of me.'

Katy beamed. 'You're great, Mum, do you know that?'

'Hush, Katy, or you'll make me blush.'

'Daisy thinks so too,' Katy said, yawning. 'She things it's terrific the way you've built the business up single-handed while raising me at the same time.' She paused thoughtfully. 'It's a shame about Daisy's mother. She is such a sad sort of a person, isn't she?'

'Who wouldn't be in her position?' Maggie pointed out. 'But she hasn't seemed so sad today. I thought she was in good form, considering.'

'She laughs a lot, but never with her eyes,' said Katy sagely. 'It's all show.'

Out of the mouths of babes, Maggie thought, but said, 'I'm sure you're imagining things.'

'I don't think so,' Katy said, stretching. 'Oh, well, I'm off to bed now.' She pecked her mother on the cheek. 'Goodnight, Mum.'

'Goodnight, love.'

Sleep eluded Maggie, for her mind was overloaded with thoughts and memories. Weary of thrashing about in the sheets, she slipped out of bed and picked her way to the window in the moonlight. It was a clear night, the plump moon beaming from the pewter sky and spreading a pearly glow over the gardens, bushes and outbuildings casting eerie dark shapes against the pale lawns.

A movement below caught her attention and, looking down, she could just make out the figure of Bradley sitting on the terrace smoking a cigar. Having spent every moment since her arrival avoiding being alone with him, she now felt irresistibly compelled to go to him and talk to him, to touch and make love to him. Instead she went back to bed, triumphing over the passionate and undisciplined side of her nature.

Unaware that he had been observed by Maggie, Bradley stared unseeingly across the gardens, inhaling deeply on his cigar to stop himself from screaming out loud at the trapped feeling inside him. This weekend had been organised by Chloe to re-establish her claim on him, like an animal protecting its territory. One couldn't blame her, of course, but she had no need. He would never leave her while she was so dependent on him. And all she had succeeded in doing by reminding him of his obligation to her was to drive him further away within himself.

It was unsettling having Maggie around. Conversation over dinner had revealed that she was still free, after all. The bleak future came vividly into focus. Chloe spent an increasing amount of time here at Bushleigh Lodge while he stayed in London. Soon Daisy would be leading her own life. What of he and Chloe then? Were they destined just to sit back, often in separate homes, with their grandchildren as their only mutual interest?

Panic overwhelmed him. At forty-four he wasn't ready for that. He

234

still had too much living to do and love to give. He looked up at Maggie's window, and was filled with a compulsion to go and see her, to be with her for just a few stolen moments. Curbing the impulse, he went inside to the bedroom he shared with no one.

Chloe lay in bed, staring at the undulating patterns on the ceiling created by the moonlight shining through the trees outside. She wondered why it was that, having invited Maggie here to make her and Bradley suffer as much as to make a point, she herself was feeling such pain.

Why did she wince as she hammered home her claim on Bradley? Where was the sense of victory she had looked for in forcing them together within Bradley's marital home? Seeing their mutual tenderness, when their eyes accidentally met, filled Chloe with sadness instead of triumph. Her emotions had become as unpredictable as British weather.

Oh God, how she longed to be free. She was tired of being a barrier between two people who must hate her for it. She wanted to bask in the warmth of affection and respect instead of feeling resented. Self-pity overwhelmed her as she remembered how close she had come to an independent life of her own. She could never have that now. Admittedly she managed well enough when she spent time away from Bradley here at Bushleigh Lodge with Joan. But she still needed to know that he was there on hand, organising people like her companion if he couldn't be with her himself. The mere thought of his not being around terrified her.

Finding comfort in the fact that she was still an excellent hostess, albeit that Mrs Brown did all the actual work, she turned her mind to the entertaining currently in progress. Perhaps tomorrow morning they might show the visitors a spot of local colour, followed by some time with the horses in the afternoon. On Sunday, maybe a trip further afield to Hever Castle might be a good idea. And to her amazement she found herself actually *wanting* Maggie and her daughter to enjoy their visit, for their own sakes and not just as a confirmation of her skills as a hostess.

The morning dawned fine and sunny and they breakfasted on the terrace, observed by tame rabbits on the lawn. Despite her late night, Maggie woke feeling refreshed and ate a hearty breakfast of grapefruit, followed by eggs, bacon, mushrooms and tomatoes. Feeling a lessening of tension in the air, she felt as if a holiday mood had descended on the entire company. They seemed to have entered a kind of limbo period which separated them from the past and the future. They were simply a group of people enjoying a weekend break together.

'I thought you might like to take a walk to the village later,' suggested Chloe, attractively clad in white cotton slacks and a baggy tee shirt which was kind to the extra pounds she now carried. 'We could have a drink at the village pub before lunch.'

'That would be great,' enthused Maggie, and her sentiments were echoed by Katy.

They set off along the lane with Bradley pushing Chloe in her chair. Maggie was wearing yellow shorts and a matching blouse that tied above her waist. Free from cosmetics, her face shone healthily, her hair casually framing it. The jeans-clad girls walked on ahead while the adults strolled behind, stopping every so often to admire trees or wild flowers about which Chloe seemed to have become an authority.

The lane was narrow and bordered on either side by banks of wild flowers. At one point, through a gap in the hedge, they could see the Weald of Kent spread before them in a magnificent tapestry. Cattle-dotted farmland; bright orchards; luxuriant woodland; all interspersed with farmhouses, oast houses and villages like playthings in the distance. Sitting on some tree trunks, they lingered awhile before continuing their journey.

It was the prettiest pub Maggie had ever seen, with whitewashed stone walls and latticed windows. Patches of ivy climbed towards a rust-coloured slate roof from which attic windows peeped over flowering window boxes, and pansy-filled gardens edged by a stream.

While the girls sat on the grass in the sunshine, the adults went inside, Chloe abandoning her chair in favour of her stick. The interior was cool and dark with the smell of ale and the feel of history. There were exposed beams and a wide brick fireplace. Pictures of the establishment in bygone days, when it had been a coaching inn, adorned the walls. The barman referred to Chloe and Bradley by their Christian names and gave Maggie a warm welcome when they introduced her. The customers wore country-style clothes and spoke with soft rural accents.

Making their way back outside to the girls, with the drinks, Maggie said, 'They seem a friendly crowd. Are they all locals or are some of them weekenders?'

'Some of each,' said Bradley. 'But it's a bit too far off the beaten track to attract too many trippers. They mostly head for the sea.'

It was so relaxing sitting in the sunlit gardens, listening to the running of the stream and sipping cider, Maggie felt herself slipping deeper into another time where the troubles of the past had melted away.

'We'd better be getting back,' said Chloe eventually. 'I've asked Mrs Brown to do us an early lunch. Nothing too heavy. We have a busy afternoon ahead.'

'Doing what?' asked Bradley.

'A riding lesson for Maggie, and Katy too if she wants it,' said Chloe excitedly. 'I'll supervise but I'll need your assistance, Daisy.'

'Sure,' she agreed.

'It all sounds far too energetic for me,' he said jokingly. 'I think I'll just potter about in the garden and leave you to it.'

'I don't know about being too energetic, it sounds positively terrifying to me,' said Maggie lightheartedly. 'I think I've changed my mind.'

'I hate to spoil your plans for a lazy afternoon, Bradley,' said Chloe, 'but you'll need to be on hand, just in case Katy needs you.'

'I can manage the horse, Mummy,' said Daisy.

'I know that, darling,' said Chloe firmly. 'You are a proficient horse-woman for your age and I'm proud of you, but you'll need an able-bodied adult on hand, just in case. I can't help physically in case of an emergency, now can I?'

'But, Mummy,' protested Daisy haughtily, 'I'm not a child.'

Chloe looked thoughtful. 'Very soon you'll be able to do just as you like. But for the moment I make the rules, especially when it comes to horses.'

Maggie had never seen Chloe so commanding. And Daisy's instant acquiescence indicated Chloe's rating as an equestrienne. What a terrible pity she could only be a spectator.

'And as for you, Maggie,' said Chloe jovially, as though the years had rolled away and they were friends again, 'I won't accept any excuses.'

And so it was that on a fine Saturday afternoon in May, townswoman Maggie Radford found herself dressed in Chloe's jodhpurs, riding boots and riding hat. 'Are you sure I need all this gear?' she queried as they assembled in the paddock.

'You certainly do,' said Chloe with the confidence of someone who knows they are right. 'The hat is essential for safety in case of a fall, and the boots are to help you grip the horse and protect your feet and legs from brambles.'

'Brambles?' Maggie queried nervously since there were none of those in the immediate vicinity of the paddock. 'How far do you intend me to go?'

'Not far, but I always insist that people riding our horses observe the proper safety regulations even if they are only going a matter of yards,' Chloe explained, heaving herself from her chair for a moment to stroke the fine chestnut mare who was to be Maggie's mount. 'She's a real sweetie, you'll be as safe as houses with her.'

'I certainly hope so,' said Maggie with a mixture of excitement and dread.

She did not find mounting and dismounting difficult. It was staying on in between that was the problem. But it was a very different Chloe to the one Maggie had known who issued instructions from her wheelchair. This was a woman with the aplomb and patience born of an affinity to the task in hand.

'Try again,' she commanded. 'Just put your right foot in the right stirrup and bring your body and left leg over, then settle back into the saddle sitting upright. That's it, you've done it! That's very good. Now remember to keep the balls of your feet in the stirrups, and hold the reins with both hands low down on the horse's neck.'

'Oh, my God,' quaked Maggie, feeling as though she had scaled Everest. 'I'm so high. I think I'm going to fall.'

'You won't,' said Chloe authoritatively, amazing Maggie with her reassuring manner. 'Now just practise getting on and off the horse once more, then Daisy will walk with you a little. You'll be all right, she's holding the rope.'

Maggie wasn't at all sure that she wanted to be led anywhere on the back of this enormous beast. But to be seen to lose her nerve would be a bad example to Katy who was awaiting her turn and watching with Bradley from the edge of the field.

Back in the saddle, Maggie listened intently to Chloe's instructions which she delivered with total command. 'Now, to get the horse to move forward, just touch her flanks with both heels . . . that's it . . . firmly but gently. To get her to stop, pull down on the reins and at the same time say "Whoah".'

'Oh, my sainted aunt!' exclaimed Maggie, dizzy with panic as the ground began to move beneath her.

'You're doing fine,' called Chloe as Daisy slowly led the horse forward on the end of a halter rope. 'Move in sequence with the horse. When she rises, so do you. When she goes down, you sit on the saddle. It's something you have to learn, particularly when you start trotting. It might seem a bit tricky at first.'

'Impossible' was the word Maggie would have used as she and her mount seemed hopelessly out of tune. But suddenly, somehow, Chloe was telling her that was enough for now and she heard herself saying, 'Oh, so soon? Can I have a while longer? I'm just beginning to get the hang of it.'

Chloe laughed, her dark eyes animated and more attractive than Maggie had ever seen them. 'OK, another five minutes.'

Later, watching Chloe pat the horse with obvious affection, Maggie said, 'I had no idea that you were so good with horses. You are a wonderful teacher. You must be if you can inspire confidence in me.'

'Thank you. I once thought I might open a riding school,' she said, the light fading from her eyes. 'Prior to the accident, of course.'

'Is there nothing more they can do to make you more mobile?' Maggie asked, wanting to weep for the waste of all that ability.

'No. Nothing,' said Chloe.

'I see,' said Maggie sadly.

The next morning Bradley put Chloe's chair into his Rolls-Royce and drove them all to Hever Castle. After a fascinating tour of the thirteenth-century, double-moated castle where Queen Anne Boleyn had spent her childhood, they ambled through the lovely Italian Garden with its ornamental walls and statues.

Lunch was chicken salad with homemade bread in the gardens of a Kentish pub, and they arrived back at Bushleigh Lodge in the late afternoon. Chloe, weary from all the activity, went to her room to take a short rest. Since Maggie and Katy were leaving immediately after dinner, Maggie went to her room and showered and changed into a plain green dress suitable both for dinner and travelling. She put on some make-up and brushed her hair and had just started packing when Katy appeared, seeking permission to go for a walk with Daisy. 'Yes, but don't be too long. You have to pack your things, remember?'

'We won't be long,' Katy promised, and they clattered down the stairs, their youthful voices echoing behind them.

Thinking back over the weekend, Maggie thought it had been surprisingly successful considering all the raw emotion that lay beneath the surface. Chloe had certainly excelled herself as a hostess, even moderating her possessiveness towards Bradley after that first day. Maggie didn't know if a revival of their friendship was possible in the long term. But she did know she would make every effort if Chloe wanted it, no matter how much it hurt seeing her and Bradley together, because Chloe needed her even though she would rather die than admit it.

She was clearing her cosmetics and jewellery from the dressing table when she noticed Bradley in the gardens talking to George. Throughout the weekend she had not allowed herself to dwell on his physical presence. Now she feasted her eyes on him properly, thrilling at the sight.

He was wearing shorts and a tee shirt, his limbs tanned and muscular, fair hair gleaming in the late afternoon sun. He was still a man with tremendous sex appeal, she thought. Reeling from a sudden stab of desire, she told herself that it was only to be expected. After all, natural instincts didn't die with a relationship, and there had been no one since Bradley. Dragging herself away from the windows, she continued with the task in hand.

Closing the lid of her suitcase, she decided to take it downstairs to the car, and perhaps have a quiet few minutes in the sitting room while it

239

was empty. Having deposited her case in the car, she made her way into the room to find Bradley sitting smoking a cheroot near the french windows and looking absently across the gardens. He turned at the sound of her entering.

'Oh,' said Maggie awkwardly, since this was the first time she had been alone with him throughout the entire weekend. 'I thought this room was empty. I saw you in the garden.'

He looked more tense now than she'd seen him all weekend. 'You're quite safe, you know,' he said grimly, 'I won't jump on you just because there is no one else around.'

'I didn't think you would,' she said, but she was inwardly quivering without the company of the others to protect her from the erotic pull between them.

'I'm sorry, that was uncalled for. Can I get you a drink?' he asked, moving to the drinks cabinet.

She shook her head. 'It's too early for me.'

'For me too really,' he said. 'But I think it is forgiveable to break the rules after such an emotionally fraught weekend.'

He poured a scotch and stood by the cabinet, looking at her standing uncertainly just inside the door. 'Do sit down, please.'

Moving into the room, she closed the door behind her and perched tensely on the edge of an armchair. 'So how have you been this long time? I didn't get a chance to ask you at the lunch last week.'

'I've missed you,' he said, looking directly into her face.

'Don't say that, Bradley,' she urged him.

'Why not? It's true.' He sipped his drink 'My feelings for you haven't changed just because we haven't seen each other, you know.'

'Bradley,' she hissed. 'Stop it.'

'Chloe is in her room, resting. She can't hear,' he said.

'But even so . . .'

'Even so, nothing! Surely there can be no harm in my speaking the truth to you, Maggie?' he said. 'Chloe's position is secure. I'll never leave her while she's so reliant on me. I'll look after her and do everything I can to make her life as comfortable as possible. But it is still you that I love.'

'It was over for us before the accident, you know that,' she reminded him. 'Even without my worries about Daisy, I could never have been happy with you, knowing what I'd done to Chloe. If you were married to a stranger it might have been different. But I love Chloe, too, in a different kind of way.'

'It will never be over for us, Maggie,' he exclaimed emotionally. 'It's still there, I can see it in you. I can feel it. If we were never to see each other again it wouldn't change.'

She fixed her eyes on her lap, afraid to meet his eyes. 'Yes,' she sighed at last. 'I know.'

And then, somehow, they were in each other's arms, the agony of the lonely years swept away in the ecstasy of a few stolen embraces. Maggie drew back before passions became too dangerously inflamed.

'No,' she cried, backing away. 'We mustn't. It isn't right.'

'I'm sorry,' he said, picking up his glass with a trembling hand. 'I got carried away. Being alone with you again after all this time was just too much for me, I guess.'

Maggie stood by the unlit hearth, an expanse of pale grey stonework with inset bookshelves adorned here and there with fine porcelain ornaments. Bradley was standing a few feet away with his back to the window. 'For what it's worth, Bradley, you are the only man I've ever loved,' she said gravely. 'The years apart have not changed that. And, God knows, I need you.' She paused, her eyes heavy with despair in her pale face. 'But Chloe needs you more. And that means ignoring our feelings for each other.'

'Do you think I don't know that?'

'Of course.'

'It's hard though.'

'We're going to have to get used to seeing each other regularly if Chloe wants to revive her friendship with me,' she remarked. 'Maybe it will be easier to cope then.'

'Maybe.'

'We'll manage.'

'We have to.'

Maggie turned and rushed upstairs to her room, far too engrossed in her own turmoil to realise that Chloe, her rest over, was sitting in her wheelchair, obscured by the door of the sitting room as Maggie opened it. She had been there for some time and had heard everything.

With a pounding heart Chloe wheeled herself back to her room, anxious to be alone with her chaotic thoughts and emotions. The conversation she had just overheard lingered in her mind as she stared out across the gardens. In all the years that she had stood between Maggie and Bradley, it had never once occurred to her that either of them might still have any regard for her. Tears welled up inside her in the realisation that they both actually cared what happened to her. Few things in her life had moved her more than Maggie's declaration of feeling for her.

But this didn't make her position any less precarious. They were both able-bodied people. They could come and go as they pleased, while she was at the mercy of others. And one of these days Bradley's feelings for Maggie might get the better of him if he got the idea that she, Chloe, could manage without him. No one realised how very lonely and frightening life was for her now. She had no alternative but to make sure he was always fully aware of how much she needed him.

If he and Maggie were exposed to each other all the time, they would get used to it. It would lessen the pull, Maggie herself had indicated that. So Chloe would re-establish their friendship. Then she could keep an eye to things and have Maggie's company too. But she was still so very afraid. She wept silently for the person she was, a woman without courage or purpose.

Chapter Eighteen

The wealthy clientele of Maggie's Knightsbridge shop certainly gave her full scope for creative floristry, she thought one day in the autumn of 1966, as she completed a special order, a gift for a man to his wife on their wedding anniversary. Having been requested to incorporate something a little more enduring into the bouquet, and been given complete carte-blanche, she had purchased some exclusive perfume and chocolates and gift-wrapped them in red glossy paper. These were then carefully arranged in a wicker basket glamorously adorned with red ribbons and filled with red and pink roses, the whole thing embellished with cellophane wrapping. It was lovely, if she did say so herself.

Maggie had been helping out at the shop all morning because of a staff shortage. Now, as midday approached and things seemed to have quietened down, she was thinking of departing. The afternoon assistants were due in soon anyway. Noticing, however, that the special order was destined for an address in Hampstead, and realising also that the van driver was already out delivering, Maggie decided to mix business with pleasure, if visiting Chloe could be called that.

'I'll deliver this special order on my way home,' she said to her manager. 'I need to make a call in that area anyway and it'll save a trip for your delivery man.'

'Thanks, Maggie,' he said warmly for her readiness to turn her hand to anything made her a popular employer.

With the fruits of her labours firmly secured on the back seat, she threaded her way through the busy London streets, noticing the long-haired men, the mini-skirted women and the increase in popularity of Eastern-style kaftans and beads for men.

According to the newspapers London was now the fashion centre of the world for the young, at the heart of which lay three streets, the King's Road, Chelsea; Kensington Church Street and Carnaby Street, once a rundown back alley behind Regent Street. *Time* magazine, earlier in the year, had reported 1966 to be the year of 'Swinging London' with its proliferation of successful artists, models, rock stars and fashion photographers.

Whilst Maggie didn't agree with everything she read in the papers, it was clear for all to see that the social revolution had reached every echelon of youthful society. Topics that had been taboo when Maggie was a girl were discussed quite openly in this new, uninhibited, sexually active culture. Even Maggie's own daughter talked without embarrassment about going on the Pill eventually. Marriage and traditional morality had become the province of the older generations.

Although in that respect Maggie clung to the traditions and standards in which she had been raised, she wholeheartedly approved of the new meritocracy which offered fame and fortune to gifted people, regardless of background. If the daughter of a London carpenter could be discovered outside her school gates and become a world-famous model within six months, as was the case with Twiggy, such things were possible, if not very probable for any pretty girl.

Maggie enjoyed making her delivery for she was rewarded by the joyful reaction of the recipient. But approaching her second port of call she tensed, for Chloe had made it impossible to anticipate a visit with anything other than dread. It was heartbreaking to watch her become more enslaved to her disability with every passing day. Since that weekend in Kent last year, there had been a steady decline in her morale to the point where she was now firmly entrenched in a trough of self-pity and determined not to make any effort whatsoever to improve her circumstances.

She refused to leave the house with anyone but Bradley, and although the doctors now said that it would be possible for her to drive a car with controls adapted to her special needs, the mere mention of this sent her either into tears or a tantrum. Her housekeeper attended to the household shopping, and her companion purchased her clothes, on the rare occasions that she was asked to since Chloe had lost all interest in her appearance.

Having, apparently, become hypersensitive about revealing her disablement in public, even when Bradley took her out for a drive she would not get out of the car. 'I'm not going to give people a free freak show,' she would protest every time the subject was mooted. 'Besides, it's painful and tiring enough getting around inside the house, let alone out of it.'

The saddest thing of all, in Maggie's opinion, was that Chloe had lost all interest in the one thing that had given her real pleasure – her horses. She wouldn't even go to Bushleigh Lodge now. She said it depressed her, yet Maggie had thought the place suited her even though she couldn't ride. So Chloe spent her days within the walls of her Hampstead home, wallowing in self-pity.

Bradley's patience seemed endless. He never failed in his support for her though she made his life hell by constantly querying his movements and making a fuss if he was late back from the office or had to go out on business in the evening. Maggie guessed that this was her way of hanging on to him, but she also suspected that her attitude had become so much second nature to her that she really believed herself to be more helpless than she actually was.

It was perfectly understandable that she should cling obsessively to her marriage. Her discomfort was considerable, after all. And no matter how difficult and tiring these visits were, Maggie would not give up on her for she truly believed that inside the selfish, unlikeable Chloe was another nicer version, longing to get out.

Now Chloe's housekeeper, Mrs Marsh, opened the door to Maggie, greeted her pleasantly and ushered her inside. Chloe's companion, Joan, who had seen Maggie arrive, appeared on the scene.

'She's in the drawing room,' said Joan, a middle-aged widow with a kindly disposition and the amazing mental stamina necessary to cope with Chloe's demands. 'She knows that you're here.'

'How is she today?'

Joan made a face. 'A bit low. She's been looking at photographs of her equestrian days.'

'Oh, dear.'

'It's a shame her riding days are over,' remarked Joan.

'Indeed it is,' said Maggie. 'But no good will come of her constantly looking back. She ought to be thinking about the present and the future.'

'I don't think she can see much to look forward to,' said Joan defensively, for she considered it her duty to be loyal to her charge against all others, whatever her personal opinion. 'The best is behind her as far as she's concerned.' She sighed. 'I can't get her to see it any other way.'

'Just because she can't ride doesn't mean she has to cut herself off from horses,' said Maggie. 'She ought to start going down to Kent again. She enjoys being in the country around the horses even if she won't admit it.'

'It's getting her to go anywhere that's the problem,' sighed Joan.

'Ummm.'

Bracing herself for battle, she made her way to the drawing room while Joan diplomatically made herself scarce. Visiting Chloe was like working through an obstacle course for someone like Maggie whose positive nature rebelled against such utter defeatism.

Chloe was sitting in an easy chair by the window, unattractively dressed in a grey sweater which hung shapelessly over a pair of black trousers. Her greasy hair was scraped back into an elastic band and her face lacked the refinements of make-up. Signs of recent weeping lay

245

blotchily on her face and her eyes were red and sore. The beautiful woman she had once been was barely detectable beneath her gargantuan form for she had turned to food for consolation in a big way over this last year or so. A dramatic increase in weight had not only ruined her figure but distorted her face too. Extra chins abounded and her lovely eyes were almost lost in mounds of superfluous flesh. It distressed Maggie terribly to see her like this.

'Hi,' she said, resolutely cheerful, 'I just happened to be in the area on business so I thought I'd pop in to see you for a few minutes. How are you?'

'Not too good,' sniffed Chloe gloomily.

'I'm sorry to hear that,' said Maggie kindly. 'Can I help in any way?'

Sighing dramatically, she said. 'Not unless you can turn the clock back.'

Since there was no useful answer to that, Maggie produced a paperback novel from her bag and handed it to her. 'I know you'd rather have chocolates, but a good read will be better for you. You really must try not to put on any more weight.'

'Thanks.' Chloe put the book on the table beside her with barely a glance at it.

Sitting down opposite her, Maggie asked, 'What have you been doing with yourself since I last saw you?'

'Oh, I've been busy, busy,' Chloe said sarcastically. 'Out socialising, training for the Olympics – you know the sort of thing.'

'That attitude won't help. You'll only make yourself feel worse,' admonished Maggie gently, noticing her friend's eyes glisten with fresh tears.

'How do you know how I feel?' snapped Chloe.

'I don't, of course. But I can guess,' said Maggie, stifling a knot of incipient impatience.

'You can't possibly know what it's like to be stuck indoors all day with nothing to do but think,' Chloe whined.

Whilst making allowances for her low spirits, Maggie did tend to take a firm line with her when she considered it necessary. Bradley was inclined to be too soft with her. Guilt-ridden, she suspected, by his resentment at having to stay with her. 'You've damaged your hip, Chloe, not lost your limbs or your brains,' she pointed out. 'I know you've had a hard time and things are still bad for you, but you'd feel a whole lot better if you made an effort. There is no need for you to isolate yourself from the world. You can go out, you can even drive if only you'd let Bradley get your car fixed.'

Her friend's eyes narrowed venomously before she laboured through the procedure of painfully rising and, with the aid of her stick, lumbering across the room in an ugly lopsided way, moving her right leg forward and dragging her left. She was breathless from temper, effort and excess weight. 'How would you like to face the world if you walked like this?' she asked.

'I'd prefer it to not seeing the outside world at all except from the window of a car,' said Maggie, feeling the argument drain her of energy. 'You'd make things a lot easier for yourself if only you'd lose some weight. Carrying that lot around is bound to tire you.'

'Easy for you to talk,' riposted Chloe, and Maggie winced at the accusation in her eyes. But how, in all conscience, could Maggie sit back and watch her friend destroy herself without making some sort of effort to stop her?

'Yes it is, I know,' said Maggie in a gentler tone. 'And I didn't come here to quarrel with you. I came to cheer you up.' She glanced towards the window. 'It's a beautiful autumn day. Why don't we go out for a walk? Not far, just to the edge of the Heath. You can go in your chair.'

A tap on the door heralded the arrival of Mrs Marsh with a tray of coffee which Maggie poured while waiting for Chloe's reply. 'Well?' she said, setting a cup of coffee on the table next to the chair where Chloe had been sitting.

'No thanks,' puffed Chloe, limping back across the room and slumping into the chair.

'All right, I won't press you,' said Maggie, not wishing to overlook the fact that the woman *did* have a disability in her anxiety to aid recovery with the suggestion of a little self-help. 'Perhaps you might like to come to see a film with me one evening? I'd enjoy that.'

'No thanks,' said Chloe, making short work of some chocolate biscuits from the coffee tray.

After several more attempts to persuade her to take the first step on the journey back to the human race, Maggie conceded defeat on this occasion and turned the conversation to the news of the day, the break-out from Wormwood Scrubs Prison of spy George Blake who had scaled the outer wall of the jail by using a homemade rope ladder strengthened by ten pairs of knitting needles.

But since Chloe was obviously in no mood to look beyond her own sorry condition, Maggie left quite soon. Always worried about her own approach to Chloe's problem after a visit, she left her car in the Hugheses' drive and walked towards the Heath in a bid to clear her mind before continuing with the day's business.

Walking through an avenue of plane trees, their colour gloriously changed by the season and enriched by the sun, Maggie considered the alarming possibility that Chloe might have sunk to such a low ebb that her role as invalid had become more of a pleasure than a punishment.

Was it possible actually to enjoy being miserable? she wondered.

These thoughts persisted as she trudged through banks of fallen leaves, skirted some ponds then took a path leading to Parliament Hill. Reaching the top, breathless but invigorated, she sat on a wooden bench in the crisp air, enjoying the superb view of London spread before her beneath a pale-blue sky.

Outlying regions of the metropolis were clearly visible from here. She could see the dark patch of Blackheath beyond grey office buildings, their windows winking in the sunlight amid elegant spires; majestic towers; the gentle dome of St Paul's, reassuring among so much new development.

It was a breathtaking sight and one that was hers for very little effort. Realising that the same thing could not be said for Chloe, she felt ashamed of her impatience. The feeling lingered as she made her way back down the hill to collect her car and go home to a working lunch, having taken too much time out from business to allow herself a proper lunchbreak.

Driving back to Ashbrook Green she was haunted by the memory of Chloe's sad face at the window when she had gone back to collect her car. The proverbial wet weekend seemed like a sunny day compared to her. Ah well, she thought there but for the grace of God . . .

Finding herself reduced to tears as Maggie drove away, Chloe stifled her sobs in a handkerchief as protection against Joan's listening ears. For if Chloe was seen to become too weepy, Bradley and Joan began to talk about the possibility of psychiatric help. And she didn't want any of that nonsense. Didn't people realise that she did *not want* to feel happy with the way things were? She did *not want* to make the best of things, or put a brave face on it, or any other damned platitude they might care to use. She wanted to stay bitter and depressed because that was her only strength. If she began to cope she would be too vulnerable.

Life prior to that weekend in Kent with Maggie seemed dreamlike somehow. She could vaguely recall occasional moments of pleasure then, despite her injury. She had liked being at Bushleigh with Joan. She had even enjoyed that weekend with Maggie. Had she really given her a riding lesson? It seemed barely possible now that she didn't even have the strength or inclination to go outside to the garden.

Recalling the touching scene between Bradley and Maggie that Sunday afternoon, she thought how much he must resent being forced to do his duty as a husband and stay with her. Well, he couldn't loathe it more than she hated being tied to him. Being reliant on someone could engender a great deal of resentment and, by God, she had learned to detest every fibre of his being. Yet, perversely, her feeling of

248

helplessness forced her, almost despite herself, into insane possessiveness towards him.

How she envied Maggie her independence. And how Chloe hated this blob of humanity she herself had become. But every day she seemed to grow weaker and more afraid. The pleasure of food soothed her. It took away the fear for short periods of time. But her dependence on it scared her too, for the more she ate, the hungrier she seemed to feel. And she was always so lethargic.

Her reverie was interrupted by the appearance of Joan. 'I've had Mrs Marsh make something tasty for lunch,' she said. 'A couple of fillet steaks with salad and jacket potatoes. It's ready for us in the dining room.'

'Thank you,' Chloe responded gloomily, for the emotion provoked by Maggie's visit and her own subsequent thoughts had robbed her of her appetite and therefore her only pleasure.

'Well, Maggie's visit doesn't seem to have cheered you up,' said Joan, waiting in the doorway to accompany Chloe to the dining room.

'She wanted me to go out for a walk with her,' said Chloe, her voice filled with implied criticism.

'And a very sensible suggestion too,' said Joan, who tried not to traverse the fine line between kindness and condescension. 'You should have gone. It's a lovely day.'

'Perhaps I'll hobble around the garden this afternoon instead,' said Chloe defensively, for she didn't rest easy in the role of recluse.

'That isn't quite the same thing,' Joan pointed out. 'You need to be out among people.'

'Don't nag,' snapped Chloe, hauling herself from the chair and staggering to the adjacent room for lunch.

'I was wondering if you might like me to make you an appointment at the hairdresser's,' ventured Joan tentatively as the two women sat down at the polished table.

'It isn't necessary,' said Chloe. 'I can look after my hair very well myself.'

'Maybe,' said Joan cautiously. 'But it could do with a trim. And a new style might perk you up and encourage you into a spot of dieting. If you were to lose some weight, moving around would be easier for you and you'd feel more like going out.'

Joan's attempts at diplomacy proved fruitless in this instance, for Chloe's meal was shoved across the long table with such force it almost slipped off the other end, followed closely by her knife and fork. 'Don't you dare to patronise me as though I was four years old,' she rasped, her hot eyes blazing at Joan across the table. 'Let's get one thing straight, shall we? I do not want to have my hair done, lose weight, or anything else that constitutes my pulling myself together. So just bloody well leave me alone.'

Being accustomed to tantrums of this sort, Joan said nothing but calmly left the room, whereupon Chloe collapsed into tears. Why could no one understand how very confused and frightened she felt? Of losing Bradley and being alone; of the world; of herself; of everything.

Listening outside the door to the sound of her employer's convulsive sobs, Joan looked at her watch. 'I'll leave her for ten minutes,' she said to herself. 'Then I'll go to her. She'll be ready to apologise by then, poor woman.'

Despite everything, Joan liked Chloe and hated to see her making her own life, and that of those around her, unnecessarily difficult. How Mr Hughes stood it, she didn't know!

Chapter Nineteen

In the spring of 1967 Sally joined millions of other fans in wishing Elvis Presley well in his marriage to long-time sweetheart Priscilla. 'I wouldn't mind changing places with her,' she joked one Sunday while joining her future relatives at Maggie's place for lunch. 'Well, for the honeymoon part anyway.'

There was a roar of laughter.

'You'd really show him what's what, wouldn't you, ducks?' teased Harry Walters, a friend of Dora's who had become a regular guest for Sunday lunch just lately.

'Not 'alf,' chuckled Sally, who still managed to maintain a cheerful front despite the agony of missing Tom. 'But I'm not complainin'. Not while I've got me honeymoon with Tom to look forward to.'

'That's the spirit,' said Harry.

Maggie was pleased that her mother had found a new companion. Harry was an independent trader dealing mostly in bankrupt stock and was reputed to be honest despite his flashy dress and quick wits. He was a widower of about the same age as Dora and they had met at a bingo hall. Since they both frequented such places as the betting shop and the pub it had seemed only natural for them to team up. Harry had the manner and appearance of a spiv but the heart of a gentleman and Maggie approved of him wholeheartedly.

Listening to the jovial chatter, Maggie glanced around the table at the smiling faces of Dora, Royston, Tim – now a fine young man of twenty home for the weekend from university – and Katy as they listened to the banter between Sally and Harry who were both cockney extraverts. When everyone had finished eating she would tell them of a rather upsetting event within her business and the way she planned to deal with it.

A frown marred her features as she pondered over her recent discovery of a rotten apple in the barrel. Being a woman of scrupulous integrity herself, and more than generous to all who worked within her organisation, she was deeply hurt to find her goodwill abused. Her suspicions had first been aroused following a series of complaints about the standard of the bouquets being sold from the Shepherd's Bush shop

251

which was under the management of Bill Wilks and his wife. It was the quantity rather than the quality of the flowers or the floristry which was in question.

Having given her guests the background to her problem, she explained more fully, 'The Wilks are ordering the same amount of stock from our buyer, and their cash turnover hasn't changed, which means they are working a fiddle. They must have fobbed the complainants off, not expecting anyone to contact me direct. That's the good thing about having my office address on all the stationery. It keeps my finger on the pulse.'

'So you think they are selling the flowers that are not being used in the customers' bouquets, as a sideline,' suggested Royston.

'I'm certain of it,' said Maggie, who had followed up the allegations by having a few trusted people, unknown to the suspected couple, make purchases from the shop. And she was ashamed to have such meagre offerings as they had received sold under her name.

'Will you confront them with it?' asked Royston.

'I'll soon sort them out for you, ducks,' offered Harry. 'I'll knock their bleeding blocks off.'

'Nothing can be done until I have proof,' said Maggie. 'And to do that I'll need to find their source of disposal. It would be too risky for them to sell through the shop without putting the money through the till, with the rest of the staff about.' She paused thoughtfully. 'This is where you can help, Harry. There isn't much goes on in the streets of West London that you can't find out about, is there?'

'That's a fact,' he said.

'Good,' said Maggie. 'Once we have proof, this is what I thought we'd do . . .'

And so it was that Maggie, with the co-operation of certain traders, hid among the rails of dresses on the clothes stall next to the flower stand in Ashbrook Green market one Saturday afternoon in June. There, among the fruit and fish barrows, the jewellery and junk stalls, she watched Flo the flower-seller do a roaring trade in choice blooms from Maggie's own stock.

When Bill Wilks appeared on the scene and said, ' 'ello, Flo, luv. I got a message that you wanted to see me. Something about upping yer order,' Maggie stepped out from a row of shirtwaisters and said, 'Hello, Bill. I think "The game is up" is what they say on these occasions, isn't it?'

He was so shocked he just stood rooted to the spot, looking as though he'd swallowed a wasp, while a cluster of people closed ranks around him.

There was Royston, Tim, Harry and Archie. And, of course, Flo,

252

who had not realised the flowers were questionable until informed by Maggie, because the culprit had had the audacity to use shop stationery as receipts for his dishonest transactions.

Flo made good her support for Maggie by swinging her handbag about the crook's shoulders with a resounding thump. 'Greedy bugger,' she growled. 'Your sort can never 'ave enough.'

Maggie did not see any necessity to involve the police but dismissed Bill Wilks on the spot and demanded that he and his wife vacate their free accommodation above the shop within a month.

'Thanks for your help, everybody,' said Maggie, as the group began to disperse. 'Particularly you, Harry, for tracking down his outlet. And you, Flo, for your co-operation.'

'No trouble at all, ducks,' Harry beamed, sucking on one of the giant cigars he was so partial to. 'Always glad to sort out a wrong 'un.'

' 'ear 'ear,' said Flo.

'I think this calls for a celebration,' said Maggie, relieved to see the end of the unpleasant affair. 'How about all of you coming round to my place this evening for a few drinks, if you've nothing else on?'

'Just try and keep us away,' was the general response.

'I won't be there,' said Archie.

'As you wish,' said Maggie. Her one-time brother-in-law didn't change for the better. He was still as strange as ever, seeming to withdraw more deeply into himself with every passing year. But the Moss Street shop did reasonably well under his management, so she had no quarrel with him. And it wasn't as though she had to suffer his company very often.

Like most impromptu parties, this one went with a swing. In addition to this afternoon's group, the gathering also included Dora, Katy, Sally, and Daisy Hughes who was spending the weekend with Katy.

The time factor meant that the food was hardly haute cuisine, but a last-minute raid on the supermarket had produced a variety of tempting tit-bits to accompany the spoils of a visit to the off-licence. Cooked meats, crisps, cheese, pickles, pork pies, things on toast and sausages on sticks had no shortage of takers.

'Mum seems to be enjoying herself,' said Maggie to Royston, glancing across the room to her mother who, smartly dressed in her new blue crimplene dress, was laughing with Harry, gaudily clad in a brown and white check suit with a yellow tie. 'I haven't seen her so happy in years.'

'Are wedding bells on the cards, do you think?' he asked.

Maggie laughed. 'I don't know. Mum says they are just friends. But whatever the situation in that respect, he certainly seems to be good for her. He looks a bit flash, I know, but he's really quite respectable and obviously makes a good living with his deals. He has a house of his own and a decent car.' She sipped a gin and tonic. 'We'll just have to wait and see what happens, but in the meantime it's good to see her having fun.'

'Too true,' agreed Royston, who had been devoted to Dora ever since that first plate of stew and dumplings seven years ago.

'How about a day out at Brighton tomorrow, Dora?' asked Harry, sipping a glass of light ale.

'I'd like that,' she said, smiling at her companion. He was no beauty, a plump, balding man with a rubicund complexion and a wide smile, but Dora enjoyed his company enormously for they had so much in common.

'We'll get there in time for a spot of lunch and a couple of drinks,' he said enthusiastically. 'If the weather is nice we'll 'ave an hour in a deckchair, a few games o' bingo in the amusement park, some cockles and jellied eels for tea, and home in time for supper. What do yer say to that?'

'It sounds just the job,' said Dora, who was enjoying the party immensely. She was grateful to Harry for helping Maggie, and glad that today had seen the end of the whole wretched business.

'Should be a good day,' he said, puffing on his cigar.

'You bet,' she said. Who would have thought she'd find someone to go around with after all these years? She'd thought she was past all that sort of thing. Now it seemed there was life in the old girl yet. And plenty of it!

Unknown to the rest of the party, Katy was suffering simultaneously from the agonising pain of first love and her first real conflict with Daisy. *The bitch, the rotten rotten bitch,* she seethed inwardly, sick with the ache in the pit of her stomach. *She's throwing herself at Tim, just like a common tart.*

Although Tim Slade had never actually indicated that there was anything more than friendship between himself and Katy, the depth of their mutual affection had led her to hope that a romantic relationship would develop when they had both matured a little. After all, the three-year gap between them seemed less all the time. His eighteen years to her fifteen had put him into adulthood while she'd still been struggling through her schooldays. Now, at almost seventeen to his twenty, she was grown and ready for romance.

Having obtained reasonable O-level grades, Katy had conceded to parental pressure to maximise on her opportunities and was now on a two-year course at a London college, working for a business diploma, after which she intended to join her mother in her business with a view to running a shop of her own eventually.

She arranged her features into a smile as she was forced to witness the appalling behaviour of her two so-called friends who were flirting outrageously. And, yes, Tim was being just as blatant as Daisy. All that eye contact and verbal innuendo. It was sickening!

'I believe you're going to be a lawyer,' said Daisy, smiling up into Tim's eyes.

'I hope so,' he replied, gazing at her admiringly. 'Providing I qualify.'

'Well,' said Daisy, fluttering her lashes and flicking her long golden hair back from her face, 'I must say I'm impressed. Lawyers are so charismatic.'

'Do you know many of them?' he teased.

'Er . . . not personally, no,' said Daisy, in the slight American drawl she had picked up from her father and which Tim seemed to find so fascinating. 'But they always seem so powerful and sexy when you see them in films.'

Feeling excluded and close to tears, Katy longed to seek refuge in her bedroom. But since self-respect forbade any such cowardly action, she forced herself back into the conversation by saying, 'I expect you'll go into your father's practice, won't you, Tim?'

'I haven't finally decided yet,' he said, turning his attention only briefly towards her. 'But I expect so.'

'I'd bring my legal business to you any day,' said Daisy seductively, leaning against him, her bosom protruding noticeably through the white skinny-rib top which she wore with a mini skirt.

'Good, I'll look forward to that,' he said huskily.

Unable to bear any more of this torture, Katy muttered 'Excuse me,' and stumbled from the room through a blur of tears.

Tim was enjoying the party, even if it was a little tame compared to the student booze-ups he usually frequented. He had had a good few drinks and was feeling pleasantly benign. Daisy Hughes was proving to be good company. He'd always thought of her as a kid up until now, being a friend of Katy's. But she had certainly destroyed that image tonight with her somnolent eyes and sexy figure.

Vaguely, on the perimeter of his thoughts, he was aware of a worm of unease, as though by flirting with Daisy he was betraying Katy somehow. But why should he feel so? The fact that he was attracted to Daisy was in no way detrimental to his feelings for Katy who was a very dear friend whom he had worshipped like a sister since he was twelve.

What he felt for her wasn't a case for the sowing of wild oats. It was far more precious. And, anyway, she was still a child. The sudden realisation that Daisy was the same age shocked him for a moment. But she was different. Like him, she was looking for nothing more than a good time. The day to settle down with one woman would come soon enough. Right now he wanted to have fun.

But why had Katy flounced off in a huff a few minutes ago, as though all the sadness of the world were on her shoulders? Even as he pondered the question, he saw her re-enter the room, tall and graceful in a green mini dress, her freshly brushed red hair flowing to her shoulders. She was growing into a beautiful young woman, he thought. Whereas Daisy was voluptuous and blatantly sexy, Katy had a real look of the times about her. She was as slim as a reed, with small firm breasts, long legs and a waif-like face from which huge blue eyes shone out.

Now she glanced across to where he and Daisy were sitting, the latter's hand resting tormentingly on his knee, then looked away and entered into conversation with Sally.

Daisy said, 'My father is collecting me at midnight tonight, like Cinderella. But I'm free tomorrow night if you're interested.'

He turned and looked into those inviting eyes. 'I'm interested,' he said.

Later, he made a point of having a private word with Katy. 'What's the matter?' he asked. 'Are you sore because Daisy and I are having fun together?'

She threw him a haughty look. 'Don't flatter yourself,' she said. 'What you do is none of my business. You're a free agent.'

It was a delicate moment and he sensed that the way he handled it was important to his future relations with her. She was obviously very upset indeed about him and Daisy. Instinctively he felt compelled to apologise, to explain that his flirtation with Daisy was just a casual thing of no real consequence. But to do so would be to establish the fact that there was something other than friendship below the surface of his relationship with Katy. And he wasn't ready to admit that, not even to himself.

He was still young. He wanted to experience life a little before he seriously committed himself to anyone. And Katy also needed to fall in love a few times before she recognised the real thing. The hurt in her eyes caused a mixture of pain, shame and claustrophobia in him. She instilled in him a need to escape, and he felt that he must establish his independence. In that moment he realised that the affectionate and uncomplicated friendship they had shared for seven years was no longer possible.

'Still friends?' he said with deliberate lightness.

'Of course,' she said, smiling a little too brightly.

'Good,' he said, stifling the urge to take her in his arms.

And as he proved his independence by leaving Katy for the undemanding pleasure of Daisy's charms, he felt a lingering sadness which he didn't understand.

Later, when all the guests had departed, Maggie stood outside Katy's room listening to her weeping. She wondered whether to go in, or if it might be kinder to leave her alone. Whilst enjoying a close relationship with her daughter, the days were long gone when Maggie could personally solve all her problems. Now she had the girl's pride and privacy to consider as well as her pain.

Dora finally made the decision for her. 'Let her come to you if she needs you,' she whispered before departing to bed in her own apartment.

Maggie was about to get into bed when Katy padded in and sat on the edge of the bed. 'How could Daisy do it to me, Mum?' she asked, her face pink and puffy from crying. 'She knows how I feel about Tim.'

'I'm sure they were just having a bit of fun,' said Maggie, who had noticed events among the young people earlier. 'It was a party, after all. People do all sorts of silly things at parties.'

'Humph!' snorted Katy. 'They humiliated me.'

'But Tim isn't committed to you, is he?' she pointed out, deciding that common sense would be of far more use to Katy than sympathy. 'So it isn't as if he's betrayed you or anything.'

'He and I might very well have become committed if Daisy hadn't poked her nose, or rather her damned great bosom, in,' said Katy. 'You'd think she'd have felt some loyalty to me, wouldn't you?'

Maggie smarted at the memory of her own traumatic involvement with Daisy's parents. 'Unfortunately, chemistry between people can't be made to flow in the direction that we might wish,' she said. 'These things happen and I doubt if either Daisy or Tim intended to hurt you.'

'Well, they have, whatever their intentions.' Her voice trembled on fresh tears. 'They're seeing each other tomorrow night. Well, I hope Daisy isn't going to come gloating to me.'

'Daisy isn't like that, and you know it,' admonished Maggie. Indeed, Maggie found Daisy to be a most delightful girl. She tended to be over exuberant at times, but never malicious. 'She's very young and she found herself attracted to Tim who is an available young man. You can't expect her to go against her instincts because he is a friend of yours.'

'Maybe not, but she did go all out to get him,' said Katy. 'And I do really love him, Mum.'

'I know,' said Maggie, sitting on the side of the bed with a comforting arm around her daughter's shoulders. 'But you'll probably experience the feeling many times again before you're through.'

'I'm almost seventeen and you married Daddy when you were eighteen,' she pointed out.

'Yes, indeed I did.' Maggie cast her mind back to her own immature marriage which had been prompted by the relentless attentions of Rupert Anderson. Her destiny might have been very different had she been free when she had first met Bradley. 'But that doesn't mean that I'd necessarily advocate it for others.'

Katy looked surprised. 'But you and Daddy were happy, weren't you?'

'Yes, we were happy,' she said truthfully. 'But not all early marriages are so successful.'

'I'd marry Tim tomorrow if he asked me,' said Katy.

Maggie was thoughtful for a few moments. 'This may seem heartless, but I'm glad that he isn't likely to. Not for a few years anyway.'

'Well, you certainly know how to make a girl feel good,' said Katy dryly. 'And, yes, you're right, it does seem heartless.'

'You need time to grow up,' advised Maggie. 'But don't be in too much of a hurry. This is a wonderful era in which to be young. Make the most of it. Meet new people, accept new challenges, broaden your horizons. Give Tim time to do the same. Later on, if you still feel the same about him – well, who knows?'

'We've always been such good friends. Now I feel as though I have lost even that,' confessed Katy.

'Falling in love always complicates things,' said Maggie, speaking from painful experience. 'But you'd be wise to behave as you always have towards him. If you're going to throw a fit of pique every time he shows an interest in another woman, you won't see anything of him at all.'

'I don't see so much of him as I used to, anyway.'

'And it's natural that you won't, he's away at university for one thing,' Maggie sensibly pointed out. 'He'll be making new friends and finding his feet as an adult. Let him go, let him have fun. Have fun yourself. You certainly won't keep him by trying to tie him down now. You may even feel quite differently about him later on.'

'I won't,' said Katy vehemently.

'Only time will tell,' said Maggie.

Later, alone in the dark, Maggie thought that she was probably the least qualified person to advise anyone on affairs of the heart, considering her own track record in that department. 'If you're so wise, how come you're thirty-six years old and alone in this bed?' she asked herself. 'Business is your forte, Maggie Radford, not love!'

Chapter Twenty

The one thing Lilian Hughes was determined to see before she died was her daughter-in-law's recovery. And she refused to accept that this was not possible. Good heavens above, this was 1968, the age of advanced medicine. If Christian Barnard could transplant the heart of one person into another, surely somewhere there was a surgeon who could do something about Chloe's hip?

It was January 1968 and Lilian and Will, now well-preserved septuagenarians, were back in Philadelphia having spent Christmas in London with Bradley and his family, a holiday ruined by the horrifying metamorphosis that had taken place in Chloe since they had last seen her. The attractive woman who had married their son now had about as much glamour and personality as a ton of hamburger meat.

Having perceived, many years ago, underlying hostility between Bradley and his wife, Lilian had guessed that theirs was not a happy marriage. But not one to insist upon perfection, she accepted this without comment and liked Chloe for all her faults, considering her well-being, as the mother of her grandchild, to be of paramount importance.

Perhaps Chloe could have coped with her disablement more courageously, she thought, but the poor woman obviously didn't have it in her to do so and that was all there was to it. The human race would be a boring species if everyone had the same degree of fortitude with which to face adversity. Oh, it was easy to criticise her for not making the effort, and for abusing her injured body by greed, but how did any of us know how we might behave in like circumstances? Lilian asked herself. Anyway, the important thing was to get something done for her. Chloe might have accepted defeat but Lilian was certainly not prepared to.

To this end she had put certain wheels in motion on their return. She and Will were not without contacts in Philadelphia society, and the United States had its fair share of brilliance in the medical field. Once she had made her requirements known in the right quarters, it wasn't long before someone had come up with the name of an expert in the relatively new field of hip replacement.

He was an Englishman, of Scottish extraction, called Andrew

Maitland who had brought his skills to the USA five years ago in the belief that there was more scope to specialise here. After an initial chat with him on the telephone in early February, Lilian invited him to join her and Will for dinner at their home.

'Will you have some more chicken and sweetcorn, Andrew?' said Lilian, having quickly dispensed with the formality of surnames. 'And there is plenty more sweet potato pie.'

Andrew Maitland raised his hand. 'As much as I'd like to say yes to a third helping, I'd like to save some room for dessert,' he said. 'It is a delicious meal, though.'

Lilian beamed for she was proud of her hospitality. 'Why, thank you.' He was charming, if a little outspoken, she thought. And quite handsome too in an untidy sort of way. His hair was the colour of coal, speckled with grey and surrounding his square face in a curly mop which matched his beard. He was a big man, tall and broad with large features, a crooked nose with a bump on the bridge, dark bushy eyebrows, a well-shaped mouth and the most piercing blue eyes she had ever seen. She thought he was probably in his forties, but beards always aged a man, in her eyes. 'Now, about our son's wife in England . . .'

'As I said on the telephone,' said Andrew, meeting his hostess's candid stare, 'it is impossible for me to say whether or not I can help her without speaking to the doctor in charge of her case and reading the medical notes. And, of course, seeing the patient.'

'They say you're the best in your field,' said Lilian.

Recoiling from the reverence in her voice, Andrew said, 'I'm only doing the work for which I was trained.'

'Sure, sure,' said Will. 'But we're hoping you'll agree to use that training to help the little lady who's married to our son.'

'And how does she feel about it?' asked Andrew, contemplating the portion of apple pie and ice cream served to him by a maid.

Lilian and Will exchanged glances. 'Well . . . we haven't actually mentioned it to her yet,' admitted Lilian sheepishly. 'It didn't seem right to raise her hopes, before you'd even agreed to take a look at her.'

'I see,' said Andrew.

There were several family photographs dotted about the Hughes home. Will rose and plucked one from the wide window sill. 'This here is Chloe. A fine-looking woman, huh?'

It was a picture of her before her accident, standing beside her horse. Andrew found himself suddenly breathless for she was indeed a striking woman. She was wearing a sweater and jodhpurs, her dark hair sweeping smoothly to her shoulders. 'Yes, she certainly is lovely,' he said, unaccountably moved by something in her eyes. Her fine white teeth were bared in a smile, but there was a haunting sadness in those beautiful eyes which reminded him of the loneliness he himself so often experienced.

'She doesn't look like that now,' explained Lilian. 'She's let herself go to fat.'

'Sorry for herself, eh?' said Andrew.

'Wouldn't you be if you couldn't do the things the rest of us take for granted?' asked Lilian defensively.

'Perhaps,' said Andrew. 'But I am constantly amazed at the capacity of the human spirit to accept tragedy without defeat.'

Andrew's dedication to his work had already cost him his marriage. His ex-wife was now married to his best friend after walking out on him five years ago. He accepted the blame for the failure of his marriage. His work was a formidable rival for any woman, absorbing him as it did and putting everything else in second place. He was quite unable to close his mind to his job. It went everywhere with him. And no woman could be expected to tolerate that.

The offer of a post as a consultant surgeon in a hospital here in Philadelphia had been just what he had needed after the divorce. Now he lived entirely for work and avoided burdening himself with the demands of a relationship. Sure, he was as lonely as hell. Sure, he got homesick. But there was always another interesting case to take his mind off himself. Work was his relaxation, his only hobby being classical music which he listened to avidly at home and in the city's many concert halls, whenever he could find the time.

'The lady in question does not appear to have your sympathy,' suggested Lilian, matching Andrew's forthright manner with her own.

'As a doctor, I try not to become too personally involved with my patients,' he said, savouring for a moment the delicious apple pie. 'My interest is purely professional.'

'But will you consider Chloe's case?' Lilian asked bluntly. 'It will mean a trip to England for you, for she'll never agree to come here. And then you could talk to her London doctors personally. Money is no object, of course. We'll pay all your expenses, plus reimbursement for any loss of earnings here while you are away, as well as your fee and the hospital charges.'

Andrew was thoughtful. He had a clause in his contract with the hospital which allowed him time out to attend to his consultancy practice. But if he accepted the Hughes case it would mean a lengthy spell in London, for he would want to monitor the patient's progress for some time after the operation. Did he want to be away that long? He glanced at the photograph now standing on the table beside him. The woman intrigued him. The husband looked a nice guy too; he'd noticed several wedding photographs in the other room during pre-prandial cocktails. Life couldn't be a bed of roses for him either, especially if his wife was a self-pitying type.

Now intrigued by the case, he searched his mind for a solution to the problem of having to charge these warm and generous people the earth for his services. An idea struck him. He hadn't been back home for five years, and he was due extended leave. He'd not taken a full vacation since he'd been here. Why not take six months' leave and make the trip to London a working holiday? That way the Hughes need only pay his fee, some of his expenses and the hospital charges, without the added burden of reimbursing him for the time he spent with the patient before and after the operation. He would use the rest of the time to look up relatives and old friends. He felt quite excited at the idea of seeing the old country again.

'All right, I'll take the case,' he told them. 'But are you sure you want to spend so much money on something that may not have a positive result? Surgical success can never be guaranteed, you know.'

Lilian gestured towards the luxuriously appointed room with its pale green carpet and fine polished furniture, and wide windows overlooking rolling gardens in this exclusive Philadelphia suburb. 'What else are we gonna do with our money at our age but spend it?' she asked. 'We've everything we need. Our son is a rich man in his own right, and he'll be even richer when we've gone. It would give us a deal of pleasure to use our cash for something useful.'

'She must mean a lot to you,' said Andrew.

'She's family,' said Lilian, as though that explained everything.

'The first thing you must do is to get the patient's agreement to see me,' he told them. 'For I can do nothing without her complete co-operation. Once you've done that, I'll make arrangements with the hospital here to spend some time in London.'

'We're mighty grateful to you,' said Will.

'We sure are,' agreed Lilian. 'Now, can I tempt you to another helping of apple pie?'

'I'd love some more, please,' said Andrew, smiling. He liked these big-hearted people. That daughter-in-law of theirs was a lucky woman, and he wondered if she knew it.

'The crowds are still pouring into the new Beatles Apple Boutique,' said Maggie to Chloe one morning in February. 'I noticed it when I was on business in the West End the other day.'

'Are they?' asked Chloe, far more interested in the doughnut she was having with her morning coffee than the pop group's latest venture. 'I bet there are more sightseers than buyers though. They say the clothes are very expensive.'

'Ummm,' agreed Maggie, sipping her coffee and preventing the remaining doughnut from finding a home inside Chloe by eating it herself. 'There will be a market for them among London's trendy elite, though, I should think.'

'Probably,' agreed Chloe absently, enthusiastically licking the sugar from her lips.

But Maggie was not here for the purpose of idle chatter. She was here, at Bradley's request, to try to persuade Chloe to see a surgeon who might be able to help her, since Bradley's own attempts in this direction had failed completely.

'What's this I hear about you refusing to see this doctor Bradley's parents have found?' she said, dabbing her sugary fingers with a fine linen napkin.

Chloe's sunken eyes turned to slits. 'Ah, so that's it, is it? You've been recruited to talk sense into troublesome Chloe.'

'Yes, that's right,' said Maggie, deciding that a firm line was her wisest course of action, 'I understand from Bradley that you won't even hear what the man has to offer.'

'I've had enough of doctors prodding me about,' she explained, making a start on a plate of biscuits. 'Why should I let some Yank start the whole thing off again?'

'Because there is a very good chance that he can change your life for the better, that's why,' Maggie pointed out earnestly. 'And you owe it to Bradley's parents to make an effort since they have gone to the trouble of approaching him.'

Chloe sank her teeth into a custard cream. 'Mmm, these are delicious. You should try one, Maggie,' she said with infuriating disregard for her friend's concern.

'Don't change the subject,' Maggie said in exasperation. Chloe was becoming more impossible by the moment. Both Maggie and Bradley were worried about her weight which she seemed determined to increase at the fastest possible rate. 'Do you not want to be cured, Chloe, is that it?'

Throwing Maggie a withering look, Chloe said, 'Of course I do. What do you think I am, some sort of a nut? But if anything more could be done for me, the doctors would have done it.'

'Not necessarily. Medical science is advancing all the time,' Maggie reminded her. 'This surgeon from the States is a specialist in your particular field. If he is optimistic enough to be willing to travel to London, the least you can do is to see him.'

'No thanks,' she said breezily, helping herself to another biscuit. 'I've accepted my fate and learned to live with it.'

'You call this living!' exclaimed Maggie incredulously. 'Sitting

263

around all day, getting more obese by the minute. Soon you won't even be able to cross the room. And not because of your hip, but because you simply won't have the strength to drag your excess weight around.'

'I knew my weight would come into it,' snapped Chloe. 'Food is my only pleasure. Why does everyone want to deprive me of that too?'

'Because you're killing yourself with it,' sighed Maggie. All this was a terrible strain, for she was not without compassion for Chloe's plight. Sympathy, however, would not aid recovery.

'It's all very well for you to sit there preaching at me,' snapped Chloe. 'You are safely in the lifeboat.'

'I can't deny that,' said Maggie, clinging tenaciously to her patience. 'But this man could put you back in the lifeboat with me. Give him a chance, please, Chloe.'

'No!'

Maggie chewed her lip, determined not to allow her friend to sink deeper into the abyss. 'Do you think you are being fair to Bradley and Daisy by letting this chance pass you by?' she asked. 'Your condition must be a strain for them too, you know.'

Chloe threw Maggie a shrewd look. 'Ah, now we're getting to the truth of the matter,' she said bitterly. 'It isn't me you're worried about but your precious Bradley.'

'All that was over years ago, and you know it.' The turn in the conversation gave Maggie an idea that just might work. 'Is that why you are so determined not to get better? Because you are afraid that Bradley won't stay with you unless he is tied to you by your disability.'

There was a tense silence before Chloe asked, 'Are you suggesting that he only stays because of it?'

'You're making damned sure he doesn't stay from pleasure at being with you,' declared Maggie hotly. 'I mean, just take a look at yourself. Your good looks and personality have disappeared under a sea of indulgence and self-pity. What could possibly motivate Bradley – or any other man, for that matter – to stay around but duty? You used to be a beautiful and amusing woman. You could be again.'

This was the first time Maggie had been this brutal in her attempts at stimulating Chloe to recovery, and she saw her words hit home. Chloe winced and pushed the remaining biscuits away.

'It's in your interest for me to get better, so that you and Bradley can go off together,' she suggested wearily.

'I've told you that that is long over and I meant it,' Maggie said, though she knew in her heart that it never could be. 'If you pull yourself together and start to be a wife to him, he won't want to be anywhere but with you.'

Knowing she had been forced into a corner, Chloe gave a deep sigh.

'OK, just to stop everyone saying how difficult I'm being, I'll see the wretched man.'

Maggie breathed a sigh of relief. 'I'm so pleased, Chloe,' she said warmly, going to her friend and hugging her. 'I'm sure you won't regret it.'

'I've only said I'll see him,' Chloe warned, 'that does not mean that I will agree to anything else. It's easy for you to talk about an operation. You don't have to go through it.'

'Yes, I know.' Maggie's tone was gentler now. She moved the telephone from a table by the window to the arm of Chloe's chair. 'Call your husband and tell him your decision.'

'Not until I've had another biscuit.'

Recognising the act as a message of defiance, in this particular instance Maggie didn't blame Chloe one bit. As she had so rightly pointed out, talking about an operation for someone else was easy.

Andrew Maitland's firm approach to Chloe's problem made Maggie's hard line seem like marshmallow in comparison, and Chloe was shaken by it.

'Of course, Mrs Hughes,' he informed her briskly at their first interview, 'surgery is out of the question unless you are prepared to lose some weight first. The strain on your heart would be too great as you are now. Good Lord above, you must be twice the size you were before the accident if the photograph I saw is anything to go by. How the devil has it happened?'

'Well . . .' Chloe felt crushed in the presence of his overpowering personality. 'I suppose I must have been eating too much.'

'I should think you've been gorging yourself from dawn to dusk,' he said candidly. 'I'd never have recognised you from the photograph.'

'Surely I'm not that bad?'

'From a medical point of view you certainly are that bad,' he stated categorically.

'Are you this rude to all your patients?' she asked tartly, suddenly goaded into retaliation by his appalling manners.

'If it's for the benefit of their health, yes,' he told her, his blue eyes resting on her in a most disturbing way.

'It's a wonder you've any left then,' she countered acidly. 'I'm sure there is no shortage of doctors in America equally as well qualified as you but with better manners.'

'I don't lack for patients,' he informed her bluntly, 'but I'm in the business of mending bodies, not toadying for social acceptance.'

It was March before he had been able to clear his schedule in the States. Now they were in a consulting room he had the use of in Harley

Street. Bradley had driven his wife here and was waiting outside in the foyer.

'Well, no one could accuse you of charm,' said Chloe cuttingly. What an arrogant man he was. How dare he speak to her this way. He'd do well to remember that it was people like her who kept him in comfort. Why, he was nothing more than a public servant! This was Harley Street where you expected the best, yet he had the manners of a yob. And she'd seen better-groomed specimens on Guy Fawkes bonfires. His clothes were creased, the brown stripe in his tie clashed with the blue fleck in his suit, his hair hadn't seen a pair of scissors in years, and as for that terrible beard . . .

'If you are seeking to have your ego boosted, Mrs Hughes, I suggest you try a beauty parlour,' he said crisply. 'Now, to get to the point. I have had a long discussion with the physician who treated you after the accident, and I have studied your X-rays thoroughly. I am confident that a hip replacement will be of value to you. Nothing can be guaranteed, of course, but the success rate of this particular type of surgery is fairly high.'

Chloe slipped into a reverie. She had come here today ready to take down a peg or two some smartass Yank conceited enough to think that he could succeed where others had failed. Instead she was buffeted by the strength of his charisma which seemed to fill the room.

'But, as I have said,' he continued, 'we cannot even consider an operation unless you are prepared to go on a very strict diet for a while beforehand.'

Her emotions were in turmoil. This man had lowered her self-esteem to zero, yet aroused her appetite for life for the first time in years. She was angry with him, yet amused by him too. He both unnerved and reassured her, it was strange. But right now he was waiting for an answer. The road to freedom was tempting, but seemed to offer only deprivation and discomfort in the immediate future. 'I need time to think about it,' she said. 'I'm not sure if I want to have an operation.'

Disappointment darkened his eyes. 'I see. Naturally you will want to talk it over with your husband.' His tone was formal. 'I shall need to know fairly soon, though, as I shall return to the States earlier than I had planned if my services are not required here.' He ran his eye over her flabby form. 'And we would need at least two or three months for you to shed sufficient weight.' He paused and Chloe smarted and thrilled simultaneously under his scrutiny. 'If you do decide to go ahead, we'll get you on a diet right away, and I shall monitor your progress personally.' He paused again as though choosing his words carefully. 'It's a depressing thought, I know. I love my food too. But no pleasure without pain, eh,

266

Mrs Hughes? Effort brings its own reward and all that.'

That was positively the last straw for Chloe. 'Meaning that I don't put any effort into life, I suppose?' she rasped, her eyes blazing with all her old spirit. 'You've got a nerve! You sit there in all your glory, probably never having known any worse physical discomfort than a hangover, and you think you have some Godgiven right to criticise me.' She drew breath, her eyes burning with angry tears. 'Well, you'll not get me down with your miserable insults, I'm made of sterner stuff. I'll go on your bloody diet and I'll make a success of it, you just see if I don't. And you can make arrangements for me to have the operation as soon as possible, do you hear?'

The explosion was far more of a surprise to Chloe than it was to Andrew, since his deliberate provocation had had the desired effect in shaking her from her trough of apathy. Quite why this case was so important to him, he didn't know since the damned woman would probably make the world's most difficult patient. But her decision delighted him. 'Good,' he said, ignoring her bad temper. Taking a sheet of paper from his drawer, he handed it to her. 'This a diet sheet I have made up for you. You get started on it right away and I'll see you once a week to monitor how you are getting along.'

Accepting it in a daze, Chloe said, 'You were pretty damned sure of yourself, weren't you? To have prepared it beforehand.'

Suddenly she found herself melting in the warmth of his smile. 'I didn't come all this way just for a consultation,' he told her cheerfully. 'That isn't my style at all.'

Imbued with an exhilarating sense of challenge hitherto unknown, she said, 'No, I don't imagine it is.'

He became briskly efficient. 'Now, would it suit you better if I visited you at home, rather than you having to get your husband to drive you here for our weekly meetings?'

'It would be simpler, yes,' she said. 'But I suppose you charge the earth for a home visit?'

'No extra charge,' he assured her brightly, radiating enthusiasm now that she was officially his patient. 'It's all part of the service.' He consulted his diary. 'Let's see. It's Monday today, so I'll see you a week from today at ten a.m. Weigh yourself when you get home, then not again until I see you.'

'Ten o'clock isn't convenient. I don't get up that early,' she said.

'You will on Monday, though, won't you?' he said, grinning roguishly. And before she had a chance to argue with him, he ended the interview by rising. 'I'll just have a few words with your husband about the arrangements.'

While she was heaving her bulk from the chair, he left the room to speak to Bradley, as though she was of no importance at all. Honestly, of all the cheek!

If she bade him a rather cool goodbye then, it was nothing compared to her icy greeting when he called at her home the following Monday morning.

'Well,' he said, ignoring the nip in the air, 'how have you been? Do you have the scales ready?'

In reply she held up the diet sheet and tore it in half. 'That is what I think of your diet,' she snapped. 'I thought you had my welfare at heart. I did not realise you intended to starve me to death.'

Apparently unperturbed, he took a replica of the diet sheet from his briefcase and handed it to her. Then he calmly sat down in an armchair near the drawing-room window, smiled seraphically, and said, 'Well, aren't you going to offer me some coffee?'

Increasingly bemused by his behaviour, she rang for Mrs Marsh. But when the coffee arrived and he insisted on serving it, thereby depriving Chloe of her usual generous helping of milk and sugar, she was close to apoplexy. 'Are you both deaf and blind?' she exploded. 'I have just made it obvious that I do not wish to keep to that ridiculous diet of yours.'

He handed her a small plastic container. 'Try a sweetener with your coffee, if it will help,' he said with infuriating calm.

Sighing patiently, she said, 'Look, I'll try to lose a little weight by cutting down.' She waved the replacement diet sheet in the air. 'But this is far too drastic for me.'

'Drastic measures are called for because you have taken things too far the other way,' he pointed out calmly. 'Now, tell me what your weight was this time last week before you popped on the scales. And no fibbing now.'

Oh, really, this was the giddy limit! 'Don't you dare patronise me,' she warned. 'I am not a child, you know. I'm hardly likely to lie about it.'

'You'd be surprised how many people do,' he said.

'Well, I'm not one of them,' she snorted. 'Anyway, I did lose a few pounds last week.'

'Well done,' he said without condescension. 'But I presume from your mood that you binged at the weekend and put it all back on again.'

She scowled. He was too clever by half. 'And what if I did? Your diet just isn't suitable for me, I've told you. You'll have to work out something less severe.'

'Not possible, given the circumstances,' he informed her. 'This diet is perfect for you because it's low in calories and high in vitamins.'

'The only thing that diet is good for is malnutrition,' she snorted. Oh, where were the simple halcyon days of yesterday when comfort was taken for granted? She looked at the dratted diet sheet. 'How do you expect me to survive on three measly meals a day without anything in between? And they're not even proper meals. A grapefruit for breakfast, a lean chop and green vegetables for lunch, steamed fish for dinner . . . I mean, what sort of a menu is that for anyone?'

'You can have plenty of fruit,' he reminded her. 'You'll soon get used to it, and your system will begin to demand less. And it won't be forever, you know.'

'This whole thing is more than I can bear,' wailed Chloe.

'Well,' he began, sipping his coffee, 'I can't make you do it. But neither can I risk surgery unless you do. It's entirely up to you.'

She spread her hands despairingly. 'There must be an easier way. How about if I take some exercise?'

'Exercise will help,' he said. 'But that alone will not be enough in your case. A strict but nourishing diet is the only answer.' He was thoughtful for a few moments. 'I think I had better see you more often than once a week. To encourage you and to stop you falling by the wayside.'

Heaven knew why, since the man was anathema to her, but the thought of seeing him more often pleased her. And to her annoyance she found his insolent assumption that he could feel free to call on her whenever he liked oddly alluring. In fact he was the sexiest man she had ever met. And since she had not measured anyone in those terms for a very long time, this realisation was something of a watershed. 'There's no need for that,' she said, but it was only a token protest.

'There obviously is,' he said. 'If this last week is anything to go by, you're not going to manage without support. Your husband has his business to attend to, he can't be expected to watch you all the time. I'll call in every morning, including the weekend if that is convenient.'

Instead of objecting, she found herself asking him where he was staying.

'Quite close actually, in Camden Town,' he said.

Damning the curiosity that prompted the question, she asked, 'Is your wife in London with you?'

'I'm divorced,' he supplied crisply. 'I'm staying with my sister.'

'I see.' She was hungry for more details. 'Do you like living in America?'

'It suits me fine.'

'Do you miss England?'

'Sometimes, naturally.'

His brevity indicated a reluctance to engage in personal conversation

269

and an awkward silence fell between them until he steered the conversation back to the purpose of his visit.

'Right, that's settled then,' he said crisply. 'I'll just give your husband a call at his office to make sure he doesn't mind having his privacy invaded for a few minutes at the weekend. Then we'll weigh you, and I'll be on my way.'

And with infuriating aplomb he used the telephone on the table next to her chair, speaking to Bradley like a fellow conspirator and old friend. 'Yes, I'd like to call at the weekends, too, because they will be difficult for her . . . more temptation about . . . Yes, we must both get the whip out to her if she goes one calorie over the top of her limit . . . Uhmm, yes, it is very important that she lose some weight.' A booming laugh. 'Keep the kitchen door locked, yes! It won't be easy, but once she begins to see and feel an improvement she'll be eager to get into pretty clothes again. That will keep her on the straight and narrow . . .'

What did he mean, pretty clothes 'again'? These loose smocks were quite attractive, and fashionable too. Well, OK, perhaps a size eighteen did look a little like a marquee. But the material was good and they were well made.

'I'll be off now, Mrs Hughes,' Andrew said, collecting his briefcase. 'I'll see you tomorrow morning sharp at ten. I'll see myself out. Goodbye.'

And leaving her feeling as though a bulldozer had just run amok in her life, she sat weakly in her chair mulling over his visit. 'All that sniping about my appearance,' she muttered under her breath. 'He's no Rock Hudson himself with his broken nose and his revolting bird's nest of beard. What some women see in hirsute men is a mystery to me.' But it was so long since she had been attracted to any man, she'd almost forgotten what it felt like. Until now . . .

'Ah, you're up and about,' he said the next morning, noticing how different she looked with her freshly washed hair worn loose instead of drawn back so severely. It had rather a wild look about it, he thought, obviously hadn't been styled for a long time. But it was shiny and thick and very attractive.

'No, I'm still in bed,' she quipped waggishly. Although she would rather die than admit it to him, there was something frightfully enjoyable about having a purpose to the day, even if she was plagued with hunger pangs for most of it.

'How has it been?' he said, plonking himself down in his usual chair by the window and looking at her.

'Awful,' she said.

'Any lapses?'

'No,' she said triumphantly.

'Well done,' he said, rewarding her with one of his rare smiles which were rather like a sudden burst of sunlight through a black stormcloud. 'Keep going like that and the scales will reward you generously.'

And they did. And as weight decreased, so energy increased. Her hunger grew less, her clothes felt looser. And she actually began to look forward to waking up in the morning.

Chapter Twenty-one

Bradley was delighted with the change in his wife. It was so good to see her smiling about the house, and a new generosity seemed to have crept into her personality. She had even inquired after his day the other evening when he'd returned from business. Even their preoccupied daughter commented on the improvement in the domestic atmosphere, on a rare occasion when she had surfaced from her all-absorbing social life and A-level swotting for long enough to notice anything.

Life was much less harrowing for Bradley now and he no longer dreaded going home in the evening. Up until recently, since the accident, he had been made to feel guilty for his good health by the tacit accusation of his wife's obvious discomfort. Her gluttony and lack of spirit had irritated yet saddened him too.

But Andrew had changed all that. He had given her back her self-respect and for this Bradley was deeply grateful. Andrew and he had become friends for the consultant made a point of keeping him regularly informed of his wife's progress. Bradley liked him a lot. He was dedicated to his job and didn't waste time with fripperies. A man after Bradley's own heart, in fact, and they understood each other perfectly.

The improvement in Chloe's general demeanour had ameliorated Bradley's relationship with her too. Not in any intimate sense, for neither wanted that, but it had led to a greater sense of companionship. Now that she was making such an effort, Bradley wanted to encourage and help her. Their outings, once so resisted by her because of her determination not to enjoy them, had been transformed into pleasant weekend interludes during which, for the first time in years, they spoke to each other as mutually respected human beings. Also, now that she took pleasure in treats, it was fun to give her non-edible gifts such as perfume and flowers.

It was refreshing for Bradley to be able to broaden the scope of their conversation to include the outside world now that Chloe was able to look beyond herself. As her self-confidence grew, so her possessiveness towards him lessened. Released from the claustrophobic clutches of her excessive demands, he found himself genuinely interested in her progress. 'How much have you lost this week?' he'd ask. Or, 'My, you're looking good today,' when she managed to squeeze into the clothes of a smaller size.

If she was prepared to make the effort to put her life back on course, then the least he could do was to support her. After all, one day they might be able to lead their own separate lives after all, he thought. And in the meantime a smiling face was much easier to tolerate than a scowling one.

The events in the Hughes household were very much on Maggie's mind as she dined with Royston in a West End restaurant on Sunday 17 March. No matter how reconciled she was to the fact that there could be no future for her with Bradley, it was still a painful experience to watch the man you loved falling in love with someone else which was, from Maggie's viewpoint, what seemed to be happening to Bradley and Chloe.

Her friend looked happier than Maggie had ever seen her. There was a new bloom about her, a fresh glint to her eyes. And Bradley had lost that strained, haunted look. He laughed with Chloe now, and there was nothing he wouldn't do for her. The change in the couple was astounding.

'Look what Bradley brought home for me last night,' Chloe would say to Maggie, brandishing the finest perfume or jewellery under her nose. 'Isn't he being a sweetie to me just lately?'

Indeed he was, thought Maggie ruefully. And he was positively boastful about the return of his wife's figure, almost like a parent over a child's achievements.

But now Royston was saying, 'What will Katy's job actually be in the firm when she joins you on a full-time basis in September?'

'Anything and everything,' she explained, forcing her mind to the present. 'I want her to have a complete grounding in the business. I'll make sure she gets plenty of experience on the floristry side, but she'll also work in the office with me, and go out to any of the shops who need her, since there is usually understaffing in one or other of them. A diploma is all very well, but she'll need actual work experience before I can put her in charge of her own shop. In a year or two I shall be ready to open another outlet. By that time she'll be ready too.'

'It sounds very sensible to me,' he said.

On the way to the car park after leaving the restaurant they noticed heavier crowds than usual and a certain electricity in the air. Suddenly, throngs of people with anti-Vietnam War banners appeared all around them, marching purposefully forward.

'They must be coming from the rally in Trafalgar Square,' said Maggie. 'I heard that there was to be one today.'

'I think you're right.' Royston's hand tightened protectively on her arm as swarms of people jostled exuberantly past them.

Inspired by natural curiosity, they detoured slightly from their course, moving with the masses towards Grosvenor Square. Here they found themselves on the hinterland of a battlefield as police fought with protestors to keep order. It was chaos! The square resounded to the thud of scuffles and skirmishes while police sirens wailed ominously. Mounted police fought to avoid firecrackers and smoke bombs, and officers' helmets were being knocked off and flung around in the crowd.

At the nucleus of the activity was an attempt by the protestors to storm the American Embassy. Determined youths using banners as battering rams charged the police cordon in front of the Embassy, but the guard remained in place. While stones and paint were being hurled towards the building, the injured were helped into ambulances, the protestors into police vans.

'We'd better get away from here,' said Royston.

'You're right,' agreed Maggie.

But it wasn't that easy with crowds swirling around them in this normally elite square, and police officers bringing down the scurrying offenders amid the daffodils and bushes. When they finally extricated themselves from the angry scenes, Maggie felt relieved but involved somehow.

As Royston drove her home, the ugly scenes lingered in her mind, illuminating her own insignificance in the scheme of things. Weighed against something like the Vietnam War, her own passions and problems didn't seem to exist.

Archie felt completely detached from the anti-Vietnam protest as he watched the violent scenes on the television news. How people could get passionate about something that didn't concern them personally was beyond his understanding.

Anyway, he had more important things on his mind. Reliving his love affair with Sheila had become his raison d'être. If he concentrated hard he could experience again the warmth of his life then, the glow of actually meaning something to someone. He took his wallet from the pocket of his jacket which he had not taken off since returning from the pub. Savouring the moment when he would bring it all vividly back into focus by looking at the photograph of Sheila and himself, he plunged his fingers into the leather compartment.

Shock buffeted him as he realised that the photograph wasn't there. Feverishly he emptied the wallet, his heart pounding and a cold sweat suffusing his skin. Without the photograph he felt alone and lost. Where was it? It had been there yesterday. Every day for the past eleven years he had taken it from his wallet to peruse, replacing it carefully afterwards. He never kept it anywhere else, and the wallet always stayed close to his person in his jacket or overall pocket. Even when the leather case had needed replacing because of wear, he had transferred the photo with the greatest care. An examination of the receptacle showed that the leather had slackened with constant use; the edges of the pockets were beginning to curl. The photograph must have fallen out. But where?

When a frantic search of the flat proved fruitless, he tore outside to the van, sobbing with the sheer misery of losing the thing that meant so much to him. Crawling around in the van he found nothing, and rushed back inside to search the shop and basement, checking every crevice and corner. It was the early hours of the morning when he finally climbed the stairs to the flat, depressed and defeated. He must have lost the photograph in the street somewhere which meant there was very little chance of finding it. It was like losing Sheila all over again!

Chloe applied her make-up carefully and brushed her new hairstyle into place. It was late April and almost two months of deprivation were now splendidly manifest in a trimmer figure and reduction in dress size. Last week Joan had accompanied her to Vidal Sassoon's where she had had her hair shaped to just above her shoulders and layered with a fringe, her sprinkling of grey concealed beneath a tint in her natural colour. Even her eye make-up seemed to have more of an effect these days, she thought, unaware that the glow in her eyes could not be caused by any cosmetic.

She viewed herself in the full-length wardrobe mirror. She was casually dressed in white trousers and a check shirt, the shirt worn loose for she still had a few pounds yet to shed. But without being boastful, she knew that she looked good.

Soon Andrew would be here for his daily visit, around which her life now revolved and which she constantly strove to prolong by offering coffee and biscuits and amusing conversation. For although her marriage was now more acceptable in that she and Bradley had become friends, it was Andrew who made her life worthwhile. And although he showed no sign of reciprocation, at least she had the security of knowing that she would receive his professional attention for the next few months.

For the first time she was really in love! But, ironically, she did not feel able to do anything about it at this stage because, for the first time in her life also, she cared about the happiness of someone other than herself. And since she suspected that a declaration of her feelings might cause him embarrassment and ethical concern, she decided to let things continue as they were, refusing to think of the day when he would fly back to America and out of her life.

In the meantime she contented herself with his keen professional interest in her. And without realising it, Bradley was aiding her happiness by making a friend of Andrew, which allowed her to invite him to dinner without seeming to contravene the proprieties of their patient/doctor relationship.

The Chloe of bygone days would not have let a minor detail like her marital status deter her from taking the initiative towards a man whom she desired as a lover. But this new Chloe was not prepared to risk losing any respect he might have for her by forcing herself on him. The only thing that mattered was to see him, even if he was the most aggravating man alive.

Right now though the sound of the doorbell signalled his arrival and by the time she'd run a final comb through her hair and made her way to the drawing room, he was settled in his usual chair by the bay window. His eyes lit with approval as she entered, but he made no comment. 'The coffee is on its way,' he informed her, seeming a little more businesslike than usual. 'I organised it with Mrs Marsh on my way in.'

'Making yourself at home as always,' said Chloe, limping to the sofa and easing herself down. She found harmony with Andrew easier to obtain if she matched his presumption with pertness of her own. 'Do you take as much for granted in the homes of all your patients?'

'It's just my way,' he said, obviously not in the mood for banter, 'but if it bothers you, I'll be more formal.'

Surprised by his strange tone, she said, 'No, no, I was only joking.'

'What is your total weight loss for the last week?' he asked with an abrupt change of subject.

'Another two pounds,' she said triumphantly.

'Well done!' He produced his diary from his briefcase. 'I have given the matter a great deal of thought and I am now quite happy to go ahead with the operation. I have, in fact, booked you into hospital tomorrow for surgery the following day. I know it's short notice, but since it is what we have been working towards, it cannot be unexpected.'

'Oh!' The blood drained from her face. In all the excitement of her new lease of life, she had pushed the operation to the back of her mind. 'So soon.'

'I thought you'd be pleased to get it over after nearly two months on a starvation diet,' he said.

'It's a major operation we're talking about,' she pointed out sharply, 'not a day at the races.'

'Yes, of course,' he said in a gentler tone. 'But you have nothing to worry about, I promise you.'

He could not know, of course, that it was the fact that the operation marked the beginning of the end of their association that upset her every bit as much as the surgery itself. 'There is always an element of risk,' she pointed out.

'A very slight one, especially for a strong, healthy woman like yourself.' He smiled. 'You'll be fine, and I shall be with you every step of the way.'

The atmosphere between them had become warm, filling the room with cosiness like the first fire of winter. 'Since you'll be doing the operation, I should jolly well hope so,' she said, concealing her emotion with a joke.

'You can rely on it,' he said.

Suddenly they were being unnaturally polite, and she perceived a certain tenderness in him. 'You'd better stop being nice to me or I'll really begin to worry,' she said lightly.

'Now you're being over dramatic,' he said, his old curtness breaking the spell. 'Can I take it that tomorrow suits you?'

'Yes, that will be fine.'

'Till tomorrow then.'

'Till tomorrow.'

Driving back to Camden Town, Andrew cursed the day he had agreed to take this case. As much as he had tried not to become personally involved, the dratted woman had got right under his skin. He had deliberately nurtured a friendship with her husband as a constant reminder of her marital circumstances. But despite all his good intentions, seeing her had become the most important thing in his life. It was just as well that surgery was imminent or he'd succumb to temptation and break his Hippocratic oath by telling her. He'd stay around for a while afterwards, then he'd be on his way. Married women were strictly off limits for him. He knew what it felt like when a partner walked out.

Andrew's was the first face Chloe saw when she came round from the anaesthetic.

'Hi,' he said.

'Hello.'

'It's all over.'

'Thank you,' she said, and drifted back to sleep.

She was in a small private hospital on the Thames near Chiswick, and she was to stay here for a few weeks to recuperate. This period of time proved to be the sweetest she had known. Never mind the post-operative pain, or the effort of learning to walk without support. The only thing that mattered was the fact that she saw Andrew several times a day, and since she was his only patient here she received maximum attention.

Situated in grounds extending to the river, the hospital became her own enclosed world, containing just herself and Andrew, the rest of the medical staff existing only on the periphery of her consciousness. Bliss-fully happy, she gave visitors from the outside only a token welcome, longing for them to leave her to luxuriate in this dreamlike, cloistered existence.

The operation had been a success, but time must be spent on winning a full recovery. Working regularly with a physiotherapist, she improved rapidly and was soon on her feet again, albeit gingerly at first. She had walked with a stick and dragged her leg for so long it had become a habit.

'Ah, here you are,' said Andrew, finding her sitting in the sunshine on the hospital terrace one afternoon in late May. 'Sister said I would find you out here.'

'It's too nice to stay inside.'

'Shall we take a walk around the garden?'

'If you don't mind going at a snail's pace,' she said, glancing at her stick beside her on the bench.

'Leave that,' he advised her.

Frowning, she said, 'I'd better not. It does give me confidence.'

'Take my arm if you need support,' he invited.

She rose and instinctively made a grab for her stick, only to find it was no longer there. 'Oh, my God,' she muttered, perspiring with panic as the ground rose towards her.

'I don't want you to rely on your stick,' he said, taking her hand and tucking it under his arm. 'You really don't need it all the time now.'

'You moved it,' she admonished him weakly.

'You didn't fall though, did you?'

'You're a hard man,' she said, without meaning it because these last few weeks had proved otherwise.

The atmosphere between them during her stay in hospital had been gentle and caring whilst entirely professional. Within his own medical environment Andrew had the perfect bedside manner. Now, as they ambled through a cluster of chestnut trees towards the river, they might have been in the heart of the country instead of a suburban hospital, for even the rumble of traffic was barely audible.

'It's so peaceful here,' she said. 'It's given me a real yen for some country air. I shall go to Kent for a while after I'm discharged, I think. I haven't been there for ages.'

Reaching a bench under some trees near the low fence that separated the gardens from the river bank, they sat down under an oak tree. The river was at high tide and the wash from a passing cruiser lapped the bank, splashing against a grey-barked willow growing crookedly towards the water, its pale green leaves trailing in luxuriant disorder.

'Would you like to live in Kent permanently?' he asked conversationally.

'I don't know,' she said. 'There was a time before the accident when I thought I might like to open a riding school and divide my time between Kent and London.'

'And how did Bradley feel about that?' he asked.

Why was he always so keen to remind her that she was Bradley's wife? He seemed almost obsessed by her marriage, and obviously assumed that she and Bradley were a happily married couple. Although sorely tempted to tell him the truth, she thought it would be unwise at this stage, for two reasons.

Firstly, he might well see any such confession by her as disloyalty to his chum Bradley, given the distrust of women Andrew had inherited from his own failed marriage.

And secondly, such an intimate disclosure might pose a threat to him by introducing a more personal note into their association while she was still his patient. One read in the newspapers of doctors being struck from the medical register after becoming too personally involved with patients. A doctor's reputation was a vulnerable thing indeed.

'I never got around to telling him about it,' she said. 'It was only an idea which the accident ruled out, so there wasn't any point.'

'It will be possible for you again now,' he reminded her, 'once you're properly back on your feet.'

'Yes, I may well give the matter some consideration,' she said. 'Daisy is off to university in the autumn, so I'll have plenty of time on my hands.'

'You must be proud of her,' he said.

'Yes, of course.' She noticed a certain wistfulness in his tone. His own lack of children had come out in conversation some time ago.

'You regret not having children, don't you?' she said.

He nodded. 'It's only natural, I suppose.' He laughed dryly. 'Still, I would probably have been a Godawful father. I'm too single-minded to keep a wife happy, let alone a family.'

Taking advantage of a rare moment of informative chattiness from him, Chloe said, 'You still sound bitter about your marriage.'

'I don't mean to,' he said. 'I don't blame my wife for walking out, since in retrospect I can see I didn't give her any incentive to stay. I suppose it was her leaving me for a man I counted as a friend that hurt. They had been having an affair for months and I had no idea. I suppose, justified or not, that destroyed my belief in loyalty between friends.' He paused meditatively. 'It's rather like your friend Maggie having an affair with your husband. Just think how you'd feel if that happened.'

The faux pas left her unaffected in the light of her love for him, but she said, 'I can see that you might feel doubly betrayed.'

'Still, it's all in the past, and I can't say that I think about it much these days,' he said.

A light breeze rustled through the trees and ruffled his hair. As always he looked squeaky clean but unkempt in a light grey lounge suit which didn't sit properly on the shoulders, his unruly hair adding to the general air of disorder. 'Have you had a beard for long?' she asked.

'About five years,' he said.

'You started to grow it after your marriage ended, I'll bet,' she said with a devilish grin. 'A sort of blow for freedom against the strictures of connubial conformity.'

'Nothing so profound,' he laughed. 'I'm just too darned lazy to shave.'

She believed him since image was obviously low on his list of priorities. But she was in the mood to tease him a little. 'You can't beat a clean-shaven man in my book,' she said, slipping into a flirtatious mood almost despite herself. 'You'd look years younger without all that hair hiding your face.'

'Some women are attracted to men with beards, so I've been told,' he laughed, infected by her levity.

'Some women are turned on by men in sweaty overalls,' she giggled, looking wickedly into his eyes, 'but I'm not one of them. Give me male grooming any day.'

'Just as well we two do not need to please each other, then,' he said, smiling at her.

For Andrew the world seemed suddenly to have shrunk to encompass only him and Chloe. Never had he felt more irresistibly drawn to her. She really was stunning today with her dark hair shining in the sun, the skin on her bare arms dark and silky against a red and white spotted dress. She was the most sexually provocative woman he had ever met. His first impression of an empty-headed, spoiled bitch had been altered by the courageous way she had faced the operation and its related discomforts.

But if she had been the most selfish woman alive, he would still want her. At this moment the factors against such a union faded into oblivion beside the chemistry which forced them together. The urge to feel those vulnerable lips against his was unbearable.

'Of course, I have never had any actual contact with a bearded man,' she said seductively. 'So I can't speak from experience.'

His kiss was like no other embrace Chloe had ever experienced. It was tender with the promise of passion, sweet with unmistakable sexual undertones.

They drew back breathlessly. 'Which just goes to show that you should never judge the goods by the wrapping,' she said shakily.

Shaking his head as though to bring himself back to reality, Andrew glanced furtively around him, grateful for the trees which shielded them from view. 'Oh, well, that's my professional reputation down the drain,' he said angrily.

'Surely you have to have someone make a complaint about you for anything like that to happen?' The moment to speak her mind had come earlier than she'd expected. 'And why should I complain since I wanted it every bit as much as you? I have been wanting to tell you something actually.'

'No post mortems, please,' he snapped, the magic gone from the atmosphere along with the warmth in his tone. 'It was a lapse that should never have happened. Please accept my apologies. It was unforgiveable conduct for a man in my position.'

'But, Andrew . . .'

'Nothing like that will ever happen again. I promise you,' he said, pale and tense.

And seeing how horribly embarrassed and worried he was, Chloe accepted that this was not the moment for the truth after all. Whilst under his medical care, she must respect his position.

'Don't give it another thought,' she said. 'Just put it down to a biological experiment on the female reaction to male facial hair. I've forgotten it already.'

'Chloe is like a different person, isn't she?' remarked Maggie to Bradley as they arrived simultaneously in the foyer of the hospital that evening. 'I can't get over the change in her.'

Armed with fruit and magazines, he beamed at Maggie. 'I can hardly believe it myself. And all thanks to Andrew Maitland. The man is nothing short of a miracle worker.'

'It must make life much easier for you too,' she said.

'Oh, yes, it has made a world of difference,' he said. Because it would have been callous, with his wife still recovering from major surgery, to have spoken of his hopes for the future to anyone, even the woman with whom he hoped to share it, he remained silent on the subject. 'You know how difficult she was being before.'

'Things will be better for you both from now on then,' she said.

'I certainly hope so,' he said, referring only to the fact that he and Chloe had now become friends.

As she accompanied him into Chloe's room, Maggie's smile was stiff and false. She couldn't know that his new solicitude towards his wife was born of hope for a future without her and a new life for all three of them.

Katy studied her reflection in the full-length mirror in her bedroom. Fashionably dressed in a white mini dress in the simple 'geometric' cut, with a black jacket, earrings and shoes, her hair worn in the latest bob, she looked a picture. A dab of perfume behind her ears gave her that 'going somewhere' feeling, and that somewhere was a discotheque in Chelsea with a boyfriend from college.

At the sound of the doorbell she glanced at her watch. It was a little too early for her date, so it was probably Harry calling on Gran. She made her way to the front door, calling upstairs 'I'll get it'.

It was not Harry but Tim Slade whom she had studiously avoided since that terrible party a year ago.

'Why, Tim.' Her inner fever was disguised by determined composure. 'How are you?'

'Fine, thanks.'

'Come on in. I'm just on my way out actually, but Gran is upstairs.' She led him into the living room. 'And Mum will be back from visiting Chloe at the hospital soon.'

Katy had taken her mother's advice as far as Tim was concerned, and during their brief rare meetings when he called at the house as a family friend, her attitude was one of casual friendliness. And she always made a point of being either on her way out or in the middle of some vital chore which needed her complete attention.

'It was you I came to see,' he said.

She looked suitably regretful with no sign of her increased heart-rate. 'You should have phoned before coming over, to save a wasted trip,' she said, looking at her watch, 'because I'll be leaving in a few minutes.' She smiled prettily at him. 'Did you want to see me about anything urgent?'

'No, no,' he said, his warm brown eyes heavy with disappointment. 'I haven't seen you to talk to for ages and I fancied a chat, that's all.'

'Hit a lull in your riotous social life, have you?' she teased without rancour.

He looked hurt and she thought how much easier it would be to continue with this strategy if he wasn't so gorgeous, his tall lean form clad in jeans and a tee shirt, his fair hair ruffled on his brow. 'Not at all,' he assured her.

'Only joking,' she laughed. 'A chat would have been nice. Another time perhaps?'

'Any chance of your changing your mind?' he said.

She shook her head. 'I'm afraid not. My date will be here at any moment.'

His eyes narrowed. 'You have a date? With a man?'

'No, with a polar bear,' she laughed. 'Of course it's with a man.'

'Aren't you a little young?' he suggested.

'At almost eighteen, I hardly think so,' she said.

'Of course, you're right,' he said miserably. 'It was silly of me.'

He looked so dejected, she almost followed her heart and offered to make an excuse when her date came to the door. But to be too easily available to Tim could be fatal at this stage. 'Are you still seeing Daisy?' she asked.

'Good lord, no,' he informed her. 'That was over ages ago. Not that there was anything to be over, really. It was only a bit of fun for both of us.'

Not knowing which was worse, Daisy's references to her relationship with Tim, or her tactful silence in respect to Katy's feelings, Katy had sidestepped Daisy's company too this past year, which was why she had only just learned of the up-to-date situation between them. And how sweet was the relief! 'How are things at college?' she asked conversationally. 'You're home for the weekend, I assume.'

He nodded. 'I've almost finished now.' He made a face. 'Finals next month. I find it easier to swot at home. There are fewer distractions.'

'And you're not slaving over your books this evening?' she teased lightly. 'Tut tut.'

'I'll be at it tomorrow, weekend or not,' he said.

'I believe you, thousands wouldn't,' she laughed.

The atmosphere between them had never been more strained, despite the superficial levity. It felt like the aftermath of some bitter quarrel where no one knows quite what to say. For all her clever tactics, Katy felt hopelessly at odds with the situation. 'Look, do feel free to stay around and wait for Mum,' she said in a bid to ease the tension. 'Help yourself to a drink. You know where everything is. I have to finish getting ready.'

'You look ready enough to me,' he said, running an approving eye over her. 'Lovely, in fact.'

'Thank you.'

Silence echoed weightily around them. 'Well, I might as well be on my way,' he said. 'I won't wait to see your mother, if you don't mind.'

'As you wish.'

The taut atmosphere was relieved by the appearance of Dora who, passing and seeing him through the open door, bounded exuberantly in. 'Tim,' she said, joyfully hugging him. 'How nice to see you. We don't see nearly enough of you these days.'

'Well, you know how it is,' he muttered. 'With exams and everything.'

'Excuses, excuses,' she laughed, then winked and added, 'Just teasing, son.'

Noticing that Dora was dressed to go out in a cream and brown crimplene dress and jacket, he said, 'You're looking very smart. Going anywhere nice?'

'Harry is taking me up West for a meal,' she said.

'I feel like Cinderella,' grinned Tim. 'With you two off out to paint the town red.'

Dora threw back her head and laughed. 'At my age it's more a watery shade of pink.' She turned to her grand-daughter. 'Katy here is a different kettle of fish altogether. She'll set the town on fire, I'll bet. You mind how you go though, my girl. There are some funny people about these days. What with men going about in long dresses and people taking to drugs.' She grinned at Tim. 'You ought to take her in hand, son.'

My thoughts exactly, he thought, but smiled at Katy and said, 'She's the smartest dolly bird in town, I grant you, but she's a sensible girl. She'll be all right.'

Dora tutted good-humouredly. 'The way you young people talk,' she laughed. 'What with girls being dolly birds and everything else being cool, fab or groovy, it's like a blimming foreign language.'

The doorbell chimed through the house. 'That'll be Harry, so I'll be off,' said Dora, heading for the door.

'I'd better go too,' said Tim. 'I'm holding you up.'

'Don't worry,' Katy said awkwardly. 'But I'd better get my handbag. I hate to keep anyone waiting when they call for me.'

He gave her a searching look. 'Perhaps I'll pop round for a chat another time soon.'

'You're welcome here any time, you know that.' She chewed her lip and decided it was time to clarify the situation.' And we'll talk. But don't expect it to be like it was between us when we were younger, Tim, because it can't ever be like that again for me. Things are more complicated now.'

'I realise that.' He walked across the room, turning at the door. 'I'll give you a ring.'

'I'll look forward to it,' she said.

His call came earlier than she expected. When she was getting ready for bed that very same night, in fact. 'I'm sorry to call you so late,' he said.

'It's OK, I'm still up.'

'I was wondering if you might like to go out with me sometime soon?'

'As a little sister?'

'Definitely not as any kind of sister.'

'I see.'

'That thing with Daisy,' he said softly, 'I think I was just using that to prove a point to you. I wasn't ready to move my relationship with you on to another plane because I didn't want to be "in love" with anyone. I'm sorry if I hurt you.'

'It's all in the past.'

'I know you are too young to make a commitment to anyone yet,' he said, 'but how would you feel about us dating to see how things work out?'

'I'd like that, Tim.'

'I can't wait to see you,' he said excitedly. 'When will you be free?'

'Tomorrow,' she said jubilantly. 'I'm free tomorrow.'

Chapter Twenty-two

Chloe's nerves were raw when Andrew arrived at her Hampstead home one wet Monday morning in September, for this was to be his last visit. Tonight he was flying back to the USA.

'You're looking very glam this morning,' he said, running an approving eye over her red jersey trouser suit. 'You certainly look good in pants now that you've got your figure back.' He sipped his coffee, his overly bright tone betraying a certain tension. 'And on the subject of clothes, I notice that dry cleaners are now charging to clean mini skirts by the inch. That just shows the heights they've reached . . .'

'Andrew, I—'

'We're all so used to short skirts now, we barely notice . . .'

'Andrew!'

'I'd suggest a last walk on the Heath, but it's raining.'

'Will you shut up for a minute, please?' she interrupted loudly.' I have something important to say to you.'

He cowered in mock terror. 'Yes, ma'am,' he said with a grin.

Chloe's skin felt damp, and her mouth was parched. She ran her eyes over his tall form, casually clad in beige slacks and a brown sweater, his hair damp from the rain but unusually tidy in what she suspected was a valedictory gesture to please her. Taking a deep breath, she said simply, 'I am in love with you.'

Her operation had been an unqualified success. She now walked almost without a limp, and her weight was back to its pre-accident level. Since that bitter-sweet moment in the hospital gardens with him, there had been no further lapses in his professional conduct. When he was alone with her his attitude was impersonally pleasant, though wholly attentive from a medical point of view. When Bradley was around he behaved like a friend to them both.

Despite all of this, Chloe felt reciprocal chemistry flowing between them. And she had finally decided that unless she took the initiative she would lose him forever. For although the professional restrictions governing their association were to end along with her full recovery, she was still the wife of another man, a man whom he liked and respected.

She had been waiting all her life for Andrew to come along, and she wasn't prepared to lose him through reticence. But now, hearing her words echo under his accusing stare, she questioned the judgement which had led her to believe that he returned her feelings.

'Well,' she said at last, 'say something, even if it's only goodbye.'

'I'm flattered, of course.'

'Spare me the clichés,' she said grimly.

Obviously upset by her declaration, he rose and stared out of the window with his back to her so that she couldn't see the expression on his face. 'It is not unknown for patients to imagine themselves to be in love with their doctor, and vice versa,' he said. 'A certain rapport is inevitable, given the close contact between them.'

'Don't be so pompous,' she snapped. 'I am thirty-seven years old, for God's sake. This is no girlish crush. I love you, and I believe that you love me, despite the fact you won't allow yourself to admit it.'

Swinging round, he fixed her with a grim stare. 'Since you are so clever at predicting other people's feelings,' he barked, 'have you worked out what comes next? Has your vivid imagination conjured up a vision of us swanning off together to eternal happiness, leaving all responsibility and moral obligation behind?'

'Of course not,' she said in a small, crushed voice.

'What do you have in mind then?' he asked. 'I take it you haven't forgotten your husband completely in all your plans.'

'Bradley and I were finished years ago as far as marriage in the ordinary sense is concerned,' she informed him.

He emitted a cynical laugh. 'Just like that, poor old Bradley is written off! My God . . .'

'It isn't like that.'

'Oh, no? Well, if you were finished years ago, why are you still together?' he asked, his voice distorted by emotion.

Chloe was taken aback by the question. The woman she had once been was not one she cared to tell Andrew about. 'It's a long story,' she said.

'And one that Bradley knows nothing about, I suspect,' he said.

Trying not to crumble under the pain of his cruel accusations, she asked, 'Does this mean that you feel nothing special for me?'

In reply he marched towards her, dragged her from her chair and into his arms, kissing her brutally before withdrawing with such suddenness that she had to grab the back of the chair to steady herself. 'Is that what you're after?' he asked. 'Does Bradley not satisfy you? Is it not enough that he keeps you in luxury and panders to your every whim? Can you not be content with all that instead of looking for a lover to boost your ego?'

'That's not how it is,' she entreated. 'I love you, and I want to spend the rest of my life with you.'

He shook his head incredulously. 'I can't believe I'm hearing this,' he roared. 'It seems that my first impression of you was correct. I thought then that you were the most selfish person I had ever met. Unfortunately that didn't stop me being drawn to you.' He paused while the implications registered. 'Oh, yes, I am only human, I have been attracted to you, in love with you even, but I certainly do not intend to take it any further. Unlike you, I am not completely without scruples.'

'I see,' she said miserably.

'It's no good looking like that,' he said gravely, 'because I will *not* come between a man and his wife, under any circumstances.'

'But Bradley and I don't love each other. He'll be pleased . . .'

His sardonic laughter filled the room. 'A man who dotes on his wife "pleased" when she dumps him! Now I've heard everything.'

'Bradley wanted a divorce years ago,' she explained.

His brows rose. 'Oh, what happened? Were you not agreeable?'

'Not at first, no . . . I had my reasons.' She was on the defensive. 'I did change my mind but then I had the accident . . .'

'And now that you're back on form it suits you to ditch him, just like that, after all he's done for you,' he said. 'Well, count me out, lady. There's no way I will be a party to homebreaking.'

She grabbed his arm desperately. 'Have I not grovelled sufficiently for you? Do you want me to go down on my knees?'

He shrank back. 'No, I don't want you to belittle yourself. I just want you to stop considering your own happiness for once and think about that husband of yours. God dammit, woman, the man does everything he possibly can to make you happy. I've been with the two of you, I've watched him. And all you want to do for him in return is leave him for another man.'

'I know it must seem like that,' she said, 'but that isn't the way it is. Ask Bradley if you don't believe me.'

'And add insult to injury? No fear.' He paused for a moment and his tone became gentler. 'There is a lot of good in you, Chloe. I saw it in the way you faced surgery and the way you behaved towards the other patients – listening to their problems, going out of your way to cheer them up. Show your strength in your life with Bradley. Make him happy. You've such a lot to give.' He came to her and brushed her cheek with his lips. 'No hard feelings.' He walked to the door. 'I'll call Bradley to say goodbye. Be happy.' And he left the room.

She started to go after him, but stopped when she heard the front door close. To pursue him would only drive him further away. Hearing his car roar out of the drive, she went to the window and stared out across the rainsoaked gardens through a blur of tears.

With Andrew's words ringing in her ears, her surroundings registered with new clarity. She saw the luxuriant autumn trees in the select avenue in which she was privileged to live; the beautifully kept gardens of her home, the sort of home the average person only ever saw from the outside; the new car Bradley had recently bought for her, sitting on the drive.

For the first time she allowed herself to view herself objectively. She saw her selfishness and unfaithfulness to Bradley, who had showered her with material comfort and received in return her denial of his right to happiness with Maggie. Her life had been one long unearned round of indulgence. She could have made more of an effort with her injury and let Bradley go. She had taken from her husband, her best friend, her parents, and even her daughter. She had plucked the pleasure from Daisy's childhood, and discarded the inconvenience. Nanny had lost sleep soothing her ills. Bradley had given his time and energy to provide the child with her sense of family, her fun, her security. He had been far more emotionally involved with Daisy than Chloe ever had. Understandably it was to him that she now turned with her problems.

Chloe saw a woman approaching middle age, self-absorbed and pampered, who had never done a useful thing in her life. Her selfishness in the past had certainly come home to roost, for by forcing her marriage to continue she had lost her chance of happiness with Andrew.

Right now Chloe felt the need of the one person in the world who loved her despite everything, the only person to whom she could turn for sympathy in her self-inflicted distress. Chloe now knew what she must do about the future, but for the moment she needed to be loved unconditionally. She left the house and drove to Richmond to see her mother.

Andrew trudged across the hummocky planes of Hampstead Heath in the rain with his hands plunged deep into his anorak pockets and his head down. He had come here hoping to calm himself before returning to Camden Town and his last-minute packing. That final meeting with Chloe had been every bit as painful as he'd feared. In fact he couldn't remember feeling this bad even when his wife had left him. He felt bruised and shaky but numb inside, as though the life had been beaten from him by a violent physical attack.

He had never hated yet loved anyone more than Chloe just now. His feelings for her had almost overruled his principles. Only the thought of Bradley's devotion to her had prevented him losing his head. He could hardly believe the casual way she had spoken about ending her marriage, with less concern than someone cancelling a dinner engagement. That was what happened to people who had too much; they valued nothing.

The thought of not seeing her again was almost too much to bear. For six months she had filled his life. Now it was over and he felt like death. Even the thought that he would soon be back in Philadelphia, where he could bury himself in his work, offered little comfort.

Rain was falling with penetrating persistence. It muddied the grass beneath his feet, dripped from the trees and soaked his clothes through to the skin. The air smelled of England – verdant, damp, misty, and unbearably poignant to him at this time of farewell.

Thank God he was leaving this city with all its nostalgia and memories of Chloe. Even the grassy hillocks of the Heath seemed imbued with her presence, for they had walked here together often during her recovery. Sadly, he climbed Parliament Hill and looked out over the city, grey and hazed with rain-mist, knowing that whether in Philadelphia or London, his life would never be the same again.

'I wanted to speak to you both together because what I have to say will affect all three of us,' said Chloe to Maggie and Bradley the next day.

They waited in puzzled silence in the Hughes drawing room. Maggie and Bradley were sitting on the sofa, Chloe was standing with her back to the hearth addressing them with ominous formality.

'You will have noticed a change in me these last few months,' she said.

Nodding, they waited for her to continue.

'Which you will have attributed to the success of my operation and my weight loss,' she said.

'Well, yes, of course,' said Maggie.

'It's only natural,' said Bradley.

Dressed in a figure-hugging jersey day dress in emerald green, Chloe looked very striking. Her hair was drawn back from her face, the dark smudges under her eyes concealed by cleverly applied make-up. 'Obviously, these two factors have made a great difference to me,' she continued. 'But they are not the actual reason.' She paused only for a moment. 'Because Bradley and I are friends and not lovers, I can say what I have to without fear of hurting his feelings. The reason for my new lease of life has been mostly due to the fact that I have fallen deeply in love for the first time in my life – with Andrew.'

'Oh dear,' gasped Maggie, sensitive to Bradley's position as Chloe's husband.

'Good God!' he exclaimed.

'Of course, it all makes sense now,' said Maggie, observing the fact that Bradley's delight matched her own. 'How incredibly unobservant we have been not to realise.'

'Alas, things haven't worked out as I'd hoped,' Chloe informed them. 'Andrew does not reciprocate.'

'Oh dear,' said Maggie, riding an emotional see-saw.

291

'I have, it seems, got my comeuppance,' Chloe told them. 'I see this as a punishment for standing in the way of your happiness all these years. Bradley and I have never been right for each other, but I wouldn't let go. I just could not accept gracefully the fact that you two had found the one thing that eluded me.'

'You've had a hard time,' Maggie reminded her. 'After the accident, you needed Bradley.'

'Sure you did,' he agreed.

'People far more disabled than I was manage without a partner,' she said. 'Now that I have experienced real love, I know what you must have suffered because of me. I hope it isn't too late to make amends and for us all to be friends.'

Maggie and Bradley exchanged surprised glances. 'Of course not,' said Maggie, her voice ragged with emotion. 'But what exactly are you suggesting?'

Chloe looked from one to the other. 'A divorce from Bradley, and a friendship with you both for me.'

'Oh, Chloe,' gasped Maggie tearfully, rushing to her friend and hugging her. 'That would be wonderful.'

'It sure would,' beamed Bradley.

'But what about you, Chloe?' Maggie asked anxiously, moving back to the sofa and clasping Bradley's hand. 'What will you do?'

'Don't worry about me,' she said with new determination. 'I plan to open a riding school in Kent. I am a rich woman in my own right with the money my father left me, and I'm sure Bradley and I will come to a fair arrangement about the Hampstead and Kent properties. It's high time I did something with my life.'

Maggie didn't recognise the woman who stood before them. She was assertive and full of purpose. It was as though she had finally grown up. But for all that, Maggie glimpsed heartbreak through the perky façade. And having had her fair share of that very thing herself, she empathised.

'Are you sure that there is no future for you and Andrew?' she ventured tentatively.

Chloe's face hardened. 'Quite sure,' she stated categorically.' I feel like hell about it, but it is something that I must accept. I have a lot more than just my recovery to thank Andrew for. He made me take a good look at myself.'

'We are all products of our upbringing to a certain extent, you know,' Bradley pointed out.

Smiling tightly, Chloe said, 'You are very kind, but I don't want to pass the blame or look back. The present and the future are what matter to me from now on.' She paused momentarily. 'On a practical note, Bradley, I'd like to move into Bushleigh Lodge right away, while things get underway. It will be a base for me while I look for a suitable site for my riding school. I don't want to have it at Bushleigh. A clean start is what I need, what we all need. Daisy can spend her vacations with whichever of us she chooses. She's old enough to make up her own mind.'

'Sure, you go right ahead. I'll give you a hand,' he said.

'Bless you,' said Chloe, sweeping across the room to the couple and kissing them both on the cheek.

'I hope this new Chloe isn't going to be holier than thou,' laughed Bradley. 'I don't think I could bear that from you.'

'They say that leopards don't change their spots,' she grinned. 'You try to diddle me out of what's mine in the divorce settlement and you'll soon find out how true that is!'

'Thank God for that,' he laughed, going to the drinks cabinet. 'I think this calls for a drink.'

'Good idea,' she said.

And they raised their glasses to the future and the success of their rearranged relationships within it.

'Have you gone off me, Maggie?' asked Bradley one evening a few days later.

'Of course not,' she assured him. 'The reason I don't want us to move in together yet is because I need time to get to know you all over again. Can you understand that?'

He looked depressed. It was disappointing to face a further delay after all these years. 'I'm trying,' he said. 'But we've waited so long, I want us to be together right away. The divorce will take a while to come through and we are both mature people, after all. It isn't as though living together before marriage isn't perfectly acceptable these days.'

They were sitting together on the couch in Maggie's living room. Dora was out somewhere with Harry, and Katy with Tim, so there was no fear of interruption. Maggie struggled to clarify her thoughts which were confused even to herself. 'Yes, I know that, and I'm not just being prudish. I think what I want, to use an old-fashioned word, is the courtship I've never had with you. Because of our circumstances we were cheated of the fun of building a relationship. I'd like to have that now before we tackle the practicalities of everyday life together. Anyway, although Katy will be wanting a place of her own soon, I still have her to consider for the moment. And Mother. What am I to do about her if I move in with you? She's happy and settled here so I wouldn't want to sell the place. And she'd be miserable rattling around in this big house on her own.'

'She could move in with us,' he suggested.

'No, I don't think she'd like that. She values her independence too much. She's not even sixty yet, remember. As things are at present, Mother, Katy and myself are three single women sharing the same house yet respecting each other's privacy. If she lived with you and me, she'd be the odd one out.'

'I could move in with you,' he suggested.

'Can you bear with me on this one for a while longer, darling?' she asked. 'Let's have fun learning about each other all over again. By the time your divorce comes through, I'll be ready to face all the problems of reality. In the meantime, I'd like to be wooed a little.' She threw him a wicked grin. 'I realise that we have had the main course. Now I'd like to enjoy the starter.'

Infected by her levity, Bradley laughed despite himself. 'If that will make you happy, then so be it,' he said, taking her in his arms.

Chapter Twenty-three

Bradley telephoned Maggie at the Moss Street shop one afternoon just before Christmas. 'What time shall I pick you up this evening?' he asked.

She looked into the crowded shop from the office. The run-up to Christmas was always frantic in the flower trade because of all the special functions, gift orders and Christmas decorations. 'I don't think I'll be able to get away from here much before seven,' she said. 'The shop is busy and we're snowed under with orders. It's a hell of a time for all Archie's staff to go down with flu.'

'Shall I call the restaurant and tell them that we'll be late getting there?' he suggested. 'To save you rushing around to get ready when you do get home.'

'That's thoughtful of you, darling,' she said. 'I'd appreciate that.'

'Will it help if I were to pick you up from the shop to save you the bother of driving home through the traffic?'

'Thank you, but no,' she said. 'If I leave my car here, I'll miss it in the morning and I'll be needed here again tomorrow. I'll see you later at my place.'

'OK. Love you.'

'Love you, too.'

She was glowing as she replaced the receiver. Bradley really was the sweetest, most attentive man, and they were having a wonderful courtship filled with presents and romantic dinners in London's most glamorous nightspots. This evening they were dining at Pinks Club in celebration of their very first meeting. She felt as excited as a young girl, and could hardly wait to see him again.

The afternoon was hectic but by about six-thirty the stock was freshly watered and stored in the coolroom for the night, the orders for early delivery in the morning were complete, and the cashing up was done.

'You can take the money to the nightsafe while I clear up, if you like, Archie, then we can both go home,' she suggested.

'Righto,' he agreed.

Her movements were accelerated by eagerness for the evening ahead as she took a broom to the shop floor. Next she hurried downstairs to the workroom where the floor was wet in places and littered with all the usual floral debris plus bits of the fern, bracken and cones they painted red and silver and used to make Christmas decorations.

Humming a tune under her breath she swept under and around the worktable, gathering the rubbish into a pile ready to be transferred to the dustbin. 'Some of this greenery clings so,' she muttered as a piece of fern got caught under the heavy table leg. Down on her haunches she pulled at the recalcitrant foliage which broke off leaving a small piece still lodged beneath the table leg. Moving it slightly she pulled the fern out and something else came with it too, a dusty card which had obviously been trapped there for some time.

I do wish the staff wouldn't drop their litter on the floor, she thought. It's bad enough with all the muck from the flowers without bits of sweet cartons too. She was about to throw it on the rubbish pile when she noticed that it was not just ordinary trash, but a photograph. Instinctively curious, she took a closer look. Why, it was Archie with a girlfriend. Well, well, so he had had his moments after all. Dusting the photograph off, she studied it, puzzled by the familiarity of the young woman's face.

It was Sheila Dawson, the woman who was murdered, she realised, trembling with shock. How could she ever forget the face that had been reproduced so many times in the newspapers and had affected her family's life so dramatically? Turning the photograph over she read in Archie's spidery handwriting: 'Sheila and me, New Year's Eve 1956.' The murder had been in February 1957, she recalled. Archie had certainly kept his friendship with her quiet.

And as the significance of this dawned, she broke out in a cold sweat. The police had been looking for another man besides Sheila's fiancé at the time of the murder to substantiate Tom's story about the man he had seen running away. If Archie had been involved with Sheila Dawson so soon before she'd been murdered, was it not possible that he . . . God, it was more than just possible! *Archie* was the man Tom had seen running away, she was sure of it. Archie had killed Sheila! He was to blame for her brother being locked up for all these years. Without stopping to consider the consequences she ran upstairs to the shop where Archie had just returned from the bank.

'Look what I found,' she said, shaking with fury and waving the photograph at him. 'A picture of you and Sheila Dawson together just weeks before she was murdered. What do you have to say to that, eh?'

He grabbed the photograph from her, flushing scarlet then turning very pale. 'You found it,' he said, dazed. 'I thought I'd lost it forever.' Seeming almost unaware of Maggie's presence, he stared at the photograph before clutching it to him possessively.

Maggie lunged at him. 'You killed her, didn't you?' she cried, punching his chest. 'You killed her and let my brother take the blame. You wicked, wicked bastard!' She was bordering on hysteria, tears streaming down her cheeks. 'I'll get you for this! I'll see that you're made to suffer. Eleven years he's served, and all because of you.'

She expected him to deny it, but he pushed her away and seemed to drift into a world of his own. 'I didn't mean to kill 'er. All I did was rough her up a bit and give her a push to help 'er on her way.' He winced as though the memory still hurt. 'She just sorta fell.'

Hearing the truth actually spoken, after all these years of anguish, was so traumatic to Maggie she couldn't speak for a moment. She just stood staring at Archie, her whole body quivering.

'Me and Sheila had something special,' he said, his eyes glazing over. 'But she had to spoil it by going back to her boyfriend after all we'd bin to each other. I didn't wanna hurt her. I just wanted us to be together.' His face crumpled and he began to sob.

Recovering from her dazed state, Maggie's actions were entirely dictated by rage. At this moment all she wanted was to strike out at the man who had caused her brother such suffering. But as she went for him, he also recovered and grabbed her by the arms, dragging her towards the door to the basement.

Only now realising the gravity of the situation, Maggie gasped, 'If you tell the police it was an accident . . .'

'I ain't tellin' the police nothing. And neither are you.'

Cursing the haste which had put her in this dangerous position, she managed to gather her chaotic thoughts sufficiently to realise that psychology was her only ally. She had to get Archie talking and play for time. But it was a forlorn hope as he steered her roughly down the basement steps into the workroom and locked the door behind them.

'Maggie isn't home yet,' said Dora, opening the door to Bradley.

'Oh!' he exclaimed in surprise as Dora ushered him inside. 'I thought she'd be back from the shop by now. It's almost seven-thirty.'

'This is a busy time of the year for florists,' Dora reminded him. 'But I don't expect she'll be long. Help yourself to a drink, you know where everything is.'

'Perhaps she's forgotten the time,' he commented, going to the telephone in the hall. 'I'll give her a ring to remind her.'

'Good idea,' said Dora, who was dressed ready to go out and listening for the doorbell, for she and Harry were going up West to see a film.

'No reply,' he said thoughtfully. 'That means she's on her way.'

'Good,' said Dora, backing away at the sound of the doorbell. 'That'll be Harry. We'll go straight off or we'll miss the beginning of the film. Have a good time.'

'And you.'

'See you later.'

'Sure,' said Bradley, making his way into Maggie's living room to wait for her.

'That will be Bradley wondering where I've got to,' said Maggie, hearing the faint trill of the telephone from upstairs.

'Let him wonder,' said Archie, standing with his back against the door and nervously puffing on a cigarette.

'Since you're going to keep me holed up in here, we may as well break the monotony by talking,' Maggie suggested, hoping to deflect his attention from herself. 'Tell me about Sheila. She obviously meant a lot to you.'

She was sitting at the worktable near the piled rubbish she had been working on before the dramatic turn in events. Piles of empty buckets stood neatly against the wall near the sink next to the wooden moss bin. The table and the workbenches around the wall had been cleared for the next day, the silent 'after hours' feel of the place adding to the tension.

'I've told you too much already,' he said.

'You've nothing to lose by telling me more then, have you?' she pointed out, struggling not to show her fear. 'You might as well make the most of your captive audience.'

Maggie knew she was in grave danger. He could destroy the evidence connecting him with Sheila, but the only way he could stop Maggie telling the police what she knew was by killing her. Without the photograph it would simply be her word against his, but she guessed he wouldn't want to take a chance, having already admitted so much.

For the last half hour he had been trying to destroy the photograph. He had lit several matches and held the flame close to the picture, but then just blew out the flame and stared miserably at the photo. It was obvious that the dead woman was an obsession with him.

'Sheila was a very pretty girl,' she said, controlling her hatred for him in a bid to keep him calm. If he lost his head now she was dead. 'You must have loved her very much.'

He pressed his back against the door, as though to increase his sense of security. Although he seemed to have drifted into thought, Maggie knew that her slightest movement would claim his instant attention. 'Yeah, I loved 'er. She had lovely blonde 'air . . . a gorgeous figure.' He fell into silent thought for a while, before suddenly narrowing his eyes on Maggie. 'Oh, no, I ain't fallin' for that one. You wanna get me talkin' and put me off me guard.'

His fear was a palpable presence in the room. He was caught in a trap which enclosed Maggie too. His dark eyes rested on her malevolently and she could read his thoughts. 'If you kill me, you won't get away with it like you did with Sheila,' she said.

'Oh, won't I?'

Her bones turned to water. Archie was a desperate man living for the moment and caring only for self-preservation. 'No, you won't. They'll know it was you. My mother and Bradley both know that you and I are here alone together.'

He flinched as though she had struck him and his eyes burned with a sudden wildness. Leaving his post at the door he marched across the room and dragged her from the seat. Gripping her by the arms and staring into her face, his mouth twisted into an unnatural smile. At that moment Maggie knew that he was no longer accessible as a sane human being. She tried to scream, but no sound came. She struggled and kicked but he held her in an iron grip.

'You can scream and struggle all yer like,' he said, his eyes vacant, 'no one can hear yer. There ai..i't no one 'ere but us. You should have minded your own business, then I wouldn't have had to do this.'

As his hands moved towards her throat her vision was dominated by that terrible, terrible smile. The air was being drained from her body and she couldn't breathe. The rushing in her head diminished the sound of the door crashing open. 'Bradley,' she gasped painfully. 'Thank God!'

Stopping only for a moment to check that she was all right, he tore after Archie and brought him to the ground by the door.

'It was a blessing I didn't wait any longer before coming to see where you'd got to,' he said a little later when things had calmed down.

'It certainly was,' she said shakily.

'I've put a board across the hole in the shop door where I put my fist through the glass to get at the door handle,' he said. 'Just until the glaziers come and fix it.'

'Thank you. How come you didn't cut your hand?'

'I wrapped my handkerchief around it first,' he explained. 'A short sharp blow made very little noise. I was worried about alerting Archie for fear he would become even more violent.'

'How did you know he had me trapped?'

'I knew he was in there with you because his van was parked near your car,' he explained. 'I guessed you were down in the basement because I knocked on the shop window several times and there was no reply. I knew you wouldn't still be working downstairs at that time. Of course, I didn't know then that the man was a murderer.'

'Thank God it's all over,' she said.

'You can say that again.'

* * *

299

There were certain formalities to be adhered to, of course, but the fact that Archie broke down and made a confession to the police simplified matters, and in January 1969 Tom was released.

He didn't want celebrations. He simply wanted to get on with the rest of his life. 'No point in being bitter,' he said. 'The years have gone. Moaning about it won't bring them back.' He and Sally had a quiet wedding in March and settled in the flat over the Ashbrook Grove shop.

The removal of the shadow that had darkened her life for so long added to Maggie's happiness with Bradley, and on her thirty-eighth birthday in the summer of 1969 she felt nineteen again.

Only a nagging unease about Chloe, who was lonely for all her newfound independence, spoiled things a little. Chloe had moved from Bushleigh Lodge to a pretty Kent house with well-planned stables which she had converted into an equestrian centre. But her rustic life had been brought temporarily to a halt that summer when her mother fell sick with terminal cancer and, leaving the stables under management, Chloe moved into the family home at Richmond to look after her.

It was in early October that Maggie discovered a way to help. It happened one Sunday when she was assisting Chloe by sitting with Lavinia while Chloe drove Daisy to Sussex for the new university term, something Maggie had encouraged since she felt that her friend needed a break.

Although quite frail, Lavinia had accepted her fate bravely. 'I'm tired and ready to go,' she admitted to Maggie. 'There's nothing left for me here without Rupert.'

Maggie held her bony hand, the fingernails painted pink by her daughter as a way of lifting her mother's spirits. Chloe had surprised everyone with her dedication to her mother at this sad time. She might have been slow reaching maturity, but she had certainly made up for lost time this last year. 'Don't say that,' Maggie urged Lavinia. 'You have your daughter and grand-daughter. They love you very much.'

'It isn't the same.'

'No, I don't suppose it is.'

To Maggie's amazement, Lavinia began to talk of Maggie's involvement with Rupert. 'I was very shocked when he told me, of course,' she admitted, her face pale and thin, her eyes seeming to protrude slightly behind her spectacles, her scalp shining through her sparse white hair. 'But it was a mere hiccup in many years of happy marriage.' She was sitting in a chair near the window overlooking the Thames, with a blanket wrapped around her knees. Her thin form was neatly clad in a white blouse and navy blue cardigan. She felt happier if she was up and dressed, while this was still possible, rather than confined to her bed. And she had medication to help with the pain.

'All those years you knew and you never said a word to me,' said Maggie.

'What was the point in dragging it all up again once the man had come to his senses?' she said. 'From what I heard, you didn't want reminding.'

'That's true,' agreed Maggie.

'I was so sorry about Chloe's marriage,' said the older woman, her head nodding slightly. 'But not surprised. They were never suited.'

Maggie was sitting on the floor by Lavinia's chair in a relaxed pose. Now she braced herself for the criticism she was sure would come.

'It's all right, my dear, I am not going to pass judgement,' she said. 'You and Bradley couldn't help falling in love any more than Chloe and Andrew. Though theirs didn't come to such a satisfactory conclusion, more's the pity. She came to me heartbroken the day he went back to America, you know. I've never seen her in such a state.'

'Unrequited love is heartbreaking because there is simply nothing that can be done,' said Maggie.

'That wasn't the trouble,' said Lavinia, 'that's the tragedy of it. He was in love with her. He admitted it to her apparently. Chloe found it simpler to tell people he didn't.' She paused and seemed to drift into thought. 'Sadly, one cannot interfere in these matters.'

'What was the trouble then,' asked Maggie 'or has she sworn you to secrecy?'

Lavinia didn't reply, but stared thoughtfully into space.

'I'm not just being nosey,' persisted Maggie. 'As her closest friend, I might be able to help her somehow if I know what went wrong.'

Lavinia clutched Maggie's hand more tightly. 'I don't suppose there is any harm in your knowing,' she said. 'The problem was that Andrew refused to come between her and Bradley. He didn't believe her when she tried to tell him how things were with her marriage. His ex-wife had an affair with his friend so he is extra-sensitive about such things apparently. And he was determined not to do the same thing to Bradley.' She sighed. 'Principles are all very well, but what good are they to my daughter right now?'

'But why didn't she ask Bradley to tell Andrew the truth if he wouldn't believe her?' asked Maggie.

'I think she was afraid it would make matters worse with Andrew if the whole story had come out,' she explained. 'You know, her refusing to give Bradley a divorce before the accident just to stop you and he being together. His moral outrage at her suggestion that she leave Bradley for him frightened her. She'd not expected such opposition.' She caught Maggie's look of surprise. 'In her trauma she told me everything about the three of you.'

Maggie nodded. But she was more interested in the present than the past. 'Andrew doesn't have to know the details surely? Just that their marriage was over long before he came on the scene.'

'Exactly,' sighed Lavinia. 'But she's unapproachable on the subject now. I daren't even mention his name. But I know she's still pining for him. You can see it in her eyes, for all the front she puts on.'

'So Andrew doesn't know that Chloe and Bradley have split up?' said Maggie thoughtfully.

'Not unless Bradley has kept in touch,' said Lavinia. 'He'd not hear it from Chloe.'

'Such an unnecessary waste,' said Maggie.

'Indeed,' said Lavinia. Clouds of lavender scent sweetened the air as she dabbed her tears with a lace-edged handkerchief. 'I know that Chloe has always been far too fond of her own way, and for that her father and I are to blame. We had her late, you see, we loved her too much.' Two large tears rolled down her wrinkled face. 'Even now I worry about her. I'd love to see her happily settled before I die.'

'Don't upset yourself,' said Maggie. 'Things have a way of sorting themselves out, you know.' And she added silently, even if they do sometimes need a little help!

Andrew Maitland lay in bed in his Philadelphia apartment staring at the ceiling and thinking of Chloe. Over a year had passed since his return to America and he still could not forget her. Her face appeared before him in hospital corridors, on the street, everywhere. That last meeting with her was so fresh in his mind, it might have been yesterday. It was just like Chloe to force herself in where she wasn't wanted!

Weary of agonising over the way he had handled her declaration of love for him, he swung out of bed and padded into the kitchen to pour himself a glass of milk. What the hell was he doing, a professional man the wrong side of forty, pacing the apartment in the middle of the night like some love-sick teenager over another man's wife?

He didn't need this sort of aggravation! He had a comfortable bachelor life with work that interested him. Why let a woman ruin it all by upsetting his peace of mind? But then he found himself smiling at the memory of something she'd said or done. Oh God, Chloe, what had she done to him? They were two of a kind, he and she. Both as self-centred as hell.

The telephone interrupted his reverie and he picked up the receiver on the wall, tensing as the operator informed him that she had a call for him from London, England. His sister immediately sprang to mind. He hoped nothing was wrong.

'Hello. Is that Andrew Maitland?'

'Speaking.'

'This is Maggie Radford. A friend of Chloe Hughes, do you remember me?'

'Sure. Of course I remember you. How are you?' His heart beat wildly and his legs turned to jelly. Oh God, something must have happened to Chloe. Why else would Maggie be calling him at this time of the night?

'I expect it's some ungodly hour over there.'

'Three a.m.'

'Sorry. I called you on impulse without thinking about the time. I tracked you down through Bradley's parents.'

'Sure, sure,' he said, breathless with worry. 'Has something happened to Chloe? Is she sick? Is it her hip?'

'No, nothing like that,' Maggie assured him. 'In fact, she doesn't even know that I'm calling you. But there are certain things I think you ought to know . . .'

Chapter Twenty-four

'Be an angel and see that everyone has a drink, will you darling?' said Maggie to Bradley. 'It's almost midnight.'

'Sure.' He gave her an affectionate smile, thinking how lovely she looked in a black velvet fitted dress with long sleeves and a scooped neckline. Her hair was worn in a smooth shoulder-length bob with a side parting, the richness of its colour contrasting perfectly with the plainness of the dress. At thirty-eight, she was stunning.

It was New Year's Eve of 1969 and the congenial clamour of a party filled Maggie's living room. A log fire crackled in the hearth, a Christmas tree lit the bay window, tinsel bells and lanterns glittered festively about the room, and Frank Sinatra crooned 'My Way' on the record player.

While Bradley was attending to the drinks, Maggie stood quietly on the periphery of the festivities absorbing the warmth of the atmosphere and observing the guests who were all so important to her.

This was a happy but somewhat nostalgic occasion as the decade drew to a close, for the 1970s would mean changes for them all.

'I can understand you two being keen to get married,' said Daisy to her mother and Andrew, who were standing near the Christmas tree. 'People of your age were brought up in that tradition, but why Katy wants to tie herself down by getting engaged to Tim Slade is beyond me. I mean, marriage is so uncool for people of our generation.'

'It can't be for all of them,' said Chloe, glamorously dressed in a flame-coloured satin cocktail dress. Her own contentment had boosted her confidence and she now found it easier to cope with her daughter's assertiveness and modern ideas. 'You've only to pass a church any Saturday to see that there's still no shortage of weddings.'

'It's still a really boring thing to do though, and certainly not obligatory as it was in your day, Mummy,' insisted Daisy. 'We are less inhibited about relationships, thank goodness.'

'Are you saying that you'd rather just live with someone?' asked Andrew, Chloe's influence manifest in his smart appearance. He was wearing a well-tailored lounge suit and white shirt, his hair combed neatly into place. Even his beard had been professionally trimmed.

'Sure I would,' said Daisy, fashionably dressed in a white satin blouse and black skirt in the new maxi length, her hair long and straight with a centre parting. 'I won't need a piece of paper to tell me how I feel about someone.'

'Well, don't expect my approval,' snorted Chloe, her own indiscretions of the past buried beneath her dignified parental status.

'Don't panic, Mummy,' laughed Daisy. 'I shan't seriously commit myself to anyone for ages yet. I'm going to get my degree, then concentrate on a career.'

'Any ideas what you might go into?' asked Andrew with interest.

'I'll wait and see what opportunities are available for a bright young thing with an English degree when the time comes,' she said lightly. 'Advertising, publishing, who knows?'

'No hankering to follow in your mother's footsteps as a horsewoman then?'

'Good lord, no,' exclaimed Daisy. 'Occasional weekends in Kent are fun, and I like to ride. But I couldn't bear to bury myself in the country permanently. Thank heavens Mummy has a house in town. At least I can make sure she doesn't vegetate completely.'

Andrew grinned. He liked Daisy. There was a lot of her mother in her. 'Chloe could never do that, even if she was marooned alone on an island in the Outer Hebrides,' he said, squeezing Chloe's hand affectionately, the mess she had been in at their first meeting long forgotten.

'Thank you for your support, Andrew,' Chloe said, 'I certainly need it against my daughter's boundless confidence.'

'So when do you two plan to tie the knot?' asked Daisy.

'In the spring,' said Chloe. 'When Andrew has finished working out his contract in the States and can come back to England permanently.'

Daisy grinned cheekily at her future stepfather. She was glad that her parents had finally decided to split up. It made for a much happier family life altogether. 'I hope you're not expecting me to call you Daddy?' she said.

'Certainly not,' he laughed.

Chloe threw her daughter an apprehensive look. 'You do approve, don't you, darling, of Andrew and me?'

Daisy smiled. 'Yes, Mother, I approve. Actually, my friends at coll think it's all wildly romantic. You know, you and Andrew, Daddy and Maggie.'

'I thought you said romance was uncool for your generation,' smiled Chloe.

'Not romance, just marriage,' she corrected breezily. She sipped her drink. 'By the way, Daddy is buying me a flat of my own. *That's* cool!'

'Real cool,' laughed Chloe.

★   ★   ★

'So you're going to make me Granny again,' said Dora, grinning at Sally and Tom.

'We certainly are,' beamed Sally. 'We thought it was time we provided you with a little 'un to spoil rotten. Now that Katy is grown up.'

'I hear you've some news of your own,' said Tom.

'That's right. I'm making an honest man of him at last,' said Dora, winking at Harry who was standing beside her.

Sally grinned at him. 'How do you feel about becoming a grandpa?' she asked.

'I'm looking forward to it.'

'And if you think that I'll spoil your new baby,' Dora chuckled, 'you ain't seen nothing yet!'

'Congratulations,' said Daisy to Katy and Tim, kissing them both on the cheek. 'There's a positive epidemic of romance around here.'

'Yes, even my father is seeing someone,' said Tim. 'A client of his with a bossy organising nature. She's just what he needs.'

Daisy threw them both a wicked grin. 'As for you two – well, I think you're crazy to give up your independence, but since there's no talking you out of it, I wish you all the best.'

'Thanks, Daisy,' said Katy, hugging her friend.

She hadn't forgotten that Daisy and Tim had once had a fling together. But she no longer saw her friend as a threat.

'I can still hardly believe everything that has happened,' said Chloe to Maggie, Bradley and Andrew as they stood together in a group. 'You know, you two and us two.' She grinned at Andrew. 'Mind you, he made me suffer for long enough before coming to his senses.'

'Have you decided where you are going to live yet?' asked Maggie.

'We'll divide our time between London and Kent, using the house in Richmond as our town house,' she explained. 'I'd like it to stay in the family. It makes my parents seem closer somehow. I promised Mummy I would before she died.'

'I think you've made the right decision,' said Maggie.

'How about you?' asked Chloe.

'Somewhere in central London. I shall be sad to leave here, but it's time to move on to a new start.'

'Is it to be a spring wedding for you and Bradley?' asked Chloe.

'Yes.'

'Snap.' Chloe looked thoughtfully into space. 'We are coming to the end of an era.'

'We are indeed,' said Maggie.

307

'Still, all the changes are for the better, eh?' said Chloe. 'I thought I'd lost Andrew forever, you know. I still don't know what made him get in touch with me again after so long.'

Andrew gave Maggie a covert wink. 'I've told you, Chloe darling. I finally grew up, that's all.'

Maggie stood at Bradley's side as the chimes of Big Ben boomed into the room from the television set, sparing a thought for those who were no longer around. Her father, Chloe's parents, the incomparable Jack who had been so dear to her in his own way. She even remembered Nelson the cat, eternally sleeping beneath his favourite tree in the garden.

Now she and Bradley stood on the brink of a new life together. What would the 1970s have in store for them? she wondered as the final chime resounded to the rafters.

'Happy New Year, Maggie,' said Bradley, kissing her.

'And to you,' she said. 'Incidentally, I had the most exciting invitation the other day.'

'Uh-huh,' he said. 'Another party.'

'No, not a party,' she said, smiling into his eyes, savouring the news she had kept until this special moment to impart. 'I had a call from the manager of the Albert Hall about the flowers for this year's Promenade Concerts.'

'Why, that's wonderful!' he exclaimed joyfully. 'Congratulations.'

'Thank you,' she said. And she had a very strong suspicion that 1970 was going to be a very good year indeed.